PIGEON ISLAND

Faraway

Also by Lucy Irvine

CASTAWAY
RUNAWAY
ONE IS ONE (*novel*)

Faraway

LUCY IRVINE

Doubleday

LONDON · NEW YORK · TORONTO · SYDNEY · AUCKLAND

TRANSWORLD PUBLISHERS
61–63 Uxbridge Road, London W5 5SA
a division of The Random House Group Ltd

RANDOM HOUSE AUSTRALIA (PTY) LTD
20 Alfred Street, Milsons Point, Sydney,
New South Wales 2061, Australia

RANDOM HOUSE NEW ZEALAND LTD
18 Poland Road, Glenfield, Auckland 10, New Zealand

RANDOM HOUSE SOUTH AFRICA (PTY) LTD
Endulini, 5a Jubilee Road, Parktown 2193, South Africa

Published 2000 by Doubleday
a division of Transworld Publishers

The contemporary and Spearline maps of Pigeon Island and the map of Reef Islands
are by Lilias Thain. The map showing the location of the Solomon Islands is by
Ted Hatch.

A catalogue record for this book is available from the British Library.
ISBNs 0 385 600119 (cased)
0 385 601808 (tpb)

Typeset in 11½/14pt Bembo by Falcon Oast Graphic Art

Printed in Great Britain by
Clays Ltd, St Ives plc

1 3 5 7 9 10 8 6 4 2

For my sons

Contents

CONTENTS

Author's Note

THE IDENTITIES OF SOME PEOPLE IN THIS STORY HAVE BEEN DISGUISED to protect their privacy. Certain events have been described differently, by different individuals, in diaries, letters and verbally. Where this has happened, I have done my best to descry fact, by seeking substantiation from as many sources as possible. Extracts from diaries and letters have been, in parts, paraphrased, and the recreation of some scenes has required a degree of liberty with dialogue and description where neither I nor a direct source of information was present. Both the contemporary and historical sections of this book are, however, based closely on actual occurrences and real people.

Place names in Reef Islands change and spellings are numerous, so I have opted, in the text and on maps, to use spellings aimed at assisting pronunciation. The names of individuals are also spelled phonetically. The meaning of Pijin English words and phrases is often clear from the context and from their sound, but for ease of reference a glossary has been provided at the end of the book.

PIGEON ISLAND

REEF ISLANDS

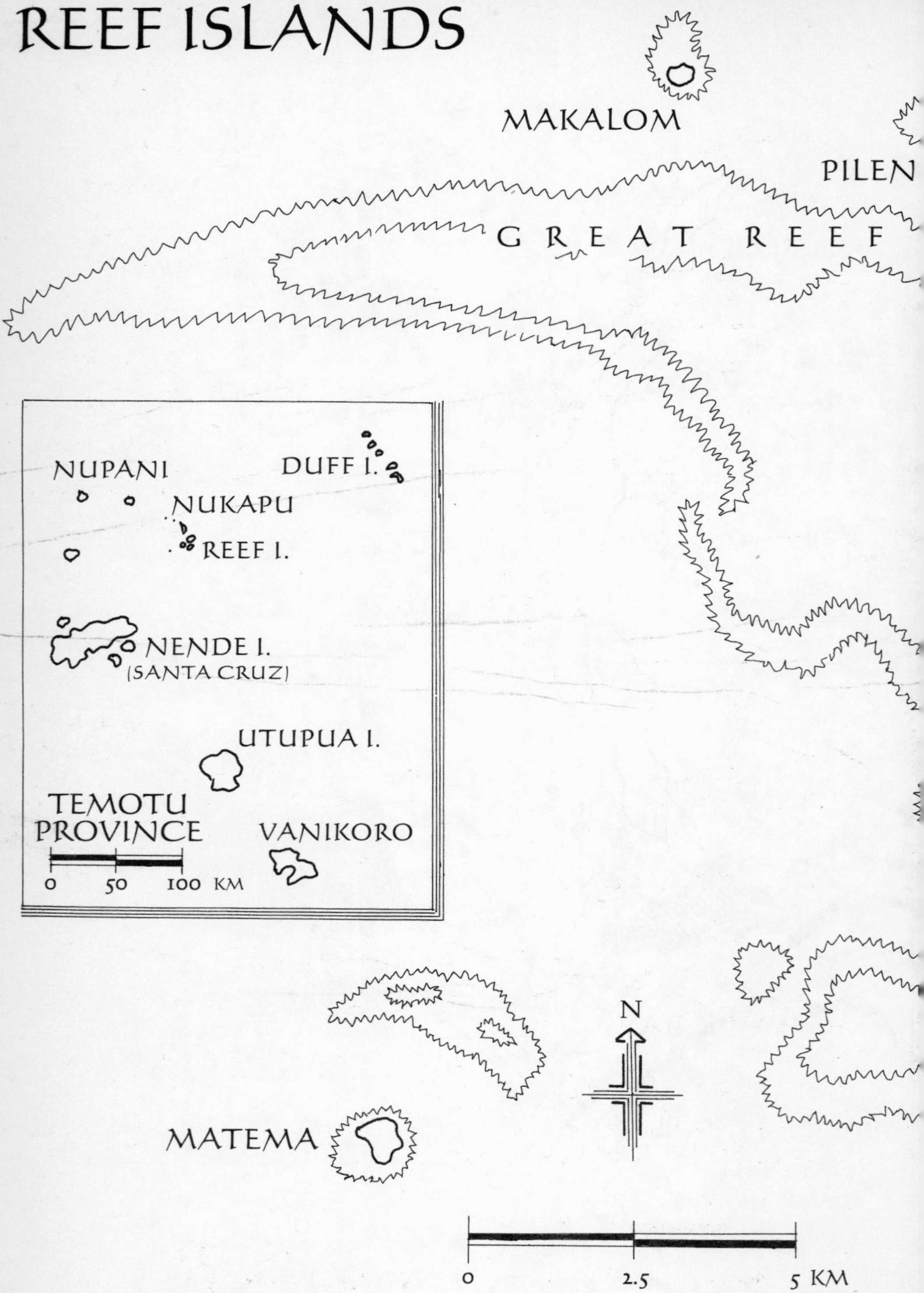

MAKALOM

PILEN

G R E A T   R E E F

NUPANI   DUFF I.

NUKAPU

REEF I.

NENDE I.
(SANTA CRUZ)

UTUPUA I.

TEMOTU
PROVINCE   VANIKORO

0   50   100 KM

MATEMA

N

0   2.5   5 KM

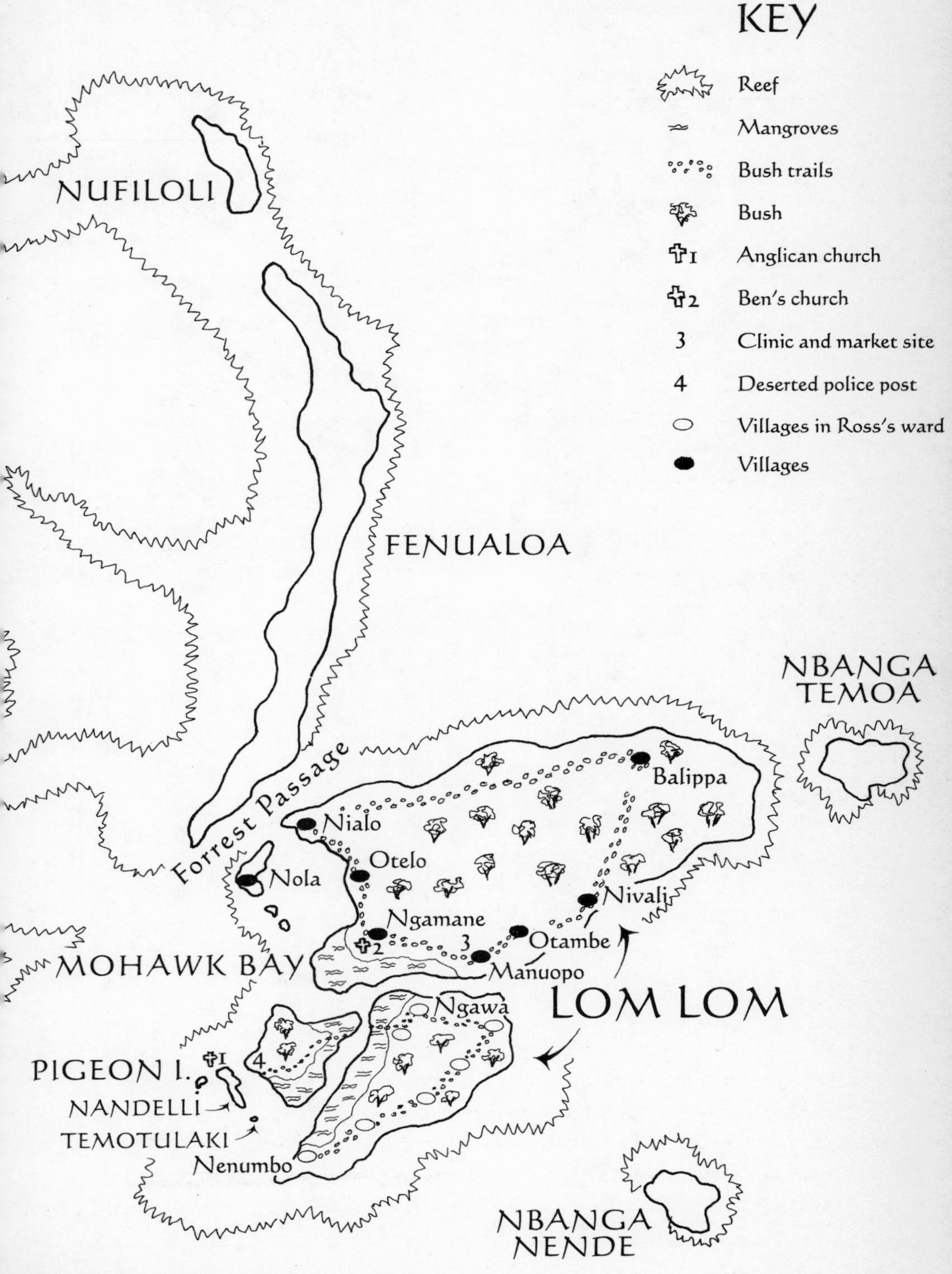

KEY

〰 Reef

≈ Mangroves

°₀°₀° Bush trails

🌿 Bush

✝1 Anglican church

♰2 Ben's church

3 Clinic and market site

4 Deserted police post

○ Villages in Ross's ward

● Villages

NUFILOLI

FENUALOA

NBANGA TEMOA

Forrest Passage

Nialo

Nola Otelo

Balippa

Nivali

Ngamane

✝2 3 Otambe

MOHAWK BAY

Manuopo

Ngawa

LOM LOM

PIGEON I.

✝1 4

NANDELLI

TEMOTULAKI

Nenumbo

NBANGA NENDE

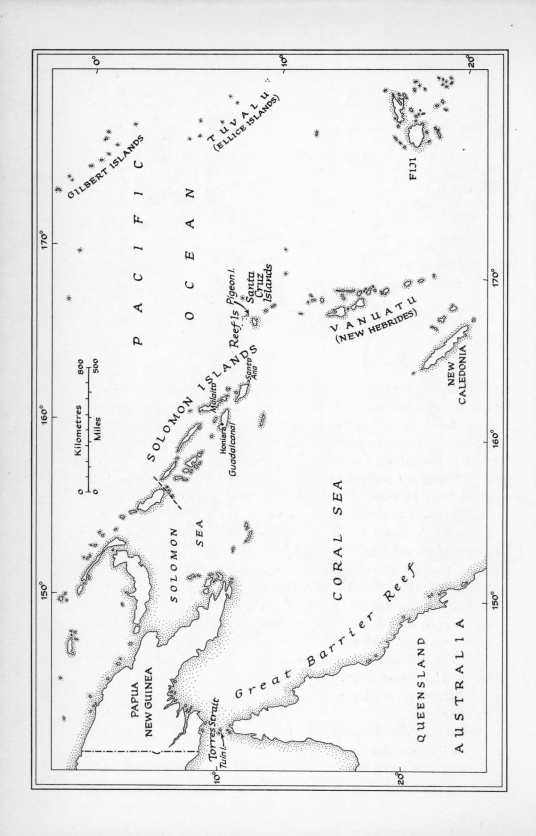

1

After Tuin

TWO WEEKS AFTER LEAVING MY *CASTAWAY* ISLAND, I STOOD IN sunshine at a bus stop on the outskirts of London, very brown in white shorts. I'd woken early, as always, missing the sound of the sea, but happy to wander round a waking suburb at dawn for the sheer novelty. Everything I did held little excitements; reason for sudden joy. I'd sung as I washed in water that ran out of a tap that morning, sighed with pleasure as I drank real milk, and now anticipated a nostalgic jaunt to the local library to borrow a book on one of my mother's tickets. I'd no desire to register for my own because my home address still felt like Tuin Island, Torres Strait, where I'd lived for the past year. It may have been half a world away, but to me it felt close, and in some ways more real than the pavement beneath my feet in their unaccustomed shoes. I carried the island's image and memories of the life I'd led there like snapshots in a wallet, facts in recent history temporarily more comprehensible and familiar than much of what I saw back in 'civilization'. It was exciting, but how real was it? The mood of people at the bus stop, none smiling on this pretty day when anything could happen, baffled me.

'Late again.'

'Time they did something about it.'

'That'll be the day.'

But a bus is going to come! I wanted to cry. Isn't it a miracle? You wait here a while, then a big machine comes and takes you where you've chosen to go. (I'd forgotten, perhaps, that many people lead lives they haven't chosen.) I rocked impatiently on legs strong from striding down to the sea over Tuin's moonscape of sandhills. I felt wonderful. I had clean hair. On Tuin I hadn't been able to wash it for four months, we were so short of water.

'Isn't it a lovely day?' I burst out.

The woman nearest to me took no notice but one beyond, flicking through a pension book, looked round.

'Only hope it lasts.'

A bus came but no-one got on. It was stopping at a terminus.

'That's the third.'

A man in an open car drew up.

'Anyone going up to town?' he asked the short queue generally. No-one seemed to be. They all looked straight ahead until I responded enthusiastically, then they all craned round to stare.

I hadn't been going up to town, but why not? Did no sense of caution make me hesitate? I had had bad experiences with strangers in cars before. But this man just looked as though he were enjoying the pretty day too. Besides, the car was open and we travelled for the most part in a traffic jam, surrounded by crowds. Everything amazed or amused me: shops, advertisements, people's expressions and clothes. I exclaimed, pointed, laughed.

'Where are you from?' he asked. He was in his early thirties, an army officer recently in the Falklands, on leave.

We speeded up a bit, and I called into the wind: 'I'm from the land where the Bong Tree grows!'

He joined in my laughter.

'Where are you going?'

I decided on the spur of the moment: 'The British Library.' One up on the local, and a publisher interested in the idea of a book based on diaries I'd kept on the island had issued me with the requisite letter for a pass. I didn't take the idea seriously, but wanted to learn about the history of the Torres Strait anyway. I agreed to have lunch with my chauffeur later.

'But you've got to wear a ra-ra,' he said. It was 1982, year of the ra-ra skirt. Gerald, my husband on Tuin, had liked me to wear stockings painted on with charcoal from the fire. He'd stayed on the island I loved longer than he wanted, because I agreed to such whims. 'I would, but haven't any money,' I said. The man gave me some, and I quickly found a silky blue number before settling down to study the findings of Alfred Cort Haddon's Cambridge Anthropological Expedition to the Torres Strait in 1898. I found his account so compelling – descriptions of the 'natives' took me back to when their descendants helped me survive on Tuin – that I phoned the publisher and an appointment was made. Then I drank champagne and ate gloriously rich steak pie in a smart restaurant with the man in the open car, who liked my ra-ra floating so lightly over my thighs. Soon my still brown breasts wanted to be bare, too.

'You really do come from the land where the Bong Tree grows, don't you?'

'Yes.'

I'd come home to find both my mother and sister as unhappy as they had been when I left for Tuin over a year ago. They were both still living in the shadow of our family's break-up. Nothing seemed to have changed for them, but everything had for me. Avoiding the sadness of the house, I accepted more invitations from the ra-ra man but refused a lift to the publishers. This was a new direction I wanted to explore alone. I had no confidence about writing, but did know what had happened during my year away, and the idea of revisiting the island by describing it was attractive, so I accepted a small advance, then hitch-hiked to Bristol to consult my greatest friend, Addie, whom I'd met when I was sixteen, during my *Runaway* days. I was twenty-six now. Addie had drunk too much at my wedding to Gerald (we'd had to marry or the authorities wouldn't stamp our visas), grabbed my newly wedded husband by the throat and told him to look after me. He'd also bet that if anyone was going to write about the island it would be me, which I didn't believe, but I loved Addie's faith in me. (Gerald, the originator of the modern 'year on a tropical island' idea, did in fact write a book, a collage of island experiences.) When I read Addie passages from my diary – how strange to sit in a city and describe spearing crabs for bait – he was matter-of-fact: 'Just do it, Lucy.' I'd never told him about my habit of lucrative escapism with strangers, but I think he knew and saw no happy future in it. I set off back along the motorway fired with purpose. It was another beautiful day, and I had a plan. When a man who gave me a lift asked me to lie down under a barbed-wire fence for money, I said no. When he insisted, I did something I'd never done before: I got angry, and swung the little leather suitcase containing my Tuin diaries threateningly. 'No!' He drove off and I had to walk eleven miles before I got another lift, but I didn't care.

I wrote *Castaway* in a converted smokehouse overlooking the Summer Isles, in Scotland. Another island setting was ideal as a backdrop for reliving Tuin days. Everything was simplified again, reduced to sea, sky and one main aim. On the island, the aim was to survive; now I just had to record how that was done. My father, running his hotel nearby with a new wife, popped in sometimes, but otherwise my existence was pleasingly solitary. Discipline, after the rigours of life on a desert island, was no problem. I produced pages without pause. But the publishers, when I sent a sample, weren't impressed. Why was I talking about starvation and tropical ulcers, and using rude words? Where were the romantic beach scenes? 'We had in mind a coffee-table book,' they explained. Weren't people interested in reality? I was staring for the last time at the rejected pages when a phone call came. 'Is that Lucy Irvine?' 'Yes.' '*The* Lucy Irvine?' 'Pardon?' 'I'm going to publish your book. Don't change a word.' My sample had been passed under a table to this godlike stranger, and I was off again. Why was the subject of life on an uninhabited island with a man I hardly knew so potentially appealing? 'It's something people dream about, you see,' he told me, 'but few do. You've done it.' I saw, or thought I did – although Tuin had felt more like a thorny personal challenge than the stuff of dreams most of the time I was there. The next challenge was how to cope with life in civilization, a feat of which I yet dream.

Fame sits strangely on the shoulders of a young woman still in the habit of regarding fresh water and electricity with reverential wonder. *Castaway* was to be sold in fourteen countries, and I was to be the chief marketing tool. After a windswept walk to say goodbye to the Summer Isles, I glanced at my oilskinned figure in a mirror. 'Chief marketing tool,' I said aloud, and wondered what exactly this meant. What was I supposed to be like? I made the mistake, perhaps, of not asking myself what I wanted to be like. I'd lived naked, inside and out, on a mile-long atoll in the Coral Sea. Now I was to be a celebrity. Moving to London, I experimented with images – county type; vamp; ragamuffin – none seemed more or less apposite than another, but it was fun trying, and a new experience not having to worry how I was going to pay – or ask men for favours. Addie sent blasts of Bach to soothe me in the high hype, jetset world I was about to enter as 'the *Castaway* girl'.

In New York, my hotel suite supplied a beribbonned welcome basket of fruit three feet high. Nervously, I nibbled a cherry and stained my immaculate designer blouse, causing a publicity escort to dash out for another. I soaked in a marble bath, more cautiously eating a banana, while I waited for it to arrive. I was soon to address an audience in Washington and rehearsed my lines: 'I can't tell you how extraordinary it is to be here.' It was truthful, but would it do? Apparently it did, backed by slides on a giant screen of dear, familiar Tuin. In Cincinnati there was a blizzard and, missing a plane, I had to appear on TV having had no sleep, make-up plastered on like Polyfilla, (who was *that* in the mirror?); in Chicago I got lost and ended up in a 'swing' bar, where women fondled women; I cried with exhaustion in a queen-sized bed with satin sheets in Boston, and laughed over a whole chicken served in a pineapple on a silver platter, when all I'd asked for was a sandwich. On Tuin, I'd sometimes had to manage on one precious cup of carefully caught rainwater per day; now I could drink a bottle of pink champagne on my own if I liked. It was fun being fêted, but also bizarre. In Milan, after being dressed in leather and given a trident to flourish for photographs, I was taken to Capri and psychoanalysed in public, in Italian, of which I understood not a word; *Castaway* in German was called *Eva und Mr Robinson* which put a new slant on it. A Swedish Braille edition came out. After a while, even discussion about my adventures in English began to seem foreign and I realized, as the novelty of plentiful food and any number of images dimmed, that I needed a place to call home. Also a question I was always asked: 'Why did you do it?' needed more than a one-line answer. Back on a flying visit to Scotland, I briefed a lawyer to find a property 'Generous for one, with no neighbours' and, after an Australian tour, began writing *Runaway*, the book which explained to myself, never mind the rest of the world, why it had seemed so natural to take the step of going to live on an uninhabited island with a stranger.

It didn't take long to find a cottage. After living in a tent for a year, then a smokehouse, I wasn't fussy. An elderly woman was wiping an ancient wood-burning stove when I viewed the home I was to buy. 'Will you manage the logs alone?' she asked. 'Oh yes,' I answered airily. What could be difficult about living in a place with a roof and walls after surviving on Tuin? The stove – a Rayburn – was the only piece of furniture left when she went, and I loved the bare rooms with their echoey floorboards, open fires and views over moorland ideal for lone wanders. The name of the place was irresistible too – Inchreoch, meaning heathery island – and I bought a car and learned to drive on single tracks near the west coast so I could move in as soon as possible. It was while negotiating a bend under a mountain one morning that I spotted a figure in a fishing jersey, hitch-hiking, who was to be the link between me and Pigeon Island years later. While I concentrated on not driving into lochs, he talked about his experiences in fish farm-ing. He'd seen an article about a tropical island and hoped the owners, an elderly British couple, might find his knowledge useful. He'd love to go there.

'And did you know that the woman who wrote *Castaway* is supposed to live round here? I'd love to meet her. She should hear about this other woman on this other island . . .'

I kept my eyes on the road, not letting him know until I dropped him at Ullapool harbour that he'd been travelling with Ms Castaway. If people had learned where I was living, now was the time to move.

At Inchreoch, I slept on the floor and used a wooden fishbox as a desk. I also sat on fishboxes, built shelves with them, and stored every-thing from pine cones to potatoes in them. When I came back from another tour, of South Africa, and found I was expecting a baby, I reckoned a fishbox would make an ideal cradle, too. But the impact of being no longer one carefree individual didn't hit home fully until my shape changed. I'd bought a bed by then, a double. When I wasn't busy writing *Runaway* or striding on the moors, I cried in that bed. And as I grew larger, with full breasts for the first time after being so skinny on Tuin, I felt no longer exotic but womanly, and vulnerable. And I wanted strong arms around both myself and my child. Leaving my unfinished manuscript in a safe place, I took myself back, one snowy night when five months pregnant, in search of what seemed so painfully missing.

I was instantly at ease in the vastness of an African landscape. I recognized the sensuous sting of the sun in the day, and the huge, cool moon lighting up the mountains at night. The red-earthed karoo with its twisted trees and flash floods and the hot, sparse plains of the Homelands to the north awed me equally. I drove miles along bright coastline and root-strewn interior tracks; stopped for tea at Afrikaner homesteads where toilet rolls were concealed beneath the skirts of dolls, and to buy peaches the size of cricket balls from Zulu women under trees. When I lost my way in a black township, women touched my belly. 'Where is the father?' they asked. 'I'm looking for him,' I answered, and they looked at me with grave eyes, as if they understood.

In Transkei, I abandoned my car in the Mkambesi river as it slipped over the edge of a ford. I had then to walk, surprising herds of striped kudu with rubbery mouths, and feeling both fear and attraction as the bare veldt filled with shadows in the dusk. A Xhosa horseman found me, and lifted me onto a tall mare. Fifteen men plucked the car from the river and slowly it dried, steaming in the sun. When I left Transkei a week later, a woman gave me sheets of preserved peaches scrolled like charts, and hundreds of tiny apples. There were fresh peaches on the dashboard too, and it is the image of all this fragile fruit tumbling and smashing that's remained in my mind over the years, from when the wheels locked suddenly and the car went into a long diagonal skid on shale downhill and turned over three times, to land on its roof in a barren field.

Now I was shaken; no longer cruising through Africa in a dangerous, yearning dream. I hung, swaying, in my seat belt. The windscreen was shattered, roof and doors buckled, making my escape route, through the front window, slim. I eased out, hair gathering glass, and wormed away. The ground was scattered with apples, split flesh bathed with juice like sweat, under the sun. I took a handful, and moved towards the road. Apart from the hill I'd crashed down, it was a flat landscape, little but sandy fields and bleached blue sky. I sat by the road, one hand on my belly, where I could feel nothing. My watch was smashed but the sun said midday, then three o'clock. I kept feeling for movement. Kicks I'd grown used to seemed to shout their absence into the air; a small voice but, to me, loud. I didn't want to be alone again. At last I heard real sounds – singing – as, like something out of a cartoon, a carload of Afrikaner policemen, all chewing boerwurst, appeared. They stopped. 'Where is the father?' 'Why are you travelling alone?' A doctor, fifty kilometres away, asked similar questions as he zoomed a machine over my skin from breasts to groin. 'Did you say you felt movement before?' 'Yes.' 'Definitely?' 'Definitely.' 'Well, I'm not getting any heartbeat now.' When it was discovered I wasn't married, I was reprimanded like a schoolgirl. 'I can feel something!' I cried, interrupting. 'You can? Maybe it's this bloody machine.' He put an old-fashioned ear to my belly, with a cupped hand. 'So OK, you're lucky, if that's what you want . . .'

It was what I wanted, and even though, when I met him two days later, it was plain the father couldn't envisage a child in his life at that time, I was clear about the future. I'd been jolted into reality. Hope and hormones had made me yearn for protecting arms around me, but if I couldn't have them I'd manage anyway.

Magnus Irvine came six weeks early in the summer of 1985. 'Are babies meant to be that small?' asked my brother, who'd now taken over the Summer Isles Hotel from our father. I didn't care. Bundling my sparrow into a blanket sewn into a bag, I took him everywhere. He watched me through the mesh of a plastic laundry basket when I chopped wood; flopped about with his head like an apple on a string on my back when I walked the moors; lay across my lap when I typed. And he grew. By the time he was four months old and we went to Helsinki where *Castaway* was being launched, he was robust and determined in his demands. He came with me to London where I went for discussions about the film based on the book. When I met director Nicolas Roeg, and Amanda Donahoe who played the part of Lucy, I got only halfway through lunch at La Caprice before I felt I must phone the babysitter to check that Magnus had had his . . . I was happy that the film should be someone else's interpretation of the story. Roeg wanted a vehicle for the exploration of a relationship between an older man and a younger woman and the island setting was ideal. Fine. I put the money away for my son's future, and returned to the Highlands to complete *Runaway*. Magnus was a red-cheeked country child when the book came out, and people asked: 'Don't you worry about him getting into trouble, like you did?' I did. More than anything else in the world I wanted his upbringing to be secure; his family, even if it was only me, absolutely stable. He mustn't have a messy background, like mine.

So why did I capitulate when, after two happy, busy years, a lonely stranger wanting arms around him appeared? The answer must be that, for all my independence and purpose, my body was lonely too. Now, so content before in all but the body's cyclical hunger – I'd stopped crying at night after Magnus was born – I rediscovered some of the confusions that had first sent me to a desert island for its blessed simplicity. I regretted my impulsive action fiercely, but there was no going back. I'd conceived again, and hope grew in me again, hand in cuff with the resultant flood of hormones, so that not one more child arrived but two – Joe first and then, two years later, Benji. All this despite my inability to give up my solitary emotional ways. Books were born between babies, and Inchreoch, described as 'generous for one', suddenly became, after a brief and mutually painful spell in which I tried and failed to share its roof with the younger boys' father, a 'cosy' nest for four.

The year Magnus turned eight, Joe six and Benji four, the one adult I felt close to as a friend, Addie, died suddenly. No more Bach through the letterbox, and no-one to receive odd lines of poetry I never had to explain. The possibility of an intimacy not just based on the body had been offered, for he'd asked if it wasn't time we got our children together, now that we were both free; but I was still in shock from recent failure and said no. I didn't want to risk losing his friendship and in fact decided then to become celibate. Mourning perhaps a double loss – for there was no hope now of the stable father figure I longed for in the children's lives – I planted, numbly, clump after clump of snowdrops and daffodils on hillocks, under trees and lining the area designated as a football field in our wild third of an acre. The boys played round me, erecting stockades and firing salvos from deep hiding whenever a car passed. We dug in as a family, but sooner or later we'd have to come out from behind our barricades and accept a degree of contact with the confusing outside world. I might have been content to become a hermit, but it would be wrong to impose such a way of life on children.

My method of re-emerging was fairly drastic. In the winter of 1994, to prove that life was still an open door and anything could happen to those willing to risk what was on the other side, I transported my sons to the west coast of Africa. Compromising on the safety front initially by placing ourselves under the auspices of a travel company, we caused raised eyebrows by finding a local driver, lining his battered jeep with mattress foam meant for sun loungers and taking off into the bush. I needed another glimpse of Bong Tree land.

Magnus gazed at the potholed red earth, bullocks languid under a thousand flies and bulbous baobab trees. He'd seen mud houses only in books before. Alligators and mangrove swamps were new too. (None of us knew we'd one day spend a year amid comparable poverty and heat, but somewhere considerably more remote, with no jeeps.) We made friends with a young Gambian and ate fish out of a communal bowl. A Marabout gave Magnus a protective juju in exchange for my gold watch, in which I placed less value. That we both wanted to believe in the juju – who doesn't want to protect their children by any means? – made it worth keeping, but I talked to Magnus about the beliefs of the ancient Greeks and Christians too. I'd given him a globe that Christmas, and a history book. I wanted him to be equipped to make his own choices later in life. Brought up without the distraction of television, he was already a keen reader. Together, in Africa, we read about the slave trade, and visited sites where men, women and children once stood in chains. It was enlightening for us both, a lesson in our good fortune to be who we were, and when. But Magnus also swam in the Kamby Bolongo with dolphins, danced the limbo, laughing, and caught crabs on the beach with Joe, Benji and African friends. He was going to become, as well as a beloved son, a friend. But my job now was to ensure he had the best of childhood. Over wild boar and yams, we discussed the possibility of his going away to school. If there weren't to be men in my private life, he must find good examples elsewhere. The plan was he'd stay in the village school at home until he was eleven, then go to an outward bound establishment we both fancied – if he succeeded in gaining a scholarship. It was a high-risk proposition to put to an eight-year-old. He'd have to be prepared to work. He was.

Joe, on discovering birds in Africa to be even more exciting than the robins and wrens he courted for his table at home, and that there were colourful lizards too, dreamed away hot days with his eyes always on the trees or under a bush. He adored the sight and sound of Atlantic rollers crashing on hot black sand. He drew pictures of animals, in silence, for hours. I was only beginning to realize then how hard this quiet middle son found it to hear normal speech clearly. His deafness was not profound, but enough to make him retreat a little. Benji was happy so long as I gave a nod to the routine the male nanny I'd employed the last year I was working had wisely imposed – stories after lunch and cuddles after baths. When Magnus and I went on a trek in the African heat that was too strenuous for his younger brothers, a beautifully coiffured woman from Mali looked after them. Benji told me, with fascination, that after lunch she'd 'taken her hair off and eaten twigs' (removed her wig and cleaned her teeth, presumably), and asked if he could stay with her again. On the night before we left, a wizened old Gambian sat up a tree to guard Benji when Magnus asked me to watch him dance. Benji thought this so novel, he wanted the old man to be his new nanny. 'You don't need a nanny now,' I said, 'you've got me.'

I won't pretend our African excursion was a great adventure, but it served its purpose. Once we were caught in a sandstorm when driving along a crazily rutted track at night. I used every piece of cloth I could find to make a covering for the boys on the padded floor of the jeep, and tied a scarf over my own eyes. When we stopped, abruptly, and I took it off, men with guns and torches were poking at the lumpy pile at my feet. 'Babies!' I blurted, and peeled back the coverings on three sleepy heads. There were instant smiles, and one of the men, in a military-type uniform, helped tuck the rags back round the boys. 'Where is your husband?' he asked. 'I don't have one,' I said, and by then I could accept both Addie's death and the death of hopes I'd harboured for a permanent relationship. But there was no sense of hopelessness any more. United as we were by this mini voyage of discovery together, the future alone with my family seemed an adventure in itself. And I didn't need my heart flung into my mouth by any more military checkpoints to make it exciting. From now on I would be happy to pursue the lessons Tuin had taught me and learn more, in the Scottish countryside, with my sons. Or that's what I told myself.

2

Attempting to Settle

OVER A DECADE AFTER MY FIRST DESERT ISLAND EXPERIENCE, I WAS still more conscious of not wasting resources than anyone I knew, and my sons grew up understanding that if we wanted a bath, first we had to check there was enough water in the burn at the end of the garden, then heat it, which meant splitting logs. I gave Magnus his first axe when he was nine. In winter, when the pipes froze, he brought buckets from the burn on a sledge; Joe half a bucket; Benji a kettle. I wrote a story for the boys about children on an island who found a gecko in their catchment barrel. They nodded seriously; pollution would be no laughing matter, but they also wanted the gecko rescued and made up more stories of their own in front of the fire. In the morning, I swept out the grate; Joe emptied the ash; Magnus replenished the peat, and Benji towed a real log behind a toy tractor. We all contributed, and nothing was taken for granted – except the solidarity of family love.

Springtimes at Inchreoch came with a mass of daffodils which sprang up, regardless of snow, in March. My benumbed planting spree when Addie died had been worthwhile, and as soon as there was a hint of warmth in the air we ate outside. Sunday lunches consisted of a hunk of lamb chucked in the Rayburn at the same time as stoking it first thing, a homemade loaf and fruit. It meant a celebration if we had crisps as well because, although we loved treats, I wanted the children to learn, as I had, that luxuries feel more rewarding if deserved. Magnus, for instance, only took *four* biscuits with his milk if he was satisfied with his training run in the woods. Out of one careless night in Africa had come an arrow shot from the bow of my desire, now speeding beyond me.

My other little arrows shot upwards, and celebrated summers with wild games in bracken and competitions to see who'd brave the cold of a loch first. Anxious to make the most of fine days, I bossed the boys to organize themselves, feeling it important they begin life with the attitude that some responsibility would always be theirs. But once we had arrived at our destination – a bluebell-filled valley or a sliver of beach along a river glittering with speckled stones – we relaxed completely, and the boys demonstrated that they needed no teaching in the art of 'living now'. The lessons Tuin had taught me came naturally to them. But I did sometimes think, lying padded with jumpers on a cool Scottish rock, eyes to the sky as I listened to their happy voices, what perfect desert island dwellers these boys would be.

Summers could be blissful, but winters were hard, and one year the struggles with buckets didn't end when the thaw came. I'd known since Magnus was born that our burn water failed environmental health tests, and we collected washing water off the roof and drinking water whenever we were near a reliable source. This was usually a toilet at a garage miles away with a tap at a suitable height. Every avenue was explored to obtain a good supply closer to home but it was fruitless, and we had to accept that, although we could enjoy deep brown baths and the benefits of a flushing loo, we must live with plastic drums for other purposes. Then an accident among forestry workers filled the burn with urea-flavoured sludge. The owners of the estate where this happened offered the use of a river on their land, but by then more stringent EEC standards prevailed and all analyses labelled the source 'unsatisfactory' on a number of counts. The home we loved was pronounced technically uninhabitable, and now all water had to be carried by hand.

To compound the impatience I felt with this, I had pressure from within. A novel I had shelved to care full time for the children was calling, and with Benji now at school I should be able to return to it. After delivering the boys to the school bus stop, I took to locking the front door and disappearing onto a fictional island, forgetting everything until an alarm ordered me to leap back into the car.

'What's for supper, Mum?'

'When can we next go swimming?'

'Give me a minute! I've just finished work . . . I can't think . . .'

Often we had to dash to the nearest town for water straight away, and I took – crossly – to buying convenience food. The pressures of a '90s pace of living had reached even my hideaway existence and we weren't geared up for it. The boys, however, thought the new tempo and its concomitant treats exciting. 'Pizza? Great! And it's good, Mum, because there's hardly any washing up.' The laundry, by then, was being taken in by a woman who thought our life extraordinary. She filled squash bottles to pop in with the clean clothes, and told me I was getting thin and always rushing, but I smiled, grabbed the bottles and dashed on. By now Magnus was in sole charge of log-splitting, but somehow, in the midst of our faster routine, we still managed to read poems together and practise General Knowledge over meals. He was my number one helper, but it wasn't right so much fell on his shoulders, and when I dropped him off for his scholarship exam I realized that, praying for his success, I was, in effect, wishing him away from my intense, isolationist ways. Warmth, love and shelter had been enough when he was little, but now he was ready for 'general knowledge' of a kind not available in books. He needed to learn to mix – better than I had – with his fellow men.

One night in the spring of 1995, I was trying to mend the Rayburn, sitting with legs braced either side of it and applying a claw hammer, when violent pain, radiating from a point in my lower spine, sent me reeling backwards. I curled up and nearly screamed; tried straightening my legs and did scream, but in my head. On my knees, nauseous and scared, I shuffled to the stove, flung in a log, then walked, still on my knees, to the bathroom, where I hung over a bucket, sweating but cold. I must have pulled something; at worst, it was a slipped disk. But I was wrong. It was bone that had slipped. In lay terms, I had a step defect, a congenital abnormality of the spine, that had presented under pressure, threatening my spinal cord and the balance of the whole column, and a surgeon I saw wouldn't operate because of the risks. Pain could be controlled to a degree but I must accept that my spine would never be normal. I tried to face this and, alone, I might have succeeded, but accepting what it did to my sons seemed impossible. There were no family picnics by rivers that summer; no sledging together in the winter, and the prospect of a miserable mum in a wheelchair ahead. Happiness to me – to us all – was a very physical thing. I asked to see another surgeon, and he said that if I accepted the risks – death or paralysis if things went wrong – he'd do it. I was to go home and be prepared to be called at any time.

Being prepared for open spinal surgery meant organizing round-the-clock childcare for months ahead, getting the house ready to close up, and making a Will. This last brought everything home to me. I wrote that I wished the funds remaining after my death to be used imaginatively with regard to my sons' care. Allowing for adventure and learning from real life seemed as important to me as more conventional education. I was trying to build 'desert island' space into their futures. My brother was supportive. Everyone would rally round if the worst happened. If only Addie could have been among them. But, holding on tightly to a blue sock containing three precious locks of hair and a plastic tiger donated by Benji for courage, I went 'under the knife' in 1996 as determined as possible to emerge not only alive and unparalysed but with a far brighter future. I wanted to be on that – so far only notional – sunny island with my boys. I regained consciousness to the sound of the surgeon shouting for me to waggle my feet. If I could, I was going to be OK. Through a fog of drugs, I made an almighty effort and believed I was paddling the air in arcs. In fact my feet moved only slightly, but that was enough and I passed out again smiling.

To be an utter invalid was at once a remote and intimate experience. Out of technical interest, since I was celibate, I asked the surgeon when I'd be fit enough to make love. It seemed a good example of all-round physical exercise requiring a degree of flow that, in my puppet-like state, must be very distant. Although he laughed, his answer was shrewd: 'You can do just about anything you want, when you feel ready.' These words boded well for the future. Wound into layers of cotton wool like a straitjacket and strapped flat, I was transferred by ambulance to a cottage hospital near the boys, and there exercised feeble hands by sewing nametapes onto rugby boots – for Magnus had achieved his scholarship. He cycled over, balancing lollipops on his handlebars, to celebrate, and we looked at each other steadily. He'd been shocked when he first saw me after the operation, gulping down Ribena as an adult might throw back brandy, but we could say definitely now that some things in our lives were going perfectly to plan.

Joe was first to take me out in my wheelchair, negotiating kerbs breathlessly, while Benji yelled warnings about dogs. If my spine was jolted in its protective brace I didn't say, but maybe my face registered something, because when we were back in the hospital Benji lay silently beside me on the bed with his arms round my neck and Joe asked: 'When are you going to get *properly* better, Mum?' With the novelty of borrowed dads, other mums' cooking and television wearing off by now, they wanted desperately to go home. So did I. A local girl, Jeanie, had charge of Inchreoch at this time, admitting water technicians and keeping the place aired. My wise doctor, generally easy-going over the idiosyncrasies of my home life, wouldn't discharge me until a shower was installed, as it would be a long time before I could use a bath. Also, I must be stronger.

Visitors came, among them the boys' piano teacher, Steve, who brought mail. I looked through the letters, and one, from the Solomon Islands, puzzled me. Who was this Mrs Hepworth, making an extraordinary proposition with such throwaway elegance? '*My late husband and I came to Pigeon, a remote tropical island, in the 1950s and raised our children here . . . People tell me it's very beautiful . . . I understand you have some previous experience of island life, and wondered if you might be interested in living in my home while I am travelling next year.*' She'd been given my name by someone I'd apparently given a lift to in the Highlands, years ago. I searched my memory until a young man in a fishing jersey, talking about an elderly couple on an island, came up. The same young man who'd talked about 'the woman who wrote *Castaway*'. What a wonderful far-flung connection, but what hopeless timing. I'd been told recovery could take a year, and even after that I'd have to be 'sensible'. Nevertheless this woman interested me and I wanted to help. Next time he visited, I asked Steve if he fancied whisking his wife to Paradise for a month or so, gratis, in return for caretaking duties. 'Are you joking?' he asked. 'No, I'd go myself if I could.' He said yes before consulting his wife. It was to be a surprise. Heartened by a compromise that would give pleasure all round, I wrote back to Mrs Hepworth from my hospital bed, throwing in a copy of *Castaway*.

Recovery was slow, when at last I got home, but having targets helped: 'Today I'm going to reach the bird table/wash my hair.' It felt like a huge achievement when I made custard for apples the boys picked – I who'd caught, killed, gutted and dried shark . . . I tottered stiffly, leaning on a walking stick and pointing with a grabstick, while the boys basically did everything, adding shopping at the nearest store, a fourteen-mile round trip by bike, to their hewing of wood and hauling of water. Benji, soon to be seven, and Joe, nine, had to learn fast because within months Magnus would be away at school. And I, one of the world's most technophobic women, was going to be taught state-of-the-art computing by Highland Disability Services, so I could go back to work.

With my new skills, and Magnus launched, I returned to my novel. In this, a woman of sixty-five, who lived on an island in the sun when young, realizes that, although when she got back she made a comfortable home in a beautiful part of Scotland, she never really settled down. She had a cat (modelled on our ginger tom, Charlie) and had once had a lover (modelled on a man of my imagination) but her life seemed all in the past. Her island experience threw a distant light over everything, which no-one could share with her. I went on writing because I was fascinated by her situation – it is true that nothing is the same again after life somewhere really remote – but I didn't like to think that the main part of my life was behind me.

Mrs Hepworth had written again, wondering if I could find a teacher to reopen the school on Pigeon where her children had been educated, as her grandchildren were now of an age to begin. I agreed to try. She'd enjoyed *Castaway* and ordered *Runaway* from New Zealand. *Runaway* describes, among other things, a frightening period when, following rape when I was sixteen, I broke down, and Mrs Hepworth seemed intrigued by my coverage of this. She had a daughter who'd had a similar experience after leaving the shelter of her island home. '*You would be the perfect person to write our story*,' she wrote. But I didn't give the idea a thought. A bill for the (still unsatisfactory) water system at Inchreoch had eaten severely into our funds and I had to provide for my family. With this in mind, I sent tapes of the beginning of my novel to a woman I knew in publishing, who was coming north in the spring of 1997. What no-one reckoned on was Mrs Hepworth's determination.

Magnus was at home when the publisher visited. Snorkelling was his latest passion, and I'd lashed out on a wetsuit for him. He wore this for our picnic by the river, and my London friend watched with a smile as boys, clad and unclad, and dog swarmed over the rocks and plunged in. My back was still frail but with the boys' help I could now reach most of our favourite haunts. I couldn't bend to collect stones but if I pointed to one, Benji would lift it for me and Joe would carry it in his rucksack. 'They're amazing!' I was told. The novel was discussed, and the thinking positive. However, the subject was small-scale. Not many people could relate to the problem of settling down after life on a desert island. I was being gently warned that my novel was unlikely to be a bestseller. Nevertheless, I was in good spirits when we said goodbye. I was to carry on.

Steve and his wife, Jocylyn, armed with telescopic fishing rods and emergency dried meals, left for their unusual caretaking position in July 1997. Following my promise to Mrs Hepworth to help further on the personnel front, I'd arranged for another couple to join them, and a student and later a geography graduate were to go out and help the mixed-race Hepworth grandchildren with their English before a qualified teacher reopened Pigeon Island's school. Unreal though islands seemed now as a serious option in my own life, it gave me pleasure to arrange stints in Paradise for others. Short-listed applicants had to find out about the island themselves, through correspondence with Mrs Hepworth, thus reducing the possibility of dangerously rose-tinted views. My job was merely to assess them for physical and emotional stamina – both essential to remote island dwelling under any circumstances. They promised to write to me. Perhaps I'd become a vicarious traveller.

A few weeks after Steve left, Mrs Hepworth telephoned. She'd seen him and Jocylyn briefly, passing through an airport on an island called Santa Cruz, when they'd landed and she'd flown out on the same plane. Now she was in Britain and keen to meet. She had a son with her, and was coming to Scotland. Her distinctive voice sounded both formal and friendly, but I shied away from visitors and made our water situation an excuse for not offering to put them up, booking them into bed and breakfast accommodation instead. I didn't know what age the son was but presumed him an adult and, planning an activity for him and the boys, contacted the owner of an estate where there was a mountain for them to climb. The landowner was welcoming, but said a map was necessary. I passed this information to Mrs Hepworth, who put her son on the phone. 'I don't need a map,' he said, 'when I have my Lord to guide me.' Oh God, I thought, he's not going anywhere with my sons, and didn't look forward much to the visit.

But because it was so rare to have guests we made an effort, arranging wild flowers and laying tea outside. I 'recognized' Diana Hepworth as soon as she stepped out of the car in which friends had driven her from Aberdeen. She was tall, for a woman of nearly eighty, and had retained impeccable poise from her modelling days. I don't know what she saw when she looked at me, but we appraised each other in silence for a considerable time. Then, with intervals only for me to drop her at the B and B, we talked solidly for three days. It was after lunch at the Summer Isles Hotel that Diana handed me the manuscript her husband, Captain Tom Hepworth, had begun to write. 'He wanted so much to write a book,' she said, 'so others could see what a wonderful life we've had.' I'd already heard enough about that life to realize it was, indeed, different. I'd lived on an uninhabited island with one other person for a year; this couple had lived on theirs for nearly forty. Undoubtedly there was a story to be told, and before she left Diana repeated that I was the one to tell it. I demurred, but suggested she meet my publishing friend. We kissed formally when we said goodbye, and she said something about seeing me on Pigeon, which I laughed off. I'd exchanged only enough words with her son, Ben, to establish that he found it necessary to put a smokescreen of religion between himself and human contact; a likeable man in his mid-thirties, but flawed. I suppose I rather dismissed him. It didn't occur to me then that his story might be as interesting as his parents'.

When they'd gone, I tackled the business of filling the boys' summer holidays. Joe attended a birdwatching camp; Magnus took part in a series of Highland Games, and Benji joined a football club. I was in the middle of slinging together bundles of clothes for them to spend a weekend at Jeanie's, so I could work, when Diana telephoned again. She'd seen my friend, who'd introduced her to several other writers. 'Oh good,' I said. 'No, no good,' said Diana. One man's hair was too long; one woman's mouth too small. I found myself smiling. I liked Diana's startling combination of autocracy and intuition. '. . . so I still hope to persuade *you*.' 'Oh.' I wondered vaguely how I managed to meet her stringent standards. She continued: 'I know you want to write your novel, but you can do that afterwards. The boys are the perfect age. They'd *love* Pigeon. And you shouldn't be lifting anything with that back of yours. A swim in tropical heat every day would do it the world of good, and we've a proper catchment system with clean running water . . .' Wow, this woman knew how to be persuasive. She'd got me on my three most vulnerable points: the children, my wretched spine and water. I blustered, arguing that Magnus was just settled. 'He could join you in the holidays.' She made everything sound so easy, and she'd been bending my publisher's ear, too.

3

Accepting the Inevitable

BENJI AND JOE WERE PLAYING WITH SPEARS MADE FROM GARDEN canes and I was removing excess packaging from a frozen pie, when I reached my decision. They'd set up targets of bags which ripped thrillingly when hit. Diana had told me that in the Solomons fishing was done mostly with spears, but children as young as six used bows and arrows. How these were used and on what, I didn't know, but it sounded the sort of thing I'd like my sons to do. Hunting for supper would surely be preferable to 'killing' Safeway bags. But the chief attraction of the island was simplification. Although I knew the boys must at some point come under the myriad confusing influences hurled at them in 'civilization' and make the choices I found so hard, I longed to solidify healthy foundations for their perspective on life before 'the world' took over. My experience on Tuin had done me good, but lessons learned there had been harshly meted out. No need for my sons to suffer like that: valuing the gift of life itself, as well as the limited resources in our environment, could equally be taught in less extreme circumstances. Wasn't Pigeon the perfect compromise? There we wouldn't be alone – apart from Diana and Ben, another son lived on the island with a young family – but it was certainly remote enough to represent an educational microcosm. And how ideal for Joe, with his dodgy hearing, to have a year at a school with no more than eight pupils, and for all the boys to have *living* lessons in the ways of another culture – for Diana had mentioned, in passing, that inhabitants of other islands in the area still lived in traditional ways.

'Did you know,' I asked that evening, 'that Mrs Hepworth has invited us to spend a year on her island? It's small, and we'd have to live simply, catching fish and finding fruit . . .'

I didn't have a chance to elaborate further. The pie stopped halfway to their mouths and they both yelled a passionate 'Yes!'

'Oh Mum, we *must*.'

'Say yes!'

'As a matter of fact, I think I might.'

They flung down their food and hugged me.

'You're the best mummy . . .'

I doubted that, but their delight brought me, as well as a slight sense of panic, great joy. Where I saw a plethora of demanding tasks ahead – including all the paperwork involved in cutting loose from civilization's strangling, protective strings – they already saw everything in simple terms.

'Only a few hours of school,' they cried, 'yippee!'

'Swimming every day . . .'

'Sleeping outside . . .'

'Hang on!' I said. 'There's a lot we don't know . . .'

'But that's half the fun. We'll find out.'

Who was telling who about the potential benefits of this mad scheme?

After supper, I took out an atlas and studied it with Benji, while Joe fetched the animal 'factfiles' he'd been assembling for years. 'There are at least thirteen kinds of gecko in the Solomon Islands,' he announced, 'and plenty of birds.'

'What about mammals?' asked Benji, then suddenly paused, looking worried. 'What about Charlie?'

I'd anticipated this. Our old collie had recently died, but Charlie, our much-loved cat who had been with me since before Magnus, needed consideration. Feeding him was no problem: suited to our lifestyle, he lived on rabbits he caught himself. But he did like company.

'I'll find someone to live here while we're away.'

While I began a list covering everything from 'deal with bank for a year ahead' to 'teach boys Pidgin English', Joe and Benji went upstairs to turn out drawers – already. It was late summer '97 and we wouldn't leave before the spring of 1998, but I'd be the last person to dampen enthusiasm for bringing possessions down to essentials. One of the most complicated things civilization foists upon us, I'd felt since leaving Tuin, is an excess of paraphernalia, when all we really need are healthy bodies and open minds.

I approached this venture, as I had others, the only way I knew how: saying yes first and worrying about the details later. It was probably fortunate I didn't examine the details first – neither the full, extraordinary history of Pigeon Island and its inhabitants nor what was involved in getting there – or I might have felt too overwhelmed to take it on. I should have guessed there would be desperation and madness, as well as sunny bliss, in the saga of a family raised in putative Paradise; and I should have known that spiriting my family from a cottage in the Highlands to a tiny island half a world away would be no doddle. But, just as I'd approached recovery from surgery by taking it in small bites, I now plotted my way through new tasks, telling myself each one ticked off was a step nearer the sun.

Pigeon Island, on any but a hand-drawn map, is so minute it's almost impossible to find. It lies on the eastern edge of the Solomons, in a scatter of atolls called Reef Islands, which in turn lie in a strung-out archipelago called Temotu Province, with a total land surface of under a thousand square kilometres in one hundred and fifty thousand square kilometres of sea . . . If you're looking for a seriously remote island within islands, within an unimaginable vastness of ocean, this is it. The distances in terms of miles from anywhere one might classify as remotely 'civilized' make Tuin, in the middle of the Torres Strait, seem a mere hop from the nearest iced beer. Looking back, I'm faintly shocked to realize I said yes before I knew much more about Pigeon than what Diana told me. Her words – *'People tell me it's very beautiful'* and *'idyllic for children'* – kept running through my head and, apart from the island's remoteness, there seemed remarkably few drawbacks. And its remoteness appealed.

Although I tried not to make comparisons with Tuin – I was going to Pigeon as a single mother on a job, not just to survive as in my woolly youth – there were, inevitably, some areas where it would make sense to draw on experience. Pigeon, covering just five acres, was considerably smaller than Tuin, and there'd been times when Tuin, a mile in length, didn't seem large. Also, there were more people on Pigeon. As well as the Hepworths, a teacher from

Edinburgh, Peter, and his wife were now confirmed, and it was hoped that several pupils would be drawn from the neighbouring community, about which we knew little. If space on land was limited, we'd need to get our exercise – and solitude – in and on the sea. The twenty-one miles of reef surrounding the island, covered with apparently safe waters at high tide, would be ideal for fishing and swimming. But what about boating? Diana had said dugouts were the local transport, but took a long time to make. I outlined our plans to a man in a canoe shop, and he introduced me to a friend who ran kayaking lessons for the disabled, where I became a regular. It took me longer than I liked to dress and undress, but not as long as some, and it was humbling to see how people with physical challenges far greater than mine struggled effortfully to the edge of the pool, then seemed to acquire wings once afloat. The boys were rolled over and over by volunteers from the RAF while I learned, slowly, how to handle imaginary waves. Later, I graduated to real waves on a chilly loch, bundled up in wetsuit, tracksuit and lifejacket, while a man with beautiful eyes called instructions from his wheelchair on the shore and another cut foam to mould to my hips in a specially designed support. After these sessions, the boys and I huddled over cocoa on the wintry moors, blasting each other with chocolate-flavoured breath, and listing the delights of an island which might, I warned them, even feel *too* hot at times.

With advice from professionals, we ordered four sea-going kayaks, with stowage space for flippers, water bottles and mending tape. We could send these ahead on a ship from Hull to Singapore; another to Honiara, capital of the Solomons, and onwards to Reef Islands on a cargo boat. We could send anything this way, and with all our needs for a year to consider and sponsorship in kind from a firm specializing in the use of Scottish produce in a range of soups and preserves, we had plenty to send. The only problem was expense. But part of the solution lay under our eyes: kayaks are hollow. Our Acadia and Freedom models travelled to the Solomon Islands with their hulls stuffed with cock-a-leekie soup and raspberry jam, padded by sleeping mats. The kindly computer wizard from Disability Services who was fine-tuning my dubious technical abilities for the year ahead took my bulky support seat to the post office. Weighing the parcel, addressed poste restante to Honiara, the postmaster said: 'Is this our Lucy, then?' There were jokes about how I missed sunny islands so much I'd sent myself to one. But in this case both the armchair and the traveller were going.

Over the next months a natural energy salesman provided a Missionary Kit lantern, plus a system of miniature solar panels to operate everything from laptop and printer to a satellite e-mail set-up through which I'd send articles to the *Sunday Times* magazine, and I began, with the boys' eager assistance, the serious job of packing a crate to go by sea and listing what we must carry. Flight tickets were already purchased – part of the 'say yes now, and worry about the details later' policy – but it was going to be a long haul for children who'd never flown more than five hours before: six days' travel minimum, and nearly everyone sent out so far had been delayed on Santa Cruz by bad weather. For the last part of the journey, I gathered, things needed to be waterproofed. Plastic suitcases and polythene went on the list, along with a careful selection of reading matter. Peter the teacher, who would set off after us in the summer of 1998, gathered educational materials, and his wife Mhairi enrolled on a first-aid course. I was too preoccupied to wonder why letters from the students who went out had been few. Steve and Jocylyn had been home a while from their brief stay but had plunged back into demanding schedules, so I hadn't gleaned much beyond confirmation that Pigeon was *very* far away, telescopic fishing rods not useful there, dried foods a welcome change from plain local fare, and the 'natives' fairly friendly but their toilet arrangements primitive. I added plastic shovels to our luggage list, and stowed away at the back of my mind one phrase of Steve's I could have read as a warning but chose not to: 'You and your kids are the only people I know, Lucy, who I'd recommend to stay a year out there.'

Into the midst of preparations came intriguing news. Diana's other son, twin of the one with heavy religious leanings, was involved in politics. He was married to a Solomon Islander, and some of his children would be attending Pigeon Island School with mine. While she'd been travelling, he'd been on an election campaign. Apparently making all his speeches in Pidgin English – known as Pijin in the Solomons – Ross Hepworth had emerged triumphant as President of Temotu Province and was coming to London to represent the interests of the Islands at a conference. Diana wrote that it would be marvellous if I could meet him, and enclosed a list of contacts for biographical background. She had been, as I was when I went to Tuin, in her mid-twenties when she set sail for 'Paradise'. I could understand the ultimate aim – to find the perfect place, away from the less desirable influences of the world, to raise a family – but what had made her take that initial step of sailing into the blue? I was also curious to know how others who'd encountered the Hepworths during their years at sea, or on Pigeon itself, perceived them. To this end, I invited eight ladies to luncheon at a hotel in London. Ross was going to be in town the same week.

For the Hepworth history luncheon, I dug into my ancient 'publicity' wardrobe, emerging in suede and silk and finishing the ensemble with a clipboard and tape recorder. And I was glad I'd bothered, for the group I encountered were as formidable as they were charming. It made sense that Diana came from a background of character. Her elder sister, also once a model, was still imposingly beautiful; her friends confident, articulate and immaculately groomed. Former sailing contacts and a woman who'd lived for a time on the island of Santa Cruz were quieter, but shrewd. There was also the wife of a government architect, from the days when the Solomons were a British Protectorate, who contributed a valuable 'colonial' view. I'd not invited men because women behave differently when men are present, and I wanted my guests to feel uninhibited. What I didn't expect was loud controversy about why Tom and Diana Hepworth had sailed away and gone to live on an island, and what kind of people they were. There were also strong views about the pros and cons of bringing up children somewhere so remote:

'We used to call them "the Empire Builders", carving out a corner of Britain under the sun.'

'Nonsense, Diana never had a good word to say for England. They left straight after the war like rats deserting a sinking ship.'

'They left because they believed there was a better life to be found.'

'They were pioneers. That place was absolute bush. Now it has a lawn.'

'Wonderful place to bring up children . . .'

'Of course we all thought it a risky place to raise a family.'

'It was idyllic!'

'But look what happened to Tasha . . .'

'And what about Ross going native?'

'What could they expect, bringing them up miles from any European society?'

'Well, at least he's moving in government circles now.'

I met the 'gone native' son next day. I'd find out 'what happened to Tasha', his sister, in due course. Like me, Ross had put on an image for London, but his mannerisms and the way he talked and walked contrasted oddly with his formal wear. I didn't know it then but lively use of eyebrows in conversation is a Reef Islands habit, and the slightly stilted speech was explained when he told me that Pijin, not English, was his first language. He walked awkwardly because he wasn't used to shoes, and said he'd had more contact with local Islanders when he was a child than with his parents. He considered himself a Solomon Islander. 'I am,' he said with a disarming grin, 'the black sheep of the family.' I knew that grin would appeal to Joe and Benji, and we spoke of our children. 'I don't want my sons going through what I did,' he said, 'being teased about their accents. That's why I want a British teacher for them.' But he seemed keen that they should understand their mother's culture as well. He also said Pigeon was a great place for children, and from what he'd heard of mine he reckoned they'd fit in – but he'd like to meet them. This pleased me. It was vitally important the boys enjoyed Pigeon, and this man, son of the senior, British Hepworths, husband and father of Islanders, would be a good person to judge.

I told the boys Ross was coming, and Benji said he'd be glad to look after the fire and carry across water if he stayed in the small studio I'd had built for privacy when working. Boldly, I agreed. This man was 'opening the door' of his island home wide for the Irvine family, and would probably have more day-to-day contact with us than his more formal mother. Also, just as I'd recognized something of a spirit I could identify with in Diana, I clicked with something quite different in him. He *was* like an Islander – like one of my old friends from the Torres Strait – and I felt no embarrassment about serving him our usual simple meals and taking him for walks as entertainment. Joe and Benji liked him immediately – Benji was thrilled to ride on his shoulders, his hands gripping Ross's head exactly like a Torres Strait child. I felt sure now that with this warm-hearted family man on Pigeon, the boys would have no problem settling, whatever new and strange customs awaited us. 'They'll run wild,' he said. 'You'll never see them.' The boys yelled 'Yippee,' and most of me exulted with them. But another question arose: would they settle when they got back? Ross said they were young enough to adapt with ease to a mix of cultures and a temporary change of home base, but like me he was less certain about Magnus, who'd be thirteen when we left. He liked school, and being with his peers. No doubt he'd like being on an island, too, with endless opportunities for swimming and kayaking. Compromise was probably safest – and what Magnus himself wanted. He'd come out and stay a while, then return to Scotland to move on, with friends, to senior school. I'd find an adventurous student to bring him out again later, and Magnus's best friend's parents agreed to become his guardians. Much was settled during Ross's visit, and he helped us choose underwater torches. He also indicated that I'd find the story of his island upbringing, and how and why he became the first white president of a remote Solomon Islands province, as worth telling as his mother's story, and I suspected he was right.

The Irvine children received no toys that Christmas. Instead of parcels under a tree dragged from the woods, there was luggage filled with sunscreen, Tilley hats and snazzy dark glasses. Fully into the spirit of both Scottish winter and coming sun, Joe dressed up in snowsuit, sun-hat and shades, tore outside and made daft faces at the frost-rimmed window; Benji wanted to pack his rucksack *now*. Magnus gave me a pot I loved, decorated with tragi-comic faces, and lifted the turkey from the Rayburn. When we sat back replete, Charlie thumping the carcass about on the roof, Joe said: 'I wonder what Christmas will be like next year . . .' We hadn't a clue, and speculated instead on yet further packing requirements, attempting to minimize and to cater for all eventualities at the same time.

'What did you find you most needed on your old island, Mum?'

I said this wasn't the same, but Joe had a point.

'Teabags and string.'

They argued I didn't *need* teabags. I agreed, and had managed with few. But this island year wasn't going to be a spartan exercise in staying alive, and tea would enhance my quality of life. I explained also that I felt no need to put myself through the hoops of a pure survival challenge again. Neither did I want them to experience that. Simplification, yes; deprivation, no. Essentially, we were going to Pigeon because my job there included being able to give them the taste of island living I'd always wanted for them – but nothing like as

raw an experience as my *Castaway* year. We'd take basic equipment –
matches, billycans, candles, fishing line – but also luxuries such as
cotton sheets and shampoo. On Tuin, I reminded the boys, there'd
been a period when I couldn't wash my hair for four months. It hadn't
mattered; shampooing isn't essential to life, but I wasn't expecting
such extremes now. Magnus's top priority was an all-purpose knife, of
which, being a country boy, he had several; Joe would take binoculars
for birdwatching; Benji was torn – for months – between teddies but
finally, to my surprise, took none, saying, 'I don't *need* one.' But he
warmed to the suggestion of taking an album of snapshots from our
lives, ostensibly to show 'the Islander children' but in fact as a
reminder, if it proved necessary in a strange land, that we did have
another home.

We had little idea what our accommodation on Pigeon would be
like, until a photograph arrived showing two uprights and a crossbeam
framing an expanse of sea, with what looked like a smoking incense
cone in the distance. The cone was Tinakula, a volcano, which
dominated the view from what Diana Hepworth described encouragingly as 'your west veranda'. But she also said building materials had
failed to arrive, and intimated tents might be wise. So the lists grew,
for both the crate to be freighted and what we were to carry. They
consisted mainly of food for the mind, food for the body and cooking
implements. If everything else that represented stability in the
children's lives wobbled, there must at least be food. Concerns had
arisen because, over the preparation months, I'd picked up oddments
of information about Pigeon that weren't entirely soothing. Not only
did the island lie within a tropical cyclone belt but it had actually been
hit once, and it wasn't impossible it might be hit again. There were
also earthquakes, and that volcano sometimes did more than smoke. A
tent suddenly didn't sound attractive, but if we had to rely on one, it
must be good. Specialists offered valuable advice, but what struck the
boys dumb with delight was an offer from another local firm to *send
out* biscuits and cakes by ship. To a mother worrying how she was
going to feed three hungry boys quickly, in what could be challenging conditions, this was comfort indeed. Into a space in our crate
between four kinds of antibiotic and film supplies (plus silica gel to
combat humidity) went a box of Paradise Cakes. There's no such
thing as cheating when preparing for life somewhere truly remote,
with children.

A long letter, at last, from the girl who'd gone out to familiarize Ross's children with English told me, movingly, that her time on Pigeon had been life-changing. She apologized for not having written before, explaining she'd wanted to let herself become fully involved with the immediate rather than stand back and analyse it – an attitude I could understand. The geography graduate gave similar reasons for few letters. Their evident absorption in island life was a further spur for us, but both mentioned that they hoped Ross would be on the island when we arrived and would organize our transport for the final leg – because his presence made '*all the difference*'.

By late spring 1998, I'd found caretakers for Inchreoch – two artists and a writer. In return for my peace of mind, the peace of a cottage in the Highlands was theirs and, with the key tucked ready for them in the woodpile and our packing complete, there was – suddenly, it seemed – nothing left to do but go. When the moment came, Joe shook out an extra helping of nuts for the birds; Benji tucked up his teddies and covered his Lego island against dust; Magnus made sure the water tank was full, and I hugged Charlie, letting him dribble and purr for a moment against my ear. Then we left our little home without a backward glance. There was so much ahead.

En route, I tried to impress on the boys that our year away wasn't going to be a holiday. It was just an extension of their life and education in a distant place, and some aspects might be uncomfortable.

'Like what?'

'Well, the heat, as I keep saying . . .'

'I love the sun!'

'Learning where it's safe to swim . . .'

'Reef shark hardly ever attack. It says in the book.'

'Insects . . .'

'Can't be worse than midges.'

Nothing put them off and I loved their enthusiasm. Stopping only to shower travel-stained bodies in Singapore, we flew to the other side of the world on a prolonged high of anticipation. I rested my spine for a week on Queensland's ultimately eco-friendly Fraser Island, while the boys dashed about happily spotting kookaburras and dingos, before we moved on, hopping over a thousand miles of Pacific Ocean, to Guadalcanal.

★

We arrived in Honiara, capital of the Solomon Islands, in the middle of the night. Wet heat pressed down through the blackness, squeezing out our energy.

'It's a bit like Africa, isn't it?' said Benji cautiously. He'd collapsed in tears when we first landed there.

'It's horribly hot,' said Magnus.

'It feels flat,' said Joe loudly and flatly. And, tired and sweaty, I nearly said, 'Shut up.'

But there was Ross at the barrier, a little golden boy on his shoulders and a smiling woman at his side. His recent brief status as President of Temotu Province still gave him enough clout to make our passage through customs easy and, to the boys' delight, he'd managed to commandeer a police truck to transport us to our modest hotel. Pegi, Ross's second wife, from Reef Islands, was totally silent at first, but had a smile which flowered every time our eyes met. The boy was Andrew, their son, who would be a classmate of Benji's and Joe's. We'd meet the rest of the family shortly.

'Rest,' Ross commanded. 'It'll take you months to get used to the heat.'

We spent ten days in Honiara, in the middle of a festival to celebrate the twentieth anniversary of independence. This included float parades, choir competitions and pop and reggae pumped day and night from loudspeakers rigged up in palm trees. I also had to chase permits for our residency in the Outer Islands and – on Ross's recommendation – purchase more food to be sent by ship to Pigeon. 'There's not much for European tastes there,' he warned. We wanted that not to matter, to become accustomed to whatever was eaten locally – with our Scottish goodies as emergency frills – but, with Joe already losing weight and Steve's comment about local fare being limited, I felt I should listen.

All we saw, during that first stay in Honiara – naked male buttocks jigging through leaf displays in a festival village; drunks at a shanty-town trade show – and all we did – including our shopping, consisting of weevily grains and musty prunes scooped from open bins in a Chinese bulk store – went by in a blur of heat and fatigue. I'd hoped the festival might make a fun and informative start to our stay in the Solomons, but we were too drained to appreciate it. It had been a mistake to encourage the children to fall in love with big, clean, rich Australia, then bring them to this. Under an inadequate punkah in our hotel room, we sweated through the nights and woke up tired. The toilet didn't work; there was a smell of old fruit skins everywhere, and after trying soggy fried bananas accompanied by flies on the first day, Joe could only manage plain rice. I accepted that adapting to the climate would take time, but prayed Ross was wrong about how long. Breathing in the heavy, damp air as I forced myself to explore un-prepossessing streets lined with peeling stores full of plastic and cafés selling tepid tinned tuna, I felt literally out of my element. It was not for this that we'd crossed the world.

The boys, although as fazed as I, were determined to find some-thing positive about Honiara. Uncomfortable at the trade show among a press of beery bodies and a babble of languages none of which resembled the Pijin we'd learned, they took a coconut to a flat piece of ground and kicked it around by themselves. As whites, and British, we were in a glaringly distinct minority. Ross's children – we met five – were in the midst of friends who spoke their language. Like Pegi, they smiled but hung back from close contact. Ross was always friendly, but clearly busy ferrying contacts about. He said we should delay our departure, give ourselves more time to adjust. 'Relax! You're on Solomon Island time now.' But I couldn't have felt less relaxed. He obviously wasn't going to be around to organize the last leg of our jour-ney to Pigeon, or to ease our introduction to the locals there either.

At the end of a week, as keen as they to get away from the crowd in which I felt like an ignorant intruder, I flopped down among weeds and discarded coconut husks and watched the boys at their valiantly improvised game. The dirt of the town clung to their sweating faces, and I knew they probably wanted only to fall into the puddle-sized pool back at our hotel. But where we were going, there'd be no hotels and none of the sweet Tropical Juice I tried to cool them down with here. I clung to what Diana had said about the climate in the Outer Islands being less oppressive than on Guadalcanal, where we were now. It was while I was thinking of this, wishing we could fly anywhere there was a breath of wind, right now, that I noticed small faces watching me, watching the boys. A group of five or six children were peeping from behind a tree. I indicated their presence, with a movement of my head, to Joe.

'We know,' he called. 'If you go away, they might come out.'

'Shall I go then?'

Magnus said: 'It might be an idea, Mum. This is the nearest they've got.'

He told me then that, day by day, these children had been creeping closer. They wanted to join in but were shy. Their culture didn't teach them to be forward.

'Will you be all right?'

'Of course.'

I left the grounds, found a driver willing to scour the town for my needs, and returned an hour later to find a lively game in progress, including three of those from behind the tree. Triumphantly, I presented the group with a real football.

'That's great, Mum,' shouted Magnus, still sweating copiously but much happier now. It hadn't only been the heat getting us down. I suspected that, like me, faced with Solomon Islanders not only en masse but en fête over a celebration of the dismissal of British influence, the boys had been wondering how they'd ever begin to cross the cultural barriers. In Africa, we'd always been approached. Even if we didn't welcome attention, people spoke to us. Solomon Islanders were quite different. The majority, whom I later discovered to be almost as 'foreign' to Reef Islanders as to us, seemed to look through us. I admired the pride, but it was also intimidating. It was probable, too, that, like many outposts that seem poor to those from the West but are an alluring Mecca to those from less developed areas, Honiara attracted not only the ambitious but the disaffected from the Outer Islands. Enterprising Chinese had the main grip on business interests, and there was friction among the disparate Islander population groups. But, as strangers just passing through en route to an adventure with a base still four hundred miles distant, we understood little, and had our own way to find. Sport has a universal language, and was clearly a good place to begin.

'How many footballs are we taking to Pigeon?' asked Benji.

'Probably not enough,' I said. If football made the difference between acceptance and isolation, we'd better take plenty. It struck me now that there was little reference to the indigenous peoples of the Islands in Diana Hepworth's descriptions of Pigeon. Clearly the island itself, not the culture of people in the area, was what was most important to her. What would become most important to us about Pigeon remained to be seen. But a guide book told me that, although the group known collectively as Reef Islands was very scattered, consisting of 'sixteen small landforms' covering in all only seventy-eight square kilometres within four thousand square kilometres of ocean, there were about six thousand people on them – which must affect not only Ross's life but the lives of the other Hepworths as well, to some degree.

Diana was right about climatic differences in the Solomons. When we left Honiara and our tiny inter-island plane dropped down to refuel in a field full of flowers at Kira Kira, even those of us who'd sicked up our anti-malarials during the bumpy flight revived. A light, delicious wind tickled the tops of picture-postcard palms and ruffled the grass runway. 'I can't wait to jump in!' cried Joe, mesmerized by twinkling sea. A fellow passenger with her luggage on her head, who'd just relieved herself discreetly behind a bush – this was the extent of the airport facilities – returned my involuntary smile. Encouraged by this friendliness, I tried out my Pijin.

'Hemi oraet nao,' I said, indicating Joe. (He's better now.) The woman had been close to us when he was sick.

She inclined her head. 'Go wea?' (Where are you going?)

'Mifela gogo lo' Rif.' (To Reef Islands.)

'Rif Aelan,' she echoed and the conversation didn't proceed further, but her smile lifted my spirits like the sea breeze. She hadn't stared through us like the Honiara men.

The next drop down, on Santa Cruz, was the nearest it was possible to get to Reef Islands by air. If a canoe wasn't waiting for us when we flew in, the plan was to contact Diana by radio that evening and arrange onward transport then. There was no canoe. Diana had, however, alerted Joanne, a VSO worker, to our arrival and we were met. Ross had said there was a place run by Islander friends of his on Santa Cruz and to stay the night there if we needed to, but a friend of Joanne's, leaving on the plane we came in on, said we could use his house. Not yet au fait with the automatic hospitality of both whites and Islanders in the more remote Solomons, we accepted gratefully, and Joanne led the way. As we walked along a path lined by a mix of woven leaf and prefabricated houses, some bright with bougainvillea, she said: 'I can't understand why Diana didn't send a boat today. It's so perfect.'

'Never mind,' I said, happy with the idea of exploring this pretty place. Children with shining eyes and dark dandelion puffs of hair stood holding hands to watch us walk by, and never failed to smile if we did. That afternoon we bought local vegetables at a market and later, floating blissfully on calm blue depths under a calm blue sky, I listened contentedly, my maternal confidence restored after the dis-appointment of Honiara, as Benji shrieked with excitement pursuing 'a spotty fish that keeps trying to bury himself' and Joe, appetite in fine fettle now, called, 'This is great!'

'I wouldn't mind staying here a week at least,' said Magnus.

Perhaps that's what we should have done.

4

Rocky Start

I WANTED TO CRY OUT TO GOD, TO PLEAD AND VILIFY, BUT I COULDN'T open my lips. I wanted to close my eyes and believe what was happening was only a nightmare. I wanted to be anywhere but in the middle of the ocean, no land in sight, in an eighteen-foot canoe with three terrified children, on waves that ceaselessly battered and drenched us. And I wanted to smack Diana Hepworth's face. Why had she let us set off today, when the wind had risen in the night and everyone on Santa Cruz had shaken their heads as they gazed out at the swell? Why hadn't I put my foot down, waiting, if necessary, weeks for a cargo boat to take us? Joe, red hair sodden against a dead white brow, bailed automatically with blanched hands. His eyes were unfocused, mouth slack. He was sitting in the water he bailed. Magnus, no less white but with eyes darkened by understanding, mouth grim, swept sea from our laps in double handfuls. He'd tried using a hat, but hands seemed faster. Benji, my Benji, screamed and screamed . . .

When we'd set out that morning I'd sat, as advised by Diana over the radio, in the stern, where she thought it would be least bumpy for my spine. 'You'll be here for elevenses,' she'd said, adding: 'I'm longing to see you.' Her voice was clear and confident, and I conjured a picture of her in a leaf-covered radio shack on Pigeon, eagerly anticipating the arrival of her biographer. Last night, I'd looked forward to seeing her again, too. To mark the occasion – the final forty-five-mile leg of our journey – I'd tied a jaunty scarf round the crown of my otherwise severe Tilley hat. Mary Kingsley with a touch of pzazz. Luckily the hat had strings. Within minutes of our departure these were tight across my throat, my head bared and soaked, and a cataract of sea obliterated all view from my Wild Fox shades. When we'd set out I'd had a camera to hand, imagining, as we crossed from Santa Cruz to Reef Islands, that I'd be able to make a record of our journey. But I could see nothing but water, with the occasional glimpse of tilting blue sky, out of which sunlight flashed like spikes of lightning on bruise-black waves. Less than five minutes from the start, my back was aching. The spinal support was too big to carry from Honiara on the little plane, so it would follow on later by cargo boat. No-one had anticipated a particularly rough crossing.

At first we hugged the coast of Santa Cruz as Tali, the Reef Islander driving, didn't want to head for open sea until we had to. The canoe was powered by a twenty-five-horsepower outboard and we rode over rather than through the waves, each one, as they grew bigger, requiring a strategic climb and plunge. At first the boys laughed at the roller-coaster effect, their voices rising gleefully like children pushed higher and higher on a swing. Sheltered by a canopy over the bow from the worst of the spray, they watched with amusement as all traces of my dignity were washed away, and I laughed back. But gradually, as the climbing and plunging went on and repeated drenchings chilled us even with the hot sun above, I began to long for the sight of a bay that Tali said we could shelter in if the weather didn't improve. There were two other Reef Islanders in the boat, with a tarpaulin pulled over them so they were just a yellow hump between me and the boys. Their bare feet were spread for purchase under wet bunches of betel-nut like giant grapes. It was hard to enquire about our progress as water entered my mouth as soon as I opened it, but Tali, after two hours of driving with jaws clamped and eyes slit to allow in the minimum of salt, suddenly said: 'We stop,' and I couldn't have been more relieved.

As we drew up in the shallows, land that had been nothing but a blur through curtains of sea revealed itself as a green bay, with a stretch of grey reef topped by a strip of sand as beach. A few huts, with leaf walls and palm fronds tied onto thatched roofs, stood back from the shore, and around these some female figures moved. I was cold and could move only stiffly. The boys stretched, quickly finding smiles as their feet found land. I bent under the canopy and searched among boxes packed at dawn for items intuition must have made me put close to the surface (as well as the suncream, unused, Diana had said was a must) – cocoa, coffee, dried milk and a billycan. These I handed to Magnus and Benji, while Joe collected kumera – a type of sweet potato – that had fallen out of the basket we bought yesterday. We filled my sodden culottes with them, bending the legs up to make bags. I told Tali I'd like to offer them to the women at the huts, if they'd kindly let us have a fire. I'd heard that, in the Solomons, it's rude to set up camp without asking permission.

Impassive stares met my bedraggled approach, but the kumera were accepted. The women wore faded floral skirts with perished black bras; their hair was dusty, feet bare. Magnus, Joe and Benji followed the men's example, taking off their wet T-shirts and laying them on coral to dry. The sun was so hot that pale patches appeared within minutes, and the edges of the cloth lifted in the wind. Quite recovered now, the boys ran off to find crabs in a gully, while I sat with my earthy-smelling culottes spread around me, collecting myself.

One of the Islanders travelling with us, Henri, a teacher, sat a little way off, preparing betel to chew. Conversationally, I tossed over the idea that it was a shame we hadn't made the crossing yesterday, when it was calm. He looked broodingly out at the dark mass of sea beyond lighter waters over the reef and lifted his chin, in a gesture I didn't understand. When the women appeared with already heated water, he accepted a cup of bracing mocha before filling his mouth with betel, then said, 'Yes,' in a delayed response, 'beta yesterday.' Tali didn't want any mocha, but munched pieces of boiled kumera the women brought. They'd misunderstood: I'd wanted to give them the kumera; they'd thought I'd thrust it at them to cook for us.

'Fo iufela!' I protested, but they shook their heads and retired behind their huts.

'It's oraet,' said Henri, 'eat.'

I pushed a piece of the greyish, waxy root into my mouth, glad of its heat, and the comforting drink which I let cool a while before calling the boys for theirs. 'Do you think we'll go on today?' I asked. 'Which way is it?'

Henri's lips were orange with betel. Up and out went his chin in what I now realized was a gesture saving words to indicate, amongst other things, direction – in this case, straight out towards the blue-blackness beyond the edge of the reef. 'Mi no savvy,' he said (I don't know) and although he stayed where he was, I felt him retire into himself.

It was Tali, when he'd rested for an hour, who suggested we head beyond the reef to the deep water ('dipwata') since Missus was expecting us, and only return to the bay if it looked bad. Sometimes it was calmer out there than close to shore. The boys and I were happy with this. After all, we did want to get to Pigeon. But, aware now of what the journey might be like, I tucked Joe and Benji well under the canopy and covered myself with an oilskin. Magnus elected – for a while – to sit upright.

We headed out, searching for that elusive calm, and by the time we realized it wasn't to be found we risked as much by turning back as going on. One moment there was the bay, receding before it was blotted to a misty outline, the next it seemed there was nothing solid anywhere. Our entire world became one of lurching blue, with the glassy edges of waves breaking into our eyes. Nothing was clear any longer, not even one another's faces. Sometimes we were pitched about so violently, I didn't know what was blue of sea or blue of darkened sky; what a minute of this madness or what an hour. Tali craned for a glimpse of land – in any direction – found none, and fingered what I thought was an amulet round his neck. He darted quick looks at it between waves that, in his exposed position at the tiller, would have knocked him flat if he hadn't been ready for them. The amulet was a compass. Benji began to cry and soon to scream, pleading, when it was too late, to turn back, and I began to ask myself what on earth we were doing in this totally inadequate craft in the middle of nowhere, with one visible life jacket – which I struggled forward to put on Benji – between the seven of us, no proper bailers and no way of calling for help.

Four hours later, I was kneeling up against the canopied bow of the canoe, legs braced, spine rigid, and so numb with cold as to be almost beyond pain, trying to make a tent of body and oilskin over my smallest son. Waves broke over the side and hit my back. I tried to take deep breaths against both pain and fear, and find reserves of strength to communicate to Benji. I longed desperately for his terror to end, but couldn't bear to imagine how it might. In the 1980s, I'd heard vaguely on Santa Cruz, an Australian had drowned in this stretch of sea. Others with him survived, but I knew that if we capsized it was unlikely we would reach land. I think Magnus knew this too, but said nothing. To bail and believe we'd make it was the only course. I thought the accident must have happened in freak conditions, and assumed the same about a report in a Honiara newspaper telling of the recent disappearance of two families, including children, between Santa Cruz and Reefs. Now I understood this was simply a damned dangerous place. Furious thoughts flooded my brain: *was Diana Hepworth – as someone I had until now ignored had suggested – slightly gaga? Was this whole book idea the mad dream of someone who'd given no proper thought to what this journey could be like for a woman with a spinal disability and three children? Did she give a damn whether we lived or died? My God, I'd never have let those students come out if I'd imagined they'd have to face anything like this . . .* But they hadn't; Ross had been in charge of their travel arrangements and had delayed their journeys when necessary. I pressed as close as I could to Benji, trying to warm him and block out the sickening sight of the sea. He was reduced to sobbing now. Between sobs, an exhausted little voice reached me:

'Why couldn't you do your writing at home, Mum?'

Through all that followed, I remembered those words. *How could I put my children into such danger?* I thought of my computer and satellite phone, currently sloshing about in plastic bags, and all the rest of our baggage I must at some point have considered vital; I thought of our car and house – there was nothing I wouldn't have happily flung into the hateful sea if it could have shortened that journey and brought us to safety. Horror and guilt fed the anger that, through my exhaustion, surfaced from time to time to quest about and land on Diana, mad or otherwise. *How dare she do this to my sons!*

It was Joe, gripping the gunwale with both hands as he peered forward to watch dipping sunlight crumpling over waves that, gradually, had begun to feel only big, not huge, who croaked: 'There's a bird. That means we're near land.' His eye sockets were mauve, as though he'd been punched, but he reached out, closed a hand on my wrist and kept squeezing. 'It's OK, Mum.'

'That's right!' shouted Magnus suddenly, looking up momentarily from his automatic bailing. 'And look – there's land!'

Beneath their yellow carapace the Islanders smiled, their dark, sea-streaming faces kind, and echoed: 'Lan'!' At that word, Benji, who'd gone limp, opened his eyes. I moved back from my protecting tent position, so he could see the smiles. The land was only a line in the distance, but it was there. 'Rif Aelan,' said the youngest Islander, a teenager named Kiyo. When things were at their worst, he'd had two improvised bailers – a bottle cut in half and a petrol funnel with his palm over the end – ripped out of his grasp by the sea, and had buried his head in his hands. But he couldn't have looked happier now, and stopped bailing to gesture enthusiastically, if vaguely: 'Pigeon Aelan.' At this, although there was still nothing definable as a single island ahead, Benji scrambled to kneel between my arms with his head just above the canoe canopy. Any land was good enough for him.

'Hurray!' he yelled. 'Hurray!'

Then he turned to me before sinking back down out of the spray.

'But you won't forget what you promised, will you?'

I'd promised to have 'a strict word' with Diana Hepworth. As we progressed gradually, still lurching over every wave, to where the dark line ahead separated into mounds, Magnus said: 'There's no way we're ever doing a journey like this again.'

It summed up what we all felt, and was the thought uppermost in my mind when we landed, at last, on Pigeon Island.

We felt relief at our arrival but were chilled, exhausted, and some of us at least in a state of semi-shock. My instinct was to get the boys into the last of the sinking sun to revive them. Nothing else, during those first moments on Pigeon, but the path of the dying sun made an impression on me. We followed it. I held Benji's hand, Joe held mine and Magnus came close behind as our feet found their way through shallows, over sand, up cement steps, along a rough path, down a short, steep hill of crumbling coral and into the remaining bars of sunlight that lay spread like towels for us in a tiny bay.

I tell a lie. Something else did impose itself, peripherally, on my battered senses, as I guided my sons to warmth: it was the sight of Diana Hepworth's tall, bikini'd figure, hair up in a little ribbon, standing in the middle of the path. Her arms were flung wide in welcome, and she was speaking. It was this vision that made me swerve down into the cove, where, with her arthritic feet, she couldn't follow. For the moment I had to block her out of my consciousness; to regroup. We never wanted to face that journey again but we might not want to spend more than one night here – never mind a year. It could all have been a mistake. Besides, right then I didn't trust myself to speak to her.

But the sun acted like medicine on us all. I lay flat, feeling the rigidity go from my spine, and with it the pain. Joe still kept a hand on my wrist, but smiled more convincingly by the moment. Benji shook himself and reeled about like a puppy that's been flung in a pool and is happy to be out – he was the first to recover fully. Magnus gradually began to look alert. Distantly, I heard Diana's voice as she told Ben, the 'religious' son we'd met in Scotland, to 'Take them to their house. It's the warmest place on the island.'

'Give them a few minutes, Mum,' he replied mildly. 'They want the sun.' I was grateful for his understanding.

When the light began to fade, as it does fast in the tropics, I clambered back up the hill and approached what I recognized from photographs as Diana's house. It was impressive, a colonial-style bungalow, with a red roof and four generous leaf verandas. She stood on the nearest, waiting, head high.

'There you are, darling,' she said smoothly. 'Supper is at quarter to six. I've put it back a bit. You have your shower now.'

I was glad I'd given myself a little time. Was she hurt I'd charged past her outstretched arms? If so, she'd mastered herself since, and so must I. I was about to refuse the supper invitation – or rather, announcement – preferring the idea of an early night preceded by a hot drink with the children, but something about her proud bearing – and the knowledge that, one way or another, I'd have to live close to her at least for a while – made me bite back the negative words. The boys would doubtless soon find their lost appetites, too. We were shown our quarters, which at that stage I barely took in, interested only in how quickly we could get into dry clothes. I opened the emergency bag – the only item brought with us from the canoe – and found something for everybody.

I later discovered Diana had had all our other bags taken to her house, and opened all those not locked. Had I known this sooner, I'd have been livid. Having lived independently from an early age, I wasn't used to being organized by anyone – or having my bags rummaged through. But I understood, in time, that Diana wasn't rummaging with any intent other than to check what needed drying out – nor, in her view, over-organizing. She was simply doing what she believed correct, and had we been guests in the sort of country house she was brought up in, in the England of the 1920s, instead of on a tropical island, she would probably have had our bags unpacked by servants.

Our first meal on Pigeon Island was served in silky evening air after sunset, on a pretty thatched veranda, with a Reef Islander housegirl in attendance. The boys sat separately from the adults, at a large painted table in an alcove, with their own covered dishes. Diana, who'd changed into an elegant full-length gown, reclined on a lounger beside a long coffee table complete with cloth and a vast conch shell filled with hibiscus flowers. Ben sat in a convenient position to oversee the needs of both tables. The 'girl' – in fact a woman – hovered, a black shadow, approaching to clear plates when called. She was thin, with cropped hair like the top of a matchstick, and wore a stained sleeveless top over a skirt with an uneven hem. The ribbon in Diana's upswept hair, which had matched her bikini earlier, had now been changed to match her long gown, and there was a touch of professionally applied powder on her still good complexion. We ate Tahitian Poisson Cru, a speciality of Diana's, off good china, and very Britishly cubed, exotic fruit salad served from a cut-glass bowl. We drank something delicious called bushlime.

While the girl washed the dishes, we sat on, chatting lightly about everything but the eight-hour canoe trip that had been such hell. I had a powerful sense of the surreal. Only two hours ago I'd been living through some of the worst moments I'd ever experienced, during which an understanding of the precariousness of life had been borne in on me with frightening force. The thousands of miles covered during the preceding days were still in my mind as we'd been tossed helplessly in that puny craft on a huge sea, promoting an overwhelming sense of distance from all that could be described as 'normal', let alone comfortable. Now here we were enjoying civilized luxury. The bizarre part was that we were still in the middle of nowhere. All that separated our dinner setting from a crazy world of water that could easily have meant the end of all our dreams was a few hundred yards of shallow earth upon coral, ending in short cliffs all round. A cartoon image sprang to mind of Diana in her immaculate evening attire, reclining serenely on her lounger atop a tiny atoll decorated by a single palm, with all the madness of the Outside World held at bay beyond the vast moat of a boiling blue ocean.

Walking through the house to wash my hands, I noticed a painting of a ship with a magnificent square rig. This was the *Arthur Rogers*, the seventy-foot Brixham trawler that brought Diana and her husband to Pigeon in 1957, when they'd already lived at sea for a decade. This woman had encountered every imaginable kind of wind and water, and built, with her own hands, a home on the island of her desire, discovered on extensive travels. It wasn't going to be easy to tell her off about our unfortunate little forty-five-mile canoe crossing.

Falling into deep sleep immediately that first night, we hardly knew where our limbs sprawled, except that there was a roof, rather than the tent we'd been expecting to unpack, over our heads. I woke once and, taking a torch, crept out of the neat, rectangular shoebox that was to be both office and bedroom, and made my way to where Benji and Joe lay on handmade beds next door, and where Magnus slept in what was to be our kitchen. I wanted to reassure myself they were all there, and all right. The peaceful rhythm of Benji's breathing, after his earlier awful sounds of fear, was like a balm, and I didn't move again until a flock of lorikeets, rising from the palms all round, woke me just before dawn. Leaving the boys sleeping but within earshot, I moved as softly as I could to the nearest bit of sea in which I could dangle my toes while watching the sunrise. The journey here, and Diana, had made an impression on me yesterday, but so far I didn't feel I had any idea what Pigeon was like.

The Little Wharf, only yards down a palm- and hibiscus-flanked path from our quarters – known as Tasha's House – was a good place to watch the day begin, and for me to begin, internally, my stay on Pigeon, pushing the horrors of yesterday to the back of my mind. From this position, all other habitation on the island was invisible. To the south, close by, sat a small, improbably perfect coral island, with nothing on it but wild, white trumpet-shaped flowers dotting a generous piping of foliage like icing round a cake – and a few tall plume-headed palms like candles in the middle. Tom Hepworth had named this Poppet Island, after the pet name he gave his daughter when she was small, because it, too, was diminutively sweet, as she had been. To the east, beyond a stretch of now calm sea, lay a low island, Nandelli, only four hundred metres distant at the narrowest point, with palms clustered thickly along one end in night-blue silhouette. Towards the centre, where the palms were less dense, hot pink light was beginning to flare, pushing slim trunks and spiky heads into sharp relief, then diffusing to a blush as great tracts of silver straddled the sea. I dabbled my toes in the water, which, like the air, felt the perfect temperature for the human body, and when I looked up again the sun had already parted from the palms and was sending out dazzling spokes as it climbed. I watched, then followed the path back to the house. The colours of the hibiscus on either side were clear now – crimson, ivory, liquid pink – and the soft cups of petals seemed to hold the glow of the sunrise. I picked four to decorate a nook among the seat-sized roots of a tree we christened our Kaikai Tree – after the Reef Island word for food.

Benji was already outside, running fingers through the coral 'gravel' surrounding our cement veranda like a frill. It seemed to him full of treasure – shapes like bones, fishes and trees.

'Look at this, Mum. When can we unpack the kayaks? What's for breakfast?'

The doors to the east veranda room where Joe and Benji slept were huge – one almost an entire wall, which, facing the Little Wharf and complete with pegs on which fishing gear would hang, could be pulled out, to make the room open to the air. Joe propped himself on one elbow and looked straight out at the dawn-washed scene of palms, hibiscus and sea.

'I can't decide whether to go fishing or swimming first,' he said.

Magnus was still dozing when I shook muesli into bowls found in a cupboard. When he woke, he opted for a water-based start to the day, too. My own first days on Pigeon would be dominated by the task of unpacking the crate that had preceded us by sea, but I wanted the boys to find all the delight they could in their new surroundings quickly so that they, too, could put the canoe crossing to the back of their minds. I was torn then, as often, between the seductiveness of living for the moment and the wisdom of planning for later. But it gave me as much joy to watch my sons take pleasure in the immediate as I'd felt myself, nearly twenty years ago, when I'd been so eager to explore my first island in the sun – before I was a mother. My current job was to make at least some gestures towards nest-building. I'd brought them such a long way.

Tasha's House – soon thought of as our own – was set among palms and bushes on a coral eyrie beside a deep gully at the southern end of Pigeon.* I began my inspection from the back, where I recognized

---

* Although technically in the south, Tasha's House was often referred to as being at the 'Western' end because it was where white residents lived.

the view from the photograph Diana had sent to Scotland of a volcano rising cleanly out of the sea. This was Tinakula, thirty miles away across twinkling waves. Often a scarf of cloud drifted just below the crater, or hovered lower, brushing the sea, so the whole seemed to float. Smoke, like the tassel of a hat, puffed frequently from the top, tweaked by the wind this way or that. The presence of Tinakula was a constant reminder of the surreality of our situation – a simmering crater on the edge of 'Paradise'. But then so was our doll's house in the blue, which had come on such strides since that sparse picture of a couple of posts and a beam. Far from being the primitive affair anticipated, our home on Pigeon was a neat structure of beams and boards with a steeply pitched iron roof, softened by leaf verandas all round. These followed a traditional design, with panels of thatched leaf supported by wiggly rafters. None of the rooms – office-bedroom, boys' veranda room, kitchen and shower – connected internally, so one always had to step outside before entering any of them. It had its idiosyncrasies but there was no doubting the amount of work put in. I was impressed and, as I peered through each open door, touched, too, at the lengths to which Diana had gone to make us comfortable. On an island so remote, who would imagine finding dozens of drawers built under each bed, and solar-powered lights, a gas cooker and a flushing loo? Where I'd expected, as on Tuin, to find problems with termites building castles on the floor, there was lino-covered concrete to keep them at bay, and anti-ant powder in bottle lids on shelves. It was truly a miniature home from home – in fact, in parts, distinctly more efficient than home: a tank outside at the proper height gave pressure through taps, and the rainwater, caught through guttering on the roof, really was clean. There were even handsewn bedspreads, pretty lamps and glass louvres.

First impressions, then, of domestic arrangements on Pigeon were of surprising luxury. Yet a glance in any direction outside showed how almost 'off the map' we were; how incongruous all the niceties, and therefore the more remarkable. Beyond Nandelli, over which the sun had risen and where the smoke of morning fires now drifted lazily along the beach, white water crashed and clawed endlessly at the edge of the coral reef; and beyond that lay deep dark blue that seemed to shelve away into nothingness, as if off the edge of the world. When I'd arranged a mosaic of glittering solar squares on the barbered leaves of our veranda roof to charge my laptop, I felt as though I were in a gilded birdcage dropped on a cliff. With a bedside table improvised from a flour tin draped with a Country Casuals scarf sitting beside bookshelves built into the painted trunk of a tree, the impression was complete, and I felt I should be unpacking crystal instead of billycans. How different it all was from *Castaway* days, when one of my first acts had been to scrape a rectangle in the sand to discourage snakes from sharing our camp area.

By late morning, I was hot from opening waterproofed packages of printer cartridges and stocking a larder-sized cupboard with medical supplies, so I found a shady place to peel the vegetables we had bought on Santa Cruz. Soaked on our crossing, they needed to be used soon. I'd half-filled a cauldron-shaped billy with kumera, enjoying the simple task under coolly nodding leaves, when the excited yells I'd heard reassuringly, on and off, all morning were suddenly close.

'Mum! Look what Laloa's caught, and they're for us!'

Magnus, Joe and Benji stood in a dripping row on the veranda, displaying a long, barbless spear threaded with multi-coloured fish. One was canary yellow, another had red fins and a third, black stripes.

'Are they all edible, d'you think?'

'Yes. Laloa says we just have to "bon 'em".'

'Bone them?'

'No, "bon 'em". I thought you knew Pijin.'

'Can you do it?'

'Of course. You just have to show us how to gut them.'

Down at the Little Wharf, I gave the boys their first lesson in gutting. Memories of Tuin flooded back as a spine stuck in the palm of my hand.

'Where shall we make a fire?' Joe asked.

I wasn't sure, and Laloa, the Reef Island boy who'd caught the fish and recommended the method of cooking – 'bon 'em' meant 'burn them' – had vanished. There was nowhere obvious near our house. On Tuin I'd had several kitchen fires – a big open 'hearth', a halved petrol drum for simmering, and embers in a stone ring for charbroiling. But here we had a gas cooker.

'What about frying them?' I suggested.

'Fine,' said Magnus, 'saves work.'

I lit the gas and put oil in a pan. It did save work, but also felt odd. I'd told the boys they must expect to improvise on Pigeon; that things we'd taken for granted back home – even in our modest, labour-intensive home – might entail hard work to achieve here. Like cooking. Now we found everything laid on. The hard work had already been done – some as long as forty years ago, when Diana and her husband cleared the bush and rigged up the first water-catchment system on Pigeon's first building. They'd used underground ovens when they had to, but graduated to bottled gas and solar power. I had to drop all thoughts of my own past experience on an island. After all, I'd really just camped on Tuin for a year; my only achievement had been to survive. The people who'd come to Pigeon Island had stayed – and evolved. Pointless to play at camping here. But what about the lessons I wanted the boys to learn from living somewhere remote? Wouldn't these home comforts decrease the value of the experience? Balancing plastic plates on knees, we ate the bony fish with boiled kumera under our Kaikai Tree, and I asked if they'd had a good morning.

'*Brilliant*,' said Joe. Benji, using his teeth to strip fish down to messy skeletons, was too busy to reply.

Magnus said they'd met Laloa in the water. He was a wontok of Ross's – meaning a relative or friend. 'Come out this afternoon, Mum. This place is unbelievable.'

Getting me away from that admirable but confusing little home-from-home was the right thing to do. One thing *I* had to learn fast, on Pigeon, was to lose any preconceptions I was carrying around.

For our first walk together, we wore hats, sunglasses, suncream and footwear and carried a water bottle, forming up on the Little Wharf as for a drill.

'Have you some insect repellent in your pocket?' I asked Magnus.

'No.'

I made them wait while I went back up to the house for a small backpack.

'What's that for?'

'We might need it. Be prepared. Do you think it's all right to leave the doors open? Shall we take a snack?'

'Yes. No. Oh *come on*, Mum!'

I smiled. I was being a fussy old fart.

'OK.'

The tide was low, dry patches showing far out on the reef, but there was still water all round the island. We scrambled down by the side of the Little Wharf, over a jumble of coral, and stood in clear sea up to our knees or, in Benji's case, thighs. Dozens of speckled crabs, so well camouflaged I hadn't noticed them before, rippled over the coral where we'd just been and tucked themselves into crevices. Joe, peering into their hiding places, wondered if they'd be good to eat. Benji grabbed my hand and pointed to a shoal of fish. We planned to take advantage of the low tide to explore locally on foot. In the morning, when the tide was high, the boys had swum before meeting Laloa, staying within sight of Tasha's House. Now we walked half way round Pigeon, along its eastern side, before heading out into the channel separating it from Nandelli.

Pigeon, we saw, was a coral island in pure, almost exaggerated form. Unlike a flat, sandy 'desert' island – of which Nandelli, only hundreds of metres away, was, in part, an example – it rose steeply out of the sea, with coral overhangs like the lips of a huge, grey, petrified anemone nearly all the way round. Only where our canoe had landed was there a small area of sand, and in the bay where we had gone to recover. Otherwise it was a jagged comma of coral, rising in places to thirty feet, with great scoops taken out of the sides by the action of the sea. When the coral was wet, it was iron grey; when dry, it turned beige, and bright green box-flower bushes, thriving on thin, sea-licked soil, sprouted over the edge in striking contrast. As well as palms, behind these there were over twenty species of sizeable native tree, not counting those imported by the Hepworths, so that despite the harshness of the coral base Pigeon appeared lush. The island stood out proud from its watery frame, on a jagged stump, and waved a frilly head. Black lizards, shiny as patent leather, as well as crabs populated its edges, and the island's namesake pigeons, with muted plumage, roosted next to emerald lorikeets in the trees.

Once we'd rounded the eastern end, passing a concrete slipway on which a wooden dugout rested beside a fibreglass dinghy, Magnus shouted that he'd found a channel. These cleared paths through loose coral were meant for boats coming in when the tide was shallow, but made handy guidelines for inexperienced feet, too.

'Aha! Mum, look at this.'

Joe picked up something black and banana shaped, and pointed it at me.

'Laloa showed us these this morning,' he said, and squeezed it, causing a stream of clear liquid to shoot out and hit me on the arm.

'Yuck!'

It was a giant sea slug, or bêche-de-mer, and the sand beneath our feet was littered with them. Dozens of live, squelchy black bananas in all directions. To balance this less than attractive discovery, there were beautiful daytime constellations of starfish – large, velvety in appearance and a startlingly bright blue. Benji couldn't believe they were real. 'They're like teddy starfish,' he said, and pointed out smaller brown ones tangled together like spaghetti and, ahead of us, darting above the coral then down into it, a plump eel with a transparent fin. 'There's something everywhere you look!' he cried. I'd just found a pyramid-shaped shell, with delicately gleaming sides whorled like ice cream: a trochus.

'Which way now, Mum?' Magnus called.

He was standing about twenty yards from the highest point on Nandelli, an area at first sight little more than a craggy pile of coral topped by a mass of green. Below the point – known as Nandelli Point – was a triangular coral boulder sticking out of the water.

'That'd be great for diving off at high tide,' said Joe.

'You'd have to be careful. The coral's so sharp,' I warned.

'Oh Mum, you always worry!'

'It's part of my job.'

'I'm glad I'll never be a mummy,' said Benji.

'Let's go all the way round Nandelli,' I suggested, keen not to appear a total wimp, 'and back along the sandy side.'

I wanted a closer look at this combination of raised coral atoll and classic desert island. This route approved, we tightened our single file where the sand shelved round the triangular rock, and Benji suddenly found himself chest deep, in water no longer clear. Beyond Nandelli Point, north-west of Pigeon – as to all points of the compass but for the diminutive interruptions of further local atolls – lay the Deep Blue. Here, as I'd seen at dawn from the Little Wharf, looking in the opposite direction, the Edge of the Reef was clear. Reef Islands lay like small pieces of a scattered jigsaw on a broken baseboard of reef, in the midst of a great deal of ocean.

'We saw trees like that in Africa, didn't we?' said Magnus, ahead. He halted so the water swirled, and we all caught up – and stared. The other side of Nandelli revealed another world. Suddenly we were in a hushed, steamy landscape divided by brown, riverlike channels lined with mangroves. From coral and desert islands waving palms against a

Pigeon Island

Robbie Cooper

Joe, Magnus and Benji, in the cottage in the Highlands where they learned to hew wood and haul water at an early age. *Lucy Irvine*

After major spinal surgery, Lucy practised kayaking on a chilly Scottish loch, in preparation for the Solomon Sea. *Magnus Irvine*

Lucy collects emergency rations before departure for Pigeon, 1998. *Stephen Cook*

Dinner with Diana Hepworth on the West Patio, served by Lanebu. *Robbie Cooper*

Tasha's House, where the Irvines were based on Pigeon. *Lucy Irvine*

It didn't take long for Benji to make friends, using the universal language of sport to break the ice. *Robbie Cooper*

Games broke out spontaneously when the pupils of Pigeon Island School went on an excursion to the island of Nufiloli. *Robbie Cooper*

Lucy searches for an e-mail connection in the blue. Using high-tech combined with solar power, she was able to send articles to the *Sunday Times* magazine. *Robbie Cooper*

Eyebrows are much used in Reef Islands conversation – so Lucy emphasized hers to make communications clearer. *Robbie Cooper*

Joe and Benji make music outside their room. Note the solidity of Diana Hepworth's carpentry. *Lucy Irvine*

Joe's hearing problem seemed to disappear on Pigeon. He sang Reef Island songs to himself, and quickly picked up subtle local gestures akin to mime. *Lucy Irvine*

Magnus kayaks round one of the many mini-Paradise islands, near Nola. *Lucy Irvine*

Ross with a kingfish caught on a line, and Pegi and Frederic Hepworth.

Robbie Cooper

Ben Hepworth with a giant wrasse he caught at night, using a simple spear. *Lucy Irvine*

Children accompanying Lucy to Nenumbo. They liked to establish friendship by touch, but were sometimes shy about it.
Robbie Cooper

The Island children could not have been kinder to Benji and Joe. Integration became total and the two young 'token whites' soon learned to speak fluent Pijin. *Robbie Cooper*

bright blue backdrop, we'd entered swamp; wide sea had narrowed to muddy delta, and the jungly call of a whip bird replaced the distant crash of reef-edge waves: 'Oo-ip!' Joe turned to me, smiled, and imitated the sound. 'I heard that,' he said. How ideal for someone hard of hearing such peace and space was. On this side of Nandelli, habitation was more in evidence than where a line of palms half-concealed dwellings on the sandy side. Here, over silty shallows, a broken canoe house on stilts, made of sticks and leaves, led the eye upwards to where biscuit-brown cubes of closely woven leaf lay like toy huts arranged by a child. Doorways, where they were visible, were black squares; there seemed to be no windows.

'D'you think there are people in there?' wondered Benji.

'I don't know.' The place was silent.

'I think they're out fishing,' said Joe.

We moved close enough, legs stirring up dark sand in clouds, to see what was evidently a kitchen area, with a carved wooden dish, some coconut husks and a tin pot draining on a stand made of sticks lashed together with twine. There was a smell of hot coconut.

'I don't think we should just barge in,' said Magnus, and I agreed. We wouldn't want people just barging into our place either. But we'd been spotted. Not far from the rickety canoe house, a little girl was squatting down, rubbing a piece of cloth on a sunken dugout. Her hands worked on, but her round, brown eyes were locked on us. A thatch of pale hair sprang straight upwards from a small, contrastingly dark face, then fell over itself to hang stiffly, immobile as a brush. She wore a wrap from waist to knees, wet from her washing. Her arms were thin and her narrow chest flat. I was about to say hello when, noticing we'd seen her, she dropped her cloth and retreated, quick as an animal, into shadow. Not wanting to disturb her further, we sloshed on by.

'Mum – there's lots of them!' said Benji. 'Boys too.'

Sharper than mine, his eyes had found rows of other eyes, all at different heights, where children sat – very still for children – along the branch of a tree, almost but not quite hidden by foliage. One boy's face was visible only through the stripes of a palm leaf; his eyes, through a slit, were like shiny features in a sharp-angled design.

'Hello!' I called.

'Oh Mum,' said Joe, 'you're so embarrassing.'

At first there was no response, but as our feet led us beyond the hiding place, there was a quick, shy, delayed echo: 'Ahloo!' followed by unconcealed, elated laughter, and splashing as small bodies fell off the branch into the water.

'Well,' I said to Benji, 'you'll know where to bring your football.'

'I will,' he said, surprising me with his confidence, 'I was planning to. But I think it would be better without you, Mum.'

His head turned back wistfully towards the children, now hidden again, as we walked on. I'd hoped the boys would make their own explorations and discoveries but hadn't expected such independence so soon. But he had a point. A mother tagging along anywhere new friends might be made could only be inhibiting. Half an hour's further sloshing took us past quadruple ranks of mangroves, from which gassy bubbles rose, adding to our sense of being deep in swampland, until, as abruptly as we'd entered this zone, it gave way again to wild Pacific. Now we rounded the flat, far end of Nandelli, all sand and palms, and saw Pigeon Island once more, across sparkling blue. For Benji's sake, we aimed to cross over where the channel was shallowest. A woman, face shaded by a cloth piled over her brow, was arriving from the opposite direction. The boys passed her, chattering among themselves, but I said my embarrassing hello. Her chin lifted. It was the woman who'd served the meal at Diana's house.

'Go wea?' she asked. It was an expression I was to hear often. Reef Island people always like to know where you're going.

'Pigeon,' I informed her. 'Iufela?' (And you?)

Up and out came the chin again, pointing over my shoulder to distant palms on an island north-east of Nandelli, close to the Edge of the Reef.

'Nenumbo,' she said, the name of a village. I hoped I might, in time, be able to visit her there. For now I just said that, having lived on another island when young, I spoke a little Pijin and would like to learn more.

'Ah-ah.' (An acknowledgement.) 'Missus lukluk iufela,' she said.

Diana either had been or was now looking for me. Tenses in Pijin are indeterminate. I thanked her and caught up with the boys, saying I'd stop by and see our hostess.

'You go on,' they said, 'we'll be fine.' I'd agreed earlier they could break out the kayaks. Just before running off, they said: 'Could you take these, Mum?' holding out a bundle of hats, shoes and sunglasses. I considered. What about cuts and skin cancer? Then I thought of the little semi-naked children we'd seen earlier, with whom they wanted to make friends. And how I'd gone without these encumbrances on Tuin.

'OK.'

My head was still full of the dreamlike quality of our wade round Nandelli when I stopped at Diana's residence. An enormous satellite dish quested its blind, concave eye, mesh reminiscent of a fencing mask, into the ether, and a handsome black and tan Rottweiler graced a swathe of lawn hedged by hibiscus just as a Labrador might grace an English garden. In fact, there was a Labrador as well – Ben's dog, Star. The Rottweiler was called Stasi – Diana's diminutive for Anastasia.

'Lucy dear, I've some pawpaws for you, and Teuna's made you bread and swept your veranda. You'll find a housegirl so useful, and these Seventh Day Adventists are less "bushy" than the girls Ross's wife takes on.'

Today Diana was wearing a blue swimsuit with a brief white skirt attached at the hips. Her carriage was magnificent. Son Ben, bare-chested, head bent, moved quietly past on long legs, with a murmured greeting. The pawpaws, big as marrows under Diana's freckled hands, were remarkably heavy, and I said, 'Oof,' as I balanced one on a shoulder.

'Teuna will carry it for you,' said Diana, and called briskly into the house. 'Teuna!'

I said I could manage, but Diana didn't seem to hear.

'She'll take down the rest of your things from the crate, too. Just tell her what you need. She doesn't talk much but she understands English.'

Teuna appeared, a diminutive woman in a dusty black shift. Shyly, she took the pawpaws, settling them in a woven-leaf basket which then went on her head. I was so tall in comparison, I looked down on them.

'Take them to house belong Tasha.'

Diana's commands to Islanders were given in English, with the odd word of Pijin dropped in. I said how impressed I was with Tasha's House, and she explained that as soon as the delayed building materials had come, she and Ben, 'with some labour,★ of course', had set to,

---

★ Islander staff were referred to as 'labour'.

determined to have it ready for our arrival. I thanked her again.

'I like having a project,' she said, and showed me what she was busy with today – painting the wooden railing that nicely finished her waist-high veranda walls. An old black and white cat lay in the sun beside the paint pot, head tilted back to watch us, and we were introduced. This was Tapushka, originally a kitten bought for Tasha, the daughter who, for reasons I'd yet to discover, couldn't live on Pigeon any more. Tom, Diana's husband, had been very fond of cats, too. He'd died four years ago, and his grave, with a miniature leaf hut over it, stood just beyond the lawn in the centre of the island.

Diana said they'd always had pets, even when they were at sea. The dogs lived on coconut and boiled fish; the cats on dried milk, fish and pawpaw. 'Vitamins are so important,' said Diana, adding: 'I hope you're taking some.' I said we didn't bother. 'But *here*, you *must*. There's no iron in anything.' Diana nearly always spoke emphatically – except to her animals, with whom she displayed gentleness. At this time I was unsure of her, with echoes of my anger during the canoe crossing and things I'd heard about her ('slightly gaga') still in my head, although I saw no signs of any impairment. I guessed she must be feeling her way with me, too, not knowing her well enough then to understand that, with small areas of exception, Diana operated from an inner world of great certainty. She'd seen and done and learned a lot in her nearly eighty years.

'The pawpaws are forty cents each. You give that to me, and you give the girl eight dollars a day.'*

The idea of having a housegirl seemed at odds with the simple approach to domestic life I'd assumed we'd take on Pigeon. But, as with preconceptions, assumptions had better be thrown out, too.

'It's a kind thought, but I wouldn't need help more than a few hours a week.'

This provoked a very emphatic response.

'No, you can't do that. They come on at seven thirty to prepare your breakfast, and stay until four thirty. They wouldn't understand about a few hours.'

Now *I* became – gently – emphatic. I didn't want anyone preparing my breakfast and suggested discussing things with Teuna, whom

---

* In 1998, eight Solomon Island dollars equalled approximately one pound sterling.

Diana had earmarked for me to share with Mhairi, the wife of Peter the teacher, who was expected in a few weeks.

'You can't discuss things with them. You just say what you want. And of course none are reliable. They say they'll come, then don't. I've told Teuna you'll have her two days a week, as Mhairi will want three for the schoolhouse.'

I wondered if it was possible to discuss things with Diana, or if one was expected just to accept being told. I said I'd think about it. Back at our house, I was surprised to find not the three pawpaws Teuna had delivered, but four, and Benji.

'Hi, Mum. That big pawpaw's for you.'

'Where's it from – and how much was it?'

'That lady with the cloth on her head gave it to me. She said it was for Mami b'long me – free.'

I started to say I hoped he had thanked her, but he was off, running down the hibiscus-lined path to catch up with Joe, Magnus, the kayaks and the gradually returning tide. Balancing the enormous gift pawpaw in two hands, I wandered down to the Little Wharf, where I chopped the perfectly *à point* flesh into four. In view of the exchange I'd had with Diana, I realized I was going to have to be decisive on this island, in unexpected ways. I wanted to be open to ideas, but it would be no good being so pliable as to be pushed in unwanted directions. I must, I saw already, leave the boys to form relationships on their own, more than I'd envisaged, and if that meant staying out of their way, I would. But I couldn't let Diana think I'd automatically be happy living in a manner that suited her, but might not suit me. The sea around Poppet Island glittered and, when I'd covered the pawpaw and set it in the shade, I headed off for a swim. Like the boys, I must learn to find my own way here.

5

Discoveries and Disappearances

THE EDGE OF THE REEF CLOSEST TO PIGEON IS ONLY STRIDES THROUGH *the water from our house. Today I swam over it for the first time, alternately frightened and elated. Is this what the boys go through privately with their new friends? It's virgin experience, a very personal thing, but judging from the smiles when they emerge, they couldn't have better guides. The children here are as born to water as to land. Under the clear blue, their hair spreads like haloes and they beckon my sons on with fingers delicate as tendrils. We know few names yet but it doesn't matter; shared pleasure in the beauty that surrounds us came, for the boys, within days.*

It's become my habit to float alone, near Poppet Island. To lie with my face in the sun-shot air and limbs just below the rippling skin of water is to leave this world. There I rest in limbo, detached but buoyed; there I am dislocated and discovered at the same time. I breathe softly, languid, lost, forgetting being, until I know I've found Now. Sometimes my head pops up, legs go down and ears fill. Then I blink round, treading water. My vision is blotted with after-images of hot light, and I draw my knees up at shadows. What else floats here? But there's nothing but shadows of coral in the shape of leaf baskets. Back goes the head and up come the feet, and waves lift me by the waist, so only pubes, breasts and chin break surface, and both after-images and ripples of water run over my eyes. A flash of lids open between ripples reveals a spinning posy of palms above Poppet, and pale pompom bushes round its sides. Below me, no more than half a dozen flips and a kick out and down, are echoing pompoms of coral, and others like swollen viscera, smooth purple, crenellated pink. Tiny turquoise fish glint in stubby trees of looser coral, like fairy lights. I dive to look, take fright at one of my own knees bumping the other, and surface, gasping, to fetch a breathing tube. On land I move stiffly, aware of my spine again as I climb. But in the sea it disappears, as whatever that thing is that is 'I' does, too. To be in this water is a separation from all I know; another dimension. At the Edge of the Reef, immersion in that other dimension deepens.

Facing the Edge, there are no palms, no mounds of island with silver sand like slices of moon in the distance; facing the Edge, there's only ocean, and colour shows clearly where the plunge begins: pale green plummets through the sea's spectrum to night blue, transparent only when you're in it. At first I stay close to the cliff edge, with only my top half hanging over the void. It's a chasm with no other side. I freeze as a fat fish with rainbow scales folds out from nowhere, showing glaucous eyes. Green fronds wave over the nothingness; hundreds of little yellow fish materialize like bubbles, then disperse. I shrink from the Edge but, just for a breath's length, dare myself over it, scattering parrotfish, flinching at the touch of rubbery-looking weed, then finding it's like silk, feeling hopelessly naked between the sharp cliff side, spiny mysteries in every interstice, and the total insubstantiality of airless blue nothing . . . Pleased with myself, for little, I return to sun on waves. I'll go further another day. But by the time I've flipped back to the Little Wharf and floated again for five minutes, I'm caressed back to calm, and find I'm smiling unstoppably.

After swimming, I rinsed in fresh water. Diana had built our shower cleverly so rainwater from a tank on the roof splashed generously from on high. I had my face upturned to this, revelling in its softness, when I heard Benji shouting one afternoon a fortnight into our stay. I'd completed unpacking by now; we'd eaten a great deal of pawpaw, and Magnus had cooked kumera six different ways. We rose with the lorikeets and went to bed not long after the sun went down, body clocks happily adjusted. The boys had tried their hands at fishing; Benji had had success with his football; and I'd formed an attachment to the heat, sea and sunrises I knew could only grow. All three boys' impressions of how life was going to work out on Pigeon were highly positive, and my own were looking good, too.

'Mum?' Benji was panting outside the shower now. 'Magnus has disappeared.'

'What do you mean?'

'We were in the kayaks and he went speeding off.'

'Where?'

'Towards the Edge of the Reef.'

'Just out here?'

'No – towards Nenumbo.'

Nenumbo was the village where Lanebu, Diana's housegirl, lived. It was less than a mile away over reef where, even at high tide, the sea would be only a little above a man's height, but close to where it plunged away to wild ocean, beyond a wall of white.

'He went towards those waves.'

I dried myself quickly.

'Where are Joe's binoculars?'

Joe was already scanning for Magnus, from up a tree. He handed down the binoculars and I ran to the Little Wharf.

'Which kayak was he in?'

'The white Acadia.'

A neat, seagoing kayak but one that could all too easily roll – spilling a boy onto lacerating coral – under those white waves, which might then with their powerful suction drag him over the Edge. I looked every way but saw only a trio of dugouts, their occupants fishing, close to Nandelli. There was a good view out towards Nenumbo from the slipway close to the schoolhouse. Dragging on a sarong, I sped past Diana's. She was up a ladder, doing something to her veranda roof, with a member of the ground staff. There was no sign from the slipway either, but the white, crashing waves were clear. And beyond them, darkly peaked endless blue – as wild as the day we came.

I ran to the easternmost edge of the island, then all over it, standing on tiptoe, scrambling to a perch in a fallen tree, scaling every rise, scanning and scanning. To run round the island like this forced me to be acutely aware of its tininess and the vastness beyond, making me feel frantic, helpless. Where was Ben? Did he have a canoe with an engine ready? Where should we start to search? Joe was now looking out from the highest tree he could climb but Benji ran at my heels, asking questions I couldn't answer. Both of us were sweating as we passed Diana again.

'Is it a ship?' she asked, seeing the binoculars.

'No. It's Magnus. He's disappeared in his kayak.'

'Disappeared? Well, of course. He's exploring.'

She had a little hammer in her hand.

'But he didn't tell anyone he was going. I'm worried he's gone too close to the Edge of the Reef.'

'The edge of the reef? Surely he wouldn't be so silly as to go there?'

She didn't sound alarmed, just disparaging at the thought of such foolishness. If I wasn't already red from running, I'd have flushed.

'He doesn't know the area well yet. And it's not like him to just disappear.'

'But you'll have to get used to that. All boys disappear . . .'

'He's thirteen!' I said, my voice rising now. 'And in a strange place . . .'

'But he saw what the sea's like beyond the reef on your way here. He wouldn't go there.'

I wanted to shout that we couldn't see a bloody thing on our way here. It was all fear and madness and sickening blue heavings. She must have seen my distress, because she said: 'It's no good worrying, you know. It gets you nowhere.' What shook me was that the delivery of these words was light and bland. 'You must learn to be philosophical,' she added.

My God, she *was* crazy! And, it seemed, short on sympathy. I didn't dare speak, so I walked quickly away. As I passed Ben, who'd over-heard our exchange from outside his bachelor quarters, he said kindly: 'I expect he is just exploring.'

'Do you think so?'

'We're all in God's hands.'

Christ!

Down at the Little Wharf, I had to swallow and swallow, masking tears from Benji behind binoculars. Magnus had been gone nearly an hour before I'd been told. They kept thinking he'd come back.

'Isn't Ben going to look for him?' Benji liked Ben, who'd promised to take him spear fishing.

'I don't know.' I didn't want to have to ask. I could hear Diana's little hammer going tap-tap. And Ben humming a hymn.

'We'll give him another half hour,' I told Benji, 'then we'll go and look, if he's not back.'

'We could all go in different directions,' said Benji, 'like a search party.'

Not all in different directions, I thought. No. I wanted us all safely visible. There were two minutes of that long half hour to go when Joe, who hadn't moved from his lookout spot, called.

'I think it's him! But he's moving very slowly.'

I scanned. Yes, the white Acadia – and I ran for my red one. Joe and Benji shared a sit-on kayak. When I saw that Magnus was un-injured, I relaxed, all the fear knotted in my belly released. Suddenly it was fun to be paddling out to meet him, in chiffon-soft air, with the sun beginning to dip.

'You've been away a long time,' I said as we drew near. 'I was a bit worried.'

'Oh, sorry,' he said, 'I forgot the time. Don't you find that happens to you here? Anyway, look what I've got.'

Magnus had been travelling slowly because his kayak was weighed down by a stem of bananas holding over fifty fruit. We tied them to a beam on our roof – two boys on the end of a rope hauling, they were so heavy – then let them down fast when they were attacked by a flock of starling-like birds. We had fried bananas with rice, banana-stuffed fish, banana pudding and banana cake, and laughed off the scare we'd had when Magnus disappeared – but didn't forget it. Yes, I told him, time tended to distort – even vanish – for me on Pigeon too, and that was one of the best things about it. Nevertheless, please would he tell me when he planned to disappear in future. Neither Diana nor Ben said: 'Told you so.' But Diana's statement that worry-ing 'gets you nowhere' kept coming back to me. She was a mother. Hadn't she ever had fears for her children's safety? I couldn't hide the coolness I felt towards her for several days afterwards, so I just kept out of her way. It had been agreed we should have time to settle before I began looking into her story. But if anyone had told me then that I'd grow not only to have respect bordering on awe for this woman, but to hold her in the deepest affection, I wouldn't have believed it. She commanded her territory with stately efficiency, but seemed to have little compassion. What had made her like that, or was it merely a front?

If it hadn't been for the Little Wharf up our end of Pigeon, it wouldn't have been easy to keep out of anyone's way, because five acres surrounded by sea is a small space to share. The boys ran past Diana's to play football in the flat area close to Ross's house – currently empty – down the other end of Pigeon, or undertake wobbly experiments in dugouts from the slipway beside the as yet unoccupied schoolhouse, but I preferred to keep my distance, wanting to establish my own modus vivendi on Pigeon before attempting to take the plunge into others' points of view. There was the history of the island and its inhabitants, and there was Pigeon now, and I felt I needed more 'now' before looking back in time. I liked Ross, and looked forward to his presence as the budding paterfamilias glimpsed in Scotland – and too sketchily in Honiara – but couldn't help feeling relieved when we heard he wouldn't be back for a while: there'd be his whole mixed-blood family to explore, in time. Then came news that Peter and Mhairi were also delayed. This wasn't a problem for us; Joe and Benji didn't object to a further spell of holiday, but the nature of their delay, relayed by Diana, who'd heard it on the radio, came as a shock. A yachtsman due to pick them up from Santa Cruz – thus avoiding the canoe crossing that gave us an unfortunate introduction to Reefs – had been killed by a crocodile. And eaten by it, in front of his wife.

The news was so bizarre that, horribly, it seemed almost a joke. But when the details began to emerge and we learned that the distraught wife was making her way to Santa Cruz, helped by a village chief from the island of Utupua where the attack happened, the whole thing became graphically real. They'd been anchored off Utupua, about seventy miles from us, at dusk when the man, as is routine for responsible sailors, dived down to check the anchor before going to stretch his legs ashore, leaving his wife on board. He checked the chain, but never reached land. Unseen by either of them, a saltwater crocodile, a creature notorious for its ability to keep all thirty feet or so of its heavy body silent while stalking its prey, crossed open water and dragged him under. We didn't know if the wife shouted, ran for a weapon or was too stunned to move until it was over. We only knew that somehow she reached shore herself, made contact with local people, and asked that his remains be buried on Utupua. Her wish was granted. Now Peter and Mhairi would have to wait for the cargo boat that was also bringing our shopping from Honiara, and the tragedy of the devoured man, as is the way with incomplete scraps of shock-horror news, went out of our lives when his wife left the care of the same VSO in Santa Cruz who'd met us off the plane. But for weeks the vision of that huge body lunging out of the deep at hopelessly vulnerable flesh recurred in my mind every time the boys went swimming and haunted me as I hovered underwater, daring myself further over the Edge of the Reef. Perhaps it was this that made me turn, temporarily, away from explorations of the sea to take a closer look at Pigeon's interior.

The best time to go for a walk on Pigeon was early, when no-one else was about. At first I set an alarm for 5 a.m., the hour the island began to wake, but I found I never needed it. The first squawk of the lorikeets' brief but vociferous chorus was enough, and one of the cockerels which lived at the eastern end soon followed, blending hints of farmyard with the tropical dawn. The boys would be asleep when I left the house, sprawled naked in poses of abandon wherever they happened to have found comfortable, inside or anywhere round the veranda, the previous night. I visited the furthest southern cliff first, to check the state of the tide, which I soon learned to judge by sound as well as sight. At low tide there were only the distant Edge of the Reef waves to hear, which before long became such a constant, it was like no sound. As the water crept higher, there was a gradually encompassing susurrus over sand and coral, culminating in a lapping at the sides of the island which increased as the sea rose, gurgling into gullies and filling pools. The southern cliffs were high and jagged, and the short, curving channel between Pigeon and Poppet filled quickly, with whooshes and swirls. Standing there at half light, no sign yet of the sun, I felt light-headed with the strength of the sense of 'island'. Pigeon was a speck in a wide, wide sea. Scents, at that time, as well as sounds, seemed accentuated – the cool tang of wave-washed coral; the close, dark scent of earth under bush; the damp, end-of-night smell of bark. And towards the centre of the island there were heady gushes of perfume, when I crushed frangipani petals underfoot. Soon it became a habit to carry one with me between my fingers, or a larger bloom from a tree by Diana's house, which overnight dropped pink tassels like fibre-optic sprays.

Before Diana's house, I passed Ben's quarters, perched like a sentry box on the highest point on Pigeon and only a stone's throw from Tasha's. If he were awake then, lying monklike on his back, as he did in the day sometimes, with the soles of his feet by the open door, head in shadow, he never stirred, and Star only wagged her tail. Stasi was another matter. If I woke her, she'd tug at her chain, waking Diana. So I learned to move lightly and quickly, skimming over lawn and fallen leaves and taking low leaps over dry palm fronds that might crackle. Once past the silhouetted curves of the satellite dish I breathed again, and pattered along an earth path with the schoolhouse on one side and Tom Hepworth's grave on the other. Beyond this central belt, dark bushes and tall trees – some looking as though they'd strayed from rainforest – clustered to make an area of shadow, where the labour huts lay, fronted by the spat-out seeds of pawpaws grown into a miniature plantation. Behind the huts, on the north-western edge of the island a single, huge tree, half its heavy trunk horizontal, made an L-shaped frame on the still dark sea, and a lattice of choked roots tumbled over the cliff. This part of Pigeon's interior, during our first months, seemed not only shadowy because of natural density, but best avoided also because of the mysterious existence of the Islanders sleeping there. On my dawn wanders I hurried past, glancing only at the fern-covered breadth of what was known as the Debbil-Debbil Tree (the ultimate Bong Tree) and moving on to a promontory on the northern end, where graceful palms nodded towards Nandelli Point and miles of open water beyond. Often at that early hour there were Islanders in dugouts fishing off the point, a silent, timeless charcoal sketch of slender wooden craft with stickmen figures. I bowed and arched with arms above my head, shaping them to the shape of the palms, stretching my spine, greeting the day, while the fishermen cast and retrieved their invisible lines.

Ross's house, part of a substantial complex with a copra dock and store, was invisible from our eyrie in the south-west, but similarly elevated, at the eastern extreme of the island. Its red iron roof caught the rays of the rising sun first, but a great tree, squeezed by and spilling hundreds of grey, snakelike lianas tangled with roots, gave it shade. Even before its tenants returned, I sped away when the sun touched it, enjoying my sense of solitude, as on Tuin. A blue, elongated cube with a red roof, echoing the shape of our house and lying close to the water not far from Ross's, was also empty at this time. This was a pair of units built for guests to Pigeon, who, I was glad to discover, appeared to be few. Perhaps my *Castaway* days, then the years at Inchreoch, had bred a habit of liking remote places sparsely populated.

But if I was in some ways isolated, inside as well as out, I certainly wasn't unhappy, and running 'home' through the silky breeze, again past the schoolhouse and the grave, past Diana's home and Ben's Box, rosy hibiscus, frangipani, spiky pandanus, languid coconut palms and the endless snapshots of sea beyond and around everything on the island, I felt better, physically and emotionally, than I had for ages. Could I really, in another existence, be called disabled? And it wasn't only the warmth of the sun, freedom from pain and the seduction of the sea that had caused this: something that had blocked the path to pleasure too often, of late, in our Scottish home had vanished. Although we'd only just begun our lives on Pigeon, an important inner change had occurred already: *tension* had gone, dropping off, on a tropical island, as easily as unnecessary clothing. To wake up eager to get up was something I recalled from youth, and Tuin; now, it seemed, in my early forties I was to have that daily joy again.

Sometimes Magnus didn't get up early because he'd been night fishing with Ben. They left any time the moon and tide were right, knives strapped to legs, torches looped on wrists. Ben said that, as in all other things, God guided him on these expeditions, but I suspected early on that Ben the man of God on land, self-effacing physically, and Ben the diver, graceful as soon as he hit the water, confident and decisive with his spear, were like two different beings. Whereas I hadn't been happy about the idea of Ben climbing a mountain in Scotland with my children, with no guidance other than the path of righteousness, I needed little convincing that, in his own element on Pigeon – and particularly in the surrounding sea – Ben was reliable. He was also amazing. A modern underwater spear had been purchased for Magnus in Australia, but Ben used the same plain iron rod and tubular rubber spring favoured by young Laloa and a Reef Islander, Matoko, who was his fishing companion. With this simple device, and a total absence of fear in the face of three kinds of shark, manta rays majestic and ominous as black sails and ferociously resistant moray eels, shy Ben secured veritable cornucopias from beyond the Edge of the Reef. Gradually the bottom of the dinghy or dugout used as a support vessel, bobbing on the waves above the heads of the divers, became studded with the fluorescent turquoise scales of parrotfish, and filled like a great shopping basket at the market of the deep with fat, blubber-lipped groupers, lurid and enormous wrasse, monkfish, emperor fish, cray, eels, squid – even turtles. Ben could catch enough in a few hours, on a good night, to feed everyone on Pigeon Island – including Ross's clan when he was back – and have enough over to distribute among the people of Nandelli. Fishing, on Pigeon, was no game, but an evolved art of survival, and Ben was a past master at it.

Other types of fishing took place on and beyond the reefs that made up Reef Islands, but none was as fruitful. Little children – I began to call them 'piccaninnis' like everyone else – toddled out from their home beach not long after they'd learned to walk, with cut-down spears sharpened by older brothers, and stabbed at shadows until they absorbed, by constant watching, knowledge of the movements of their prey. For a sardine-sized snack, arrows were used, not aimed at one fish but loosed upwards, over where many swam as one. The fish might only be stunned by the falling arrow, so the youngsters ran to finish them off with a sharp shell or their own teeth. Not many had knives. The Nandelli Point fisherfolk – only there in the season of trade winds – used line wound round a Y of wood or a bottle, bringing up slender garfish or small snapper, and spending many patient hours on the rocking water before achieving the makings of a meal. Trolling – pulling a line behind a canoe – was practised too, not only by those lucky enough to have access to an outboard motor, but from swiftly sailed or paddled dugouts.

Magnus enjoyed his night-fishing trips with Ben, but clearly felt like the boy he was, among men, when it came to the use of a spear, despite some successes. And I felt an aching gap, on his behalf, where a father should have been. Tropical islands make wonderful playgrounds, and Magnus loved the dazzling world of sun, waves and mirror-calm depths that was better than any theme park, but a caring man could have broadened the experience for him. I've never believed single mothers can do it all. I'd get up and make Magnus cocoa when he finally came home, snorkel dangling over one shoulder, salt-thick hair impenetrable to a comb. Joe and Benji would be long gone, off on missions of their own, before Magnus's later daytime began. The difference in ages and temperaments between Magnus and his brothers, already marked in our previous life together (that's what it began to feel like, another life) became a clear division during our time on Pigeon. Magnus, child of another land of sun, was entering the zone where young boy falls away to make room for budding man – the twilight world of the teenager before the party begins, and to be on a small island, cut off from others of his ilk going through the same phase, was not something I'd wish him to experience for too long. Wiser heads than mine in Scotland – and Ross – had been right: although I dreaded his departure from Pigeon, I knew that it would be the right move for him.

Meanwhile Magnus enabled me to begin the task that, apart from indulging isolationist whims and giving my children a taste of remote island life, I'd come for. I'd become aware that, in an environment where time was easily forgotten, the 'living now' I wanted more of was potentially endless, and must therefore be compartmentalized. I pointed to imposing rows of leather- and canvas-bound books lining the boatlike shelves of my office-bedroom: Tom Hepworth's diaries from the 1930s all the way up to 1994.

'There's a helluva lot more to go through here than I'd thought,' I said.

'Don't worry, Mum,' said Magnus telepathically. 'I'll cook and keep an eye on Benji and Joe. You get on.'

And Magnus was as good as his word. From a well of flattened grasses beside a cliff where I began to rustle, at first tentatively, at the edges of Pigeon's past, I heard my eldest son's mock-ferocious tones:

'Get back under the shower, Benj, and rinse off at least half that sand. And you, Joe, deal with that cut *properly*. And don't shout. Mum's working.'

He was a dab hand at squid and bushlime bake, too. God, I was blessed with my boys. So, unable to make excuses any more, I took the plunge into Hepworth history.

6

The Hepworth Story Begins

CECIL HEPWORTH, KNOWN AS HEPPY, MADE THE SORT OF SILENT movies in which heroes with kohled eyes lean towards swooning girls with parted lips, the picture fades to black and up comes a screen with the legendary words '*Came the Dawn*' – instead of a sex scene. He also shot the first footage of a royal funeral – Queen Victoria's – and pioneered location filming. His success was huge, but his rise to fame was matched by his downfall when 'talkies' came along, and inevitably his personal disaster affected those closest. Tom Hepworth was born in 1910, several years junior to two sisters, Elizabeth and Margaret. Their mother was so firm in her faith and belief in routine that she insisted her children attend chapel twice daily, and when she died, Tom was immediately sent away to a new set of routines at boarding school. In his autobiography,* Heppy wrote just one line about his son: with reference to the death of his mother, when Tom was seven, he said: '*The boy was too small to know much about anything.*' Elizabeth and Margaret took over the running of the home. All their lives these girls, who never married, operated as a team. Their formal education ended early, home duties for girls being the priority then, but they never stopped feeding their minds with art and literature, and liked nothing

---

* *Came the Dawn*, published by Phoenix House Ltd, 1951.

better than to share their interests with their little brother. They looked after Tom during school holidays in an almost maternal capacity, and later lavished care on him that they might in other circumstances have lavished on beaux.

Tom was the apple of his sisters' eyes, but to Heppy his tendency when he left school to drift from job to job and spend every spare moment 'messing about in boats' was a cause of anxious irritation – even though he used to like boats himself. Once a bold entrepreneur who worked and played hard, Heppy latterly became conventional, wanting to see his only son established in a sensible line of work. He was pleased when Tom took up photography, but where Heppy saw work with film as an art to be tirelessly pursued, Tom saw it only as a way of earning enough to keep his weekends free for what meant most to him: sailing. And as early as 1933, the ledger Tom used to record what he paid in models' wages contained jottings of doubtful application to photography. Less than inspired by the requirement of his job to '*snap endless glamour girls*', he made lists of items for use on a sailing trip round the world. In an expenses column '*9d for Messenger to Harpers Bazaar*' sits beside a diagram of a helm-to-bunk buzzer system, and a description of how to splice rope. By the mid-'30s Tom's lists filled three ledgers and, for all Heppy's doubts about his son's ability to commit himself to anything, Tom had pursued his vision doggedly enough to acquire a vessel. The *Arthur Rogers*, Tom's dream ship, spent the war tucked into a mud berth, awaiting the day the affairs of the world, and Tom's purse, would allow the next steps towards faraway places. Tom spent the war on Thames sailing barges and deep-sea rescue tugs, learning much that would be useful in future years.

When pressed for funds to maintain the ship, Tom approached his father, now remarried, for a legacy left by his mother. Heppy, feeling the boy's adventurous scheme epitomized his unrealistic attitude to life, disapproved, and a rift opened between father and son that would last the rest of Heppy's life. A letter of reconciliation Tom wrote years later, from the other side of the world, arrived just days after his father died. Would Cecil Hepworth, who himself went through enormous swings of fortune in pursuit of visions dear to him, have finally found something in Tom's achievements to approve? They were, after all, both pioneers in a way.

★

While Tom was designing shelves in gimbals for the sailing ship he didn't yet possess, in the early '30s Diana Field-Hart was learning carpentry. Born in 1921, she was the youngest daughter of a gentleman poultry farmer. Mr Field-Hart kept his wife and three daughters in style – their home had a walled garden and tennis courts – and devoted himself to his business. He was one of the first to simulate a twelve-hour day, anticipating the battery hen, but he had a spiritual side too. Following a case of jaundice, when a Christian Science practitioner cured him, he became – for a time – a follower of Positive Thinking, with the upbringing of his daughters informed by his beliefs, so they had no vaccinations and were given no drugs. Tough immune systems developed, but couldn't prevent an accident to Diana when she was two, in which her feet were run over by a truck and received no treatment – possibly a contributary cause to her semi-crippling 'arthritis' later in life. When Diana was four, Mr Field-Hart, whose fittingly positive family motto was Una Via Cor Unum – one way (with) one heart – decided to move to California and buy a ranch. He sold his home and business but headed for America before being paid. The buyer went bankrupt, and the formerly well-heeled Field-Harts suddenly found themselves living in tents in Connecticut. The search to find ways of regaining their former position took them far, and involved many repitch-ings of tents and much 'making do', but Diana loved the adventure of it all. Dashing outside in a thunderstorm and dancing naked in the rain to flashes of lightning, she discovered she revelled in storms.

Eventually Mr Field-Hart found a job with the *Christian Science Monitor* in Boston. His position improved steadily until, after four years, he was able to transfer to their London office, moving his family back to English country life. After a brief period at conventional school, the Field-Harts sent their daughters to a progressive establish-ment which named among its aims the encouragement of pupils to pursue '*the power of self-realization*'. Personal success was of paramount importance, self-discipline was emphasized, and the development of '*perfection of physique*' was considered as vital as the development of the mind. But Diana was endlessly teased by fellow pupils for having an '*over-confident*' manner, which was mimicked until she cried. Emphasis on individual achievement enabled her to work out her frustrations creatively, and she soon shone in her chosen field, producing perfectly constructed items of furniture in spite of frequent tears. Then she made the lessons in self-discipline work for her, too, deciding at the beginning of one term not to show her feelings any more, however much she hurt inside. She succeeded.

When Diana was fourteen, her father, questioning new directions in Christian Science, lost his job. Once again funds were low and Diana had to leave school. Mr Field-Hart found new work, but the proceeds went to keeping up the country house. Social life at that time was fun but not frivolous, weekend house parties centring round a task such as cleaning the pool or weeding the tennis courts, in which friends were expected to participate. All three Field-Hart sisters attended the London Theatre Studio, where Diana learned, as well as elocution and deportment, prop making and stage management. Did the fact that her father now immersed himself – wholeheartedly – in the teachings of Krishnamurti affect her outlook? Where Christian Science had a firm set of tenets for the adherent to follow, Krishnamurti flung all the great questions of life back at the individual – a 'sort yourself out and everything will fall into place' philosophy. But also enshrined in Krishnamurti's 'way' was a distancing from worldliness. The accumulation of possessions took second place to the condition of the inner man. But Diana had little chance to discuss his spiritual changes with her father because he died when she was still in her teens; her mother retreated to a cottage, and when the two elder sisters married the family dispersed.

Diana was teaching riding at the outbreak of the war but quickly volunteered for the Women's Auxiliary Air Force. There, it was a shock to be plunged among women of mixed backgrounds. Diana, classy, horsey and, by her own admission, bossy, was made, by women her parents might have declined to employ as maids, to drill endlessly and clean lavatories. When the chance came to 'look after her mother' instead, she took it, and later, when conscription started, she found a reserved occupation as a programme engineer at the BBC. Diana had found it difficult to blend in with others in the WAAF, and so uncomfortable did she become with humanity en masse that all through the war she avoided entering bomb shelters, preferring to go on walking to her job while the sirens wailed. She admired, too, theatre performers who went on with the show as long as they could, whatever happened.

As the war continued, Diana felt trapped in England and longed only to get away to a better climate and the wide open spaces she had glimpsed abroad as a child. Out of her £3 10s a week salary, she started to save, building, with the frugality and determination that was to mark her future, a modest nest egg towards adventure, and in 1945 she took a job as a cook on a Swedish yacht. But this jaunt was by no means smooth. The skipper's nerves were raw after wartime service, and he worked out his anger at the human condition by insisting on sailing at night, with a skeleton crew, in storms. Making no bones about what she thought of his foolishness, Diana nevertheless rose to the occasion and discovered, as she struggled with flapping canvas and fought to keep the ship on course, the thrill of challenges at sea. Back in London, she trimmed nails ragged from hauling ropes and sewed herself an outfit in which to look for new work, so she could add to her adventure fund. One way or another, she was determined to find a way of leaving the post-war Britain she found so grey. And like her father, she pursued her aims fully, in the spirit of the family motto – with her whole heart; something she was to do all her life.

September 1946 did not find Tom a happy man. After demobilization, he'd dusted off the *Arthur Rogers* and was now living on her in Newhaven. His diary shows his state of mind: '*A pig of a day, blowing hard and raining . . . I've been here alone a fortnight now and am completely at a loss about my future. Both physically: where shall I take the boat? – and spiritually: what now? Alternatives seem to be: live on board and write for yachting papers; or, return to the photographic racket. Main objection to Plan A is I haven't the strength of character to lead the life of a hermit-author, and, besides, I want to sail, not just talk about it! . . . I suppose it's back to Nine to Six. Oh Hell!*'

Tom did return to town, but spent every weekend on the *Arthur Rogers* and soon tried out her paces on a trip across the Channel, passing thoughtfully along the invasion coast: '*Sandy cliffs edge a featureless countryside, to me each mile identical. Yet the success of the assaults here depended on each detachment landing on a particular beach and each furlong must have been mapped minutely . . . some men landed on strips of beach just a few feet wide, and beyond, scaled vertical cliffs manned by a desperate defender. It looks impossible but it was done.*' Those words – '*it looks impossible but it was done*' – must have stayed in Tom's mind because next time he was on the *Arthur Rogers* alone his gloom had gone and he was back to planning how he'd manage, if necessary living off salt horse-meat, to make his dream come true. Meanwhile, before the winter, he'd get the *Arthur Rogers* into her mud berth again. A pleasant way to do this was to make a weekend party of each shift along the coast, with anyone willing to lend a hand. A model he was working with heard about this and said he should meet her sister, who was '*mad about sailing*'. The sister, who had herself recently started modelling, was Diana Field-Hart.

Tom, in his several starts to a book about his life, takes liberties with the facts surrounding his early contact with Diana, but never varies from consistency in his inner response. '*Do you believe in love at first sight? I didn't, but from the moment I set eyes on this tall girl with the magnificent figure, she filled all my waking thoughts.*' Something clicked pretty rapidly for Diana, too. With this slight man whose shyly sensual mouth smiled frequently and whose sailor's crinkled eyes lit up when, with quick movements of small hands, he sketched his vision of the future in the air, she found instant rapport. She was used to men appreciating her beauty, but those who shared her recognition of the possibility of a life quite unlike that perceived by most of her con-temporaries had so far been hard to find.

Although Tom and Diana were both based in London for work, they were more frequently to meet on the *Arthur Rogers*, dressed in oilskins on chill autumn weekends, than at the fashionable cocktail parties to which they had access in town. At first there were always others with them. Tom would go down on a Friday, to whichever little south-coast harbour they'd managed to tuck the seventy-foot bulk of the *Arthur Rogers* into last weekend, stoke a stove decorated with fat cupids in the saloon, and fetch Diana and the rest of the temporary crew from the nearest station. And Diana soon impressed Tom more than visually. During a rough trip in November she pro-duced a hot meal from a single primus ring in a tipping galley and, already a competent small-boat sailor, soon adjusted her skills to the requirements of a larger vessel. '*A girl like this is precious above rubies,*' Tom mused, and concluded he must find a way of being alone with her.

The opportunity came in December when, by an inching process, the mud berth was finally reached. In the bleakest of British weather, in a damp dinghy in the dark, when he'd rowed Diana to shore after the triumph of finally delivering the *Arthur Rogers* to safe winter quarters and heard her voice still light with laughter despite a soaked skirt and flattened hair, Tom asked Diana to share his dream. Without a second's hesitation, she agreed. Fingers they promised each other would, in time, entwine under a tropical moon laced tightly, slippery in the cold rain.

'Better get an extra-tough ring,' said Diana, ever practical. 'I shan't want to lose it.'

'I will,' said Tom, gently lifting a long tendril of hair that blew across her mouth, 'and you won't.'

Fade to black.

They were married from Leigh-on-Sea the following spring, having already made the *Arthur Rogers* their home. Laughing at convention, they raced up to London to an informal reception in the photographic studio of Tom's best friend, Dennis. Back the following day on the *Arthur Rogers*, they set about the monumental task of preparing her for a voyage that could take them anywhere in the world. Not many young women would relish spending their honeymoon heating rusted rigging screws in a furnace, then working them free with vice and crowbar, but there was no aspect of work on the ship to which Diana wouldn't turn her hand. To have a shared vision was wonderful (one way ahead but with two hearts as one now) but to her it wasn't something 'up in the air' so much as a plan with many stages, all of which would go smoother for a disciplined approach. From the beginning of their marriage the Hepworths followed a daily routine. 'R and S' (rise and shine) in Tom's diary was with the dawn; a proper breakfast was de rigueur, then steady work, with a short break for elevenses, until lunch. Work continued, stopping only for English tea, until supper-time, and bed was rarely after 10 p.m.

Diana used her nest egg to furnish the *AR* (as the ship became known) with paint and anti-fouling substances. But a boat gobbles cash, and she still modelled when she could, picking up, en route, a stunning Hartnell gown which lived in a sail locker. One assignment, for *Vogue*, took her – and the *AR* – to the Isle of Wight, where she posed for a glossy piece on rough sailing. Next day, imagining the excitement to be over, she let her hair uncurl and got back into dungarees. But word reached press circles that a model and a photographer were about to do something unusual in a boat, and soon Diana's long legs featured in further eye-catching if more downmarket snaps. It was these, accompanied by an erroneous article stating that they were headed for the West Indies later that year, that suddenly landed the Hepworths, who'd so far had little luck recruiting crew, with three hundred letters from people wanting to join them. They had, in fact, considered starting their sailing plans with a trip to the Greek Islands to fish for sponges, but their eyes met over their bedtime cocoa and they quickly agreed that, if people preferred the West Indies, why not? It was bound to feel closer to Paradise than post-war Britain in a winter freeze.

7

Tropical Routines

I'D REACHED THE POINT IN TOM AND DIANA'S YOUNG LIVES AT WHICH they were about to set sail from 1940s England when my attention was drawn back forcibly to the Outer Solomons, 1998. It was the sound of a Boo shell, a resonant blast unchanged as a means of summoning the people of Reef Islands for centuries, that brought me from my desk. Not one but several Boo shells were being blown on Pigeon, Nandelli and Nenumbo, and Benji, who'd got hold of one, was trying to join in. Specs tied on with twine and pencils poked in my topknot, I wandered, barefoot, to where he sat elflike on the wharf, the conch at his lips.

'Listen, Mum. I can nearly do it.'

Mournful little farting sounds emerged.

'Sounds like a pigeon with problems,' I said. Pigeon's pigeons, we'd discovered, didn't coo but moaned gently, as though it were just too hot for them to bother opening their beaks. The Boo shells called to each other like foghorns and the high, curtailed yodels of Islanders joined them.

'What's happening?'

'Boat,' said Benji briefly and, screwing his face up, applied himself to the shell again, managing to produce a sustained note. Joe was down in the schoolhouse arranging a welcome for his new teacher, expected to be on board.

'Our stuff might be on it, too, mightn't it?' said Benji. 'Yippee, tomato sauce!' and he pelted away, butter-cookie brown with a peeling nose and sun-bleached hair.

'Excellent,' said Magnus, joining me, 'more ingredients.'

We made our way to where Ben was fixing an outboard motor onto a canoe. Already several dugouts from Nandelli were heading out into Mohawk Bay, where the boat would anchor. At the moment it looked like a postcard image on the horizon, squat with fat funnels.

'If you've any mail to go,' said Ben, 'I can give it to the captain for you.'

I rushed to take advantage of this opportunity, plastering envelopes with stamps depicting crabs of a kind with which I was now very familiar, and was back at the canoe just in time to jump in. Joe and Benji sat on the canopy with Laloa, Magnus on the gunwale below. This was the first time I'd been in anything motorized since our crossing but the boys were evidently used to perching on the front, a practice which would break every safety rule in 'civilization' but was considered normal here. The cargo boat, battered, rusty and no less tubby close up than distant, sat in the bay like a mother duck surrounded by ducklings as dugouts jostled at her sides. Some of these were paddled by naked children who'd been out fishing and just wanted to join in the fun; others by women waiting for a piece of cloth (called, as was any kind of clothing, 'kalico') from Honiara or a leg-sized root of taro from Santa Cruz. But most dugouts held men, heads of families, there to collect relatives who'd been away, or sacks of Australian-grown rice that had recently become nearly as much a staple of the Islanders' diet as kumera.

'Look, they're there!' cried Benji.

High up on deck, Peter and Mhairi, white arms easily distinguishable in a mêlée of plum-black, brown and golden Polynesian skins, were waving. How far they'd come, from the security of nine-to-five jobs and the very different pace and stimuli of Edinburgh city life, to tiny Pigeon. After a quick greeting, the activity of finding their luggage and our supplies among baskets of vegetables and roughly tacked together cages of hens took over. Once they were on land, Mhairi was whisked away by Joe on a conducted tour of the island, but Peter, Magnus and I went back for missing bits, and to witness some of the exchanges that went on between the central Solomons and the far-flung satellites of Reef Islands, which, in terms of development, might still be in another century.

One or two Islanders unloaded a mattress, or kerosene for lamps, but the majority collected such age-old items of inter-island exchange as bunches of betel-nut or a piglet with its legs bound. Magnus, balancing upright in the rocking canoe, received, among other things chucked by smiling, sweating crewmen from massive hand to hand down the side of the boat, tin kitchenware wrapped in hobo bundles, parcels of frilly greens scarce in Reefs, and striped watermelons to pass on to people in dugouts, who called out, gesticulating with the object, until it was claimed. Only the people of Pigeon Island received embarrassingly burst cartons of goodies from the capital, revealing their contents to stares: Benji's tomato sauce, spices for Magnus's culinary experiments and olive oil to dress our kumera. Coming to this corner of the globe, they were riches indeed.

Although well outside our neighbours' culture at this stage, skirting the edges of villages on my walks and still exchanging little more than shy greetings with women I met on the reef, I was aware, through the increasing contact Joe and Benji had, as they shared games on land and in the sea with piccaninnis their age and inevitably met relatives, that the people of Reef Islands were deeply different to any I'd encountered anywhere before, including in books and during my year in the Torres Strait. On first acquaintance, the adults seemed like aloof but volatile children and communication to consist of cries echoing like bird calls from island to island, with undertones rippling like shallow waves over the reef, and esoteric facial signals. Wild fruits never seen in the Outside World's most exotic stores were plucked from trees, coconuts quenched thirst, fish was roughly burned over coconut-husk fires and the sea was a communal toilet as well as a source of sustenance. And the style in which Diana lived, with Elgar in the background during English tea, a dress code for dinner and Shakespeare on video, underscored the 'primitive' side of the difference.

'It's amazing. There's no way anyone could be prepared for this,' said Peter when we'd found his things – but gave the impression, smiling at a piccaninni so shy he hid his face behind a dugout paddle, that he couldn't wait to welcome his first class.

Now I'd started looking into her and Tom's backgrounds, it had been arranged that I'd spend an hour each evening with Diana, going through old slides. The more I learned about her as a young woman, the more interested I became in the Diana I saw in 1998. But it was also impossible not to be intrigued by the people within whose orbit she had elected, albeit at carefully circumscribed arm's length, to live. And I could see, as I skirted her domain on my walks, heading for the reef and the edge of that other world, that her history of Pigeon Island might not be the only one to examine, if I were to emerge with a full picture. I was going to have a busy – and possibly sharply divided – time ahead.

With the reopening of Pigeon Island School under a qualified teacher for the first time since Ross, Ben and Tasha Hepworth had attended it under governesses thirty years before, our days fell into a routine. Rising, for me, was at 5 a.m., when I crept out for my pre-dawn dance round Pigeon or, if the tide was high, a solitary swim. As light spread from above Nandelli, I'd be boiling breakfast rice, and the boys stretching luxuriously in the perfect air, by six o'clock. Magnus, if he hadn't been night fishing, would hustle them to have their bowls cleared from under our Kaikai Tree and the veranda swept of crab bodies skewered in the night by seven, and Joe and Benji filled the waiting time before school, which started at seven thirty, with scrumping. They learned early on from local friends which trees harboured tasty fruit and never hesitated to try something new. I knew when school had started because Peter found that the best way of combating the reserve of the shy Islander contingent, wild on the reef with Benji and a football but clamming up when expected to use English for lessons, was to play games outside before classes proper began. For the first few days, only Peter, Joe and Benji's voices carried, but within a week Ngive and Elisha from Nenumbo, Patteson from Otelo, and Simon Boga, from a village beyond Nandelli, joined in. I always tried to be at my desk with Tom's diaries, or in my study dell on the south-western cliffs, before 7.45 a.m. and we all broke for lunch, which Magnus prepared and often caught as well, at twelve. Teuna, the housegirl Diana had wanted me to take on, was happy, it transpired, to come once a week and, apart from attending expertly to white ants that threatened the books in the boys' veranda room, she was hardly needed. But I liked her gentle presence, flicking round dreamily with a bunch of twigs; she brought us pawpaws and when, once, water was short on Pigeon, she took the washing, and Joe and Benji, over to her island, where there was a well. The three of them stayed away for hours, the boys eventually returning scrubbed and full of tales of village life. They were walking ice-breakers – and un-intentional ambassadors for my future relations with Reef Island people. Magnus continued to find pleasure in solitary explorations, when he wasn't wave-skiing in his kayak, and became well known locally as 'fasbon b'long Lusi' (Lucy's firstborn). Seldom was he permitted to leave any island he visited without a gift of fruit.

I took a generous break in the middle of the day, knowing Joe and Benji would be back in school until two, and then busy coaching athletics teams of hermit crabs, swapping kayaks for dugouts or trying to learn, with as many giggles as scraped bellies, how to shin up palms, until Magnus rounded them up for a rainwater rinse and to help with the evening meal, which we ate around sunset, at five thirty. Often I wasn't back from my lunchbreak until three, because this was my 'living now' time. Far out on the reef where, at low tide, curlew-like birds dined delicately, a solitary black heron rose and a white line of breakers was a scrawled flourish on a dazzling blue blank, or a little deeper every day under the darker blue below, I found that, without trying, I could shed my mind.

They say the landscape under the sea here is mountainous, with Tinakula a hollow peak, Matema like an epaulette on a sunken shoulder, and the main Reef Islands like small plateaux and the bushy tops of ridges. But however you look at it, Pigeon always emerges as eccentric, a frozen grey mushroom with a flounce. When the tide is right out, it's an island in a desert of coral-strewn sand, and at midday I detach myself from it and wander, almost shadowless, over the grainy yellow sea. The sun is spread, hot and arched above the reef like a woman in abandon, sky shimmering like glistening skin. And I abandon myself beneath it. My bra goes when I'm equidistant from Poppet and Nandelli and the trunks of palms have become blurred. I tie it on my head. Shells pop and crackle – small sounds underlining noon silence – and I roll my shoulders to tilt my breasts at the sun.

When I became celibate through a process of elimination after failure and Addie's death, I found an acceptable plateau, a numbed plain more middle-aged than it need have been, perhaps, before my spine crumpled – and with that all the suppleness and flow that makes a woman a woman. But here, as on Tuin, even if that was years ago, before babies and at a time of expected sensuality, something I recognize is happening. The sun has placed a warm hand at the base of my spine and massaged gently, flaring sure fingers all over the bad bit, moulding the lump of transplanted bone and implanted metal that felt so alien into something better than a spare part – into a part of me. And

my feet, brown and sure as they were on Tuin, toes curling in timelessly
trickling sand, have become almost as sensitive as another pair of hands. Far
out on the reef, nudged deliciously out of sense and into sensuality by the mid-
day sun, I remove the strip of kalico round my waist and hold it up in the wind
so it floats like a magic carpet. Coconut oil slides on my all-over-browning
body, and sun catches the wild white whoosh of the distant waves that
circumscribe this huge crucible for the distillation of inner space, making my
mind slide too . . . Far out on the reef, I am ridiculously happy.

And occasionally, when I was out on the reef, images of others
came to mind, men mostly, and all the longings and evasions I'd come
to associate with them – but I thought of one woman, too, Diana.
Had she felt what I felt there, or experienced similar transports and
transformations before, during and after her childbearing years? She'd
been beautiful as a young woman, and even now she had poise that
said she still was. Had the sun that was dissolving me dissolved then
moulded her, too? Sometimes such questions were still in my head
when I went across for our evening sessions at six thirty. Joe and Benji,
well stretched by morning school and a long afternoon of play, were
often already asleep when I came back to write up my notes until my
own solar-powered lantern went out, usually before nine.

Diana, as I'd learned from Tom's early diaries, had always liked
routine, and soon our evening slots acquired a special shape of their
own, her practical approach to our archival explorations suiting the
way I worked, too. The 'little difference' we'd had over Magnus's disappearance was smoothed over by a shared task, but many of her
attitudes, and the strangely hard philosophy that dismissed maternal
worry, remained unexplained to me for some time.

'There you are, dear,' she'd say, long body nestled into a lounger
pulled inside but the great barn doors of her home open on tropical
space, and she'd pat an upright chair, which my back preferred. From
this I could see not only her and the images she showed me but the
hugeness of the night beyond, setting her words into context, always
reminding me that whatever had gone before, Pigeon was where
she'd ended up – and my job was to find out how much it had been
for her a haven, an escape, the base of further dream building, and
what else. There were always two squares of Ben's home-made fudge
on top of the pile of pictures and papers I was to look at, which we
ate while dealing briefly with contemporary matters, before devoting
ourselves to history. Had Laloa been round with the insect spray? Yes,

thank you. I should remember to give only single-use quantities of washing powder to the housegirl or it would disappear. Fine. Any chance we could find out when the next boat taking mail was due? (This was me.) Diana: 'No chance.' Never mind. I rarely needed to ask Diana what she'd been doing during the day; with her home being so open and her workshop close to my office, it was usually obvious.

In 1998 Diana still adhered to the daily timetable Tom had outlined for the two of them in the 1940s, only the hours were all earlier – 'elevenses' at 9.30 a.m. and tea at three instead of four because we were in the tropics. She left her bed, not long after I did, at 5.15 a.m. and began the day with exercises performed in knickers on her east veranda, where she could view the sunrise at the same time. I'd spotted her from the side and back, arms boldly outflung, legs wide for balance and chest open to the dawn as she bent and swivelled vigorously from the waist. Her legs would be swung like a ballet dancer's, and at a certain stage all that could be seen above the veranda rail were her feet, the only imperfectly balanced, damaged part of her, as she raised and lowered them, toes curled in on themselves but neatly together. Those little feet appeared and disappeared against the backdrop of a tropical sunrise seven days a week; she kept herself in trim to match her Eden-like home. Breakfast with Ben followed, when they discussed the main aims of the day. Perhaps, if he wasn't weighing baskets of copra locals brought to Pigeon, he'd concentrate on a repair to the solar electrics or fix a leak in a water tank, while she spent the morning measuring wood for new stools for the school-house, overseeing the filleting of fish caught in the night or mending a roof. They'd meet again at lunch – prepared by Lanebu – and catch up on progress, returning to their tasks until tea. That's an eight-hour day already, with house and ground staff to supervise constantly too, and the jobs never ran out. In the evening, after a shower and supper, before I came Diana either read, listened to music or, power permitting, watched a video. It was a busy existence, and I noticed she never seemed to venture outside for pleasure. Not even on a Sunday, which – again echoing habits begun early in her marriage – she kept as a strictly non-working day. 'When you live in the tropics,' she said once, 'you don't seek the sun.' But I couldn't believe she'd always felt like that.

8

The Sailing Years: 1947–1957

THE HEPWORTHS WITH A CREW OF FOUR CAST OFF TO CROSS THE Atlantic in November 1947, singing as they waved Britain goodbye, but only ten days out Tom wrote: '*Whatever made me consider this mad voyage?*' They'd hit weather that poured freezing water onto their bunks and made it '*an athletic feat to stand up*'. But that first fortnight at sea, no blue skies in sight, turned out to be the storm before the calm, a trial by ice and seasick misery before the gods relented and, in mid-Atlantic, sent a school of dolphins pulling the sun after them one dawn, '*like a blazing chariot!*' Then Diana climbed to the end of the twenty-foot bowsprit, swung underneath so she was dunked in every wave and called: 'Come on!' Some crew members joined her but Tom, happy to let them enjoy themselves while he took the helm, listened to the laughter and told his diary: '*I'm a very lucky fellow.*' He'd thought about his dream so long, the birth pangs of its realization were perhaps more difficult for him than for Diana, who'd already discovered she thrived on challenge. But now they were in mid-ocean, in what would be midwinter in Britain, the sun hot on their backs, and when Christmas found them still miles from land, Diana was at the helm after sunrise, when a shower produced a rainbow Tom described as '*arching over five-sixths of the sky, and seeming to meet under our feet*'. Diana wrote of that rainbow that it seemed to glow all round her, like a sign. At that moment, married to a man she loved and with the world, if she were prepared to take the grit with it, her oyster, she felt pure happiness.

First landfall, after thirty days, was at Madeira, where Tom admired Lilliputian fields '*where a man might draw from the earth, in all this beauty, enough to feed his children, and owe no-one*'. This vision was key to Tom's dream. Nothing about the competitiveness of the world they'd left attracted him, and his father's criticisms of him had made him stall rather than acted as stimuli to lead a 'sensible' life. '*Diana and I wanted to live a down to earth life, not hemmed about with rules and conventions, or worried about "keeping up with the Joneses"* . . . *We didn't want to work fifty years in the hope we could* then *retire and enjoy ourselves* . . . *Better to enjoy life as you go along, for you may not live long enough to* have *an old age. Somewhere in the world there must be a place where a man could raise his family in peace, and in the way he thought right.*' This was the final aim, but the search proper didn't start yet. '*For years I dreamed of sailing down the blue seas in the hot sunlight, and when at last I achieved it, the reality was as good as anything I dreamed* . . . *This swinging, lunging ship, so small a speck on the ocean, is our world for now. The far lands await, but we should be content to have them moved ten thousand miles.*'

This blissful passage brought them tanned and triumphant – but penniless – to the murky brown waters of British Guiana, where they needed to find funds for the next leg of their voyage. '*The lap of the Gods is tilted and slippery and each must scrabble for his place.*' But this is where Diana's schooling, with its emphasis on practical as well as social skills, proved such a boon; she didn't mind scrabbling. Tom placed advertisements for yacht charters in Georgetown, then looked for any kind of work in the interim. He returned proposing to re-convert their home to a trawler, to carry out a fishing survey. 'We'd need to find space for an ice hold,' he told Diana, 'for four tons of ice.' This was no fridge freezer to be fitted into a cupboard, but she drew up plans at once, doing away altogether with saloon accommodation and keeping just a cubby-hole cabin for herself and Tom – consisting entirely of a curtained-off bed – to use only when it rained. Once the hold was complete, they dragged their mattress up every night and slept on the great double hatches, under the stars.

For the survey, a trawl net was cast, pulled up and tipped out over the deck, where a hose separated mud and debris of the deep from those fish that needed to be counted. As soon as the hold was full, they headed back to port, cleansed it of guts on hands and knees, replenished the ice and set out again. Once more the Hepworths, yearning for the freshness and freedom of space and sun, experienced trial by ice and stench before their goal came nearer. But, brought up to respect the virtues of the stiff upper lip, they didn't discuss how much they loathed this job, only celebrated when it was over, despite not greatly bolstered funds. Riches didn't mean money in the bank but six months' worth of foodstores on board. For the time it took to reconvert the *AR* into a vessel fit to charter, they moored up the Mazeruni river, where Tom wrote: '*We were unworried by being broke and out of work because the conditions were quite different. At home, if you lose your job you're in trouble. Even if you've a well-stocked larder, there's still rent or mortgage to pay. We had none of those worries, and something would turn up before we ran out of food.*'

It did. By mid–1949 they'd found a couple who wanted a trip round the Caribbean and were off, cruising round a dozen then minimally developed islands until Christmas, which they spent in feudal grandeur in Jamaica, where they completed their ménage with a ship's cat and dog. Diana was coming up to thirty, Tom forty, but their wanderlust had just begun. Stopping for Mardi Gras in New Orleans, then sailing on towards Panama to pick up the next clients, they treated long sea passages as casually as others do motorway journeys – only with infinitely less restriction, never a tailback and many pleasurable picnics in the middle of the blue en route. But plain sailing for long was rare, and they hit major setbacks. First, a crew member, saying he was taking laundry ashore, wrapped Tom's photographic equipment in a sheet and vanished. Then, delayed by blown-out head sails and Tom's lifelong enemy, '*bloody bureaucracy*' in the form of a '*little Hitler*' at Honduras who demanded cash in lieu of documentation they hadn't needed elsewhere, they missed the appointment in Panama, and consequently the charter fee upon which they'd been depending. They had less than twenty dollars between them when they finally limped into harbour, and Tom sent a cable to his friend Dennis asking for a temporary leg up. They were to be stuck now, for over a year, close to the Panama Canal, but before they reached a safe mooring in Gatun Lake the *AR*, with Tom and Diana asleep on deck in each other's arms, was raked by machine-gun fire. Dumb with shock, hearts hammering, they touched each other's faces in the dark to see if they were still alive. Then Tom, tousled and furious, got up and swore. The mistake had been made by a sentry, jumpy at the outbreak of the Korean War. Inches higher, the shots would have been fatal. It took Diana weeks to fill the holes and made Tom keener than ever to 'get out of the way of other people's wars'.

But Dennis didn't let them down and, anxious to repay his debt, Tom went to work for Kodak in Panama City, while Diana greased every ball-bearing on the ship. Their troubles weren't over – Tom developed malaria in Panama, but while in hospital he met an American who fancied the idea of a cruise round the Galapagos and helped to find three other crew members. This group shared many miles of sailing, and trekking on foot and by donkey, during their trip round eight of the Galapagos Islands, which received on average no more than two yachts a year at that time. Diana stood on a giant tortoise, cuddled a flamingo and held a rare iguana; craters in which lakes nestled, vertical pinnacles of rock and battalions of sealions were duly admired. But what really interested Tom was how the few Europeans who'd settled in the islands fared, because one day he and Diana would simply stop sailing, as some of these had done, and make a home.

On Floreana, they learned of a dentist who came in 1928, with a patient, seeking ultimate power over his own life. Judging from his early writings, he believed he'd found it: 'We two are the absolute masters of our destiny as you who remain in Europe and America can never hope to be.' And (after Nietzsche): 'This is the best of all possible worlds for if it were still better, it would no longer be earth, but heaven.' After several years, he'd adjusted his sights inwards: 'Paradise is not impossible for attainment. It is only a state of the soul within one's self.' How carefully did Tom study these words? His aim was still to find the perfect place to rear children away from the 'noise' of the world.

Other residents of Floreana were the Wittmers, who, despite the scarcity of traffic, offered hospitality to passers-by. Not an easy enterprise, as even the intrepid Hepworths were 'happily lost' for most of the eighteen miles they walked to find the remote homestead, but the island had a special attraction for voyeurs of escapism. In 1932, a woman calling herself a baroness arrived with two lovers in tow, pistols, silk underwear, and plans for a hotel and golf course. She built a three-man bed with a roof, calling it Hacienda Paradise, is said to have shot a passing sailor who wouldn't sleep with her, whipped her bedfellows, and honed her own arousal by watching them fight. But she drove her men too far, for one eventually murdered her, and her other lover, then desperate to escape, took the first available lift off Floreana and died of starvation on another island. Outside the laws of civilization, remote islands are little worlds of their own and freedom can be a dangerous toy.

But it was on the life to be had near Academy Bay, the centre of the archipelago, that Tom made his judgement as to whether setting up home here appealed. He was impressed by the industry of a family who, starting from nothing, had built a farm which now provided the island with fresh produce. A refugee from Germany had also done well, and could endorse his claim that life in the Galapagos had all he needed by showing a letter written by a film director who'd sent him to Hollywood, saying he was '*the handsomest He-Man ever. He is BOX OFFICE!*' But the bright lights couldn't compare to Galapagos phosphorescence, and back he came. Other contented island dwellers said they lived on a dollar a day, a point Tom noted in his diary, but that didn't persuade him they'd found their particular Paradise. '*Not enough water,*' he wrote shortly, and '*The Ecuadorian populace look a dodgy lot.*'

The charter had, however, been a success, and only a few more dollars were needed before the *AR* could cross the Pacific. These Tom earned by bringing a fleet of shrimp boats from Miami to Panama. A crew member passed on word of the impending ocean voyage to Amalie Stone, winner of the Amelia Earhart Award, who was dropping down in her Cessna aeroplane on university campuses throughout America to encourage girls to fly. In March 1952, Amalie, the Hepworths and a young author, Bill Crealock, cast off.

Swooping from South America right across the great swag of blue that is the South Pacific, to Tahiti and Tonga and finally New Zealand, the *AR* rocked in its berths people who were living out their fantasies, and Bill Crealock detailed the first part of that trip in his book *Towards Tahiti*.★ But in this, Tom and Diana are only lightly sketched. The picture of Tom's daily life that emerges through his own notes, scribbled between navigational sums, is of constant activity – maintaining the thousand components that together make a ship – interspersed with odd moments, during night watches, of immense peace, when ship, man and ocean seemed to meld as one. Diana

---

★ First published by Peter Davies, London, 1955.

worked solidly too, but it was around this time that Tom, borrowing a camera, photographed her nude, on a log over a river inland of some sunny Pacific shore, which says much about the pleasures of an island-hopping life. In that picture, black and white and made ragged by time, a woman at the height of her beauty, whose days were filled with physical challenge and nights with silken air and stars whose constellations her husband could name, reclines in perfect natural abandon, eyes closed, and the tiniest, intimate smile on her lips. There was not an aspect of her youth's longings unfulfilled at that time, and all the adventure of the future ahead.

Journeying among the islands, they anchored not only at the landmarks of Typee, where Herman Melville had been as stunned by primeval Eden as they were, and Fakarava, where Robert Louis Stevenson stopped and stayed, but just wherever they found (another) perfect cove. And everywhere they went, they were fêted. The sight of a ship, in the Tuamotus, was rare, and not only the indigenous peoples, decking them with flowers, found something to celebrate in the arrival of strangers. Lonely expats straight out of Somerset Maugham, some content with their isolated postings, some 'gone peculiar' (Tom's words), fell over themselves to offer hospitality. At Nuka Hiva, Tom lost his heart to an anchorage with untouched land all round, and the notion of Hepworth's Happy Holiday Hacienda was bandied. But not for long; they weren't ready to stop yet. Ua Pou's mad peaks amid green baize hills appealed to Amalie, who learned to sail an outrigger canoe, and all had a chance to reassess the values of the Outside World during an unscheduled stop on the uninhabited island of Nengo Nengo, where they ran aground and had to wait for spring tides to help them out. They observed, from their travels, that the average Polynesian's expectations of life were infinitely simpler than the average European's, and therefore it was easier for them to be happy. But they also saw the locals' lifestyle as one-dimensional and felt that their simplicity of outlook couldn't be borrowed successfully by people from another culture, so they had no desire to 'go native'. One can't have diversity of choice without the stresses that go with it, but if diversity is what a man's been brought up with, he may 'go against his own nature' to try to forget it. Selectivity, Tom considered, was the key, and his ambition was to make a life incorporating the best of both the natural and the evolved – but well away from what is usually seen as civilization. Bill and Amalie, with other commitments, left the *AR* in Tahiti and, after a pleasant six months' rest there, the Hepworths sailed on alone to Tonga.

This trip took twenty-eight days and Tom was too busy to write much, but he did note that one of the worst moments he ever experienced was when he was convinced Diana had fallen overboard in the middle of two thousand miles of empty ocean. Frantically he ran up and down the deck, calling: 'Darling, where are you?' over and over. They were making good speed, and if she'd fallen and been unable to grab the safety rope trailing from the stern, it was unlikely he'd find her. Then she hallooed from her invisible eyrie at the top of the mast, where she hadn't heard him because of the wind, and he, perched precariously on a rail as he craned upwards, nearly fell overboard in surprise and relief, terrifying her . . . They hadn't spent more than a day out of each other's sight since their wedding. And not one night.

Tonga, for the Hepworths, was a blend of formal social whirl and filthy ship's repairs, a mix that typified their land adventures. Queen Salote was away in England at the time, but Prince Tungi took them spear fishing and asked them to train a countryman in navigation, to which they agreed. But, the Tongans excepted – because of their openly classist system of rule – Tom had by now formed his own ideas about the majority of 'natives' in the Pacific. The greatest mistake Europe made, he believed, was to attempt to bring Western-style education to people who couldn't benefit from it, and whose formerly simple, happy lot was muddied by a little dangerous knowledge. The idea of equality that was fashionable in the West could only be a red rag to the unsophisticated. People under a respected hierarchy knew where they stood; their expectations didn't exceed possibility – ergo they were content. It may be, too, that Tom was still reacting against expectations implicit in his own background. He would never equate himself with a 'native' – whom he saw as a different breed of human being – but didn't ally himself to the general perception of a rounded European man either.

Diana was about to undergo a transformation. When they arrived in New Zealand in 1953, they had to earn some money. Advertised as '*One of London's leading models*', Diana hit the scene when boatloads of new gowns had just arrived from European fashion houses, and after only briefly traipsing round with her portfolio she found herself in demand. A motor scooter was added to the dog kennel and punt stowed on the *AR*'s deck, and she rode on this from the harbour, make-up and stockings strapped on the pillion, to stalk the catwalks. Tom was less lucky, giving up '*pursuing poverty through photography*', as he called it, to settle for better pay as a house painter. While they worked and saved, the Hepworths' by now professionally worded advertisements appeared in the press until five crew members had been picked for a six-month cruise. In prim, early '50s Auckland, the fact that all the successful applicants were girls caused a flutter. '*Tom Hepworth's Harem*', read headlines on the women's pages.

The *AR*'s all-girl crew, who made entrances to exotic harbours in the Pacific scantily clad and cunningly deployed on spreaders and yardarms up the rigging, were to hold pride of place in Tom's memories of his happiest sailing days. Navigation classes and a charm school – to prepare the girls for a ball hosted by the Governor of Fiji – formed part of the daily routine on board as the *AR* sailed first back to Tonga, where the trained navigator was delivered, then on to the New Hebrides. Each girl also took her turn manning the anchor winch and washing dishes in a bucket drawn from the ocean by rope, and discovered life at sea was full of extremes. Seasick for a week, some found the Hepworths' rule that they stick to their roster harsh. But Diana, who believed the best life to be full of challenges and contrasts, taught them how to rig up canvas slings by their bunks to prevent them falling out, and within days the sun burst from behind the clouds and the girls bathed their shocked bodies in buckets on the deck, wan smiles turning to laughter. With their smalls hung in the rigging, the *AR*, with Tom playfully pampered by all, took on the atmosphere of a holiday camp, and when the crew had been through further trials and joys together, the girls flung off their swimsuits whenever it rained, and washed nude on deck while Tom read. If blue jokes ever passed between Tom and the officers of a passenger ship, the *Tofua*, that kept bumping into the *AR* after the girls had found their sea legs and picked up hula skirts to show them off, they weren't recorded, but he did note a signal exchange that took place:

AR (Tom): '*I have six women in grass skirts aboard. Headache severe.*'
Signals Officer of *Tofua*: '*I am requested to say boys all have lawn mowers for the grass skirts.*'
AR: '*Girls say they'll need to be sharp.*'
Tofua: '*Boys all at razor edge now . . . Sweet dreams.*'

During six months among the prettiest of Pacific islands, the girls spent hours scraping decks for painting, then, light-headed from sun-bathing to the strains of Mozart blasted over the ocean, opened oysters collected on reefs or, on lucky days, simply picked flying fish off the deck for supper. One evening, thrillingly, they attended a kava (local liquor) party with 'natives' on shore, crawling jelly-legged up the *AR*'s side late at night; another time they caused a sensation among expats starved of female company at a fancy-dress party. Tom, in drag for this, had a substantial bosom thrust upon him by his crew, who snapped a picture of him coyly '*adjusting a boob*'. A life of contrasts it was, and they all finally adopted Diana's philosophy that tough times only enhance pleasure.

But to one girl, Cathy, a nurse, adjustment of boobs had special meaning. While the others took his charm school lightly, Cathy listened to every word Tom uttered that might help her feel less susceptible to 'making boobs' on formal occasions. As they shimmied past him, books on their heads to keep their necks graceful as swans', Tom taught them the golden rule of how to handle men: '*Ask them questions about themselves, and curb impulsive comments, and you won't go wrong.*' Cathy put this advice into practice, with success, at the ball in Fiji, where she'd been afraid she'd feel too tongue-tied to say anything beside Diana, whom the girls referred to as 'the Skipper's Skipper', in her Hartnell gown. Tom was delighted when, later, Cathy wrote: '*I left New Zealand very unsure of myself, but my experiences on the* AR *gave me the opportunity to change all that. That six months set me up for life.*'

The principle of 'live now' characterized this period in the lives of most of those just passing through the cabins of the *AR*, but Tom and Diana kept a weather eye on the future. While in the New Hebrides, they made enquiries about copra trading and concluded that, if con-verted again, the *AR* would make a fine trading vessel. And if they were making major changes to their floating home anyway, why not add facilities for a trade store – in their deckhouse bedroom? They'd use the bed to display their wares and keep their stock in a chest of drawers.

Trading in the New Hebrides in the mid-1950s was the first occu-pation that allowed the Hepworths to break even regularly. They visited inlets, stopping to 'yarn' with locals and gradually working round to the subject of copra. Tom explained to his sisters how the operation worked: '*We buy copra (the dried meat of coconuts, children, used for soap and margarine) from natives, and sell fish hooks, stick tobacco, ammunition, aspirins – a thousand and one things. It's rather fun. Often we take back in the store all the money we've paid out for copra, a highly satis-factory state of affairs.*' But there were risks attached: '*Loading copra in remote spots in an ocean swell, one backs the punt in, paying out rope from an anchor, then, on the top of a wave, a bag weighing 150 lbs is chucked from the shore, and the chap in the bow hauls frantically to avoid the next wave and the rocks.*' This persuaded Tom to have the *AR* insured, but he expressed no worries in his letters 'home'. '*Changed, I have, sans doute. I could no longer bear to live in a city, or anywhere, I suspect, outside the islands. It's not a question of comfort, but climate makes a difference . . . I think it's chiefly this: the civilized world is rollicking into chaos, irretrievably in my view, and since I no longer think anything can be done about it, I no longer care . . . Music and Art aren't enough for me. But sunshine and sea and a job to be busy on apparently are . . . By the way how are you financially? It would be stupid to starve in a garret with a wealthy brother in the Tropics.*'

It must have given younger brother Tom, who'd always been looked after by his sisters, a sense of pride to be able to dangle this largesse, and although copra prices rose and fell his spirits remained buoyant. If he wasn't actually living his final dream, he was close to it, and his passionate relationship with Diana made any discomforts inherent in his chosen job – a trade as opposed to the profession his family had hoped for – easily bearable, and heightened every joy. An intimacy begun one cold December in the *AR*'s dinghy in pouring British rain had only grown deeper with time. He jotted a note as the new year of 1957 dawned: '*We* can't *have been married ten years!* . . . *It's still like a honeymoon.*'

Tom's sisters wrote as often as he sent a poste restante address, but they had busy lives too. In the latter half of the 1950s, Elizabeth Hepworth held a painting show which led to a photograph in the *Lady*, and an interview in an evening paper in which she mentioned her adventurous brother Tom. Within weeks, Tom received a com-mission to write articles and a letter from André Deutsch, the publishers. '*Never heard of 'em,*' wrote Tom to Elizabeth. '*Oh my dear,*' she wrote back, '*say yes!*' But Tom had now expanded his operations to include twenty 'natives' diving for trochus in the Banks Islands. '*I'll get down to it when I can,*' he wrote, and after a successful trading trip in 1957 he and Diana decided to take a busman's holiday, with stop-offs in coves for writing en route as part of the plan. Their destination was the Eastern Outer Islands★ of the then British Solomon Islands Protectorate.

★ Later known as Reef Islands.

9

Current Contrasts

SOMETIMES, AFTER EVENINGS WITH DIANA, I LET MY PRECIOUS TEA GO cold, I was so busy jotting down the essence of what had passed between us. Diana's reminiscences and Tom's diaries had brought the Hepworths close to Pigeon now – forty years ago. What had changed in Reef Islands since then? What hadn't? To add to interest that grew the more I learned, Ross, not even born where I'd temporarily left his parents' past, was now back, and Pigeon in 1998 had altered dramatically, for Ross didn't just bring his family; when he returned, a village sprang up overnight at one end – and a dividing line appeared across the middle of the island. Although Tom's grave held the most central position, the schoolhouse felt, to Peter and Mhairi, bang in the middle of two radically different cultures. This was perhaps appropriate since it was a mixed school – but it wasn't easy for them at times. Ross saw himself as a Solomon Islander, but his children's paternal grandmother couldn't have been more different from other grannies in Reef Islands, and Stasi the Rottweiler had a problem distinguishing who was allowed up the Western end and who she should discourage in no uncertain terms. She'd learned to recognize regular staff, such as Lanebu, and Tangypera and Nupanyi, the two main grounds 'boys', but would bark at the grandchildren and other Islanders who passed – or tried to pass – Diana's house. Joe and Benji couldn't understand at first why she didn't bark at them in daylight, but did at night. Then Joe said one day:

'It's because we're white, isn't it? The others are really frightened when she barks at them.'

'I tell her to sarrap,' (shut up) said Benji. 'Why *does* she chase the Islanders anyway?'

At that time I didn't know why Diana felt it necessary to keep a guard dog either, and it was sad to see men, women and children shrink from Stasi, when all they wanted was to deliver a bowl of coconut to Diana (for the dogs' supper) or pop along to see me with a fruit offering.

'A lot of elderly people like a dog around,' I told Benji vaguely. 'You feel vulnerable when you're old.'

'What's vulnerable?' asked Benji.

Joe was quick: 'It's how Elisha and Patteson feel when they have to pass Stasi.'

Benji and Joe, growing closer daily to their Islander friends, didn't approve of what they perceived as an old-fashioned, prejudiced side of Diana. At the same time, they were glad to have their own little eyrie to retire to at the Western end when they wanted to indulge their European side – for instance, by having a quiet read. Pigeon, I discovered, was not only educational in the matter of natural resources, but encapsulated problems of race and territoriality seen throughout the history of the Rest of the World, from which, in other ways, we seemed so remote. I'd hoped it would prove a microcosm, and so it did. But why should humanity's struggles be different from elsewhere just because Pigeon was tiny and pretty? Why do we connect tropical islands with some Utopian ideal? Problems in a small space tend to be concentrated, not diluted.

No such questions troubled the boys' minds when, after two of their schoolmates, Patteson and Simon, had been installed for the year at Ross's house, returning to their families by canoe at weekends, and Ross and Pegi's eldest son, Andrew, joined their class, Joe and Benji took to spending nearly all their time down the Islander – or Ross's – end. There, with guidance from Pegi, on her own territory the confident epitome of Melanesian motherhood, Joe and Benji learned how to eat whole fish tidily in their fingers, handfeed Pigeon Island pigeons, and join in crab hunts at dusk resulting in joyful, impromptu bonfire bakes.

Ross and Pegi's house, unlike mine, which had to have quiet hours so I could work, was always open and welcoming. Originally it had been built as a cargo shed – in 1959 – by Diana, and still had massive doors either end, never closed, except against wind. A low wire fence surrounding the sprawling yard was supposed to keep poultry out, but often ducks, kittens, lorikeets, toddlers and mild-tempered cockerels mingled happily under the leaf veranda, or played on a mountain of petrol drums outside the back of Pigeon Island Traders (PIT) store. And there were always plenty of adults around to scoop up a toddler about to trip, or dip a small bottom in the sea. These were Pegi's wontoks – family, friends and clan members – whose main activities in the yard were weaving leaf mats, mending twine and bamboo fishing nets, stripping the bark from trees cut for building or simply sitting around companionably. Often Pegi's mother, from Nandelli, was present, and there were several ''ousegels' who sat over buckets washing kalicos or peeling kumera but were treated like friends. Covertly flirting with the girls were youths who carried copra or helped with Ross's building projects, and older, experienced Islanders who rammed the copra into sacks. Uncles, cousins, brothers, aunties – all with their own entourages of piccaninnis, naked or clothed – came and went all day. A critical eye might have observed that baskets of copra, laundry and vegetables sat about waiting to be seen to, twig brooms were only occasionally wielded seriously and litter tended to accumulate. But what overflowed most from that busy yard – people busy 'stori-ing' (exchanging anecdotes), grooming each other's hair, grating coconuts to make cream for fish someone had just caught, checking an underground oven – was a sense of deep physical and emotional ease.

Joe and Benji, accustomed to a mum who, for all her dreamy island past, had succumbed as much as any in the end to wound-up Western ways, fell into that unhurried, unworried atmosphere as though it were a homecoming. I looked at Ross one afternoon, sitting under a palm outside his ever-open home with a pigeon on his wrist, a baby on his knee, two toddlers at his feet and a lorikeet sidling round to nibble his ear from the back of his chair, and understood I was observing that too rare phenomenon in this stress-filled world: a happy man basking in the bosom of his (impressively extended) family. The fact that he'd been through much to reach this point – and I didn't know how much then – added to the impact of the realization. Catching my look, Ross indicated a scene taking place behind me. There, Pegi sat on a stool that was also a coconut grater, broad legs spread with Joe kneeling between them and her hands delicately at work pinching nits from his floppy red hair, which she popped between strong nails with a sound that made everyone grunt with satisfaction. In front of him sat Patteson, nine, in whose dark curls Joe's hands were buried, and in front of Patteson, Benji, his blond head being expertly explored. Last in the train, picking hopefully at a kitten's fur, was Ross's and Pegi's youngest, Frederic, aged two.

'I told you they'd fit in fine with my family,' said Ross.

I said how grateful I was that he and Pegi had more or less adopted my sons. If there was a football match on another island, they automatically included Joe and Benji in the outing; if anyone was going trolling for tuna, they'd be invited. And if a bishop happened to be visiting for breakfast, they joined in the feast laid on for him, too. Joe became so friendly with one local man of the cloth that they regularly shared the same mug of Milo – a malted hot drink popular in the Solomons – dunking Hard Navy Biscuits in turn and discussing the satisfactions of various types of fishing.

'We're not doing anything special,' Ross said. 'It's just part of the culture. Mum keeps you locked away the other end too much! You should spend more time with us to see how it all works.'

I wanted to do that, and to go beyond Ross's end of Pigeon in my quest to understand more about Reef Island life and the Kastom beliefs that still held sway, as well as the modern religious side of the culture. As it happened, two opportunities to begin this process occurred almost simultaneously. First Ben, always a distant figure for all he lived only yards from us, asked if I'd like to go to the church he attended, the only white in an Islander congregation. This was arranged for the following Sunday. Then Magnus, returning one afternoon from a banana hunt on Nenumbo, said thoughtfully:

'Mum, you know that guy who works for Diana, the small one with bandy legs?'

'Yes, that's Tangypera. He was struggling with a pipe in our cesspit all morning. Don't throw any more pawpaw skins down there.'

'OK. Anyway, in his village I think he's quite a "Bigman". People seem to respect him; he chews betel with the elders a lot, and several women look after him. You should talk to him.'

I planned to, but was beaten to it by Tangypera himself who, a day later, as if by telepathy, suddenly materialized as a shadow subtly altering the light through the window of my office, so that I looked round casually but didn't get a fright. He'd managed to slip past Diana's, and Stasi, without making a sound, an implike figure not much taller than a child, but with two of the most compellingly adult eyes I'd ever seen under hair tight and thick as a stamped circle of coir. Those eyes, though bloodshot, were steady and shrewd, but his large mouth, prominent as a puppet's on a jutting jaw, was given to extravagant twists of humour – when we got to know each other. That first time he visited, until I got up and walked round to where he was, he just stared in at me, as though assessing what he saw and coming to some inner judgement.

On the veranda nearest the cliff edge outside our house, with Tinakula puffing in the distance, Tangypera stood with a grubby Solrice (Australian rice) bag between his feet, making a gesture with his eyebrows that indicated, in any language, that we should move to where we wouldn't be overheard. I followed him to the edge of the cliff, where we perched on lumps of coral.

'Missus no savvy mifela visitim . . .' he began cautiously. (Diana didn't know he'd come.) I said that was all right, and he settled more comfortably and asked if he should 'stori' first, or if I'd begin. It seemed formal, for a chat on a rock, but I did my best to comply with what was evidently a pattern for 'toktok' (discussion).

'Iufela stori fastaem,' I suggested, and he happily took the lead. In a roundabout way, and with great seriousness, he told me in Pijin he'd seen my piccaninnis looking for shells on the reef. Having heard that under Kastom law certain reefs were owned, I wondered if they'd unwittingly breached some code, and started to apologize. Then the smile I was to grow accustomed to broke through, and the red eyes danced.

'It's all right. They just don't know where the good ones are!' I got the message and, on cue, Tangypera rooted in his bag, producing a huge, beautiful, peach-coloured spider conch, with delicately splayed spokes making a perfect vase. It was a queen of shells, with great lips pouting from its base ideal to kiss the stems of hibiscus. I lusted after it, and Tangypera smiled. Then I noticed there were other, smaller shells in the bag, but these he dismissed as being 'jas' kaikai'. This interested me, and I thought quickly, under the guise of considering his request for tobacco in exchange for the shell.

'Suppose,' I said finally, 'I'd like to learn about Reef Island food . . . ?'

Tangypera wanted to know why. If I wanted to try the shells local people ate, his wife would bring them, because I was busy. He'd heard, through piccaninnis who were Joe and Benji's intimates by now, that I was writing a book.

I decided honesty was best. 'I want to learn about your customs, to better understand your life – and how you feel about certain things.'

Tangypera's face gave nothing away. I was talking about Kastom now, not just kaikai, and I tried to sell my case harder, asking how I could give a proper account of Pigeon's history if I talked only to Diana. The people of Reef Islands obviously had their point of view too . . . The non-committal expression in Tangypera's eyes remained. Then he announced he'd discuss the matter with the elders at Nenumbo. In the meantime I could have the shell. I felt on tenter-hooks waiting for the judgement of the elders. Would Tangypera explain why I wanted to learn about Reef Island life as I'd explained it to him, and what sort of reaction would that provoke? The round-ness of my view on Pigeon's past was heavily dependent on whatever verdict was reached. If the Islanders decided to clam up, I might live close to them for a year, as Tom and Diana had for forty, but end up knowing very little about the people whose home Reefs had been for centuries.

When Sunday came, I'd still heard nothing from Tangypera and, although the shell was filled daily with hibiscus by Benji, the strong-smelling sticks of tobacco I'd bought in exchange sat untouched.

'If Tangypera appears,' I told Joe, 'could you give him those sticks?' Joe had elected not to go to Ben's church that day as Pegi had invited him to the Anglican service on Nandelli instead, with kaikai to follow.

'Yes. But you could just leave them out. No-one else will take them.'

Joe and Benji had already found that if they left possessions around at the other end of the island, they would be carefully collected and returned. Once, when a comb fell out of my hair, a child retrieved it and brought it to me, after diving for hours in the area where it was lost. Yet Diana had locks on everything, and I noticed Ben wore not a cross but a bunch of keys round his neck, too. '"Do not lead us into temptation . . ."' was the quote used when I enquired about this, but he didn't elaborate. Normally clad only in shorts, he wore a shocking-pink shirt decorated with black palm trees when he came to collect me for church, and I was glad I'd made an effort too – hardly hat and gloves, but at least clean culottes. As we were about to leave, Diana called out. Wind had damaged a duck pen, and it needed fixing. While Ben saw to it, I chatted with his mother.

'He never used to be like this, you know, church all the time. I suppose he just has to cling on to something, after that awful brainwashing in Australia.'

'Brainwashing in Australia?' It seemed an odd subject to come up with on this beautiful morning, on an island miles from anywhere.

'Yes. He was got at by a cult. They tried to take everything from him.' A look I hadn't seen before on Diana's sometimes hard-seeming features softened them, and she seemed, just for a second, bewildered and anxious. This was her son. 'He was so innocent, you see, brought up here where it's so idyllic for children. I suppose they saw that and pounced . . .'

I didn't know who 'they' were, and it was a while before I found out more about the brainwashing, although I observed what could pass for symptoms of it. Meanwhile quiet, obedient Ben, who at other times bopped shark on the nose and wrestled with moray eels, had mended the duck pen and was ready to go. Star followed as we set off into the blue. Maybe Ben was genuinely more at home with real sharks than those produced by civilization. His father's diaries would reveal more about the idyllic childhood and what happened in Australia in due course.

The walk from Pigeon to the Church of the Living Word was something of a Pilgrim's Progress itself. The tide was out when we crossed the channel towards Nandelli – where worship at the Anglican church was already in progress, women and children's voices winging over the reef – but when we veered north, straight out to sea, it seemed, I had to tuck my culottes high in my knickers and carry a Solrice bag, containing an offering in case there was a collection, on my shoulder. We progressed at first along one of the cleared sea paths, no more than a foot wide, with ankle-piercing coral either side. Directly ahead were two tiny islands as perfect as Poppet, the sun pointing up their palm topknots, and the flow of current around them making them seem to float. After twenty minutes, our path curved towards an area thick with mangroves. Here the heat, pouring over our shoulders on a stiller scene, made me pant, and Star, swimming, panted too, saliva on her pink tongue in glistening threads. Ben moved on in silence, not panting, but occasionally allowing a murmured hymn to break from what was perhaps already a state of spiritual repose. Star's paddling paws made watery noises, but the great cathedral dome of the sky and the heavy, muffling mangroves absorbed them. When we reached mud, beyond the end of the path, I had to concentrate on what was directly underfoot. Here the water was dark and the ground full of potholes. Here also was shade, for the trees grew so close along the channel we entered, they almost closed over our heads. I glanced behind, and the broad space of bright sea we had just crossed seemed miles away, another country. There was the whip bird's jungly cry, and the popping of muddy bubbles close to our thighs. Small brown jellyfish hung in the soupy water between the red and grey hoops of mangroves and dotted our way ahead. I moved among them cautiously, understanding they carried a sting, but as the water parted with our strides, they slid by. The channel was long and we saw no-one but Ben responded, in Reef Island language, to a voice that greeted him out of the dark mesh of mangroves, once, and we saw a dugout bobbing, with crabs trying to climb out, under a branch.

How often had Ben journeyed here alone with his dog? It was a bizarre rather than beautiful landscape – or waterscape – where the swamps began, but a ready backdrop for the growth of spiritual leanings. It was like a beginning of the formation of a world, the first muddy steps towards the making of an earth where man might dwell. But it was also, in a sense, unearthly. It was a heavy, impassive setting, where a vulnerable mind might expand – or snap.

The third change of scene along our progress towards worship came when we stepped out of swamp into jungle. A slight elevation of land caused the brown water to drain away, leaving a plain of compacted sand, out of which short magenta spikes of embryonic mangroves protruded. Beyond this, tall trees, some wound about with lianas, lined a narrow track and spread away on either side, with clumps of stubby banana plantations breaking the density and patches where vine vegetables grew under pale-leaved pawpaw trees. The odd pandanus and broad-trunked sago palm brought the atmosphere of tropical island inside the jungle. It was a wild green hotchpotch of growth, with everything vying up towards the sun, as in rainforest, but from thinner soil. The morning smell of damp earth and leaves on Pigeon was heavy here, and enriched by vegetation trodden down by tethered piglets met at intervals in clearings scattered with edible offerings, like wayside shrines. In one, an enormous black sow reclined, her head among coconut husks and a bright banana skin flapping over her snout. Ben walked swiftly, long legs almost in a lope, and I struggled to keep up, images coming and going quickly as we passed: a woman with a stack of branches on her head supported elegantly by one hand, eyes sliding sideways to return Ben's greeting; a naked boy with hair and tiny penis dripping as he smiled from under an upturned red plastic bowl; an old man tramping in silence with a rice bag hanging down his back, its handle round his brow. Then we were in a hamlet where leaf shacks seemed to have grown organically from where leaves still fell, and babies and piglets rooted among fruit skins. From the low doorway of one of the huts, a little girl with a hugely swollen head stared at me. Other children stared too, but a woman squatting over a small fire seemed incurious until Ben spoke, when she smiled. She was young, but the faded strips of kalico she wore hung as if half grown into elderly skin, and her opened lips revealed wet, blood-orange-stained, broken teeth as though she'd been punched.

'They chew too much betel,' Ben remarked, as we moved on along the narrow track flanked by lush greenery. I'd gathered Ben disapproved of all intoxicants — tobacco, beer, lust. Was laughter on the sin list for him, too? His brown eyes looked as though it might not have been, once. The church, when we finally reached it, was just a leaf hut larger than the rest, but beautifully kept. A conch to summon worshippers and a diver's air tank on a rope hung outside, and on the ground lay rows of plastic thong slippers, kept for Sundays. Ben's and mine joined them. Inside, women and babies sat on leaf mats on an earth floor on one side of the hut, men on the other. There was a cluster of little girls, some in rags, some in handmade frocks looking like angels, close to where a bare table served as an altar and — fantastically incongruous in this jungle clearing — a young woman in immaculate white, polished brown face upturned, with closed eyes, doodled soft organ sounds from a shiny battery-operated keyboard. She was one of several leaders of worship, vassals to a man in a scarlet shirt, who welcomed Ben and 'Sista from Pigeon Aelan' in ringing tones when we entered. Every shadowy face was turned to take me in, the toothless, the beautiful, the malformed and the serene — and every one smiled. I smiled back, blushing, and was relieved when a woman previously fanning a sleeping baby with a leaf massaged space on a mat beside her, and I sank out of exposure. But, as though the worshippers had been waiting for our arrival to begin, the scarlet-shirted man, chest puffed out like a pigeon's, immediately commanded us to 'Stannup,' and up everyone scrambled; only a few sleeping piccaninnis were left on the floor. The light was low, and chopped into a filmy checkerboard by overhanging leaves outside. Abruptly, in this bare box woven from surrounding nature by the hands of the people in it, the service began.

'Oraet evriwan, mek prae!'

Following a song of praise, people addressed God individually, but all at once, so the hut slowly filled with a babel of sound. One woman close to me said only, 'O tanggio God,' (thank you) over and over, but older men made quite elaborate speeches in respectfully cajoling tones, and children went through lists of friends they wanted brought to the divine attention. A sense of brother- and sisterhood was promoted by the congregation shaking hands. As though in a dance, thirty or forty men, women and children glided around the small, hot body of the church, palms outstretched to clasp. Women came to me first, then pushed children forward, some paralysed with shyness but eyes shining when contact was made. Damp fingers touched me lightly from behind; garments worn to shreds and small heads of stiff hair brushed me.

When settled back in our places, we sang and prayed in turn. Some of the songs were in Pijin but others were in the local language,★ and during these I could only hum, sway and clap my hands, as others did, humbled by the unforced passion that rose around me until voices, arms and old cheeks shook as God's presence was felt. The young woman who played the keyboard abandoned it as the spirit entered her and, arms extended, opened her heart in soft exultation to her Lord, like a bride. Her throat pulsed, and from it issued little warblings of intimacy that finally came together in a crooning cry, echoed by others trembling on the air in the shadow-filled light. Men's voices, no less fervent, throbbed in lower tones, and tears burst from one youth asking for help for a brother who was ill. Sorrow was as open as joy, but God's mercy was the keynote of this service, and the congregation sat rapt as a Father told the story of the Good Samaritan in Pijin.

★ Over sixty-five different languages are spoken in the Solomon Islands.

'Tif stripim evri kalico b'long dis pua fella. Hemi nekked nao!' (The robbers stripped the traveller naked.) Sympathetic voices murmured in soft indignation. The victim was described as 'third-grade copra man', a person of low status, and yet, the message implied, one who also had a soul. It was the same in Reef Islands, said the Father, and we should examine ourselves for behaviour that didn't come up to the standard of the Good Samaritan's. Every other human being was a brother or sister and none deserved to be abandoned by the side of the jungle track.

I glanced at Ben as we stood up for the last hymn and the clapping and stamping resumed. His pale face was soaked with sweat, hair spiky with it, but his darkly shadowed eyes were soft and calm. Did attendance here every week nourish some part of him life on Pigeon did not? Was it the vehicle for him, as it clearly was for some, to an inner catharsis close to ecstasy? Outside, women came to touch my shoulders and hair, and ask about my piccaninnis, and my husband. Their faces were so open, I felt any answer I gave must seem evasive. Finally I just said: 'Mi no garem,' (I haven't got one) and was treated to instant commiseration and told it was 'oraet'. Even if it did lower my status – as in Kastom, I discovered, it would – they were Good Samaritans.

'Come back next week,' they urged, as I divided a bunch of bananas I'd been given among a semi-circle of politely unclamorous piccaninnis, and I felt a fraud, nodding, for although genuinely moved by the sincerity I'd witnessed in church, something disturbed me, too, about this offshoot of happy clappy-ism in the jungle. It was as though Ben, child of Paradise, needed to succour a yearning soul with a mode of religion that was, essentially, infant formula. And his need of it, to me, expanded his aura of loneliness.

The village of Nenumbo, from where Lanebu paddled in a dugout to make Diana's fruit salad and wash walls that, if neglected, grew mould, could be reached on foot if the journey were judiciously timed. By now I was attuned to the movements of the tide, and a glance at the level by the Little Wharf before breakfast informed me whether my midday 'walk' would be a wade, kayak or swim. The day I planned to see how long it took to reach Nenumbo was so hot and still, it was as though a plug had been pulled in the great cracked basin of the reef, and all the moisture drained out – except that which dripped from my hairline. Magnus was busy writing when I headed out into the glare.

'Sure you don't want to come?' I called back.

'No, I'm fine. I'm writing to biking friends. Can't wait to get suspension forks.'

I felt both sorry and relieved. Since there were only weeks left now before he would set off back to Britain, it was good part of Magnus's mind was already there.

Along the palm beach end of Nandelli, beyond which a broad plain of coral and sand stretched, at low tide, almost to the breakers at the Edge of the Reef, kingfishers streaked, bright as airborne scarabs, and, further out, herons flexed ragged wings, and small wading birds with long beaks fed fastidiously. Otherwise the plain was bare but for one distinctive landmark which became, for me, a personal totem – a natural 'church', perhaps, which I associated with inner peace. This was Temotulaki – meaning small island – and the essence of small island is what it was. The first time I saw it, when high water lapped at the coral base, a breeze stirred the feathery branches of its single tree, an enchantingly strayed casuarina, and the sky formed a panoramic backdrop, I thought this must be somewhere I'd come often, but without conscious intention the walk there – or swim, or kayak – became a daily pilgrimage. As life on Pigeon began to look more complex, with its current divisions and a history that grew more absorbing daily as I read Tom's diaries, I found that half an hour in the vicinity of Temotulaki made a perfect break. It was simplicity in concentrated form, around which I could walk and onto which I could climb, so that all that intruded on my consciousness, if I lay on my back under that tree, was – space.

But today my eye was drawn away from Temotulaki to other figures on the plain: three distant bodies bent like croquet hoops as they searched for something in the sand. To a stranger from the West, the lives of these people appeared incredibly simple, matching their surroundings. They rose, found food, ate and slept, altering the routine only to build a leaf hut, plant kumera or prepare a feast. Or so it seemed. I wondered if this was what Ross had found attractive when, after excursions into the Outside World as a youth, he'd come back and settled here. Life 'out there' did seem inordinately complicated in comparison. But simpler doesn't necessarily mean easier. And to get a clear picture, I must learn. Why hadn't Tangypera been back yet?

Perhaps it was because my head was down, musing, with the sun on my neck, that I saw and heard nothing to warn of what occurred next. One moment I was walking alone towards Temotulaki, across a plain empty but for those distant figures, the next the man I'd been thinking of was at my side.

'You were looking for me?' asked Tangypera politely in Pijin. Beyond his extravagantly carved, dark face, the canopy of the universe shattered into winks where it met the Edge of the Reef.

'Yes!' I blurted. 'How did you know?'

'I was looking for you, too.'

'Were you behind Temotulaki?' I couldn't think where else he could have hidden.

'No,' he said with a small smile, 'I was in the mangroves, then in your shadow.'

With the sun still high, my shadow was too small for Tangypera to have been invisible in it, but I could hardly argue. And to prove he'd come from behind me, he held out the sticks of tobacco I'd left at home for him. Improbable materialization, I came to learn, was his favourite trick. I tried some more telepathy, asking loudly, in my mind, whether the elders had agreed to Tangypera imparting what I wanted to know about Reef Island life and the local view of Pigeon's history.

'It's oraet,' he said casually, half in English, half Pijin. 'Sekhan'.'

Solemnly, in the middle of the plain, Temotulaki's single tree waving like a flag above us, Tangypera and I shook hands. I'd no idea what I was letting myself in for. But it was, in one way at least, like every other arrangement made in connection with our year on Pigeon: say yes now and worry about the details later.

It's hard to believe I'm sitting in front of a computer when, only half an hour's walking distance away, seriously primitive ceremonies are taking place. I suppose it's still going on, the singing and the gorging, but if there's any more screaming to come, I won't hear it from here, thank God. What did I imagine when I made my little arrangement with Tangypera — that we'd sit down together and he'd explain everything nicely and I'd take notes? Hardly that . . .

My introduction to Reef Island Kastom began in a dugout paddled by Ben's diving partner, Matoko, who had one eye. That eye was alert, under a bright bush of sun- and sea-bleached hair, watching me with interest, but the other, and the whole of the right side of his face, looked as though it had been clawed, seared, then sealed up. He sat on the floor at one end of the roughly gouged craft, I at the other, with our legs stretched out along the narrow bottom so our feet nearly touched. His soles were thick, looking as though they'd never seen a shoe; mine were patched with plasters covering coral cuts. He was taking me to where I could view a welcoming ceremony for visiting Islanders with Reefs connections, but on the way we came upon preparations for the feast to follow. The tide was well up and the water calm under a hot sky. Matoko was leaning forward to ask me something, when out of the stillness, space and peace of the sunlit scene, drilled a shriek I thought would never end. It seemed to divide the heated air into quivering layers, and enter my skull to fragment sense. *Eeeeeeee!* Didn't whatever was being tortured need to draw breath? Palm trees tossed airy heads on picture-postcard isles and our dugout drifted on, leaving a soft wake through limpid depths. And the screaming continued. Reluctantly, I looked towards the source of the sound. From out of the jungly interior of a bay we were passing, three youths were manhandling a large, upside-down, flesh-coloured form with limbs tightly bound. One of the captors held a bushknife, another a cleaver, its square blade bright. As they waded into the sea with their prize, they laughed. For a few seconds, as the pig's snout was submerged, the shrieking faded, but when it began again it was at a fresh pitch. Panic and something mechanical combined in that noise to bring phlegm to my throat. 'Are they going to kill it?' I asked Matoko, my Pijin deserting me. The good side of his face screwed up, trying to understand, and his mouth, teeth darkly stained and breath strong, hung open.

'Uh?'

'Pikpik gohed fo dae?' I almost pleaded. Pikpik is too sweet a diminutive for these gross, hairy, helpless things that pain and fear reduced to shrieking monsters. As they must, at one time, have reduced human victims. First they must wash him, Matoko explained, then burn him to take off his hair, then they'd cut him up to put in the umu (underground oven). On and on went the shrieking, and my own voice quavered. But when do they *kill* him, I wanted to know. Surely it was before they singed off the hair? Matoko shrugged: 'Sometimes.' Children on the beach clustered in an excited semicircle, which broke when the still struggling but now weary body was brought back to land. It hung swaying, streaming water, from the youths' shoulders, then stiffened to shriek again. Above the trees, smoke rose.

'Lusi,' Matoko's voice was softly urgent and he was leaning forward, as he had been before we were interrupted, a hand exerting gentle pressure on my wrist. On the shore, foliage closed over the crowd ready to watch the burning, and the drilling noise receded momentarily, but continued in my head. 'Iu marrit? Iu naes . . .' (Are you married? You're nice . . .)

Appalled, and appalling myself, I froze for a moment, then guffawed, nearly tipping us out of the dugout. The live flesh would be nearing the fire now, and I made fast paddling motions to Matoko, which he understood. When I'd collected myself, I explained I was celibate, the Islander word for being by oneself – seleva – sounding close. And made it clear that's the way I preferred to be.

'O,' he said, 'oraet,' and began to sing, in a strange, falsetto voice, as he paddled on. Ahead of us, after half an hour in which quiet settled over the mangroves sliding by, and blue sky danced sunlight once more on an innocent scene, I saw the bay fronting Nenumbo village, where Tangypera had told Matoko to bring me. Two canoeloads of people coming directly from Nandelli, on the route I walked when the tide was out, were headed that way too, and skirting Temotulaki when we landed. There was no visible welcoming committee on the shore, but Lanebu stood up from where she'd been sitting at the edge of the bush – it was her day off from Diana's – and held out her hands for my bag. Ever since I'd shown her the scar from my spinal operation, she'd offered to carry things for me, running her finger down it, as children did, in fascination, and clucking softly. It was good to see her now, and I was about to chat when, with juttings of her chin, she indicated I should follow – quietly. Where was Tangypera? I whispered, not understanding why everything was so hushed. 'Hemi bisi,' she answered quickly, 'hemi Kastom chief.' So Magnus had been right about Tangypera having high status at Nenumbo, even if he was only a houseboy on Pigeon.

Lanebu led me through thin bush, with village debris of fruit pits and shells underfoot, until we were parallel to a path leading to the Kastom circle. Is that where the welcome would take place? I asked. But Lanebu merely flicked her eyebrows in a non-committal gesture and said Tangypera wanted me to watch from here. A watery swish

and a scatter of cheerful voices on the air let us know that the visitors
– a youth group from Santa Ana in Makira Province, led by a deacon
– had landed, and soon they appeared, marshalled into two lines in the
distance, heading towards the Kastom circle. Their chatter had
stopped when they found no welcome, and they moved forward in
a subdued fashion, as confused, it seemed, as I was. The leader, in a
European shirt, looked very young. Next to him, at the head of the
quiet procession, was a hatchet-faced elder, chest decorated with
wreaths of shark's teeth. Another man wore a pair of boots as a necklace. At Nandelli, I'd gathered, the youth group had been serenaded
with traditional songs as a welcome, and this was what I'd expected
here. But, as if at a signal, a lone figure suddenly stepped into the path,
feet from where I was – an old, old woman, naked but for a loincloth,
with legs like withered lianas. She was clutching a wooden staff and
had an intense expression on her shrivelled features, eyes glittering in
the direction of the visitors. No sooner had she put in this appearance
than she melted back into the bush. As my eyes tried to follow where
she vanished, something made me look upwards, and there my gaze
remained, for crouched on a branch overhanging the path was an all
but naked man, body dappled by leaves and camouflage markings,
pointing a bow and arrow at the approaching deacon's chest. He must
have sensed me looking up, because he looked down, eyes impassive.
Now there was someone else on the path, an ancient with a ring in
his nose, sitting cross-legged. His arms were spread like crab's pincers,
hands on thighs. Would the procession divide to pass him? I craned
my neck to see how near they were – and a fourth figure revealed
itself, flattened against a tree trunk, a youth with a shaven head
crowned by a tasselled leaf band. His body was streaked with earth, he
carried a spear as tall as himself, and his profile, pointing like an
animal scenting quarry, held an expression so cold, I drew in breath
sharply.

Lanebu laid a hand on my shoulder and jutted her chin up and forward. I was just in time to understand that the entire canopy of trees
over the path was thick with hidden bodies, all armed, when the
deacon, now level with the furthest of them, stopped his slow march
abruptly, spreading arms over his companions, and staggered backwards. He'd been hit with a long stick by a minute elder who now
rushed into his path yelling and shaking the stick furiously. The
visitors attempted to shrink back, but were mobbed by more yelling

figures which sprang in front of them, hemmed them in at the sides, encircled them from the back and dropped out of the trees on their heads. And with the hurtling bodies came a battery of war cries, guttural whoops and ear-splitting yodels. The last I saw of the deacon before he fell to his knees was his shocked face, from which his glasses had fallen as he was walloped again, and his hands opening helplessly as his camera was knocked from them.

If it hadn't been for Lanebu's hand on my wrist and a smile playing about her lips, I'd have been very afraid. It was true the men in the trees hadn't loosed their arrows but leaped on their prey bodily, felling them more with fear than injury. But there was nothing held back about the fierce emotion displayed, and the smell of men's bodies, heated with excitement, was scarily animal. The group around the deacon still pressed close, but his obvious submission and the trembling silence of the entire procession of thirty or more must have been enough for them, because the beating and yelling stopped as suddenly as it began. But it was only the appearance of another procession – every female of Nenumbo village carrying leis (floral necklaces) of frangipani – that completely convinced me what I'd witnessed was a deliberately planned display of enmity rather than the real thing. Now the deacon was allowed to rise to his feet, his trousers were dusted, camera picked up and fragrant frangipani flowers placed round his neck. And everyone broke into smiles. Tangypera materialized, in his usual implike way, and walked me to the edge of the Kastom circle. From there I had a view of the youth group reforming themselves into a confident crocodile – with the deacon wobbling along grandly in front, on a flower-bedecked chair hoisted high on the shoulders of his former attackers.

'Why,' I asked, as the space around the beaten-earth floor of the Kastom circle filled up with the men who'd so cleverly hidden themselves before, 'did they pretend to attack the visitors?'

Tangypera was never precise in his explanations, but the gist was that anyone coming from beyond Reef Islands, even if they had former connections, was potentially an enemy, so precautions must be taken. There was also the assumption that within the village itself was an element, often with vendettas going back generations, who didn't welcome the return of these people, and whose anger must be given expression. In times gone by the degree of feeling on the ground would have been assessed before the visiting party reached shore – and arrows loosed then should it be decided, on balance, that their presence wasn't wanted. But had the deacon and his party today really not known what was going to happen? Mischief danced in Tangypera's bloodshot eyes. 'They knew nothing,' (Na–rtin'!) he said with satisfaction.

In the Kastom circle a headman with stars scraped deeply into the flesh of his cheeks was giving a shouted address in Reef Islands language, which was answered politely by the deacon, now wearing three necklaces and a circlet of flowers on his head, in a mixture of Pijin and English. He was still a little shaky and wisely chose to be brief, and frank.

'Mi no got ani wud (words). Wud fly out from head b'long mi . . . !' – here he rubbed his head with a smile – 'Bat tanggio fo spesol Kastom welkam. God bless evriwan.'

Several Nenumban elders now moved into the centre of the Kastom circle carrying a wooden shield, which they arranged in front of them on the ground as a drum. A small boy – in training as a drummer, Tangypera informed me – joined them, and the oldest raised his head high, shaking his wattles, and gave utterance to a chanted phrase that hushed the crowd. The chant, which sounded like '*Bumjiyay, bumjiyay ooh!*' was repeated, and on the last '*ooh*' a troupe of little boys pranced into the ring and stamped their feet like ponies. Among them were two of Joe's and Benji's schoolmates, looking very different in warrior guise from the quiet, T-shirted pupils struggling with phonetics at Pigeon Island School. All the boys wore loincloths, some of bark, some of rice bag, with wrist and ankle leaf decorations that shook like pompoms and individual arrangements of leaves on their heads. Round and round they danced, to no more accompaniment than the elder's quavering voice and the thump of the drum, but boldly forceful in their actions, all of which told a story. When the children raised their arms above their heads, they were shielding a man's eyes from the sun; when they made a downward thrusting movement, they were digging the end of a bamboo-and-twine fishing net into the reef, and when they rubbed their bellies, they were expressing the anxiety of a woman as she watched her son climb a tall tree. A rolling movement of the arms indicated the making of an ankle brace for climbing palms – of the type I'd seen made for Benji. These dances went back centuries, but I saw nothing enacted that wasn't still part of the Reef Islanders' everyday life.

After the boys, it was the men's turn. Women sat quietly with babies, or tended the underground ovens baking puddings – and pikpiks – for later. I'd relaxed by now and was enjoying this part of the welcoming ceremony more or less like any other show, albeit on a small island with little but four thousand miles of Pacific in one direction beyond the Edge of the Reef. But I was aware that the line between the Reef Islanders' studied performance and real feelings could be thin. These dancers still wore their masklike red and black streaks, and pointed their weapons stylistically with much rippling of polished muscles which was, for the one white woman in the crowd at least, disturbing because it was frightening as well as beautiful. My eyes were riveted by the undulating sheen of one particularly magnificent set of thighs, when their owner stopped abruptly in front of me and, without moving his unsmiling eyes from my face, pointed his arrow between my legs. In that instant, I felt not like someone from the computer age at all, but just a different-coloured stranger, and a vulnerable woman, from any age, a long way from home among people who hadn't hesitated to kill intruders on their shores, whether their own kind or on missionary, recruiting or trade business, in the not so distant past. I'd heard glee in youngsters' voices earlier that day as they prolonged the sufferings of a fellow creature – that was genuine bloodlust – and witnessed the potential for an effective guerrilla-style attack in the warriors so cleverly concealed in their natural habitat only an hour ago. We think as we enter the twenty-first century that we've come a long way from the primitive, yet the churning in my stomach during the seconds when that young man, with no reason to feel friendly towards this spectator from the Outside World, pointed his arrow at me was plain, primitive fear, in response to a plain, primitive threat. And the 'natives' were probably only 'friendly' because their grandfathers had experienced reprisal massacres when arrows had attempted to defy the might of the gun.

My startling introduction to Kastom practices still very much alive in Reef Islands added a new slant to my studies of Pigeon's white settlers. It was, after all, only a couple of decades after the last murder of a foreigner in the Outer Islands – an Englishman attempting to collect taxes for land indigenous people considered their own – that Tom and Diana anchored the *Arthur Rogers* in Mohawk Bay. There had been an intervening world war, in which Solomon Islanders and British were supposedly on the same side, but the Outer Islands are a long way from Guadalcanal and the people there had few allegiances, or reasons for them, beyond their clans and the ancient laws of Kastom.

10

Arrivals: 1957–1959

ON THE WAY TO REEF ISLANDS, THE *ARTHUR ROGERS* PASSED ANOTHER
trading vessel, a 'te puke'★ or traditional voyaging canoe with a crabclaw-shaped sail made of panels of pandanus, ropes of coconut fibre,
and a basket on a platform between outriggers like airplane wings as
accommodation. It was heading back to Duff Islands for a fresh cargo
of light dugouts to be exported to Reefs. Reef Islands were traditionally exporters of women. Diana photographed the te puke and Tom
marvelled at the ancient navigation skills its sailors used, but soon their
eyes were drawn away from the retreating sail, towards a bay where
they hoped to anchor for the night.

'Lot of shallow reef, I reckon,' said Tom. 'Would you mind
conning, darling?'

Diana climbed the mast and looked ahead. Late afternoon sun
gleamed in dimples on the surface of transparent depths, and the
islands were cupped in soft auras of light, airbrushing the sand on their
beaches pink and haloing feathery palms. She called instructions to
Tom, guiding them between coral castles looming up through the
water, but then stayed in her perch a moment, drinking in the
tranquil view, and noting in particular one small, densely green

---

★ Pronounced 'te puki'.

island standing high above its neighbours on a base of silvery cliffs. Diana had contained her urge to start a family for years, but now, as she approached forty – and they entered the most enchanting lagoon she'd ever seen – the call was loud. This is where I want to live, she thought, and something in her face must have said it too, for when the rumble of the anchor chain ceased, bringing them to sway gently in silence in the bay, Tom stood with his arms around her at the rail, looking towards the same island. A silky breeze lifted hair over his temples which was just beginning to grey.

'Do you think this could be it, then?'

Diana kept the intense, intuitive feeling she had about that little island to herself, but said: 'You never know.' And he knew her well enough to smile.

Musings ended when movements on a larger island close by – Nandelli – indicated they'd been seen. Tom knew from experience that when it was learned they had tobacco and cloth aboard, they'd be popular, and so it proved. A flotilla of dugouts soon surrounded the *AR*, the subject of copra came up and sales were brisk. Then, Tom noted, the following ensued:

"Wiss-way, Master?" All whites were addressed as Master in those days – or Cap'n. "You savvy stop? Me want im . . ."' (The Islanders had no regular copra buyer or store, and hoped Tom might serve the area.) ' *"No can do," I said, but discussions continued until Diana half-jokingly said, pointing: "If you'll let us have that island, we'll come back." Next morning a delegation returned, led by a Headman wearing an armband and shield. Solemnly, they informed us they'd deliberated all night and decided Yes, we could have that island . . .'*

The Hepworths circumnavigated their future home, which had a native name, Ngarando, meaning 'the far place', but was also known as Pigeon Island. They spotted two beaches and at least one mango tree among the palms, and reckoned the whole was roughly three by one hundred yards in size. The richness of the underbrush suggested fertility but it was too thick to make detailed exploration possible immediately, pressed as they were to catch the tide. With little to go on but aware of what most small Pacific islands had to offer, they decided it suited them – and the deal with the Islanders was clinched when Tom handed over fifteen pounds to their spokesman, Tambi, with some sticks of tobacco. The government would be contacted about an official lease.

After this stop in Mohawk Bay the *AR* sailed back to the New Hebrides, where trading was resumed. If Diana was excited about Pigeon, she kept quiet about it as there was no point in making plans unless and until officialdom moved. Nothing was heard about a lease for so long that they assumed it would never happen and concentrated, as ever, on making the best of the business in hand, which consisted of preparations for an extensive pre-Christmas trip, with the deckhouse store open long hours. Contact with expats in the capital of the Solomons had yielded little beyond the discouraging comment, when they'd discussed settling in Reefs: '*You won't like it – there's no-one there*.' The speaker, of course, meant no European society.

But those who were there, the Reef Islanders – in particular Tambi's clan – hadn't forgotten the visit of the *AR* and when, months afterwards, a 'gummint' ship appeared on the horizon, they asked the District Officer aboard to follow up the lease request, which he did. It was recognized that a copra trader was needed in the area, and Christmas 1958 brought the Hepworths a rare gift: a ninety-nine-year lease on the island of their dreams at £2 per annum. The sum paid to the Islanders in 1957 was assumed by Tom to cover the matter of any Kastom land ownership involved.★

If the Hepworths had been cautious in their enthusiasm for Pigeon before, they now threw doubt to the four winds. This was what they'd always wanted, the prized piece of land on which '*a man might draw from the earth, in all this beauty, enough to feed his children and owe no-one*'. The first thing Diana did was toss overboard the Dutch cap she'd always used before, so they could revel in spontaneous lovemaking in lagoons along the coast of Espiritu Santo. Diana's girlhood dreams of adventure had been more than realized; now would begin the joys of maturity. And, at nearly fifty, when many men wonder where the best years of their lives have vanished, Tom saw only more challenge, excitement and satisfaction ahead. The idea was to carry out a few more trading trips on lucrative routes, then gather materials for a house, stock up with goods and set sail once more for the Solomons. But fate intervened. Over the years, the Hepworths had made many sailing friends, and loyalty to these was fierce. They heard one

★ Under Kastom law, land, which is held to be of great value, is passed on, within families extending to clans, over generations, unless a change of arrangement is mutually agreed.

evening, while at the *AR*'s chart table drawing up plans for an eight-sided homestead beside the mango tree spotted on Pigeon, that a fellow sailor had been badly burned when gas exploded on his yacht, and was fading under inadequate care in Vila. Swiftly they modified their plans. Diana would fly at once with their friend to Auckland and rendezvous with Tom later, to load up ready for the Solomons. In New Zealand, too, they'd have the pick of materials available and be able to bring the old ship up to the peak of condition, ready for an even more remote life than she'd been used to. Diana didn't know for certain and Tom didn't know at all but, when they parted for the month it would take Tom to sail to New Zealand, Diana was pregnant. She'd conceived within a week of wanting to start a family.

When the injured friend was comfortable in Auckland's burns unit, Diana addressed herself to the immense exercise of planning for a home, and a baby, on Pigeon. There was everything to buy, from machetes for clearing bush, seedlings to plant and cement for the house's foundations, to a medical kit, household linens, marine and roofing paints, a baby bath, and food and clothes for an indefinite period. They were equipping themselves for life on land as a couple for the first time, with a blank sheet, only the vision of that dot of green so far away as an outline. It was a heady experience. Everything was entirely up to them, a whole small world to create with no restrictions. And, wanting to do everything independently, Diana applied herself to the current bible on natural childbirth. The dream now, to crown the joy of finding their place in the sun, was for their baby to be born there.

The first thing Tom did on arriving in New Zealand's winter was to kit out his shivering New Hebridean crew from a thrift shop. He was, as he wrote to his sisters, '*cock-a-hoop about the baby*' but anxious, as Diana's tall form grew bulgier, to move maintenance work on the *AR* forward swiftly, because he'd no desire to carry out the instructions in a midwifery pamphlet he'd been given in the middle of the Solomon Sea. So keen were they to get away – hoping to have the house partly built before the baby came – that work on covering board around the stanchions was still unfinished when, with Diana six months into her pregnancy and the total makings of their future home in the hold, they set sail from Whangaroa. But three hundred miles out, the waves rose so high that the unsealed board was soaked and Diana had to spend hours on her knees, close to the engine room's fumes, keeping the bilgepump clear of muck threatening to clog it. Reluctantly, Tom decided to turn back, wait for better weather and complete the work. But it didn't occur to Diana that this meant an end to her hopes of giving birth on Pigeon. With further reinforcements made to the *AR* and more stores aboard, they set off again six weeks later. But the doctor only let Diana go on the promise that 'if it gets choppy' she'd stay in her bunk.

It got choppy. In that same confused patch of sea three hundred miles from New Zealand's North Cape where ocean currents mix, a storm with three centres that sent a battle cruiser limping back to port caught hold of the *AR* and, as Tom told it, '*tossed her about like a chip of wood*'. It was impossible to heave-to in the pyramiding seas, so the crew, unable to help, huddled together praying while Tom tried desperately to keep the ship upright if nothing else. And in the madly swaying deckhouse of that chip of wood, with great green seas sweeping in over her, Diana, now eight months pregnant, was wrenched from side to side, with arms outstretched, hands grasping a pole one side, a shelf the other, in the double bunk where so often she and Tom had lain entwined and watched the moon. Underneath her, water tanks sloshed queasily; from the hold, where everything needed to make a life on Pigeon was stowed, came ominous crashings, and so violent was the bucking and rolling of the ship that she daren't let go her hold even to relieve herself or fetch fresh water to rinse the nauseous taste of salt from her lips. Because the deckhouse was close to the helm, where Tom wrestled with the tiller, Diana could see him, but it was impossible, with the shattering noise of the storm all round, to hear each other speak. Just once in thirty-six hours he managed to struggle close enough for the question on his white, soaked face to be clear: ' "Are you all right, darling?" '

Diana could feel wetness between her legs, but as waters were breaking everywhere anyway, with the deckhouse floor awash and her mattress sodden, it was impossible to tell if this were a sign, and she didn't want to worry Tom.

'I'm fine,' she called loudly, although to him it seemed only like mouthing against the rage of waves that sucked at the weighted hull below her and sent claws of spray into her eyes, 'just wish I could help.'

'You damn well stay put . . .'

Tom was knitting admonitory brows and Diana smiling at the order when a sudden darkening, like a curtain pulled, and a heavy, sideways lurch told them that – to Tom's disbelief – they'd been drawn inside the curve of a giant comber, and were in danger of being rolled over. Those on land, including the all-girl crew of '54, biting nails as they listened to reports of the storm on the radio, were by now convinced the *AR* was lost. Through a vertically hurtling screen of sea, Tom saw how a dinghy to be delivered to a mission in the Solomons, secured to the deck by eye-bolts and double lashed, was ripped free and tossed over the side to be swallowed at once. At the same time, the steel battens above Diana's head, on top of the deckhouse, buckled and, with a crack like a gun report, the seven-foot-long, four-inch-thick oak tiller snapped, and the *AR* pitched so far over that sections of the bulwarks disappeared under water – and were torn out as, after sickening minutes, in which imprecations to many gods rose from that tipping hell, the broken, shuddering but still game old ship righted herself.

Diana's bunk – shared with a terrified cat – was on the side to which the *AR* had rolled, so she'd been flung into the wall, rather than across the deckhouse, with much pelting down on her. But the waterlogged mattress and cushions padded her belly, and by the time Tom's haggard face reappeared – he and the crew, as soon as movement was possible, had broken out house timbers to jury-rig the tiller so it could still be used – she'd heaved herself back into the middle of the bunk, cat under one arm, and was performing relaxation exercises with eyes closed. When she sensed his presence, she looked up brightly, or thought she did, but Tom, horrified by what had happened, later noted that '*on her face were deep lines of strain I'd never seen before*'. With all that was most dear to him threatened, for the first time in his life Tom felt nothing but loathing for the sea. Their child, if only they could turn the boat round without another of those waves opening its jaws to swallow all dreams, would be born a Kiwi. And Paradise could wait.

An article Tom wrote about the storms that prevented them reaching Pigeon as planned, in 1958, was edited to dramatize the romance of 'a race with the stork'. In fact, although she'd had a 'show' during her ordeal in the bunk – where she'd lain, in all, for three weeks – Diana didn't go into labour for another fortnight, and they made it back to Whangaroa with her up and heating soup. The damage the storms had done, however, was not only to the boat – hailed in New Zealand papers as a miraculous survivor – and most of their equipment for a home in the South Seas: Tom's passion for sailing had died. He didn't have to tell Diana, she just knew. Side by side, during the remaining days of her pregnancy, they lifted every item from the hold, rinsed off the salt water with fresh, and laid out the entire material contents of their future in the sun. The last water stain faded from the carrycot just in time, and an elated Tom was at Diana's bedside within minutes of Jenifer Natasha Diane's birth, arms round them both. '*Now I've got two glamour girls,*' he wrote to his delighted sisters, '*we're headed for a life in the sun, and I feel like the luckiest man alive!*' Diana said the birth had been 'a piece of cake', and proudly held her little daughter up to the porthole of the *AR* for the world to admire. Tom wanted her to grow up as beautiful and brave as her mother; Diana for her to be as kind and wise as Tom, and as fine a sailor. Maybe she'd even rekindle his love of the sea as she grew up on an island surrounded by it.

When Tasha was six weeks old, Diana flew to join Tom in the New Hebrides, where he'd sailed the newly repaired *AR* on now calmer seas. While he was waiting for her – the plan being she'd join him in time to revive depleted funds with another pre-Christmas trading trip – he met a trader who convinced him he'd be better joining an established business than risking all on a speck of bush miles from anywhere in the Outer Solomons. Tom was vulnerable to such a suggestion at this time, and enthused about it to Diana when she arrived. Everything looked set fair and, with a house included in the offer, the loss of Pigeon, in which little had been invested financially, didn't seem too great. They'd still be living among islands a long way from the rat race. But Christmas came and went with no trading trip, as the new plan to become partner-managers didn't allow for absence, and the trader, at first so keen, proved unable, as months passed, to show Tom anything confirming the success of his enterprise. The Hepworths' funds, already low, were in a parlous state when they discovered that the 'thriving' business was in fact close to bankruptcy. Tom, who'd thought to make life less hand-to-mouth now he was a father, was furious. They should've stuck to their original idea of going it alone, however risky. The sea might be treacherous but at least he *knew* it was. His fellow man was always an unknown quantity. Deeply stung, as he told his sisters, '*by being taken for a dupe*', he and Diana revived the Solomons plan. But this time they had no house in the hold and less than £100 worth of store goods, for they'd sold every stick of timber when the proposed partnership looked good, to repay friends who had helped them in New Zealand after the storms.

'Never mind,' said Diana. 'We can use local wood – and live on board as long as we need. We've got our island – and Tasha. Let's go.' She refused to be despondent about their bad luck, her optimism soothing away his doubts, and immediate tasks absorbed them both once the way ahead was firmed up. Using scraps of wood, Diana made stock display trays as they sailed, and Tom wrote to every company in Melanesia that might pay for cargo or labour transportation, eventually securing a contract with a timber firm in Vanikoro. There was another delay, when the engine broke down and they had to wait months for a new part, still nowhere near their destination, but during that time Tom completed the series of commissioned articles and Tasha, to his delight, took her first, staggering steps on the deck of the *AR*. '*She's just a Poppet*,' he wrote, and when at long last they sailed once more, in August 1959, into Mohawk Bay, that's what he christened the tiny cake-shaped islet off the southern end of Pigeon. He thought it as beautiful, and perfect, as she was.

The sight of the *AR* on the horizon caused a stir among the locals, and when Tom opened the deckhouse store on arrival, record sales were made. '*I've got myself a slice of Paradise*,' he wrote to Dennis, '*and run the only shop in the islands for five thousand eager souls!*' After counting the take the Hepworths rowed a dinghy ashore, ferrying the first of many loads from ship to land – including a small cement mixer. They planned to show Tasha round her new home before the sun dipped away behind the volcano which had been one of their chief landmarks en route. Tom gathered up his little girl, holding her face forward as Diana secured the dinghy where it wouldn't be stranded by the tide. He strode through the shallows towards the beach, telling Tasha elatedly that this was Pigeon, their very own island, but waited until Diana was at his side before setting foot on shore. He was lowering Tasha from his shoulder, so in fact her feet would be the first to touch home soil, when Diana laid a hand on his arm.

'There's someone on the island,' she said. 'We can't have that.'

As they moved up the sloping beach to where the island proper began, a figure separated itself from a tangle of bush on Pigeon's northern promontory, overlooking Mohawk Bay. It was a short, heavily built Islander carrying a spear.

'Cap'n,' he said in Pijin as the Hepworths drew level, 'this land belongs to me.' He tapped the earth with the blunt end of his spear, and swept an arm round encompassing a sizeable swathe. Diana, much taller than the Islander, stepped forward, about to remonstrate – she'd been dealing with 'natives' for years – but Tom quietly motioned her back, handed her Tasha and said he'd settle the matter diplomatically. After all, there could be no real problem: he had all the paperwork to back up his position as rightful occupant of the whole of Pigeon Island for the next ninety-nine years – his government lease. Besides, he'd paid for the island directly to the Islanders. This fellow evidently hadn't understood the arrangements made back in 1957, and simply had to be put straight. When Tom joined Diana shortly afterwards, he adopted a determinedly breezy manner. Nothing must spoil this first evening on the island home they'd been searching for so long, and which had cost them so much, when they finally reached it only after battling through the worst storms of all their years at sea, disillusion over the New Hebrides affair, and financial disaster. They'd paid for it all right, and now would have to work from scratch to transform wild bush into the home of their dreams. They had enough on their plate without '*damned locals bugger-arsing about*'.

'All sorted out,' he told her, suggesting they look for the mango tree spotted in 1957. But later, in his diary, he scrawled angrily: '*Dealt with Gorilla Willy by flashing 3 quid at him, which he hesitatingly took. Hope that's the last of this . . .*' Diana, always careful with funds, might have baulked at the sum – large in Islander terms – but Tom just didn't want trouble. Beside the mango tree they agreed on an area of bush to be cleared before anything else, and Tasha, set down to toddle among the palm trunks and vine-tangled undergrowth, found a long pink and white flower on the ground, pretty as a satin tassel.

'She loves the place already!' said Diana. Tom was making a list of the order of items to be brought to land. Maybe first should be tools to manufacture a lock-up dock. Stories had reached them about the 'unreliability' of Solomon Islanders. They should start as they meant to go on: with a no-nonsense approach. But before they rowed back to the *AR* they unloaded the cement mixer, and its silhouette at the top of the tideline, squat, with the hand crank like an animal's tail, baffled and absorbed a small group of Islanders paddling past in dugouts as the sun cast up its final hot pink glow, and Pigeon's lorikeets completed their noisy evening chorus.

By the end of the Hepworths' second day on Pigeon, fully sixty yards of bush had been cleared, using labour recruited from customers paddling to the ship's store when it was opened briefly in the morning. And Tom and Diana had staked out a site for the eight-sided dwelling they planned, comprising three bedrooms, sitting and dining rooms, kitchen and bathroom positioned for optimum use of water catchment, and leaf verandas all round. By the end of the first week, the dock had been completed, and Islanders from beyond Nandelli were bringing baskets of copra, which Diana inspected, noting quality, quantity and place of origin, so they could build up a picture of their future catchment area for both customers and copra. They also made it known they were interested in turtle shell, greensnail and trochus, and would buy fruit and vegetables brought to the island to supplement their main diet, still reflecting a life at sea, of carefully numbered tins relieved by occasional fish.

But during those early days on Pigeon there was barely time for Tom to jot a hasty addition to an ongoing letter to his sisters – he'd no idea when this could be sent, but used it as a diary when keeping no other notes – let alone go fishing. Together, with Tasha gathering shells nearby or pottering after the Islander labour force, Tom and Diana knelt for hours in the heat smoothing cement mixed with loose coral and sand; worked out the angle of pitch for roofs; dug holes for posts, and devised a gravity-fed shower below what they referred to as the cargo shed, on the eastern promontory. They also built a hut for their workers so they didn't have to live cheek by jowl with them, and Diana sewed curtains for the *AR*'s portholes, finding that otherwise curious faces peered in from dawn to dusk. They continued to live on the *AR*, commuting daily by dinghy to Pigeon and with every journey unloading more and more, so that the dock had to be expanded and the cargo shed took on the dimensions of a warehouse. Tom's jottings can only hint at the pace of life – and his relations with the neighbours: '*Rain all night so early start delayed by bailing . . . boys all day painting 9 roof irons and Diana had done 15 by teatime! . . . 19 bags copra landed, but refused three, as not dry . . . Argument with cutters over Saturday work settled for 30 cigs each, except for two, who declined. Who can understand a people who say they've no need to work! . . . Unloaded plants now Diana has completed crab fence round her garden . . .*

Twenty posts brought, but where are the straight ones? . . . First brush through finished now. Good work, but Oh how flakers!'

As well as opening the store twice daily, building six-by-ten-foot door frames, cooking for her family and apportioning rations to the workers – bully beef, rice, tea and Hard Navy biscuits – Diana was creating both kitchen and decorative gardens. She'd collected seeds and fruit trees of many varieties, so that soon Tom was able to boast to his sisters that they had hibiscus, frangipani, pawpaw, citrus and avocados all flourishing, and that Diana was building a pergola to festoon with passion flowers. *'You spit out a pip and it turns into a seedling as you watch – just about. Sounds exotic, don't it?!'* and when at last they allowed themselves a quiet Sunday, he set down his feelings clearly: *'We've quite forgotten our former disappointments in our delight in Pigeon. It's even bigger than we knew, and has much character . . . a rocky promontory one end, then a flat part, with good soil, where the house will be, then a "timber belt" with big trees . . . Round the sides it climbs to fully 30 feet above sea level and there are aspects over the surrounding sea in every direction. It couldn't be better, and we love it. Even financial prospects are bright, but we anyway feel it hardly matters, we're so happy with our island.'*

Huge progress had been made by November, when the time came to take the *AR* to Honiara to deal with official entry to the Protectorate. Shortage of funds, and of hours in the day, had enforced temporary abandonment of the plan for an eight-sided house, but it had taken only three weeks for Diana to adapt the now substantial cargo shed into both home and store, so now they had two retail and receiving outlets, one afloat and one ashore. Pigeon Island Traders' first land store consisted of little more than a plank raised as a counter dividing the public area from private living space. Another plank, set lower, with a basin on it served for hand and face washing when there was no time for a shower, and Diana cemented a space for laundry close by, where water drained conveniently off the island's edge. Although she lived in a bikini, and Tom in shorts, there were dozens of nappies to be washed. She happily allowed Tasha to live as clothes-free as local piccaninnis during the day, but wetting of precious bedding at night was to be avoided. The new double mattress they'd promised themselves – for the first conventional bed since their marriage – would take six months just to reach Honiara. In the meantime Diana made the base, painted it rich magenta and scattered its generous surface with cushions from the *AR*. On this arrangement, covered only by a sheet, with the great barn doors of the shed wide open, they slept the sleep of the fully stretched mentally and physically – and of the just. For it didn't occur to the Hepworths that their presence on Pigeon could bring anything but benefit to their neighbours. And they weren't aware, at this stage, that the swathes they'd cut through every quarter of Pigeon had violated land belonging under Kastom law not to one but to four local clans, with members extending over most of Reef Islands.

11

Farewells: 1998

TANGYPERA HAD BEEN 'ROUNABAOT' TEN – LIKE HIS SON NGIVE, NOW
at Pigeon Island School – when the *Arthur Rogers* anchored in
Mohawk Bay to stay, and remembered the excitement. He and others
had followed progress on Pigeon avidly, and his eyebrows bounced up
and down in awe recalling the 'riches' that passed in the dinghy
between ship and shore. The *AR* seemed as bottomless as Mohawk
Bay itself, so much came out of it. The entire population of Reefs
surely didn't own as much as this English pair, and they built such
impressive dwellings – where they slept alone was larger than the
Sapulo (Men's Single House) at Nenumbo, used by forty or more. In
Tangypera's tone was more amazement than envy, but I knew there
were shadows, too. Avoiding the use of Tom's term 'Gorilla Willy', I
asked if Tangypera knew the man who confronted the Hepworths
when they arrived to settle. This caused a narrowing of those intense
eyes and I could see I was on tricky territory, so I changed the subject.

'Tangypera, you know Magnus must leave soon?'

'Oh sore sore . . .' (I'm so sad . . .)

'I wondered if you could put word out we'll have a party on his last
evening here, and would like friends from Reefs to come . . .' – here
I reached down from our Kaikai Tree a rice bag I knew Tangypera
knew contained money – 'but it'll be difficult to arrange by myself.'

'We'll all help,' said Tangypera. 'It's our Kastom to sit with one the night before he travels on the sea.' And he graciously accepted the contribution I made to the catering. It was a respected move for anyone wishing to 'cut ice' in Reef Island society to start the process by donating livestock or funds for a communal feast. Just as he was getting up to go, Tangypera mentioned casually he would toktok to the elders about the other matter I'd mentioned. This was what I'd hoped might happen. Then he dropped a nugget: Nupanyi, Diana's oldest worker, who'd originally served under Tom aboard the *AR* on trading trips, owned, through marriage, some of Pigeon's best ground – where Tom's grave house now stood, and not far from Diana's house. I thought of Nupanyi, an old man personifying human dignity in its most stripped-of-embellishment form. He paddled at sunrise from Nola, rammed copra all day and dug out Diana's cesspits, then paddled back to his leaf hut in the dark, while she sat in comfort amid what must surely appear to him great wealth, carved partly from his people's property. Did he ever feel angry?

'Jas sore,' Tangypera said. (Just sad.)

I was to learn more about Islander feelings towards the Hepworths' development of Pigeon in time, but history vied with the present for attention in the too few hours in a day there seemed to be for me, as well as Diana, on the island. It was Joe who ran to my office window – pelting in a handful of alite (wild nuts) opened with a stone – to deliver the news that we were going to Nbanga Temoa for Magnus's last weekend – Diana had arranged this with Ben – then Magnus and I were to dine with her before he departed on the Monday. He would sail on the *Southern Cross*, a mission ship still plying regularly in the Outer Islands. By the way, added Joe, Diana wished to see me for tea. Then he was off, stopping only to collect the spear Nupanyi, unasked, had spent an hour sharpening for him, before I'd time to say we'd be doing something else the night before Magnus left. But perhaps it was best not to involve children in the darker complexities of island life. After all, their lives on Pigeon were beautifully uncomplicated: they relished their condensed schooling and the hours spent with Islander friends. Only those less innocent had to tread with care among the variety of viewpoints held by the grown-ups on and around Pigeon.

When I arrived for tea that afternoon, refreshed by a lazy swim round Poppet after a morning delving into Kastom land law, Diana was asleep, head back, beside the ready tray. She'd had a long morning clearing white ants from the shelves she'd built into what had once been Tom's office. One of her hands was resting on a sheaf of photographs in her lap. I was about to creep away, not wanting to break her unscheduled siesta as shadows under her eyes suggested she needed it, when she stirred.

'Ah, you're here. Lovely. Sit down. I thought you should see these.'

By now, as we'd gone through the bulk of the Kodachrome slides relating to the Hepworths' pre-Pigeon adventures, our evening talks had become less frequent. These days, I went for tea just twice a week, or when requested, as now. Diana had come across the pictures during her cleaning blitz. 'I'm afraid some were damaged in the cyclone,' she said, referring to Cyclone Nina which had flattened Nandelli in 1993.

'Tom took this of me giving Tasha her first swimming lesson.' Usually stiff-upper-lipped and strict, Diana was shown here with a look of total tenderness as she supported her naked child in the great, pristine pool of the Pacific – into which, nowadays, Ross and Ben tipped crates of empty beer bottles. So much of life on Pigeon now, as in the past, was a paradox. Another picture showed Tom taking a sight of the sun on the *AR*. Behind him were crew boys, solemn faced beside copra sacks, avoiding the camera's eye. Was one Nupanyi? Tom's body was tipped back and his face screwed up, but he looked full of zest for life – the ideal pioneering sailor and settler. Now Diana held up another snap of Tasha, all but destroyed by mould which cloudily framed a perfect portrait of a baby Eve, clad only in a necklace, and expressing utter contentment as she explored the treasures of the reef beneath her, standing in crystal water under the echoing arc of blue I knew so well from my own sweet, dazzled wanders.

'She was such a happy little girl,' Diana said simply.

I'd have preferred to leave it there, to retain the vision of this delightful child revelling in her South Sea backyard, but it was impossible not to look at the last image proffered. This showed a fat, blunt-featured creature with an institutional haircut and institutional clothes being propelled round a dance floor, clearly in an institution, by another woman, unnaturally thin and with a painfully ravaged face.

'She's still pretty, don't you think?' said Diana.

It was a horrible moment. Both women in the photograph had something grotesque about them; the special quality of the freak. But evidently not to Diana. Suddenly I recognized something in the fat girl's eyes, a glazed sheen that was a parody of the brilliance that had made Diana shine as a model.

'What amazingly tiny hands she has,' I said, avoiding a lie, and as anxious to preserve whatever image Diana had of her daughter as she must be herself. Then I handed the photographs back. So much had happened and was happening on Pigeon, and I could only handle one thing at a time. Tasha's story must wait. Right now there was the question of Magnus's final evening to tackle; another rejection for Diana, because I guessed he'd prefer to party with his Islander pals than eat a stately meal with her. But she took it well, skiing on smoothly to the subject of Nbanga.

'You *must* go there,' she said in her emphatic way, 'because it's where we had such wonderful times when the children were small. And Ben would love to take you. It has such happy memories for him.'

The tea ended with Diana suddenly exploding into a diatribe against Ross and Pegi and 'all their wretched wontoks' who, she believed, had ruined the lawn she and Tom had put in with such care all those years ago. The real reason Diana was so exhausted was that she'd made one of her rare sorties – using her parasol as a walking stick – down 'Ross's end', which was where she and Tom had lived during their hectic but rewarding pioneering years when the only Islanders allowed on the island were workers or customers. It was evidently important to hold onto happy memories, on Pigeon.

Graham, son of the guardian angels in Scotland, arrived to take Magnus home in time for the start of a new school term, and after he'd spent one night in our tent in a tropical deluge Ross unlocked the guest units and let him and Magnus camp there. Graham, admirable product of an Outward Bound education and thoroughly steady parents, took to island life with panache, organizing jumping competitions over bamboos on the beach for local youths, and proved as ready to eat out of a banana leaf as to charm Diana with impeccable manners. I asked Peter and Mhairi if they'd like to come to Nbanga, but they declined. A peaceful weekend without hordes of children around would make a change. But they'd be there for Magnus's farewell party.

Parts of Nbanga, Diana told me, reminded her of coastlines in the New Hebrides which had inspired Tom to have the *AR* insured. I saw why. Nbanga – barely an hour's motorized canoe run from Pigeon but strikingly different – was wild indeed. If Pigeon looked on a fair day like a cupcake perched on the Pacific, Nbanga was a craggy slab of pudding with sides aswirl in foaming cream. We approached the proposed landing spot from the Deep Blue and I saw with a shock that what looked from a distance like a dream swathe of sand beyond the foam was edged all along – except in two slender channels – with fingers of jagged coral, hidden when the waves swept over them but exposed as bared claws to tear small craft – or flesh – when the seas fell back. Did Ben plan to take us into that? There were broken coral boulders scattered like mines along the beach and half submerged in the shallows, too. I looked at his often strangely empty face, hair blown about boyishly for once instead of flattened into its neat church style, and wondered what was going through his mind. I knew he believed we were all in God's hands, but surely to risk a light-hearted group of campers on a seventh-wave dash between a whole phalanx of Scyllas and Charybdises would be madness.

'Wow,' said Magnus. 'Great place for surfing if it wasn't for all those rocks . . .'

So he was wondering too. Graham sat calmly, sure Ben would follow the right procedures since he'd been brought up here. Joe and Benji were relaxed, too. They'd been night fishing with Ben by now, following his torch beam into depths filled with shadows – some alive – with total trust, and returning only thrilled by feeling 'a *bit* scared', and triumphant at having overcome the fear. Now Ben held the canoe back from the waves sweeping shorewards, where it bobbed and strained like an excitable horse. Figures had appeared on the beach, clusters of thin, shock-headed girls and boys. There was no village visible, only this wild shore with a fringe of wooded cliff concealing any possibly more hospitable interior. The landing beach ended where the island curved away past hectically piled broken-off lumps of itself, glimpsed only for seconds under explosions of foam. Some of the figures raised their arms straight up, and perhaps Ben responded to a signal from them, for he drew the canoe further back and put out an anchor. So be it, I thought, relieved, for even if we succeeded in getting safely in, how, with those seas endlessly thrusting us back, would we get out? The boys would be disappointed – we'd brought billycans for cooking and planned a palm-frond fire to light the night – but there was always the farewell party still to come. Ben was busy at the outboard, I presumed refuelling it before preparing to fight the tug of the waves to take us back to the now surprisingly safe-feeling Deep Blue. But he was tipping it up. Then he removed his shirt and put on flippers, long body perfectly balanced, almost languid, in the bouncing craft.

'We can snorkel in,' he said. 'Just count the waves and aim for the channels.'

But the waves were surging into the beach, shock upon shock of them, and the undertow would be as powerful. Did he see my face? We'd come here for fun, not to be battered.

'Benji can come with me,' he said. And there was Benji, soft-bodied in the sunlight and looking terribly small, busily checking the suction of his mask.

'You could stay here, Mum,' said Joe, surprising me with his perception. Graham was ready, so was Magnus and – incredibly – Islander children were flinging themselves like seals under the waves to surf out, using the violent suction, towards us – with no snorkels, and spending long periods invisible. One boy was using a sea-sucked shard of smashed outrigger to keep his face above the surface, complete with welcoming grin.

'I'll have a go,' I said. If any of my children got dragged over that coral, I wanted to be there to bind them up, not watching helplessly. Ben had done this before, and I had to place my trust in him. We'd packed a sit-on kayak at the last minute – just for fun. Now Ben suggested those who weren't strong swimmers use this to float in closer, to where we could judge the right wave and best channel. He asked me which items in the boat I most needed ashore, and I tried a joke: 'Medical kit!' but he just asked flatly which box that was in. In the water, outside where the main push and pull of waves began, Ben checked the children's masks, then mine. Joe and Benji were like frogs by now, and Magnus coolly competent, but I'd only ever snorkelled for pleasure, on calm days. Treading thick, dragging blue, trying to stay upright, I almost hated Ben when he laughed as salt made me splutter. It was the first time I'd heard him laugh. Our thighs touched accidentally as we bobbed for a moment face to face, and the muscle that coincided with my softer flesh felt startlingly strong, belying his languid looks. It made me even angrier with him – then. Seconds later, we were all propelled into a watery dance. Graham and Magnus hardly bothered with the kayak, following Ben, who used the waves to swoop forward strategically, with apparent ease, while supporting Benji – whose short legs appeared briefly at one stage flippering the air, before he vanished again, for what to me seemed unending seconds. Joe hung onto the kayak until he saw some of the first Islanders who'd battled out to us reach shore again. 'That must be a good channel, Mum,' he called as he let the next wave take him.

I hung onto the kayak as long as I could. Ben and Benji were close to shore by now, fangs of coral projecting all round them and underneath their skimming bellies, too. Then I saw Ben lift Benji bodily ahead of him, into the air, so that as they were flung forward, it was a warm breast of sand Benji's body hit, not coral, and he immediately scrambled higher, without turning round, while Ben let himself be rolled in lightly as hollow driftwood, to emerge from the water dripping and pale but to me at that moment transformed into a saint. I hadn't seen Graham and Magnus land, but saw them now standing together as I followed the tip of Joe's snorkel, and was aware blood was running down Magnus's leg but he was also laughing. Joe surfaced inside a circle of Islanders close to shore and was guided in. Then I was doing what they'd all done, but far less ably. My spine, all but forgotten on Pigeon, now felt a horrid liability and the blue, when I stuck my head under it on the edge of my chosen surge, swung crazily, but was clear enough to show the clutter of coral getting closer all the way in. If there was beauty in all those spiky flowers of the deep with waves romping carelessly over them, it eluded me that day, and as I reached the shallows, I called on every instinctive resource I possessed to forge a path between, rather than across, the heads of the coral sea mines. Close to shore, I lost my breath and, foolishly, attempted to stand. At once my flippers were sucked off and I was scooped backwards rapidly. Like Benji, I didn't look round as I crawled, scrabbled and fought forwards any way I could before being clouted by the next wave. When I finally made steady enough contact with the sand to stay on my feet, I found I had one fist and one eye full of it. Everyone was recovering on a high bank, and I joined them, thanking Ben for taking care of Benji. He said nothing, but motioned with his chin, Islander fashion, to where a black hand rose out of a whooshing wave, balancing my medical kit like a waiter's tray. Beyond it were others, supporting, on thin arms, water bottles, billycans and my polythene-wrapped notebook in a surreal procession across the swirling deep.

Among items brought ashore was a football, and whenever the

piccaninnis of Nbanga weren't actually tearing after it, they gently held Joe and Benji's hands in silent demonstration of goodwill. Magnus and the men searched for a quiet spot to dive for supper (Magnus's shin was torn, but not badly) while I, after washing the sand from my eye – observed closely by forty others under fantastic stacks of hair – found many helpers to build a fire. I began by making a circle of coral under the edge of a broad cliff overhang. Instantly, an 'ah-ahh!' of understanding went up among the assembled women, and they deputed dozens of little girls, who'd sidled from behind boulders like pretty spindly-legged crabs, to collect wood. Even the tiniest, barely toddling and wearing only a piece of green twine in her baby fuzz of hair, solemnly placed a brown coconut husk at the edge of the circle, reminding me how Benji had copied his brothers as they'd performed tasks in Scotland, bringing a single log when too small to manage more. Two of the young women, Kabi and her 'sista' Dora, were bolder than the rest. Kabi was handsomely built, with a great mass of stiff hair sticking straight up from her head and tribal scars engraved into her cheeks like blurred kisses. Lips folded, she reshaped the fire for me into an oblong and laid along it two green palm-leaf stems, perfect as a barbecue. In the meantime a tripod of sticks was erected to hold billycans, and fresh water fetched from a stone bowl elevated on a cairn of coral beneath a hole in the overhang. While the billy boiled (could I squeeze tea for twenty out of it? I needn't have worried: they passed round our few cups taking only a sip each), I told the women I'd be honoured to meet their chief. I'd brought, on Tangypera's advice, ten sticks of tobacco. Kabi sent a small boy to inform the chief of my imminent visit, then began a detailed inspection of my hair – made into rats' tails by the sea – and jewellery and clothes.

'Naes 'air,' she said, separating the tangles carefully. 'Iu messabaot wetem Ben?'

This bold suggestion that I might 'mess about' with Ben provoked merriment among the group, but I was slightly perturbed. We'd already established I was unmarried – there was the usual sympathy – but evidently the news of my *happily* lone state hadn't penetrated as far as the ladies of Nbanga.

'What about you?' I countered. 'Are you married?'

She giggled, and her warm flesh at my back, redolent of all the grit and sweat in her life as well as the coconut oil rubbed into it, shook. 'Dadi b'long mifela lukluk 'usban.'

Her husband would be chosen for her. Would it be a local boy? She shrugged with careless magnificence, then joined in her friends' peals of laughter: 'Mi no savvy . . .'

When the fire was going nicely and could be left to burn to embers, Kabi and Dora accompanied me to meet the chief, while others stayed to watch the football and receive any fish caught. Dora put her hand shyly on my back as we walked along. No-one shrank from my scar here. Did I fall from a tree, she wondered? Injuries – and deaths – from tree-climbing, as well as sea journeys, weren't uncommon. Not long ago, a young woman widowed by the sea, with five children, died after falling from a tree at Nola where she'd been gathering tevi – wild fruit. There had been all-night wailing, and Pigeon's staff requested time off for the funeral – but within hours her children had been taken in permanently by 'sistas', blood or otherwise, and a breast offered to the youngest, who would automatically share it and its owner's maternal affections. If anything happened to their parents, children quickly went 'into care' here – but the care of extended families, not strangers.

Things were different, however, for girls past puberty. If a father, adoptive or otherwise, had enough land, his daughters were married off for an agreed price of red feathers* – cash was often involved as well, nowadays – and this, contrary to my preconceived Western ideas, seemed often a happy arrangement. But some girls – Dora among them – were less fortunate. Her father had no land so she might never marry, even though she was pretty. In days gone by, when women were the chief export from Reefs, she could have been sold as a concubine but the missionaries had banned this practice so she'd probably end up as Kabi's housegirl/confidante when her friend married. And if she wanted relationships with men, she'd have to 'messabaot'. If this chief I was to meet proved elderly and seemed approachable, I decided to enquire if the practice of concubinage was missed.

Perhaps another Scot had visited Nbanga in the past, because the well-grizzled chief greeted me graciously at the door of his palm-thatched hut, wearing, with dignity, what was unmistakably a

---

* Red feather money, made from the plumage of small, bright birds of the Islands formed into a roll, remains a valuable form of currency in parts of the Solomon Islands.

woman's Fair Isle sweater over his loincloth. We shook hands, I presented the tobacco and he sent women scurrying off for a reciprocal gift of fruit. It seemed rude to raise the subject of the territory's past reputation for selling women without preamble, so I asked if I might meet his wife.

'Dae finis,' (she's dead) he said, and inclined his head when I commiserated. Then he gave a yell into the blackness of the hut and, shyly, there emerged not one but three of the sistas of the deceased, who were now, I understood, looking after him in lieu. We exchanged smiles, and everyone watched me drink a coconut. By this time there were several elderly men around, an opportunity not to be missed, but how to begin?

'In our society,' I said, in best Pijin, 'we no longer have many laws governing relationships between young people after a certain age. Some older people wonder if this is wise, as it can be hard for the young to make the right choices on their own.'

There was an encouragingly sympathetic murmur, then one old man voiced evidently shared feeling.

'You mas' have plenti strong law, or evriting buggerup!'

'We used to have a system in our society,' I said, risking my homeland's reputation rather than seeming to cast aspersions on theirs, 'whereby marriages were arranged between landed families' – now for the shock tactics – 'and men could buy the use of women's bodies before they got married – or if their wives were . . . busy.'

'Olsem olo Kastom,' offered the chief. (That's how it used to be in Kastom.)

The English-speaking elder spoke up again.

'Young pipol nowday,' he said, making me smile, 'no gud. Messabaot allataem . . .'

It didn't take much probing to discover that the system of concubinage *was* missed – but not only for the obvious reasons. These elders believed it had had a healthily limiting effect on sexual conduct. A man slept either with his wife or with a concubine. Not his neighbour's wife or any other unmarried girl. One of the old women at the edge of the circle, smoking a pipe, grinned at the turn of conversation. The suspicion crossed my mind that the system of concubinage can't have been all bad for the wives, either. How many Western women, worrying about the latest nubile colleague in their husband's office, would prefer he used a no-threat-to-the-family legal prostitute if he wanted extramarital dalliance? Solomon Islander wives took things further and looked after their husband's concubine's feminine needs – including any children she bore. But what about the concubines themselves? The old men were emphatic that concubines had enjoyed life. As many as twenty men would club together to buy one, and she would wear the finest shell jewellery and never be short of food.

Suddenly the chief's face closed. They were Christian now, he said. That business belonged to 'befoataem'. Perhaps he clammed up because the next question might have been why concubines were quite so valuable – costing ten times as much as a bride. The truth was that they were usually exported from Reef Islands to bigger, more powerful Santa Cruz, as objects of propitiation. 'If you stop attacking our villages, we'll send you a beautiful girl.' These girls may have been mere bodies for barter, but they could prevent – or halt – raids resulting in slaughter and the acquisition of human bone for arrow tips, not to mention human flesh for kaikai. And one thing most Islanders were not keen to discuss was that particular aspect of their pre-conversion past. Cannibalism and headhunting were evil, the white men with the all-powerful God decreed, a practice only of *savages*. (Tangypera's face was a study when I told him how our one-time Queen of Scots had her head chopped off in cold blood.)

With the arrival of gifts of fruit – and the rest of the European contingent, minus Ben – rounds of handshaking began, and the women exclaimed over Joe's red hair. I left the group after being proudly shown leaf shacks constituting church and school, and descended the narrow access from the hidden clifftop village, once more in the company of Kabi and Dora, who'd half hidden behind a palm tree while I was talking to the 'Bigmen'. I gave Kabi a clasp out of my hair which nestled fetchingly in her wild bouffant and Dora a phial of scent – maybe unwisely if the only pleasures she could have must be illicit.

At the near end of the beach was a shark, freshly landed, and further along excitement surrounded a wizened elder who was balancing a dugout just beyond where the surges broke over the coral, and appeared to be towing something. The former football teams divided efficiently into two lines, dashing forward at precisely the right moment first to haul the dugout in safely, and the old man – then risked their skinny bodies right in the surf to grab the enormous sailfish on a line behind. It was twice the size of the little old man who'd caught it. Everyone beamed as my camera flashed.

The sea calmed slightly as daylight began to fade, and after checking the fire (now in Kabi's charge) I took myself off to bathe – and
pee – in the sea, for there was nowhere else to go. I chose the smaller
of the two safe channels in the coral minefield, and there squatted
discreetly, kalico spread. When the automatic flush of swirling waves
had operated, I sat on a while, the water, like a giant bobbing bath, up
to my ears. There was something pleasurable now about the way my
body was clasped and let go, clasped and let go, by the surges. The
force was considerable, a fearsome all-over caress, but the sinking sun
glowed on my face and it was pleasant to bounce gently on my
bottom in that warm sea. It was more than pleasant. It was sexy.

In this extraordinary spot, it seemed natural for unusual things to
emerge from the waves, and now I saw another. I'd thought Ben had
gone off for a nap somewhere, as was his way. Whenever he wasn't
mending things for his mother, studying the Bible or night fishing, he
slept. Or dozed. The soles of his feet sticking out of his Box on
Pigeon, as he lay in full sight of anyone passing, were something of a
joke between me and the boys. He was so often 'resting', rising only
at his mother's calls, when he'd go about whatever she wanted with
total patience – dumb animal or martyr, I'd thought once, cruelly. But
earlier today I'd thought him a saint for protecting Benji from the
madness of the sea, and there had been no unkind overtones in my
head then. And if Ben believed he received personal protection from
on high, what business was it of mine? The man was basically good,
and now I saw he was also beautiful. For Ben wasn't napping at this
magical moment before sunset; instead he was pouring his perfectly
balanced body again and again onto and through the seventh wave.
He was so intent on what he was doing, I don't think he saw me or
anything other than his chosen trajectory as he made each fresh, prolonged plunge, using the power of the sea to drive forward the slender
body that, in this setting, became magnificent. Diving headlong
through huge surges, with skill honed by years of practice, Ben was in
his element – because, clearly, Ben's element was the sea. Diana said
all three Hepworth children had climbed the cliffs at Nbanga and
dived thirty feet into waves below, but Ben was always keenest. I
believed it, but wasn't thinking of him as a child now.

When night had claimed Nbanga with sudden blackness and bellies
were full, Islanders who'd joined wontoks for their share of sailfish in
the village returned, guided down the cliff by torches of dry palm

which they placed near our camp, and settled down to watch us – and sing. I'd heard Reef Island singing before – when the wind was in the right direction, gentle waves of sound, taking their rising and falling cadences from the sea, washed over Pigeon from Nandelli – but the singing of the Nbanga people by the fire that night held a special charm. Perhaps it was because the way into that now softly starlit beach had been so fearful, through dangers these patient people lived with constantly, perhaps because Magnus must leave soon, and I knew he was enjoying what would be his last weekend excursion in Reef Islands for a long time. Ben was back in his napping pose, shut off from the world. He didn't join in when young men formed a slowly moving circle, feet stamping a rhythm in the sand that matched the song, but Graham and Magnus did. The girls were thrilled, fists shoved against teeth gleaming in the torchlight to stem streams of happy giggles, then clapping efficiently as white feet found the same beat as black.

I watched my son, at thirteen looking the youngest in the group but obviously considering himself no longer one of the 'little' ones. At his age Islander boys had often already passed through initiation rites into the responsibilities of adulthood. But he still seemed young to me, the image of his tininess as a newborn child – a feather fallen out of Africa – fresh as yesterday. After a while older men joined the singers, beating the side of a dugout as a drum. The tempo rose and girls made cricket-like hissing sounds, with tongues tight against teeth. This signalled a free-for-all, the hissing falling into a new rhythm for feet to follow, and first bare-breasted older women, then children, then – perhaps this only happened when safely surrounded by others – young women joined in too. Joe was pulled in unreluctantly by laughing piccaninnis, who continued to hold his hands – as many were holding hands, boy and boy, old woman and old woman – and the circle became a warm jostling mass, stamping companionably through half the night, with the moon at its highest casting only a glimmer – just enough to throw a sheen over the deceptive deep – on this craggy fragment of sunken mountain adrift in time.

The singing of the Nbanga women sustained me when we left their shores next day. Again Ben took charge of Benji, and I was aware of the seal-man in him taking over from its pale, shore shadow as he led a trusting child through real perils of the deep. He saw everyone else safely into the canoe too, and Islanders performed acrobatic feats to ensure most of our gear remained unsoaked. Kabi sensed my apprehension. Her wontoks stood close to the edge of the surf, offering silent support as I fastened on my mask, then Kabi unwound my kalico, handing it to a boy to carry out on a plank, and she and Dora took hold of my arms and literally launched me when the right wave came. They were lost to sight for a while, as, once more, I struggled in the swaying blue, but when I surfaced, there they were, a circle of women treading water, hair dilating on the waves, singing their hearts out to wish us well. The sound – and their beauty of spirit – gave me strength, for although gasping when I reached the canoe, I was elated. Ben pulled me up, not laughing at my spluttering this time but with a wry little smile.

'Well done, Mum,' said Magnus, who'd known it had been difficult, with my spine. But Benji just said: 'Wasn't that great? We must come again – I've promised those boys we will.' He waved madly and dozens of hands waved back, faces playing hide-and-seek among the waves. And I found myself saying yes.

The *Southern Cross* was spotted sixteen hours ahead of Magnus's planned departure. It hung there, a dent in the horizon, as Magnus stuffed crude carvings into his rucksack along with an unused jotter in which we'd thought he might keep a diary. Instead, I'd used one page to try to express my belief in him and my love, which would always be with him, however far apart we were physically – or in other ways as he moved naturally into the next stages of his life. I told Magnus not to bother looking at it until he was well on his way. It was just a babble – a mum being a mum. 'I'll be all right, I think,' he said. Then we got on with the party preparations.

Tangypera, judging from constant paddlings to and fro between Nenumbo, Nandelli and Pigeon, had taken his task of 'putting out word' seriously. Not knowing how many to expect, I'd made enough bushlime for about forty. I'd also cooked pots of 'savvy savvy rice' – a dish picked up during *Castaway* days, using the shaved inner 'seed' of a shooting coconut. Mhairi had made masses of banana cake. But one always underestimates the number of children accompanying each adult, and Joe had secured a sheaf of sugar cane from a schoolfriend's dadi, which he hacked into portions, so at least there'd be something for every piccaninni. I also raided my shortbread supply, fanning ten boxes onto leaves. But all our efforts were as nothing compared to the Islanders'.

When we made our way, at Tangypera's summons, to 'Ross's end', I was humbled by the sight that met our eyes. The veranda, the steps up from the water and the tiny sand beach topped by coral beside the units were all lit up by tilley lamps, and thronged with Islanders. Dugouts lay in jumbled ranks in the shallows and there were leaf mats spread on the ground. Most splendid of all, there were tables pulled together to form a buffet overflowing with baskets of boiled and baked kumera, leaf platters displaying fish of countless kinds, cauldrons vouchsafing delicious aromas of kokoroko (chicken) and – a great honour – steaming pigflesh mounded high on seaweed-dark frills of wild cabbage.

A coo of welcome – like Pigeon Island pigeons sighing together – rose from women already in place fanning away flies, when Magnus appeared and was led by Tangypera to sit closest to the best food, on the best mat. The rest of us were ranged in an amphitheatre-style semi-circle many deep before him. Ross and Pegi, beaming at having been instrumental in pulling off this coup, motioned for the im- mediate family to face outwards too, which we did, so the 'audience' could watch us eat as well – and include us in their prayers, for the parting of a family from one of its members who must travel was familiar in Island life, and there were rituals to follow. As a catechist made a short speech expressing the pleasure felt by all in Magnus's presence among them, and the sorrow that must follow his departure, I noticed familiar faces in the crowd only glimpsed previously in the shadow of trees or on the reef, fishing or picking shells, during my wanders. Small children who'd yelled my name: 'Mami b'long Magnus!' then hidden, were now here in shyly smiling rows, their mothers with yet more feast offerings in baskets beside them, and fathers in a proud phalanx of most of the local men I knew – includ- ing Kiyo and Henri who'd been with us on the original canoe crossing. Tangypera whispered that some elders, among them Nupanyi, were there because of my interest in more than the Hepworth history of Pigeon. My monetary contribution to the feast – although minute in the face of this largesse – was all part of the form that led them to trust my respect for Kastom ways.

Magnus was unwrapping the dripping banana leaf placed in his hands by Pegi, with more waiting, laid at his feet by women from Nandelli and Nenumbo, when he said in an aside:

'I'm surprised Diana's not here yet.'

'Diana?'

I'd sent Magnus and Graham to tea with Diana earlier to say their farewells, and made it clear the evening meal was an Islander affair of the sort she usually shunned.

'Do you think she'll come?' I asked, concerned this could stymie my plans to increase the confidence of the elders. If they thought 'Missus' was a close wontok of mine, they'd surely never risk giving vent to their true feelings about the Hepworths and Pigeon. Others were filling their leaves now, men first.

'Well, she should, shouldn't she?' said Magnus.

I wanted to understand what he meant.

'Well . . .' He paused to move a particularly large piece of pig from one side of his jaw to the other. 'She kind of *is* Pigeon Island, isn't she? It's just a shame she doesn't mix with the Islanders more – a shame it's so "her and them".'

It was as simple as that to him, and I felt vaguely ashamed. A great gulf of difference in class, education and attitudes made it impossible for Diana to mix on an ordinary level with the Islanders – seeing them, as she did, only as customers and servants – but I also saw what he meant. Indeed it was sad to think of her in that grand house watching a video alone, and Ben in his Box, separated from the Islanders by his censorious fanaticism, while we partied. But I needn't have worried. Just as youths were stepping up to fetch food there came out of the darkness the yellow flash of an electric torch – and a rumbling growl. Diana Hepworth, Stasi the Rottweiler and Ben the ascetic were on their way. Tangypera shot me a look which said several things at once: 'I didn't know about this'; 'Forget about talking to the elders for the moment' and 'That lady really takes the cake, doesn't she?' The look, beginning with alarm, ended in a grin, and he pattered away silently, first whispering to men in the most senior ranks, then – with amazing speed, before the torchlight flared over us as Diana checked out what was in progress – he was at her side, transformed from respected Kastom chief to humble houseboy, and shouting for others to fetch her a chair. It was impossible not to admire his acting skills, and her chutzpah. This was transparently a gatecrash – unthinkable vice versa, Islanders invading one of her dinner parties – but she knew she'd not only be accepted but treated as an honoured guest. And she was. Within seconds, the veranda was all but clear of Islanders who'd made way for her lounger, on which she reclined, with Stasi alongside whimpering confusedly, making piccaninnis hide their faces in their mother's kalicos. Some silently melted away into the dark. The older men held their places, but managed with body language to look suddenly deferential. And I found myself not only endorsing this process but taking it further. I offered to fetch Diana's food – in a daughter's place – and didn't fill a banana leaf but used the plate Pegi offered.

'Not much pikpik for me,' called Diana gaily. 'It can cause belerun, you know.'

This was not intended to offend, indeed, may have been an attempt at a joke. But pikpik was the food of honour. One simply didn't say 'not much'.

There was no doubt the crowd come to attend Magnus's farewell party shrank when Diana appeared, but only as far as the darker end of the landing beach. A full belly, to a Reef Islander, equates to happiness, and although they couldn't relax so easily in front of Missus, their boss, they were still determined to have a good time. Benji and Joe took loaded leaves to their friends in the dark and Magnus chatted with Peter and Ross. Ben ate in silence on the flank of Diana's lounger not occupied by the dog and, perhaps inevitably, I spent the meal talking to her. Very English small talk. It was now an all-white central group on the veranda – as in feudal or colonial times, with the serfs or servants seated on the ground at a respectful distance as the literally lower orders. But the Islanders hadn't finished their formalities yet, and Lanebu left her mistress to kneel, with two of her sistas, in front of Magnus and sing.

'Isn't that lovely?' said Diana, and it was, but I was silent, the purity of the voices and the feeling behind them almost bringing tears, as they'd brought courage, at Nbanga. 'God Be With You', they sang, raising a chorus from the Christian element present, then those Reef Island songs which are like the voice of the reef itself. After this, Diana tapped my shoulder.

'Give me a hand back, dear, will you? I expect the young will stay up, but I'm off to bed.' Again, this could have been an attempt at diplomacy, and my emotions were mixed as I supported her awkward steps along the crab-strewn path back to 'the white end'. 'D'you see this?' she said, stabbing with her parasol at the ground. 'Just as I told you, they've *ruined* my lawn . . .' And she didn't mean the crabs.

After I'd seen Diana home, I thanked the Island ladies and suggested

Magnus enjoy himself with the young crowd gathering to dance on a strip of sand revealed at low tide, now the moon was up. We'd meet again at first light, when he had to go. And then it would just be a quick hug.

'That was fantastic, Mum,' he said. 'Everyone was so kind – Diana too.'

I went to bed that night feeling my fasbon might have the makings of a valuable diplomat in this muddled world. He'd just wanted *everyone* to enjoy his party, and they had. At dawn, every Islander on Pigeon and many from Nandelli and Nenumbo got up to see him go and Pegi and her sistas stood with me on the shore waving, then held my hands for an hour in gentle silence until and after the *Southern Cross* was out of sight.

12

1959–1964

AFTER THE INITIAL JOINT JOYOUS BUILDING SPREE ON PIGEON, TOM WAS frequently away on trips to Vanikoro, where he was contracted to carry labour (workers). He also took the ship's store all over Reef Islands and Santa Cruz, where he bought turtle shell and started crocodile hunting. Being separated from his new home – and Diana – hadn't been in the original plans for Paradise, but was essential if sufficient business was to be generated to keep them there. '*Apart from the chore of running the ship, I love the life, so does Diana. It's not idle beach-combing, we work from dawn to dusk, and if being paid wages should complain of Exploitation . . . We make probably less than the average truck driver, but live in a spot millionaires might envy, and WE envy no man.*' But the periods of separation – months if the *AR* had to go on the nearest slip – were difficult for both. Diana kept a journal mostly for practical in-formation, such as the week's store take or which 'boy' was on what job, but that she missed Tom is transparent. They had an old wartime radio, and when she wasn't flat out building or selecting and rejecting copra she spent hours hunched over it hoping for news of Tom. '*Tried again to raise Tom. No joy. Hope you're all right, darling . . . Still no Tom . . . Try again later.*' What kept her going was the thought of how lovely it would be to have the projects of the moment complete for his return. '*Lovely*' was Diana's strongest superlative, in capitals when-ever the ship was sighted; '*awful*' her most expressive negative, but she was too drained even to write this, when, after what both described as a '*wonderful first year*', despite the separations, she suddenly lost a second child while working alone on Pigeon. On that occasion, all she managed to scribble was '*Thank God you're coming home soon.*'

Diana was working on the roof of a room for Tasha, extending the cargo-shed home, when she felt the wrench in her womb. The pregnancy hadn't been confirmed, but she and Tom had been delighted when the familiar signs manifested themselves, and even when nauseous she'd insisted he stick to his trading routine. 'You go on. We'll be all right,' she said, and always stood with Tasha on the southern extremity of the island, waving until the sail of the *AR* was over the horizon – then calling to the 'boys' that it was time to bash on. After a while she rigged a bell, made of an engine part, that echoed widely when struck with a spanner, so she didn't have to yell so much. It was this she used to summon whatever help might be forthcoming when she felt the blood – and strength – drain from her on the roof. By crawling to the edge, she was just within reach, and hit the bell repeatedly. But no-one came. It was the Islanders' kaikai time (lunch hour) which they observed religiously. Or maybe the wind was in the wrong direction for those nearest, on Nandelli, to hear. Tasha was too engrossed in scooping the soft flesh from a young coconut with her fingers to be alarmed by the prolonged din, and when she did finally look up, Diana stopped the useless ringing and smiled, saying she'd be down in a minute. So she lay alone on the baking roof irons and lost a baby under the wide blue sky, the worst of the flood soaking into the unfinished leaf thatch. When she managed to climb down, she held a handful of stained rag, which she took into the sea, where the red flowered briefly, then was gone on a current. She described the tiny thing she and Tom buried later as '*little more than a blob of blood*', but the fact she waited for him to come home and they dug the grave together argues that it felt like more than that.

When the Islanders returned to work in the afternoon, she told them to fetch a woman to do the day's washing and mash kumera for Tasha, as she couldn't trust them with the key to where she kept tinned supplies and by now couldn't move from her bed. The *AR* reached Mohawk Bay at sunrise the following morning, and Tom was immediately worried when he saw no Diana on the beach, waving a square of sail in welcome.

'Where's Missus?' he asked the first Islander to paddle out.

'Mi no savvy.' (I don't know.)

'Where is she?'

The old man in the next dugout took time to hawk up and deposit a betel-stained gob in the water before replying: 'Mi no savvy.'

And that's what everyone said, until Nupanyi, Tom's chief crew boy, spoke to another PIT employee.

'Missus sick.'

Stowing gear quickly – for nothing could be left out safely –Tom asked if she was 'lelebet' or 'propa' sick, and his relief when told lelebet (little bit) must have been profound. If anyone on Pigeon was propa sick, there wouldn't be much hope for them with between three and ten days' sailing, weather permitting, to the nearest half-serious medical aid in Honiara. During the next fortnight – for she developed an infection in the womb – Tom left Diana's side only when she pushed him out to chivvy her workers. His own crew were told to get on with copra bagging, after he'd weighed it. Nupanyi proved one of the best.

'You work too hard,' Tom told Diana, agonized this should have happened in his absence and hating even more the fact that he must leave her again soon.

'Nonsense,' she said, but did accept the idea of taking on house staff who would stay on Pigeon – where they couldn't pretend they hadn't heard the bell. Although the Hepworths had built labour huts early on, Islanders had proved reluctant to use them because of local lore. The great cycad tree that, in its 'primitive' grandeur, had been for Diana a discovery of delight held a quite different meaning for them. To the Islanders it was a Debbil-Debbil Tree, to be left alone, except by those whose personal god (or devil) inhabited it – and which might manifest itself in frightening guises at night. There were also beliefs about Mohawk Bay, the portal to and from the Outside World – with all the good and evil that might mean.

'It was just horrid bad luck,' said Diana, referring to the miscarriage. But among Islanders there were whispers of the awakening of Mohawk Bay's Debbil, and some suggested it wasn't surprising Diana's early gardening efforts had failed, too. These 'punishments' may have been the Debbil's doing, but petty thefts were more directly retaliatory. Tom thought their neighbours must just be a particularly perfidious brand of 'native' – they hadn't had such problems elsewhere – but some of the men of Reefs with Kastom claims on Pigeon Island were making the only kind of statement they knew how, in the face of circumstances beyond their control. There were those among them whose grandparents had been killed when they refused to respect the British flag. White meant might.

While Diana was recovering, as well as ordering store goods from Hong Kong she wrote to her family – less of the loss of the child than of successes: '*Even old women produce copra now. I tell them how to do it when they come for their stick tobacco (ugh!) . . . locals are drying fish for us now, too . . . Tom's off to Kira Kira with a load soon, so he'll post this then . . . Send some of those wonderful plastic training pants, would you? . . . No, Tasha isn't talking yet, but you should see her in the sea, quite fearless, and my housegirl has a really very nice child for her to play with . . .*'

The new system of help in the home freed Diana for more building work, for the women who came to sweep, scrub clothes and peel vegetables, and the men, automatically kept an eye on Tasha, too – it was their Kastom. Soon there was a cookboy to prepare breakfast – pawpaw with cereal and dried milk – and Islanders were taught to care for the grass that would one day become a flourishing lawn. And a whole new world opened out to Tasha. When she was but two, Diana watched her determinedly tackling the four hundred metres of shallows and exposed reef that led to Nandelli at low tide, on her own. Tasha knew her piccaninni friends came from there, and didn't want to be without them for a minute. When she was three, Tom wrote to his sisters: '*She still isn't talking, and we're still not worrying . . . she's very physical, like her mum.*' That third year on Pigeon, when the lucrative crocodile-hunting side of the business took off and Diana was once more pregnant, so both her parents were smiling and unworried, must have been truly a spell in Paradise for Tasha, playing as she did all day on the reefs and being welcomed in the leaf huts that were her friends' homes. Life was good and could only get better, Tom and Diana believed, when the new baby came.

Tom occasionally played patience when he was away on the *AR*, or listened to a cracked forty-five of Chopin, courtesy of a generator still going strong from pre-Tahiti days, but more often than not he spent his evenings writing to his sisters, under a swaying hurricane lamp and the stars. How exotic his tropical existence must have seemed to two middle-aged ladies in London, though they were hardly stereotypical spinsters. Elizabeth Hepworth, in particular, making a name for herself

Diana Hepworth aged about twelve.

Diana modelling in the 1940s.

Anthony Buckley

Diana in 1946, around the time
she met Tom.

Tom Hepworth at the helm in the 1940s.

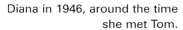

(*Top left*) The *Arthur Rogers* becalmed in mid-Pacific, 1950s.

(*Above*) Tom taking a sun-sight on board the *Arthur Rogers*.

(*Left*) Diana and friend riding the waves under the *AR*'s twenty-foot bowsprit.

(*Below*) Diana relaxing during idyllic island-hopping days in the 1950s.

(*Top left*) 'Tom Hepworth's harem' – the all-girl crew, 1954.

(*Above*) The all-girl crew reunion, 1984.

(*Left*) Members of the all-girl crew working on the *Arthur Rogers*, 1954.

(*Below*) Diana, pregnant with Tasha, ready to set sail for Pigeon Island in 1958 accompanied by a New Hebridean crew. *Bingham Green*

Tom bathing his 'Poppet', Tasha, soon after setting up home on Pigeon in 1959.

Tasha Hepworth, born October 1958, gets her first glimpse of the sea from one of the *AR*'s portholes.

Tasha and friends, late 1970s.

Tasha, 1960. A happy little Eve in a South Sea Eden.

Diana and Tasha at a home for the handicapped in New Zealand, 1990s.

The first house Diana built on Pigeon in 1959. The same roof is still on it over forty years later.

Loading copra from Diana's handmade slide, early 1970s.

Pigeon Island Traders' shopfront in the 1970s. *Bertram Follett*

The boat- and bunkhouse swept away by Cyclone Nina in 1993.

Christine Clement, Pigeon's first governess, with Hepworth and Reef Island children, 1970.

Bressin (Ben) Hepworth with the first fish he caught using a bow and arrow, 1960s.

Lapoli, the housegirl Ross and Bressin spied on when she lay sleeping in the nude.

Bressin and Ross as choirboys at school in New Zealand, mid-1970s.

Sipikoli with Bressin/Ben's child,
Diane, 1990.

Ben and Ross with Ross's son
Andrew, 1993.

Teimaliki, dressed up for the photo, with Ross and Christine, the year Tasha
was 'taken away'.

Tom, in latter years, at work on his book.
Bertram Follett

Tom and Diana in New Zealand, 1984.

Diana, 1999, with pictures of Tom and the *Arthur Rogers* in the background. *Robbie Cooper*

in very unspinsterish paintings, had an astute eye for detail. All her little brother's effusions about how perfect life was, despite the tedium of endlessly stripping down engines and the maddening '*slowness of the native mind*', couldn't conceal from her the fact that it was odd a child of three wasn't talking, and she traced a specialist in New Zealand he might look up when, as was the plan, Diana went there to have the next baby.

Maintaining old contacts was a forte of the Hepworths', however rarely mail came or went. Now, as Diana expanded, they made arrangements whereby a couple met in the New Hebrides should come to Pigeon and hold the fort while they were away. Tom would sail Diana to Vanikoro as her time approached, and from there she'd take the timber company's ship to the New Hebrides and fly to New Zealand. Tasha would come along for the ride as far as Vanikoro. But when Diana was thirty-three weeks pregnant, Tasha went down with '*a bout of malaria, poor mite, in the course of which she threw a convulsion, nearly driving us mad with fright. It was terrifying, eyes rolled up, face blue, limbs twitching.*' It wasn't the first time Tasha had had a convulsion. She'd shown the same symptoms around Christmas 1959, when the Hepworths were sailing close enough to Honiara to have her seen quickly. Nothing to worry about, they were told, but Diana agreed when a doctor suggested taking an X-ray and sending it to New Zealand. When she heard nothing further, she assumed there really was nothing to worry about. In fact, the X-ray was never sent. If it had been, Diana might not have had to wait until she had twin baby boys feeding at her breast to hear the news that Tasha had been born with a hole in the heart, plus a blockage in the same dangerous area, and must come to New Zealand for tests – and possibly surgery – at once.

Diana's telegram to Tom in the New Hebrides, announcing the births of Ross and Bressin,★ crossed with his to her saying he was on his way urgently with Tasha. She was suffering from '*ventricular septal defect and infundibular pulmonary stenosis*', according to an X-ray finally sent to New Zealand over two years after concern was first raised. A further reason her speech was slow might be because Tasha was also partially deaf. '*I'm over the moon about your nephews,*' Tom told his

---

★ Ben Hepworth was called Bressin originally. He later changed his name.

sisters, but Tasha's condition horrified him. It was true she was unusually small, had suffered recurrent 'fevers' since birth and couldn't speak. Why hadn't they recognized these as signs of abnormality? Was it because there were no other European children around for comparison? Worse, Tasha, '*chirpy as a bird*' on the island, was totally fazed by suddenly finding herself amid a host of white-uniformed, *white* strangers in an Auckland hospital ward. It was like taking an innocent Eve out of Eden and locking her in a glass box into which dozens of strange faces leered, and hands loomed, wielding sharp, intrusive instruments, from all sides. Tom was only able to stare from behind the ward window at her small face, eyes huge with shock and brimming with unshed tears, while inside he wept himself. Within a day of her admission, he found a job as a painter in the hospital, with a box-like room thrown in, to be near her, but was still restricted to visiting hours only. In between visits – agony for both – sitting with Diana and the twins and stints of work, he took himself for walks, sun-browned neck muffled against the New Zealand winter chill. His little girl, his Poppet, needed him, and he 'wasn't allowed'. '*Bloody, bungling bureaucrats.*' Diana, still emotional from the birth but calmly livid when she learned what was happening, telephoned the ward where Tasha was kept and, armed with iciest BBC English, intimidated the night staff into some concessions. But it was no good. Two weeks after she'd entered hospital for tests, Tasha was returned to her mother '*a bag of bones*'. She'd stopped eating. She'd even stopped crying, only responding slightly when a Maori nurse with familiar bushy hair came on duty, and when her dadi came. When at last she was reunited with Diana, she clung and clung, as needy as her newly born brothers – and regressed almost to their stage.

Diana's mother came out from England; it would be the last time she saw her daughter and only time she saw her grandchildren. Diana, hands full with thriving twins and an ailing Tasha, found little time for this woman she considered weak-willed and who complained Diana should have a trained nanny, not 'native housegirls', to look after the babies. No member of Tom's family saw the children when they were small, so a more nuclear white family there could hardly have been when Tasha was recovered enough to return with her parents and brothers to the Solomons, land of families extending to tribal clans who were nearly all hands-on carers of their virtually communal young. The hospital had agreed that, although it was essential Tasha have heart surgery, it couldn't be undertaken now, when she was so traumatized. She must come back when she was eight or nine.

It had been hoped that the couple who'd held the fort might be able to relieve Tom of the long trips away from Pigeon he so disliked, but this was not to be. The man was a competent sailor, Tom reckoned, but unable to pass the requisite written test. Fouled by the rules of bureaucracy again. So this pair departed, and within weeks of having reinstalled the now much happier Tasha among those she'd come to see as her own, Tom was away across the Deep Blue once more, to bring home crocodile skins to be made into handbags for women like Diana's model sister, the 'Contessa'. She was now married to an admired squire, regularly featured in gossip columns, who housed her in splendour in a grand priory where he also kept a collection of jade. '*Do come and see my home*,' wrote the remarkable Field-Hart sisters to each other. What comparisons they might have made. Somewhere out there, too, in the world beyond Pigeon the Beatles were finding fame, Marilyn Monroe and Andy Warhol were getting together over Coca-Cola cans and Claude Lévi-Strauss's *The Savage Mind* had been published. But none of this affected the inhabitants of Reef Islands. At a hand-made table on canvas chairs under their mango tree, the Hepworths ate the same combination of Fray Bentos pies and fresh fruit and fish they had eaten since leaving Britain in 1947, and the Islanders, under their mango trees but on the ground, ate the same food their forefathers had eaten for three thousand years. The only item missing from the Island diet was long pikpik (human flesh) but maybe that was made up for by the odd tin of spam from PIT.

What went through the Reef Islanders' minds when they saw Missus and Cap'n return with twin boy children to their forefathers' time-honoured portions of Pigeon? Did it feel a further threat? It meant more jobs for those who wanted them, anyway. Some were hired to hold torches that blinded the crocs Tom shot; others assisted Diana in the creation of an impressive playground-style slide for the copra. One night she heard a break-in taking place on the store roof, and boldly shone the torch to see which of her disloyal workers it was this time, but the man leaped away along the beam of the torch, dashing on bare soles the length of the forty-foot slide and diving headlong into the water beyond. They were after tobacco, mostly, but also aspirin, meths and, when it came, liquor. They also stole Tasha's little money box twice, and it becomes easier, in the light of this litany of offences, to understand why soon Diana was never without a large dog trained to bark at Islanders. But Tom, eroded by anxiety over Tasha and a dose of malaria to eight stone ten in New Zealand, soon bounced back to his normal ten and a half, and wrote merrily to his sisters of a sudden shower of fanmail from Holland received after publication there of old articles about their search for and discovery of *'the perfect place to raise a family in the sun'*. *'You are living our fantasy,'* wrote total strangers. *'How wonderful for your children to be brought up away from all the madness and pettiness of the world'*. . . *'We are your ardent admirers'* . . . *'Can we join you?'*

Tom sifted through the outpourings, looking for any half-serious enquiries, for, with the various arms of PIT expanding and the question of the children's early education to consider, they could do with another European couple on the island, preferably with young of a similar age. In the end it wasn't a Dutch but an Austrian couple who met the Hepworths' requirement of having *'something to put into the business'*, as well as sounding *'thoroughly pleasant types'*. This family would come out when Tasha was five, by which time her speech would surely have caught up and she'd be ready to start elementary school in the company of a chosen Islander companion the same age, as well as the European children. Diana made enquiries in advance about correspondence education, and set her team to work on the beautiful leaf building that was to become the schoolhouse, herself setting in all the posts because Islanders, she believed, were incapable of seeing straight lines as all they ever saw was the horizon, which wasn't straight.

Tasha's general health improved by leaps and bounds – Diana had been told that if she didn't have heart surgery, she might live a normal life until she weakened, then died, at around twenty-one – but problems with speech persisted, and not, it seemed, just because of deafness. *'Perhaps it's her exceptionally long tongue,'* mused Tom, as ever, to his sisters. *'Most consonants are beyond her, so Pussy is "Hoo-hee" and so on . . . But she can manage "n" and sometimes "b" – her triumph is "ban-an-na" . . . But of course it's mainly psychological . . . Consider: infancy with mother constantly present, scenery (Pigeon and the ship) unchanging . . . Suddenly mother disappears . . . then there's competition for Mummy when she finally sees her again, and that ghastly time in hospital . . . easy to see how insecurities arose . . . The books you sent are helpful, particularly*

Child Care and the Growth of Love, *but we're both sure nothing can be gained by further uprootings in search of "treatment" . . . Love, patience, peace and encouragement are what we're giving her. The only thing that scares me is the possibility the boys may overtake her. If they really talk before she does, she might give up . . . At the moment she plays with the babies as a baby, crawling . . . Could you send* Jemima Puddleduck?*'*

Throughout the children's infancy, Diana took all three down to the little beach in front of Pigeon. '*Tasha and Ross have marvellous crawling races,*' she effused to her American friend Amalie from crossing-the-Pacific days. '*Bressin tends to go off on his own . . . Tasha calls the twins "Orse" and "Bahin" respectively, which we've turned into "OssBiss".*' 'OssBiss', as they grew past the crawling stage, played with miniature dugouts like the local piccaninnis, but theirs had pretend outboard engines from the first, complete with string which, to Tom's delight, they seemed to know naturally how to pull in the proper fashion. Sibileh, the Reef Islander child selected as Tasha's companion – and adopted by her with joy – came to live on Pigeon full time. Tom described her as '*the arch-typical Picaninni: fat as butter, bright button eyes, fuzzy top, and a big smile. Her mother works in the local "hospital" – you should see it! – and only visits her daughter occasionally. They don't appear to miss each other at all.*'

The 'hospital' Tom referred to was a shack manned from time to time by a nurse qualified only to bandage wounds, but who held a sporadic supply of antibiotics to which Tom, with a persistent tropical ulcer on his leg, had frequent recourse. When packing for trading trips on the *AR*, he also took a supply of sleeping pills, as nights in remote anchorages were often plagued by mosquitoes as well as noisy parties ashore fuelled by beer now available from PIT. Tom may have been kept from sleep by business worries, too, for it was around this time that government-run co-operative societies began to operate in the Outer Islands, buying copra from small-scale producers, and Tom found impossible competition on his doorstep. '*Of course we can't pay the same prices as a subsidized operation,*' he complained to Dennis, his old friend, '*but the current DC is a stinker. I believe he goes ahead of where I plan to stop and tells the natives he'll take their copra at a better rate . . . one of those jumped-up righteous beggars who reckons he knows what's best for Johnny Native when he's barely out of short pants and I've been in the trade years.*'

This probably well-meaning servant of the Protectorate also proved less than understanding over matters relating to a licence to sell beer, and proper 'protection' of the Islanders from the abuse of methylated spirits. Islanders were meant only to purchase meths if they had a spirit appliance, which they must show. Common practice was for the same appliance to be presented on numerous occasions – in different hands. '*Of course I intended to pay my bloody licence,*' Tom exploded. '*These people have no idea how hard it is to mail cheques out here, let alone on time, and know* nothing *about the tricks these so-called "noble savages" get up to . . . What does he take me for, a lowlife criminal?*'

Tom was incensed – and perhaps afraid, too. In a furious letter to the same District Commissioner he outrightly accused him of '*attempting to use your position to run me out of business*'. It didn't help that occasionally an inspecting officer in Honiara turned PIT's copra away, with scathing comments: ' *"It's copra we wish to buy, Mr Hepworth, not mould."*' Again Tom railed that these people knew nothing of conditions in remote areas, and had no notion of the trouble he took to keep every bag of meticulously examined copra dry. The DC of greatest opprobrium visited Pigeon in Tom's absence, but refused Diana's invitation to lunch – delivered, startlingly, in a bikini in the government ship's saloon – or even to be taken on a guided tour of the little estate the island was becoming. '*Classic case of the envy of the herd for the individual,*' Tom concluded. '*We've met it before . . . you have to stay in your rut to be accepted . . . don't worry a button if a tidal wave makes a clean sweep through Honiara . . . no loss to anyone*' (this to his sisters who'd expressed worries about weather conditions) '*and we're unlikely to be affected on Pigeon, because the path of a cyclone is generally so narrow. Hah! Famous last words.*' It was perhaps fortunate that Tom couldn't see into the future.

There were always enjoyable family outings on Sundays to look forward to – a walk through dapple-leafed glades to show the twins the tethered pigs on the neighbouring islands, or a picnic in an exquisite bay a dinghy-ride away – but Tom began to set great store by the coming of 'the Austrians', as he referred to their new partners, a family named Wien with three children. Diana's enthusiasm for every new project, as well as her religious attention to maintenance of the island, never waned. She was utterly content in her little world, and said 'Pooh!' to whatever the – increasingly distant, for her – Outside World might think. '*She'd never dream of popping up to Honiara for a spot of shopping, or to meet other whites, from one year's end to the next.*'

But until there was someone else to do the ship's runs, Tom still had to go, and another thing niggling below the sunny surface of his life was the condition of the *AR*. More than once she'd been thrown onto reefs and sustained damage, and it was nearly time for her Certificate of Seaworthiness examination again. Would she make it? 'Roll on, the Austrians,' he'd say to Diana on the happy but increasingly rare occasions they had a peaceful night together, without Tasha or the twins disturbing them or the dog barking at passing Islanders.

'I know, darling,' she'd say, 'it will be wonderful.'

Diana's own letters of this time reflect cloudless fulfilment. She was, as ever, living up to her father's motto — one way, one heart — and a happy family life on Pigeon was her chosen path. But things had to get worse for Tom before they got better, it seemed.

While 'OssBiss' and Tasha were lapping up the benefits of endless sea and sun one perfect day in 1964 — the twins now walking, talking and nearly swimming — a distressing radio message crackled into their mother's ear. The floor of a shed Tom had built at Vanikoro had collapsed, and large amounts of copra — some belonging to the co-operative societies but handled by PIT — had been ruined, and Tom was blamed. Alone on the *AR* but for his labour, some of whom he described as '*bolshie*', Tom, his ongoing ulcer streaking his leg with red lines from ankle to groin, vented his frustration in letters to officials in Honiara, denying responsibility for the freak weather conditions which he believed caused the collapse. In private notes, however, he expressed less injured *amour propre* than weariness with the seemingly endless practical problems that bedevilled so-called Paradise. But Diana, ever resilient, was out in a canoe the minute *AR* was sighted, to supervise the task of salvaging whatever might still be usable of the now reeking copra. The redrying took days, and capricious tropical showers sent the Hepworths running day and night to cover what was laid out. '*Thank God Tasha's so busy with Sibileh*,' Diana wrote, expressing every working mother's dilemma of dividing time between children and work. Then even that happy relationship seemed threatened. While Tom was away again, to petition, scowlingly, the '*office beggars*' for mercy over their demands for compensation, word reached Diana that Sibileh's relatives had taken offence at some suggestion the child had stolen a biscuit, and would no longer allow her to remain in the Hepworths' charge. '*I'm MAD AS HELL*,' wrote

Diana in her diary, adding: '*I love little Sibileh! She's such a friend to Tasha.*' It had been planned, when the Austrian family came, that Sibileh would share Tasha's schooling, for nothing, and it was this that finally persuaded her wontoks to allow her to return to Pigeon. If Sibileh sobbed and flung about as miserably as Tasha did when separated from her sista, this could have helped, too. There had never been any objection to her friendship with Tasha, and the 'offence' at the stealing suggestion may have had more to do with brooding discontent over the Hepworths' use of stone, sand and mangrove wood, without always bowing to the ritual request process demanded by Kastom, than any actual accusation. '*They're* incapable *of being straightforward,*' raged Tom futilely when Diana radioed him about the problem. On his return from an unsuccessful trip to Honiara, during which his consignment of dried fish was also turned away, he attempted once and for all to settle the ongoing annoyance of 'natives' questioning his right to use local building materials by attending powwows that bored and exasperated him, and handing out a few more pounds. And things did seem to simmer down – for a while.

So much went on in, as Tom put it, the '*Hepworth Family Robinson's*' day-to-day lives that major natural events are mentioned only en passant. In 1963 there was an earthquake followed by a tidal wave which had considerable impact on other islands, including evacuations on Guadalcanal; in 1964 another quake and a dramatic eruption of Tinakula caused stirred seas in the immediate vicinity, and much speculation in leaf huts all over Reefs as to their cause. But these happenings took up no greater space in Tom's diaries than records of shells packed for sale by Diana in those years – thousands of tiger cowries brought to the store by piccaninnis and exchanged for sweets. Islanders who found old tins of coins buried under a dead man's hut knew these could be exchanged for more useful items, too, at PIT. The Hepworths took advantage of whatever came their way, because they never knew when the copra prices were going to plunge or when there might be another 'tambu' (ban) on the store. These sudden cessations of business usually had to do with the personal grievance of a headman, who'd tell people in his village not to go near Pigeon again until the ban was lifted. Tom's method of dealing with this was to call upon an Anglican Father to remonstrate with his congregation about how unchristian the tambu system was, and this often worked, accusations of old heathen ways upsetting the faithful. The kindly

Father also exorcised a 'Debbil' from one of Diana's labour huts, and blessed the new leaf house she built for a full-time cookboy, Paia, who joined the family in 1964. Tom had no Christian leanings, but was not against using religion if it helped smooth local relations. Diana didn't go to church either, but had a soft spot for the Father, who in turn knew he could rely on her to dress a wound if there was a drunken fight on Nandelli, and agree with him fervently about the evils of liquor. She did not, however, call on him for help when an event occurred on Pigeon that in other parts of the world might have made ugly headlines. When she was five, Tasha disappeared one day for some time, and was next seen crying in the doorway of her parents' room, with blood on her skirt. Her hymen had been broken by a man's hand.

Tom was away when it happened, and Diana, as at the time of the miscarriage, had been working alone through the Islanders' kaikai hour while the twins rested. She'd assumed Tasha was having a nap, too. Now she put down her tools and took her small, incoherent daughter into her arms. 'What happened, darling?' didn't bring a response, so she laid Tasha down and examined her. It was all quite clear, once the mess was cleaned up, and so was the identity of the culprit, because there was only one Islander on Pigeon at that time – one Jimson – and Tasha, Diana learned, had come from his hut. When Tasha was finally resting quietly – face to the wall in silence for the first time since her hospital experience – Diana opened her diary and talked herself into what may have been the only possible course of action. There were twenty other 'boys' in her labour force at the time, all due back to work in a quarter of an hour. *'Jimson, damn him, and how he's hurt her . . . bleeding still . . . I've got to try not to appear too furious, so as not to worry Tasha – but HE MUST GO . . . think quickly . . . I'll send Jimson, as if nothing's happened, to get another boy to work tomorrow . . . don't want to finish him too suddenly as I'm frightened Tasha may attach too much importance to her experience, then.'*

Next morning, when all three children were watching newly hatched chicks a short distance away, Diana, who hadn't been able to raise Tom on the radio and was the only European woman for hundreds of miles, in a deeply vulnerable situation, assembled and addressed all the men on her staff, announcing that something disgraceful had occurred. Flinging an arm out dramatically towards Jimson, and naming him, she told everyone exactly what he'd done –

and that she must '*finis' him*' (fire him) – because she wouldn't have workers who couldn't be trusted with children. For someone who'd not taken a deep interest in the Kastom practices of her neighbours, it was a masterly piece of psychological play. Jimson slunk away and wasn't seen for months. In earlier times, he might have been prevailed upon by his tribe to commit suicide, because that was what men did who committed a shameful act, and to hurt a child was shameful. As it was, he seldom reappeared in the Hepworths' lives until – with terrible irony – nearly twenty years later, when he was the only man available to assist an ageing and ailing Tom with the removal of his by then violently disturbed daughter from Pigeon Island to permanent psychiatric care.

It's not recorded if Diana allowed herself to weep in Tom's arms over Tasha's torn virginity at age five. '*I want to kill him*' was all that appeared in Tom's diary, and it's not hard to imagine his fist clenched round the precious Schaeffer pen his sisters sent, on the desk Diana had made specially for the writing of his book. '*It wasn't meant to be a story like this . . .*'

The Wien family arrived not long afterwards, exhausted but elated after their long trip from Austria, to follow their own dream of the perfect place to raise a family in the sun. Their first impressions, like the Hepworths', were that a more idyllic setting for early education than Pigeon would be hard to find. And Diana still believed this to be true.

13

Dreams

THE BOYS HAVE A PERFECT CAMPSITE FOR HALF TERM: POPPET. IT'S
like something out of an exotic Arthur Ransome dream – a raised green islet
with frills of foam at its base, box flowers all round and a ring of feathery palms
in the centre. No wonder Diana fell in love with Pigeon. Undeveloped – and
in all-softening evening light – it must have looked just like a larger version of
Poppet, with all its potential waiting to unfold in her skilled hands. Plus, she
was with the man of her dreams, and following the dream they shared . . .

Did the Wiens, who'd corresponded with Tom before quitting safe
jobs and a home to cross the world, have a clear picture in their minds
of Pigeon and the life there when they came, or only a hazy idyll?
What had their sea journey been like? Had they first seen Pigeon, as I
did, through eyes of fear and anger, or sailed up to it like the
Hepworths had done, when it resembled everyone's desert island
fantasy come true? I was wondering by now if it was possible for anyone to have a clear picture of Pigeon – from inside or out. But there
was no denying it *could* be idyllic for children. I had the evidence in
my own sons. Contrastingly, I was appalled by what had happened to
Tasha as a little girl, and it took a while to accept that how Diana had
handled the assault was the only way. Tangypera had another slant on
it. The culprit, Jimson, *was* metaphorically 'cut', even by his own clan
for a time, but, just as the Hepworths' store was considered fair game
for theft, their offspring were less liable to attract vengeance for

wrongs done to them than the Islanders' own. I'd consulted Tangypera, in a roundabout way, about safety before allowing Joe and Benji alone on Poppet. His response was both flattering and revealing:

'I've already told you, the elders have decided in your favour.' This meant that we, in some obscure way, were under a form of protection the Hepworths were not – or at least not Diana and Tom and Tasha, all those years ago. It also explained why nothing was stolen from our place.

'Eniwae,' concluded Tangypera, 'evrifela lav piccaninni b'long iu.' He shrugged and picked his teeth, throwing away this announcement of general affection for Benji and Joe, as if it were unnecessary to state. I asked about Ross's children, and received the expected reply that they were Reef Islanders, whatever shade. There was more hesitation about Ross himself, Ben and Tasha. Tangypera went distant, then said succinctly:

'Ross oraet. Ben samtin'-nartin'. Tassa sik.'

I would pursue Tasha's story in due course and I knew Ross was popular, but the dismissive attitude to Ben was curious. 'Samtin'-nartin'' was hardly a compliment, meaning loosely: 'neither here nor there'.★ But he'd donated money to the church and was a fine fisherman. Didn't these notch up points in his favour? Tangypera explained. People didn't think much of Ben because he disparaged Kastom ways. He did not, in local minds, belong to Reefs in the same way Ross did. How had one twin come out more or less wholly 'Islander' in his outlook and persona; the other so unequivocally 'white'? Both brothers had played with Melanesian friends under the palms when little, and speared fish to cook over campfires for snacks just as Islander children had done for three thousand years or more – and like Benji and Joe did in the 1990s.

The night Joe and Benji went to Poppet for their half-term camping expedition it poured with rain, blotting out the islet behind a heavy indigo curtain, so I was unable to see if any frantic little silhouettes were waving. But we'd discussed this eventuality – several hours' rain in the twenty-four were normal – and the boys had our tent. They also had a cauldron, with rope attached, for hauling

★ Like many Pijin expressions, 'samtin'-nartin'' can mean different things at different times: 'storm in a teacup', 'nothing to get worked up about', 'unimportant'.

goodies up the side of the steep coral cliff that was Poppet's base, and a stack of banana leaves picked on Nandelli earlier in the day as plates and pillows. At dawn, I glided out in a kayak on the high tide to check they were all right. Poppet had its own red feather birds, geckos and squeaky flying foxes, and an inimitable view over the blue horizon. I 'trod water' with my paddle at the Edge of the Reef until the lorikeets had completed their morning flap, the sun was beginning to run lazy fingers of warmth up my back, and the natural moment arrived for the boys to wake.

'Hi, Mum! Have you brought more bananas? Something squashed ours, and crabs got into them . . .'

I'd brought fresh water too, although they'd wisely caught some in their cauldron. Could it really be true, I wondered vaguely, gazing up into Joe's improbably shiny morning face, haloed by a palm against the lightening sky, that houses in Scotland didn't have water catchment systems built in? Did Scotland still exist? It had to.

'I'm going to see if there's a message from Magnus yet. See you later.'

'Yup.'

Benji hadn't bothered to get up but muttered, 'Yerp,' sounding contented. Later he explained he hadn't slept much due to noisily scrabbling crabs, but after Joe had gone round on a dispatch mission with his spear in the morning, they'd both lain in a dry spot munching bananas under dopily dripping palms and nodded off again. Just as well, as they were out late that evening attending preparations for a feast in honour of a friend's first significant haircut – and away again to be present at the opening of umus before the following dawn. At Pigeon Island School, Peter organized lessons for Joe and Benji that would keep them on track with peers back home, but outside school they were learning other things, too. Like how Reef Island children, with no television in their leaf huts, no money and little hope of education past primary stage, had an endless capacity for self-invented fun – and basic survival skills down to a fine art before they were ten.

I'd had a message from the guardian angels but nothing from Magnus himself yet, and longed to hear. Tilting my satellite phone dish skywards was routine. So long as I'd stored sufficient solar energy in batteries the day before, there was rarely a problem making a connection in the great blue beyond. My laptop had a voice which let me know, in seductive tones, if I had mail. Sometimes, on my bumpy coral perch in the middle of nowhere, I giggled when I heard this, but today I whispered: 'Yippee!' because there was, at last, word from Magnus. He described how he and Graham, when it became 'choppy' on the *Southern Cross*, had lain steadying each other across a row of seats on deck, because it was unbearable to go below where everyone was puking. Then he'd eaten vast amounts of Vanuatu-grown beef in Honiara, and floated home to Scotland in a blur of freebie airline computer games. It was another world, and some of the influences he would come under there I dreaded. Despite some of what I read in Tom's diaries, I still thought remote islands, on the whole, safer and simpler for children than the Big Wide World. But I'd accepted that the Big Wide World (albeit with carefully organized shelter) was the place for Magnus now. It just seemed too long until I'd see him again, and – as had happened frequently over the years since he came into my life – I found myself wishing I had someone to share parental feelings with. Maybe not only parental feelings either. Intense working hours interspersed with lazy reef walks under hot sun, and reading and dreaming through warm, moonlit nights, filled my time richly, but still left an ache. I was familiar with the peculiar tug of a vacancy in the heart, but now my body, so long latent, seemed to be making tugging movements of its own, too. In a disturbing direction.

Tuin, in my twenties, taught me how to walk: the heat, and soft sand under my feet, rolled a new, softer rhythm out of me, unlike anything a pavement could do, and now Pigeon is renewing the process – with dance steps added. I'm golden from head to toe; sharp angles are gently rounded by massive consumption of pawpaw; my topknot is blonded to a bright plume, and even my pubes are sun-streaked. I accepted all this as my due on Tuin. I was young, the island was exotic, and bursts of sensuality not surprising. But now I'm a mother of three, in my mid-forties, with a peculiar spine. Only it doesn't feel peculiar here. With unlimited hydrotherapy at every high tide, this is the ideal environment for it. And something in the atmosphere is working on other parts that haven't felt quite happy with themselves for years, too. I'm startled in the night by dreams full of intimate slidings with other heated, slippery bodies, and when I wake the dreams don't end. I duck under the leaf thatch round to the bathroom and give my face a cool morning splash with rainwater, then nip into the kitchen to heat water for tea. But my fingers follow, and stroke, almost unknowingly, where droplets of water have run down over my breasts, and I return to the bathroom to stare with sleepy amazement at a face in which the eyes seem larger, and the mouth sensitized, so that a finger tracing lips then strays to discover a hipbone too long ungripped. My breasts are swollen too and much of the centre of longing. When I wake like this, I seek the comfort of the sea, which can't grant the release I crave but touches me all over with gentle pressure, easing the ache . . .

My fantasies were graphic and had a lot to do with Ben's copious chest hair. Perhaps there was something of the skewed missionary spirit working in me too, for I imagined that, with arousal (and boisterous fulfilment), his smokescreen of over-protested faith might somehow be cleared and he'd accept his place, with a lighter, gladder heart, among more normal men. But of course it was just his 'difference' that attracted me. Had he been an ordinary, lusty thirty-eight-year-old, who perhaps cast the odd flirtatious eye over his parents' aunty-aged biographer, he wouldn't have appealed. It was the secrecy of the man, the mystery – and his beauty revealed only in the sea – that drew me, night after night, into heady tunnels of erotic imaginings. Even at my desk in the daytime, sometimes, I felt suddenly scorched with desire and could no longer work. Then I walked it off – or went to see Ross. Ironically, Ben's twin and I could crack naughty jokes cheerfully for hours, with no sense of awkward-ness. Ross emanated healthy fulfilment; he was safe. It was his near-silent, apparently lustless but deeply sensual and physically promising brother who felt dangerous to me. I don't know how attuned Diana's antennae were, but sensed she wouldn't be averse to her troubled son receiving a little womanly therapy.

'Take your tea up to Ben's office,' she'd say. 'I'm sure he'd like to talk to you. Or Lanebu could put two chairs on the West Patio, if you'd prefer.'

It made me smile, it was so obvious, but also so ingenuous, and behind it, I knew, was a mother's care. Also, Diana desperately wanted things to work out right on Pigeon. Even after all these years it was still her dream island, and she wanted it to go on being a dream island, through one of her children, after she'd gone. Maybe, subconsciously or otherwise, Diana was even hoping I'd take her place eventually, as First Lady of Pigeon.

Joe and Benji, whose total absorption into Island life left little time for more than an affectionate hair ruffle for or from boring old be-spectacled Mum, announced out of the blue after their half-term break that Pigeon Island School had a new pupil, older than the rest and keen to meet me.

'Can she come now? We want to show her our photos from Scotland. One day she wants to travel – like us.'

Christine Hepworth, who'd been living until recently with her mother in Honiara, came as a big surprise, and no surprise at all. She was Ross's fasbon, his eldest child by his first wife, and was – as far as possible for a golden-skinned girl with cascades of rippling black hair – the image of her paternal grandfather, and seriously attractive as a result. There were Tom's wide-set clear brown eyes and his strong, compact body – but in female and half-Melanesian form. It was entrancing, but confusing. And that, I was to discover, was Christine all over. Within half an hour at Tasha's House, she'd announced she wanted to come and live with us in Scotland, and asked if I'd be like an aunty for her, to talk about women's issues ('evrisamting b'long mere') because her mother was a long way away, and it was against Kastom to talk to other wontoks first about such things. I said I'd try. She was sixteen, and named after the Hepworths' first governess, who taught Ross, Bressin and Tasha on Pigeon after Tasha had finally had her heart operation in New Zealand in the late 1960s.

14

Disasters: 1964–1971

FROM THEIR CORAL EYRIE ON NANDELLI POINT AND FROM DUGOUTS passing to fish at the Edge of the Reef, Islanders observed the new arrivals on Pigeon, in the season of Bigwinds (cyclones) in 1964, and reported to one another on their every act – and that of Missus and Cap'n Tom. The Austrians, in a family group, waded across the channel between Pigeon and Nandelli to church their first Sunday, looking very white, and gave fervent thanks for their safe arrival. They also made an impressive donation, and shook hands with the Anglican Father. It was noted they prayed every night on Pigeon, too, and some Islanders wondered if they'd bring the Hepworths to church next time. But although at first they kaikaied with Missus and Cap'n and toktokked quietly, with smiles, it was still the season of Bigwinds when the man with the moustache's voice – and that of Cap'n Tom – grew louder, and there were frowns. When there was shouting, the new white woman hustled her pale piccaninnis away and cried alone on a rock.

'Wanem hemi hapen nao?' the Islanders asked each other (what's going on?) as, soon after New Year 1965, the man was seen paddling a dugout to the side of the visiting *Southern Cross* and whispering to the bishop. Money changed hands, and the man sent many letters. Cap'n Tom, seen watching it all through binoculars, talked to the bishop himself afterwards, and looked at the envelopes.

After less than four months on Pigeon, the Wiens were desperate to get away, and Tom, who'd so looked forward to their arrival, couldn't wait to see the back of them either. He couldn't let them leave, however, until some of the jobs they'd agreed to share were done. Wien, he wrote his sisters, was '*100% useless*' when it came to mending engines, '*pretty hopeless with crocs, too . . . AND has a foul temper*'. The wife had seemed prepared to muck in at first but had been '*odd*' about teaching Tasha alongside her children, and displeased Diana by administering first aid to Islanders without consulting her first. Wien even thought it should be up to him to decide when a store trip round the islands should be made. He expected to be treated like a partner, not an employee, and objected to the lack of autonomy in his position. A proper partnership may have been the Hepworths' original intention, but there were financial controversies, as well as personality clashes, from the first. The point of the Wiens' coming was to ease matters by spreading the workload – and putting something into the business – but, owing to a demand by British officials on Guadalcanal for a sizeable deposit against possible repatriation costs, they arrived not only penniless but in debt. The Hepworths, accustomed to the vagaries of officialdom, might have been content to live with this situation until the Wiens had worked off the debt, but had little patience with their fussiness over rations offered for sustenance in the meantime. '*You can live on a couple of dollars a day,*' Tom had enthused in his letters to the couple when discussing their imagined mutual dream of contented co-existence. This was true. What was difficult for the Wiens to accept was just how simple 'the simple life', Pigeon style, was. Diana may have been operating an anachronistic system, based on wartime rationing memories, but if she could live happily with it – and look how healthy she was – why couldn't they? If they weren't fit, it had nothing to do with diet – here she cited the improved health of the nation on rations during the war – they should exercise daily like her, and drink more rainwater and bushlime. But the Austrian children's faces puckered at the unaccustomed sour drink, and they devoured a week's worth of sugar in two days, their mother asking for more. Tom recorded an exchange that took place when he took Wien for a '*man to man*' on the beach one evening, after Diana and Mrs Wien had virtually come to blows over cookies that had been consumed too quickly.

It had been raining, and the palms shone like snipped black satin against the sky. To Tom, this was Home, and beautiful, and he couldn't understand why these people were objecting to some temporary '*making do*'. He'd try to '*bring the fellow round*'. Wien slapped insects from the latest coral nicks in his shins, and snorted phlegmily. He claimed that, among other ills, he had tropical flu, and said the island and the life there wasn't what they'd been led to expect. Stung, Tom denied any misleading, and brought out copies of letters to prove it. '*Of course it's not Heaven all the time*' was written in one, causing Wien to explode. Pigeon was very far from Heaven, in his view, most of the time, which caused Tom to bristle with injured territorial pride. '*I told him he must control his temper and learn to adjust to us if he wants to stay. Not vice versa. He expected me to go halfway to meet him. I said No, why should I? and he started yelling again . . . good riddance, I say.*' It was agreed that they should part. But leaving Reef Islands in a hurry is easier said than done. The Wiens had made their arrangements with the bishop – and, as Tom suspected, written off in nineteen directions looking for another position – but still had to wait until the next ship's visit to pack their bags. And during that waiting period, separated from each other because Tom had persuaded Wien to make a trading trip – on a small sailing boat, the *Seaspray*, acquired for local sorties – they had a serious storm to ride out. The storm in which the *Arthur Rogers* was lost.

In a folder marked '1964', Tom kept copies of letters to companies which promised wonders from timber treatments. As predicted, the *AR* hadn't met the requirements for her seaworthiness certificate that year, and Tom had been told she must have the worst wood replaced – an operation out of the question financially. We don't know how the 'miracle cure' manufacturers responded to Tom's entreaties to '*save a good old ship and, incidentally, my livelihood*' nor whether she would have passed her test second time round, for, in March 1965, '*Ole Debbil Sea finally caught up with the* Arthur Rogers', and Tom wrote an in memoriam:

'*She was in her usual anchorage in Mohawk Bay, when wind and sea got up. I went aboard to move her to a sheltered spot, slipped the cable to save time, and put her into gear, but the engine stalled . . . Three times I restarted it, and each time it failed. . . . The ship drove swiftly down the wind, and struck . . .*' Despite this first injury, Tom thought there was a chance of refloating her when the weather moderated. But it worsened. All night there were vicious squalls, until one great violent rush of sea lifted all seventy foot and thirty-odd tons of Brixham trawler, complete with store goods, copra and memories of over a decade as a home to the Hepworths, a ship's length further up the reef. '*An unlucky coral head took the full weight amidship, and stove her side in for several feet.*'

Diana looked out, saw the racked frame arched like a body in mortal pain over the coral, and said quietly: 'That'll be the end of her.'

But it wasn't quite. The *AR*'s bulk lay with spine broken, battered in front of their eyes a little more every day, until one morning they woke up and saw her mast crumpled over her in defeat – not waving any more, but ready to drown. The weather was calmer by then, and so were feelings Diana had about this loss, for she rowed the children out to '*view the wreck*' and started the long, painful but practical process of salvaging anything of use.

'Look, darling – silver lining,' said Tom, roping the generator to shift it ashore. Now they could have electric light on Pigeon, and Beethoven. Diana nodded and they clasped hands briefly – the *AR* had been the scene of their first lovemaking – then set to and cut out so much planking they could floor a house with it in future years. It was like butchering the carcass of a loved one for recycling – brutal but necessary on occasion, at sea – and, in a sense, it meant she never died. Anyone visiting Pigeon today may find themselves standing on part of the deck of the ship that brought the Hepworths to it, half a century ago. '*Requiescat in pace*', Tom ended his elegy, and circulated it to all who'd sailed in her, eliciting pages of commiseration from members of the all-girl crew. But on the copy sent to his sisters, he added: '*For your ears alone, it is in many ways a "happy release". She was getting ever more expensive to maintain – and of course, is insured, though only for £10,000. I say "only" because that won't go far these days to buying a new ship. So maybe we won't bother.*'

They didn't bother. The *Seaspray* was adequate for short trips, and the insurance money was invested in land in New Zealand, on which Tom and Diana would build flats to generate enough income to enable them to send their children to senior school when the time came. In the sort of life the Hepworths led, perfect rainbows, terrible storms and surprising silver linings were fairly familiar phenomena. And when they mourned, it was never for a moment longer than they needed. But the Islanders of Nenumbo, Nandelli and Nola slapped their own cheeks, gasping, when the *AR* drove onto the reef. How could anyone doubt now that the Debbil of Mohawk Bay was fully roused in wrath? The more thoroughly converted scurried to church and said prayers, as at a funeral service, over the *AR*. But who knows what went on in the hearts of the Kastom landowners of Pigeon, and what other gods they'd been petitioning to strike at enemies on their behalf since 1957? The death of the *AR* may not have been only the answer to Tom's secret prayers.

On the departure of the Austrians, Diana became headmistress of Pigeon Island School. By the time the twins were five, she had them beginning to read and do simple sums, and Tasha, at eight, and the Island children (a companion for each of the boys was chosen) weren't too far behind. In the face of what others might consider a double disaster – the '*unfortunate mistake*' of the Wiens, and the '*tragedy*' of the *AR* – Diana's resilience triumphed again, and Tom found time to doodle a word sketch to his sisters, demonstrating the solid domestic happiness underpinning everything in their lives. '*We've recently installed our treat of the decade – a bath, which involved shipping a water tank and cementing a base, not to mention plumbing . . . I help, but the bulk falls to Diana, because I have the accounts and operation of Seaspray, but this sort of project is fun, and there are no Building Inspectors to interfere. Little of our house would "pass" but it suits US . . . The bath is a huge success. On Saturday nights it's filled, heated by an outsize primus, and all three kids enjoy a lovely wallow together. Then it's refilled and reheated, and it's Mum and Dad's turn. Afterwards, all the small wounds, known as "Ows", are dealt with because, in the Tropics, every scrape has to be watched or will go septic. The children then have a splendid screaming dash-about, and are ready for bed . . . By the way, did I tell you about our pet Pigeon Island pigeons? Ross has a lorikeet, too, that sits on his head.*'

Beyond the bath, the snug beds lengthened with planks as each child grew and the palm-thatched cargo shed they now called home – although they'd not given up hope of building a better one – the Solomon Sea roiled, swallowed its bounty, and soon cast up a pleasurable new challenge for the Hepworths in the form of an avalanche of letters arriving on the copra ship, which – usefully – now visited every few months, obviating the need for Tom to trek to Honiara frequently. These were replies to 'homeswap' advertisements Tom had placed in New Zealand, where, before long, they must return with Tasha for her operation. There was no shortage of couples ready to open their semi-detached suburban hutches to the Hepworth family in exchange for a South Sea island for six months, but Tom didn't want another Wien fiasco, so sternly weeded out anyone sounding remotely idealistic. In the end he opted for a practical conjuror/carpenter and his wife – the bubbly lady in a sequinned costume he sawed in half. In the absence of the Hepworths, it can only be imagined what a hit this professional couple's practice sessions made with the Islanders.

Diaries were abandoned during the six-month stay in New Zealand while Tasha underwent heart surgery and the five-year-old twins had their first taste of 'civilization'. But Tom did tell his sisters of the wonder on Ross and Bressin's faces and, free as they were from the distress surrounding Tasha's first exposure to the ways of the West, implied it was all a grand adventure. Tasha was sad to be parted from Sibileh, with whom she played at 'being brides' at Kastom weddings, but her parents assured her that this time there was no question of her being shut away – Diana had organized a job for herself in the hospital kitchen – and that she'd feel so much better after the operation it would all be worth while. The last six weeks on Pigeon had seen Tasha laid up on a lounger with a high fever. She'd been carried about the island by two girls employed for the purpose, and Diana had been obliged to administer massive doses of streptomycin by injection, as she'd been warned the 'fever' might be endocarditis, which in Tasha's condition could be serious.

The operation looked, initially, as though it had been an un-qualified success. Within weeks of the mass of stitches on her small chest healing, she was running along a beach holding hands with her dadi and scrambling up a hill near the hospital for a picnic of such exciting luxuries as sliced bread and – oh joyous discovery! – chocolate. Tom and Diana couldn't have been more thrilled, and arranged for Tasha to experience some conventional schooling during the months she still had to stay within testing distance of the hospital. But here they struck a problem. The school announced unexpectedly that Tasha was 'disruptive' in class, and that dealing with her dis-charging ear was difficult for them. (Tasha had also had an ear operation, in the hope of relieving her deafness.) Then they said she had a 'learning block' – possibly as a result of her surgery. Angry at the school's rejection of her vulnerable daughter, Diana took Tasha riding with the twins and started work on a DIY sailing dinghy for the three of them, while hospital papers were shuffled and investigations made. Nothing very illuminating resulted, but it was confirmed that Tasha had 'learning difficulties', and the Hepworths decided that a governess must be found who would live on Pigeon and bring her up to normal standards gradually, in the environment she loved. Tom found a site for the flats they were to invest in, and the rainbow was without doubt encircling the whole family the day Christine Clement, a twenty-two-year-old teacher with a passion for challenges and total commitment to all-round childcare, walked into their lives.

As soon as Tasha was pronounced – physically – fully recovered, Tom took her home. Diana was to follow shortly with the twins. Father and daughter had a serene trip up from Honiara on a cargo boat, with Tom relieved not to be at the helm and Tasha chatting nineteen to the dozen to Islander friends in her own special brand of Pijin English. Once back, they were meant to pursue a little learning, but as Tom found this tedious and Tasha frustrating, they soon gave up. Now the homeswappers were gone, when Tom wasn't working in the store they played with the kittens they both loved, and enjoyed tin-and-fish combination cookery. As he confessed to his sisters, Tom spoiled his beloved firstborn unashamedly at this time. 'She's not gormless,' he wrote, 'but who knows if she'll be "stuck" with a six-year-old mind, or if her "block" will crumble now she's back where she's happy?' He concluded on an upbeat note: 'Well, Dumb Blondes seem to get by OK.' The holiday ended when Diana, Christine and the twins arrived, and Tasha once more faced competition for her parents' attention from her brothers, as well as the thousand and one jobs awaiting Diana – and not yet begun by Tom – on Pigeon. But she found a sympathetic friend in Christine, who welcomed the more shyly offered affections of her Islander pupils too, and it wasn't long before the bikini'd figure of the pretty young New Zealander was constantly surrounded by worshipful piccaninnis of all ages – but with Tasha always closest, and often clinging physically, to her gentle heroine.

Under Christine's hands, a garden of scented flowers sprang up outside the leaf schoolhouse (all Diana's early gardening efforts had failed, with the exception of the hibiscus hedges – Debbil, said the Islanders; poor soil, said Tom) and exotic collages of land- and seascapes soon covered the classroom walls. Puppets with hollowed coconut heads were fashioned, and theatrical shows performed; music and maths were taught with the aid of shells, and Christine petitioned Diana and Tom to let her take the children for an 'educational/fun' trip on a mission ship all round Reefs. They said yes, delighted with the progress they saw, especially in Tasha, and everyone was happy. Christine was contracted to stay on Pigeon for two years. In the course of that time she made learning such a pleasure that Bressin, in particular, often stayed in the schoolhouse studying long after hours, and she transformed even days of lashing rain into something to look forward to, by making a cosy corner and reading Tolkien out loud. But at the same time as extending to the children the benefits of semi-conventional education aimed at helping them fit in wherever they found themselves later in life, Christine acknowledged the unique educational attributes of microcosmic island living, not only on Pigeon but further afield, among their neighbours. Kite-flying in a tropical gale, from miles of bare reef, was a special perk of remoteness, as was observing how the resources of the area were consumed, regenerated and conserved. Christine taught the Islanders of Nandelli to do the Twist (it was the late 1960s now) and, in exchange, learned from them how to make leaf jewellery and cassava pudding, and sat up in a Kastom circle with an entire village, plus the three Hepworth children, watching the moon and explaining about the American landings there. The Islanders found the idea of human beings in non-spirit form reaching the mother of tides hard to believe, but that they liked Christine was in no doubt, and 'stori-ing' with her was immensely popular. To them, myth and fact were as real as each other, in many cases. She laughed, they laughed, and they all held hands. Perhaps the Islanders hadn't realized white people could be like this – joining in, sharing, and respecting Kastom ways. What is certain is that when the Mohawk Bay Debbil struck again, it hurt everyone in Reefs, and, unlike the loss of the *AR*, on this occasion there was genuine mass sorrow – and fervent attempts to help – as well as fear. One night when Christine was floating under the stars she loved to study, her small dugout drifted away. And the Debbil tortured her for five days and nights before what was left of her was washed up and found, by other Islanders, seventy miles away.

This time, Tom wasn't away on a trading trip when the horror happened, but in Honiara sorting out paperwork that would allow Christine to stay a third year. For once he was making promising progress with bureaucracy, when a garbled message reached him that this girl of whom they'd all grown so fond was missing, believed drowned. Frantically he tried to contact Diana, but radio communications were down and air-sea rescue services would divulge little beyond the fact they understood the young woman had been missing a full night already, so had conducted only a brief search during the morning then given up, as survival was deemed impossible. It had been a blowy night, there was a swell on, and if those hadn't tipped her to the sharks, her dugout would have been smashed on the reef. What was she doing out in it at night anyway? Hardly sensible.

'Where exactly did you search?' Tom demanded, containing his irritation at their admonitory manner. He may have looked to the neat, disapproving officers like a scruffy Outer Island oddity, but he knew the waters around Reefs like the back of his hand. His was coral-head-and-tiny-landing-channel knowledge, not guesswork based on an old Admiralty chart.

'We followed the course of wind and current – naturally, Mr Hepworth.'

'*Captain* Hepworth,' Tom snapped. 'Are you aware that the current patterns in that district are unique – that the drift may have been anti-clockwise, despite what your books say? That's certainly the local belief.'

They didn't give him much of their time – a captain who'd lost his ship and gave credit to 'local beliefs'. But while he was in their offices, another message came. It was second-hand but originated, Tom knew at once, from Diana. '*Don't believe dead. No dugout found.*'

'There!' said Tom. 'A broader search should be conducted at once.'

But as far as the officers were concerned, it would be pointless. Not unkindly, because they realized sentiment was involved, they explained to Tom that *scores* of dugouts had gone missing between Reef Islands and the larger groups over the years, and the vast majority had never been traced. It was impossible; not so much a needle in a haystack as a matchstick in the ocean. Sorry, captain.

Tom would have given anything, at that moment, to have the *AR* back. The *Seaspray* had been lost too by now, but that was such a minor event in comparison it rated no more than three lines in his diary, plus the strongly worded avowal that there would be no more sailing ships for the Hepworths. Now he cursed his helplessness. He knew Christine was very able in a dugout, a strong swimmer, and – most important – not someone to give up. If she were out there still, she'd be fighting for her life, singing to keep up her spirits at night, dousing her head with water to prevent sunstroke in the day . . . Tom sat down with a whisky in the G Club, an expatriate hangout where he was rarely seen, and Diana never. There he was befriended by a government architect who pulled a few strings, but it was still ten days before Tom learned properly what had happened. And during that time he'd been forced to accept the 'missing believed drowned' theory, and had written both to Christine's parents – a eulogy on her qualities – and to his sisters. '*Our darling Christine dead. I can still barely believe it.*'

Diana, cut off entirely from contact with Tom, and frequently from Honiara, by faulty radios, refused flatly, at any point, to give up hope. While the children paddled daily in their dugouts to the clinic at Manuopo, where inter-island news could sometimes be picked up on a hand-wound radio set known as 'the hurdy-gurdy', she talked as perhaps she'd never talked before to Paia, her cookboy, his wife Doroti and the housegirls. 'Mi b'lieve 'em stap' (I believe she's still alive), she said repeatedly, in her awkward Pijin, as she went distractedly about her tasks – flaking fish for the dog; varnishing an occasional table – and, whether or not they said so aloud, they agreed. And through extended families all over Reefs, they put their belief into action.

The alarm had been raised when, after spending the evening celebrating Diana's fiftieth birthday with her, Christine had failed to appear for school the following morning, and the children said she couldn't be found anywhere. It was Paia, at breakfast, who noted the absence of the dugout, and mentioned that 'Miss Kistin' had been looking at the night sky. Diana stared at him and he gazed levelly back, an understanding passing between them. She didn't want to worry the children, but was immediately very worried herself. Christine was utterly reliable. Even if she'd gone for a morning dip, as she liked to, paddling to the Edge of the Reef, diving in to thrill and dare herself, then rushing back full of bright energy to start the day with salt water still shining in her hair – she was never late.

'Go and look at your books,' Diana instructed the children, 'and I expect Christine will be back presently. Go to Manuopo,' she said to Paia, 'and ask.'

'Doroti's already been,' answered Paia. 'People are looking everywhere.'

'Thank you, Paia. You may clear the dishes now.'

This was when Diana desperately tried to charge the batteries of the one radio that might get through to Honiara, achieving just enough power to send a Mayday at once, then to get a reply at midday about the abandoned air search and cable her objection. At lunch it was impossible to hide her feelings from the children, but she channelled her anxiety in such a way that there was no question of despair, only a need for patience – behaviour of the sort Christine would have approved – and frequent visits to Manuopo. That journey is an eight-mile round trip, and Tasha, Bressin and Ross made it morning and evening for over a week, believing, as their mother did, it was only a matter of time until there was news of Christine. Islanders from Nandelli and Nenumbo made up parties of dugouts, and paddled the sixty miles to Tinakula and back; further, to Ndende – their name for Santa Cruz – and extensively round the likeliest coasts of the nearer islands. And they risked much to find this white woman everyone loved; the air-sea rescue men were right: 'stakka' (many) dugouts and canoes of all sorts had been lost over the years; plenty of families drowned. During the day they paddled, passing on word through the bush grapevine to anyone met at sea or glimpsed on shore, and at night they sang. No-one recalls what the words of those songs were, but the spirit of them may have reached Christine, for Tom was right: she herself was singing, while she still had a voice, and when her voice gave out, her exhausted muscles kept her tipping craft upright, buoyed by the belief that others were still singing or praying with and for her, too.

She'd fallen asleep looking at the stars, but when she woke they'd receded, and she knew at once, by the swell and silence, she'd drifted beyond the Edge of the Reef, and could be anywhere within a hundred miles, depending on speed of wind and current, of Pigeon. She fought back panic and decided to try to rest while the sea was calm enough to allow her, without risk of capsize. She'd need all her strength to get herself to land, once she saw where it was, when dawn came. But before dawn she heard surf and knew she'd drifted near an island. Which island, though? And there was no comfort in the sound of surf in the dark, for if it was pounding over coral, she'd be better off staying in deep sea. By first light she was paddling with long, strong, determined strokes away from land, whatever land it was, for the particular crash of the waves was familiar to her. Christine, in her journeyings around the islands, had seen many a shoreline where not even the hardiest Islander would attempt to land, and this sounded like one of them. Midday found her far out on the deep, and exhausted. But she didn't dare stop paddling for fear of being driven back towards the coral, so she paddled on, hoping to see, each time she lifted her head, a kinder shore where she could rest. No shore appeared before the sun went down, and she allowed herself a few minutes' rest from the paddle which had blistered her hands, to put them together.

'Dear Lord, look after me, please. There's still much I have to do.' A simple plea, uttered with conviction, for Christine trusted God and his knowledge of her. She closed her eyes, and may have dozed for moments or hours. When she opened them again, the stars were out, and so were the sharks. 'Dear God,' she whispered, and lay rigid, arms clamped to her sides, feet folded in on one another, in the slender dugout swaying carelessly over the waves. But her rigidity in the little scoop of wood made it tip about. She knew about breathing and the art of balance, and knew she must try. That's when she began to sing again, but softly, not to hurt her voice, on the second night, when she also collected a little rainwater. The singing forced her to breathe deeply, so the more easily laden dugout floated gently between its consort of fins. Christine knew a shark's anatomy precisely, having inspected those landed near Pigeon: the skin like a rasp; the inbent teeth that ripped. Sometimes they came so close she could have touched one; sometimes vanished, then zoomed at her, only to swerve off course, as though teasing, at the last minute. No sound came from her mouth by midnight, and the moonlight was so thin its revelations only added to terror. She counted eight fins, dreading one would bump under her and pour her out to the rest. She shivered uncontrollably for minutes on end, then took deep breaths, went limp and poured sweat. Repeatedly.

Twelve hours later – another midday – her face was blistered, and she'd tied her bikini on head and shoulders against the sun. The shark had left in the morning, and she'd sighted land – a dark bouffant of green, promising more than coral – and begun paddling frantically. But it was as though for every twenty paddle strokes made, she was flung back nineteen, because the wind had risen now, and there was a scattering of white over the waves that pushed her easily, like little rippling fingers, back, and always back, to what she now knew, when the sun went down, would become her nightmare zone again. And it came, again and again, for three more nights, until she no longer knew what time was, or which was the worst horror, the grinning sun, under which her tongue swelled when her water supply evaporated and the tops of her feet bubbled like lava, or the black night, bringing the grotesquely beautiful arrival of the fins, trailing streamers of phosphorescence.

'I'm sorry, Tashi . . . Mum . . . Dad . . . Dear God.'

But she never totally gave up, and when an Islander on Utupua's remotest shore found her, she was curled around her dugout, holding it to her like a man, on her side. He carried her light body, and her paddle, which he couldn't wrest from her fingers, to his village, and the women laid her gently in the shade, on their newest leaf mat.

Tasha lay at night, a week after the disappearance of her teacher and friend, face to the wall, thumb back in her mouth. She only stared at the lessons set her by a new girl, fortuitously passing on a yacht, and only roused herself to get into her dugout after school. But her paddle dragged now, and the twins had to cajole her to keep up.

'Come on, Tasha, there might be news of Christine.'

'Sarrap,' she said.

The twins liked the yachties. The man was building them a tree-house overlooking Mohawk Bay.

'Hurry up, Tash.'

'Sarrap! Sarrap!'

For all their efforts, the children never did manage to gather much from the hurdy-gurdy radio, but the Islanders were still busy.

'Missus,' said Paia to Diana a few days later, arriving a little late to peel kumera for the evening meal, 'fela tokabaotem Kistin'.'

''Wea?' cried Diana, thrusting her paintbrush aside and striding towards him. 'What are they saying? *Where?*'

'Mi no savvy mas . . .'

'Don't say that bloody "mi no savvy", you fool!' She looked as though she'd shake him, but Paia stood his ground. Doroti was there too. Diana turned away, more miserable than angry. 'Just tell me what you heard – please.'

''Emi sae 'em' oraet – 'lo Utupua.'

Word said she was alive, at Utupua.

'Oh Paia! Doroti!'

Diana had spun round and her eyes were full, shining like lamps in a face gaunt from sleeplessness, and Doroti, beaming, stepped forward to hold in silence the trembling hands she'd seen so often clenched, or pointing at her, at Paia and all the Islander staff. It was – almost – an embrace of mutual joy, with Paia smiling beyond, and the Boo shell on Nandelli beginning to trumpet out the good news.

But on distant Utupua the first news Christine heard, when she came to, was that she'd been reported dead. And she realized her parents, in New Zealand, would be thinking this too. It was three weeks before Tom was able to reach her, and bring her back to Pigeon. Her body was much recovered by then, with little-and-often feeding by the Islanders, who'd pushed mashed pawpaw – the baby-food of the islands – carefully between her cracked lips when at first she couldn't eat, and applied coconut cream to her sun-shredded skin. But she was to re-experience her living nightmare whenever she tried to sleep, over the next month, and even though Diana moved another bed into the schoolhouse to be with her, and sponged her face when she cried out and shook, Christine could find no way of escaping the memories of the shark, and the sharklike sun, and the particular horror of the announcement of her own death, with her parents mourning prematurely. Mercifully, Tom believed, a coma broke this pattern. When, after thirty-six hours of being unrousable, Christine opened her eyes once more, she was calmer, but her paddling arm was paralysed, and she couldn't write a line home with her other hand without weeping. Although she half protested she was all right and couldn't leave the children, there was no alternative but for her to return to New Zealand. She needed to touch her parents, and for them to touch her.

'I'm sorry, Tashi . . .' she whispered to the suddenly sullen eleven-year-old '. . . but I'll find someone else nice to teach you.'*

That Christmas, celebrated with fewer of the shell decorations in casuarina branches Christine had been so good at, Cathy, the nurse from the original all-girl crew, who'd gained so much from her time on the *AR*, came to stay on Pigeon. She described Tasha at twelve as noticeably retarded – and her behaviour, slavishly affectionate one minute, moaning the next – as distinctly disturbed. Although her

---

* The above account of Christine Clement's ordeal was drawn from Tom's notes, Diana's memories, study of the area, and discussions with Islanders and with Christine herself, who would like it known that, despite her terrors adrift, her main memories of her time on Pigeon are highly positive.

speech had improved hugely under Christine's care, her thumb was often in her mouth now, shoulders hunched forward and toes turned in. It was impossible for Tasha to understand properly why she'd had to be parted from this big sista she loved.

15

Excursions

'YIPPEE! NO MATHS TOMORROW. WE'RE GOING ON AN EXPEDITION.'

Benji echoed Joe's pleasure by making his eyebrows dance, Reef Island style, to the pipings on his recorder. They were supposed to practise in the morning, on the Little Wharf, but tootled any time. Over a supper of turtle liver – not a favourite, but eaten for the iron – they told me Pigeon Island School was to be present at the arrival in Reefs, from Duff Islands, of the first traditionally made te puke (voyaging canoe) since Tom and Diana saw the last one still trading in 1957. They would set off with Ross at dawn to the expected sighting spot, and would not require packed lunches as there'd be a feast as soon as the te puke's bow touched the shores of Nufiloli, some six miles from Pigeon across the Deep Blue. The te puke itself, skippered by an eighty-three-year-old descendant of the legendary creator of these craft, must travel more than sixty miles, with only stars and wave patterns to guide him, through the night. A Hawaiian anthropological team, including a priestess, would video the event. I was invited along with the school.

Peter, quietly making an excellent job of bringing an initially speechlessly shy class of Reef Islanders close to the level of British primary school pupils the same age, had assembled his troupe by 5 a.m. at Ross's house. Mhairi had to dash back to pen chicks she was rearing out of the way of Stasi's jaws, then we were away, chugging at first between coral heads, then opening out to a cheer when we crossed the Edge of the Reef. Sixteen-year-old Christine Hepworth sat astride the bow of the motorized canoe, voluptuous in a black T-shirt sculpted by the wind, with dark ripples of hair streaming behind. Joe smiled when the hair tickled his cheek, and Kiyo sprawled full length beside her in the attitude of a devoted slave. There was a competition to see who'd be first to spot the te puke's crabclaw-shaped sail, and bets laid as to how many Duff Islanders would be aboard. Eight set off but only six arrived, and I thought of the first Pigeon Island Christine – Christine Clement – who'd suffered so, on this stretch of water, thirty years ago, when we gathered what had happened in the night.

The te puke, its hull blessed by a bishop, set off as planned, loaded with Polynesian-style offerings to Melanesian hosts waiting in Reefs. But Pacific Island generosity, when it weighs down a delicately balanced craft with vegetables heavy as stones, can be as dangerous as it is charming, and before they were halfway across from Duffs the sailors were in trouble. 'Throw out the women,' shouted the ancient navigator over the wind, twitching his kalico more comfortably around shrunken loins, and the anthropologists in the accompanying yacht, meant only to observe, had the unenviable task of bowing to tradition (women were less important than food on sea voyages, unless colonization was in the offing) but also behaving in a humane, twentieth-century manner. 'OK, but throw them this way,' yelled the tattooed Hawaiian priestess, spokeswoman for the chief anthropologist who was also the yacht's skipper. And time after time, across the moonlit deep, a rubber dinghy was passed on a rope close to the floundering outrigger, and the figures of two silently submissive Polynesian girls were waved, on strong arms, in its general direction. But the current was fast, and the proximity of the solid hull of the yacht a constant danger to the leaf-and-twine construction of the te puke. And when at last the two waterlogged women made it from te puke to dinghy to yacht, they were instantly sick in the anthropologist's bunk – for the next four hours. They weren't used to sailing in an enclosed space. When the te puke still wallowed, Paramount Chief Coloso Cruso Kaveia shrugged philosophically and turfed out some yams. With this sacrifice to the sea, the perfect proportions of the craft found their balance and the great leaf sail caught the wind, leaving the modern yacht behind. Perched on our bow, Christine spotted the speeding te puke first – looking from a distance like a raffia basket rigged with a knotted handkerchief – and gave the age-old Islander equivalent of 'Sail-ho!' Then we were all waving.

At Nufiloli, Peter promoted numeracy among his pupils by using leaf food parcels laid along mats for impromptu games in addition and subtraction. Language was also on the learning menu, with a child helping to translate speeches made by Nufiloli elders to welcome the Duff Islanders and us to their shores, but lessons were over for the day once the tasty mathematical units had been breached and the easily comprehended instruction to 'Fillimup beli b'long iu!' rang out. A mix of around seventy Reef Island hosts plus six Duff Islanders – the women were recovering in hosts' huts – and a sprinkling of Europeans tucked in, and afterwards a green lorikeet offered to clean people's teeth. Joe, flat on his back in the sun with a bird eating out of his mouth, was in seventh heaven.

In the afternoon, when the tide was out, a football pitch of sand lay in front of the village. On this, with the te puke drawn up at its edge like a mascot, members of the Duff Island crew teamed up with Nufiloli stars and soundly but in the best of sporting spirits beat the Reef Islands team, including Peter, Ross and almost all of Pigeon Island School. (Christine, understandably, didn't want to be the only female playing; besides, she was basking in the admiration of every shining-muscled Nufiloli youth not in the team.) I sat with Mhairi, who was sketching the pretty skeleton of the te puke with its furled sail, and drank in a scene I never wanted to forget. Beyond the football pitch, its size absorbing the cheerful players, tiny islands like Temutolaki played their trick of seeming to float on the horizon, and uncountable acres of brightest blue-green rippled away under glittering points of sun.

'Your Joe's fairly come on,' said Mhairi. 'You'd hardly know he had a hearing problem out here.'

'I know.' I hardly knew I had a spinal problem either. We were in another world, and I could see that Mhairi had 'fairly come on' too. Some people don't tan in the tropics and she was one of them, but she shone, kissed all over by the warm air, and her unfettered body, in a light wrap, was deeply relaxed. There was a sensuality about her now that I hadn't seen in Edinburgh, and when she rose laughing from the sea, with the last caress of a wave gleaming on her bosom, she was a great deal more wild water nymph than nine-to-five bank employee. I hoped she'd find ways of hanging on to what Reef Islands had given her when she finally got home. Peter maintained more formality – necessary in his position as instigator of some kind of discipline – but found personal expression through the mellow voice of his alto saxophone, which he played, adding to the surreality of island life, standing alone, in clean shirt and Oxford bags, on a coral outcrop near Pigeon's north-eastern tip. Often I'd stroll back from the reef or swim ashore to the dreamy accompaniment of Miles Davis.

Before the sun sank on the day of the Pigeon Island School expedition, the children raced through the shallows, cheering, as the flying fox population of Nufiloli flapped into the darkening blue like so many broken umbrellas, and I was invited by the Duff Islands chief to 'siddown' while he chewed the best of Nufiloli betel-nut, and the Nufiloli chiefs chewed the best of Duffs', and they 'stori-d'. At the end of a lengthy interweaving of myth and fact, involving the suckling of the creator of the te puke on the tail of an eel, and vivid mimicking of the forest bird carved on its prow, the chief told me his craft was strong because it was bound, not only by six hundred fathoms of natural cordage, but by the unbroken skin of a grandaddy ('granipapi') lizard. 'If people work like that, binding their strength into one, instead of making separate knots that chafe against each other, the spirit of our islands will be revived.' This was the aim of the Duff Islanders' te puke project, addressing concerns among elders that the younger generation was losing touch with Kastom values – and not finding anything satisfactory from the Outside World to replace them. I spoke to the chief anthropologist too, who believed in the benefits of reviving traditional arts but was aware that her presence, while necessary for co-ordination and funding, was not the ideal catalyst, because the Islanders would prefer to secure the continuation of their 'endangered' culture themselves. *'These Islanders were the most intransigent in the Pacific,'* an HMSO book said of Reef Islanders.* This implies belligerence, but may simply indicate a reluctance to bend the knee. The questions that came to mind after my toktok with the chief, and discussions with the anthropologist, were large, and none easily answered. All that was certain was that everyone on Nufiloli had a happy time that day – even the rescued women from the te puke, who finally emerged to have their hair wound into beautiful shell shapes by Christine.

---

* *Western Pacific Islands*, by Austin Coates, HMSO 1970.

★

One day not long after this, Diana sent a piccaninni to Tasha's House with a weathered-looking floppy disk which had 'Towards the Book' written on it in Tom's hand. She'd found it in a bag hanging out of ants' reach in his office, dated the year he died. But when I slipped it eagerly into my laptop, it revealed nothing – and wrecked the floppy-disk drive. Wanting it replaced if remotely possible, I made enquiries, under slanting columns of moonlight, on the southern tip of Pigeon that night. What a challenge to Compaq's Worldwide Care package. Did Reef Islands count as being of this world? My answer came back, under fuller moonlight, two nights later. They could get help as far as Honiara, but no further. The Outer Islands, it seemed, were not just on another planet inside my head. That same night, I had such an out-rageously erotic dream about Ben, I feared I might rise in wanton nakedness in half-sleep and attack him like a succubus. The mantle of my reawoken desire hovered dangerously over this vulnerable young man, whose own history I'd barely touched on so far, and I needed to get away to regroup. The school holidays were imminent too, and Peter needed a hepatitis jab, only obtainable on Guadalcanal. A good time for a break all round then. Christine gasped when she heard I planned to take a yacht past Tinakula, across the blue to Santa Ana and onwards, stopping off at dots on the map whenever we felt inclined, and eventually heading for the capital of the Solomons, to keep a date with Compaq.

'Can I come, Lusi? O please!'

I said yes, sensing a need in this stunning youngster to stand back a bit herself. She'd asked me recently how contraception worked, and her probable path was only too clear if someone didn't do something soon.

The vessel is fairly unspeakable – holes in the spinnaker, bent boom – but we're reaching some wonderful spots in it. Benji's learning to sail with a palm leaf, Joe's been swimming with dolphins, and I'm studying the history of these islands as we pass them, starkers beyond the mizzen. Only trouble is we told our latest host at anchorage, the chief of the Fanalei, about the dolphins, and now he's getting up a hunt. They decorate their daughters with the teeth here-abouts. What are you going to decorate me with, when we get back? You can't say I'm not giving your grandsons a rounded education . . .

I seldom wrote to my father, but this voyage made me think of him.

He'd have been amused by the Danish barman who'd hitched a ride in exchange for stints in the grubby galley, and would have enjoyed the sight of Benji at the helm of a forty-five-foot ketch, however decrepit, bawling out depths and holding an erratic course by the wobbling red anemone of a compass in gimbals, while the stars of the southern hemisphere streaked by. Organizing our temporary escape from Pigeon hadn't been easy, but past experience of life on an island had served me well. You get what you can out of anyone dropping by, in a remote situation, and when a yacht appeared in Mohawk Bay not long into our stay, I'd taken an e-mail address and traded shortbread for the promise that a batch of 'Pigeon Posts' (articles I'd written for the *Sunday Times* magazine) would be mailed for me. Then, when things had begun to crowd in on Pigeon, I'd tried out the address – belonging to a posher yacht – and word eventually reached the itinerant postman, who agreed to overhaul his vessel, fit in the trip before the onset of the cyclone season, and have us back in time for Magnus's Christmas visit.

It didn't occur to me that behind the sun-crinkled Nordic eyes and mahogany tan of Sven the skipper lurked a mind half kindly clown, half pirate. His idea of an overhaul, it transpired, was to fling just enough violet and lime paint – in suitably rough diamond shapes – onto a background of scraped hull to make it look as though *Loki II*, his ship, were in motley. Drinking water was caught through a Heath Robinson arrangement of Tahitian supermarket bags feeding hoses stuck down portholes, and the (very) token toilet, flanked by bulging nets of exotic fruits in various stages of ripeness, was presided over by a full-sized carving of a fierce-browed 'Vele man' (traditional hired killer) with no penis. Benji and Joe, excited by the idea of a month under sail, liked this strange doll, the dubious boat and their owner, who kept Asterix books by the chart table, and were thrilled Christine was part of the crew.

'We're like explorers!' shouted Benji gleefully as, on our first night, we anchored off Matema. One hundred years ago, this was one of the few islands in Reefs to be annexed without confrontation – a bottle containing the Proclamation was buried without resistance on the beach – which wasn't surprising, for its thin bush offered Matema's small population scant cover. When the wind was high, they were obliged to dig themselves shelters in the sandy soil – in which they were helpless if caught. There was no scope for the guerrilla tactics used on other islands to meet gunfire with spears. Even the tiny church was a square scraped underground. Here I was taken to 'mek prae' for the chief of Matema, who was unwell, then asked to examine him.

I was ushered past low leaf huts with lace curtains of purple convolvulus, behind which huge-eyed piccaninnis stared, to a hut set apart from the rest, its neat 'front yard' the size of a blanket tidied, as I approached, by a bevy of silently stooping female figures scratching the earth with twigs. Still stooping, they parted, making a corridor as one, like shoals of fish I waded through on the reef, and the eldest grasped the corner of a bin bag spread over a low entrance and pulled it back. It was dark inside, but the chief's eyes gleamed feverishly at me. He was young, with a beautifully sculpted face, but far too thin. Wordlessly, he held out a sweating palm for me to clasp, and ducked his chin for me to sit down. I'd been told his trouble was, loosely translated, 'a pain and a big testicle'. In fact, he had a swollen gland in his groin – displayed like a child, with more anxiety than embarrassment – but I guessed this was only an indication of deeper trouble, he looked so gaunt. Above our heads, wind tickled the palm leaves latticed to the roof of his hut with twisted twine. How terrifying Matema must be in a Bigwind – with no place to hide but the church, which I learned was usually flooded by waves surging from one side to the other. This man's clan had ridden out the last major cyclone singing, up to their waists in sea water, in that church, with piccaninnis perched on beams. They couldn't remember a year when they hadn't had to take cover at some point. But, unlike Mohawk Bay, Matema was said to be lucky. If it had a Debbil, it was benign.

I indicated that fresh water should be boiled, and made up a Lemsip sachet to try to bring his fever down. An old man with a ring through his nose, sitting in the shadows, rocked enthusiastically when I spoke of reducing fever (outim hotwan). This was the Kastom medicine man, who'd already sent to Tinakula for leaves that should do the same as the Lemsip – which he sniffed cautiously. Would I come back in the morning to see if either preparation had helped? In the meantime, please would I accept small offerings from the chief's piccaninnis; sorry there were no pawpaws, their trees had blown down. Shrinking the doorway now was a fuzzy ring of heads, and in a dozen outstretched hands were coconut husks brimming with lavender cowries. A woven basket was added to the gifts, and I was escorted back to the boat. Sven tried to radio Ross to say I thought the chief was seriously ill, but – like Diana trying over and over to contact Tom all those years ago – we had no joy. All we could do was keep trying. How many pic-caninnis must have died of infected coral wounds for want of a course of antibiotics; how many succumbed to malaria. But Matema was so small – a deceptively soft-looking cushion of green rimmed with white sand, supporting little fruitful bush – it couldn't have catered for a larger population; couldn't have supported families all of whose members survived to adulthood. Impossible questions arose in my mind again and, again, were put out of it by the sight of simple happiness *now*. Christine, Benji and Joe were sitting in a ring of Matema children on *Loki II*'s deck, peeling pana (a species of yam) and grating coconut on a spiked board, for Christine's delicious cocopana soup – and giggling their heads off, all adorned in freshly made leaf jewellery that would shrivel by morning.

After Matema, we passed as close as we dared to Tinakula, to feel its heat and our timbers shiver in the tremulous water round it, like a pan threatening to go from simmer to boil. In 1898, HMS *Mohawk* – whose officers annexed the volcano, though they raised no flag as it was uninhabited – were treated to a display *'which knocked Brocks Firework Display into a cocked hat'*. All we got was the curious pleasure of seeing plumes of smoke form and rise – at one point dividing evenly into one black, one white, decorative as holly on a Christmas pudding. Then Christine hooked a huge emerald fish on our trolling line, and in the time it took to get it aboard and its thrashing reduced to quivers, Tinakula was passed. Christine gutted the fish on deck, transparent scales shining on her brown thighs like sequins – and I noticed Sven looking the same way, caught his eye and gave him a lightly reproving look.

'All right,' he said, without resentment, revelling in the role of connoisseur of women, 'but she's almost overripe and will lose her freshness soon.'

I wondered if this was the way European men had viewed women of the Pacific over the ages – fruit to be plucked, then discarded when the 'freshness' had gone. Perhaps this was true of Polynesian girls, but no report I read of reprisal raids carried out by colonial powers included the ravishing of Melanesians. To the common sailor there seemed something forbidding about them: *'You would never know they was women apart from their bosoms . . . one place we saw, all their hair was cut short with bushknives, and the men's was long.'* The same diarist, William Cock on HMS *Mohawk*, describes strongholds built by Islanders in trees, with a *'twine ladder swinging no white man could set foot on'*. Whole clans took refuge on high, drawing the ladder up after them when headhunters came, and hurled sharp coral down on the trophy seekers, for heads were used to decorate huts and the more you had the 'bigger' man you were deemed to be. Certain European ships, finding resistance to recruiting in the South Seas, carried out head-hunting raids themselves, using firearms, and presenting swag bags of heads to chiefs in exchange for live young men as slaves. The Protectorate wasn't only conceived with power in mind: a *Daily Mail* 'special' of 1898 boasted 'Fourteen Islands for the Empire' and mentioned the administration of 'stern lessons to intransigents', but its creators saw a need to protect the 'savages' from less savoury examples of their own kind, too.

Watching chains of phosphorescence stream from the bow by moonlight or dozing in the shade of a sail after lunch, Joe fell into a dreamlike state on *Loki II*, but also became expert with the anchor chain, and was our luckiest fisherman. Benji was more excitable, but adapted no less easily to the simple routine of days and nights spent moving slowly over the bare blue camber of the Pacific. He loved taking the helm and attempting to furl flapping sails with his short arms, but at night he, too, returned to some cradled sense of earlier years, and insinuated himself onto my lap or Christine's.

'I love you,' he'd say matter-of-factly, and fall asleep.

'And I love all you guys too,' Christine would say. 'Take me to Scotland!'

It used to take Tom, in the *Arthur Rogers*, anything from one day to five to make landfall again after Tinakula, depending on the weather and his crew. We, hitting a lumpy sea and being mostly inexpert, took the longer time, and Christine and I were frequently to be found at the rail, re-offering raw fish suppers to the deep. Benji and Joe were happily oblivious, stuffing quantities of pancakes into their mouths and climbing as far up the rigging as Sven would allow, to be the first to spot the next island group. I'd never craved a wash so ardently as when Santa Ana was sighted, and could not have found a more ideal place to indulge the desire, for the speciality of this island was its freshwater lake, an unlikely oasis beckoning as alluringly as a mirage in a desert of sea. Christine and I, punting ashore bedraggled, were welcomed by bands of children who ushered us to a great brown pool glistening like a limpid eye, and there watched us soap ourselves all over, falling off overhanging tree trunks at the hilarity of the sight and, unasked, rubbing our clothes with stones to clean them. There was nothing the Makiran inhabitants wouldn't do to add to our comfort: please take some coconuts aboard; did we need our bushknives sharpened? Of course they'd make an umu for us to bake bread. All the facilities offered were stone age, but felt luxurious. I could have basked longer with my feet on terra firma, but Sven's schedule of having our trip over before the cyclone season made us press on.

We stopped briefly at Star Harbour, where we were discouraged from swimming as a male crocodile had recently been speared and his angry mate was still around. After this we were at sea proper again, but by now I'd found my sea legs and lay with my book absorbing the sweet sting of salt-laced sun on my skin, and letting it nuzzle away all thought until I felt like nothing but a vessel myself, for the silky attentions of warmly insistent elements. Unfortunately Sven, sensing my state, thought he could provide the final key to the unlocking of physical joy, and waved it at me fairly insistently one night, until I was cross. 'Come on, baby, live now,' he said persuasively, rocky muscles at my back, hands roguishly at roam. But though I might have burned for Ben's body – albeit without the complication of his head – in my lurid fantasies on Pigeon, I felt no desire for this freely offered slab of lust. I could see the beginning, middle and slightly grubby-feeling end of the story. Inevitably, this rejection caused temporary tension, but Sven was – or so I thought – 'free-spirited' enough to let it pass. Nothing, anyway, alloyed my sensation that we'd truly found a chip of heaven dropped in the ocean, when we approached Ugi Island.

Ugi conforms perfectly to the desert island dream. Sparkling water furls and flies over reefs guarding a sweetly ample bay seductive as an angel's breast for a boat to nestle in; palm trees loll so louchely they kiss the blue; dolphins frolic and dugongs quietly graze . . . I wrote this at anchor, at Ugi, while everyone else was away snorkelling, and before I knew that in the rainbow-hued channel between reef and beach killer currents ran; dead trees banked along the shore were cyclone barriers, and for every playful dolphin there was a shark in that candied-citrus-segment bay. Nothing is perfect, perhaps, except in the longing eye of the beholder

– even one as experienced as Diana Hepworth, who'd first seen Pigeon in its best light all those years ago. Yet she'd stuck it out through thick and thin, and still held that first image in her mind – the one she'd offered me in Scotland, and which I recognized, but not without some harsh realities as well. To date, Tom's diaries had recorded the loss of two Hepworth-owned ships to Mohawk Bay's Debbil, and I was beginning to suspect he felt that in some way he'd also 'lost' not one child to sinister forces, or even two – but all three . . . Between lovely, lethal Ugi and an uninhabited island, our next stop, I retired out of the sun's – and Sven's – glare to the aft cabin, where I journeyed back in time to look at some of the different angles from which people involved in Pigeon's history came.

From the diary of a Royal Marine, HMS *Mohawk*, 1898: '*The natives of these islands are different to others . . . Let a copper coloured savage shave his head in parts . . . gather such of his woolly hair as is not cut into frizzly tails which stand out like a fixed bayonet, dye some white, some scarlet, smear his face with soot and yellow streaks . . . put a grass mat round his loins, squeeze a dozen bangles upon his arm, hang a tortoiseshell ring through his nose and give him twenty arrows tipped with poisoned human bone, and some ornamented club . . . and this is the sort of ruffians that swarmed upon our quarter deck.*' Often a twenty-one-gun salute was enough to subdue Islanders into not molesting the hoisted flag and acceptance of Queen Victoria's protection, and those who showed defiance were '*filled with holes like the tops of pepper pots – and how they jumped!*' But pockets of objection, if not overt resistance, remained. Silence doesn't always mean consent, and the Islanders were practised at waiting – for generations if necessary. When a splinter group of the old enemy – such as the Hepworths – 'commandeered' Kastom land, it must have been tempting to wield whatever small powers still lay in 'intransigent' hands: a vested interest in the might of ancient Debbils – and the magic attributed to Reef Island women. For Tom, I'd discovered, was not beyond being persuaded that his sons had been led astray by more than fleshly passions. The sensual succubus of whom I'd been given a glimpse – from the inside – on Pigeon was not, apparently, a new phenomenon of the area. Ben, he reckoned, had been 'got at', as well as the more obviously 'gone native' son, Ross . . . But I'm jumping decades. I took myself away from Pigeon partly to view things there in the clearer light of distance, and ended up with a more complex picture by glancing both backwards and forwards in time. It was a relief to leave research alone and go walkabout on a small island which reminded me nostalgically of the real simplicity of Tuin, my old remote stamping ground in the Torres Strait, which had little history other than that of its gum trees and goannas. Joe, Benji and Christine accompanied me ashore and scampered up the sandy end of the island, while I headed for a patch of jungle.

Did I really live for a year on an island with not much more on it than this – a few sea-sucked bars of driftwood, smooth as soap; a spider's web of coral spreading in petrified grey skeins; a shake of greenery one end and sea, sea, sea all round – with not one yacht in sight, ever? I scrambled over the bony spine of the atoll to sit alone on the windward side, with nothing before me but sea and sky – and all that imagination could throw up from such emptiness. No wonder island peoples through the ages brewed creation myths from water. In parts of Europe, a maiden danced on the waves, coupled with a sea serpent, and from foam splashed out of them, like frogspawn, grew men; Tangypera's tribe, on the other hand, believed their ancestors were spewed fully formed from the deep, off the wildest tip of Nenumbo – complete with particularly impressive dugouts. And what of the godless, less certain of their origins or purpose, who found in small islands some kind of refuge from an Outside World that they, unlike the Islanders, had seen but feared more than loved – the Tom Hepworths, even the Lucy Irvines, of this world? Where I longed for some kind of faith, Tom seemed a purer cynic. Although he leaped onto the bandwagon of natural energy use, adding a wind generator and, later, solar power to back up the *AR*'s salvaged generator on Pigeon, it felt more like plain practicality than part of any philosophy. If you'd asked Tom Hepworth to 'Save the Whale' he'd have laughed, (*'and who'll save the human race from its own damned road?'*). Arrogance and affluence, he believed, were what bred such sentimentalism, and to want to 'save the world' or to believe there was a Saviour built in, you perhaps had to care about it more than he did. What he did love, transparently, was first his wife and little girl, then the twins. Whatever was important to them he'd work to keep, which basically boiled down to Pigeon – and bugger the rest. Tom thought it possible the Outside World would destroy itself with a third world war before his children grew up, so retreated from any sense of responsibility to anything beyond his island. Horrors such as Christine Clement's experience – brutal not only to her but affecting Tasha too, and staining 'Paradise' – served only to deepen his distrust of the idea of any well-meaning Higher Being.

I had a quick massage in a channel overhung by a cat's cradle of lianas dangling from palms, then padded along a vein of sand towards the beach end of our 'playing at *Castaway*' island, in search of the boys and Christine Hepworth. When I found them, I had to smile. With ruthless efficiency Christine had plundered the island of every useful item on it, regardless of yesterday or tomorrow, and was sitting proudly beside her booty, showing the boys how to plait twine ropes to carry pillaged firewood and knotting into a bunch all the coconuts from the single yielding tree. We like to think people who live on remote islands are natural environmentalists, and to a degree this is so – but they're natural survivors first, Hepworths and Reef Islanders alike, and if a genuine castaway found himself thrown upon this barren cay now, he'd die of thirst and be unable to kindle a fire because someone else had got there first. Simple as that.

'Well done,' I said to Christine. 'Your grandfather would be proud of you.'

'Grandfather?' she said, smiling, then looked away. 'O, you mean Grandpa Tom. I don' ting he liked me very much.'

She spoke English but with the lilt of a Reef Island girl, and frequently broke into Pijin. 'Granny doesn' like me, I know.'

I would have preferred to have this conversation away from Joe and Benji, but they were already more au fait with local gossip than I'd ever be.

'It's true,' said Benji, wriggling up to Christine on the sand and hugging her tight. 'Diana made her cry.'

'Stasi growls at her too – it's horrible,' added Joe, and I wanted to say, stop it, all of you, Diana's had her pain too . . . but I knew, from my own distant *Runaway* experiences, that a sixteen-year-old girl is all turned in on herself, when she isn't superficially flaunting, and there'd be no room in Christine's heart for her granny's point of view now.

'Let's get in the washing together when we're back on board,' I suggested, giving her a woman-to-woman look, and she agreed. It was while we were unpegging unusual male underwear from the rigging that Christine confided, as well as that Granny Diana frightened her, she had a boyfriend in Honiara she was longing to see. She also tried to make me understand that she knew, after our talks, how to 'look after herself'.

'He will use a condom if he loves me, won't he?'

'I hope so,' I said, but resolved to get her on the Pill if I could. We all make mistakes.

The Fanalei tribe, at the end of Small Malaita, were the ones who decorated their daughters with dolphin's teeth. Christine hid under Sven's sail-mending bench when we anchored in their bay, for in Reef Islands it was said there were still people in Malaita who'd cut your head off and kaikai the rest of you, and the Fanalei had a ferocious reputation. When the first *Southern Cross* had dropped in, hoping for conversions here, no-one had survived to tell the tale.

'Don't worry, I expect they'll just want anchorage money,' I said, but with Sven and the barman mate asleep when the dugouts came, I too felt vulnerable. The men looked like the 'savages' described by the *Mohawk* diarist – except that some had full heads of two-tone hair, and most wore shorts or rice bags instead of leaf loincloths.

'Lo' wea?' (where are you from) said a spokesman with huge arms almost cut in two by bracelets. 'Scotland,' I answered primly, and went on to eulogize the reputation of his kin as an admirably in-dependent people – 'Olsem man b'long Scotland' (just like the Scots). He looked ready to parley on this, but still wanted to know where we'd come from *recently* and if we had any Islanders aboard.

'My sista from Reef Islands – fasbon of the chief Bigman there – I'm looking after her on our way to Guadalcanal.'

This was a precautionary tack, as revenge was well understood among the Outer Islanders. If you offended someone journeying away from their homeland, his or her whole tribe might come down on your head.

'Oraet,' he said, and by now at least a dozen antennae-haired faces were peeping into portholes. 'Do you want to stay?'

We hadn't decided then, because so much depended on the reception, but Benji suddenly popped up beside me like a puppet and asked the still knit-browed speaker if he had any good cowries. All the best had gone from Reef Islands, he added, shrugging dismissively. This casual query from a cheeky piccaninni transformed the purse-lipped frown into a toothless beam, and the spiky head inclined to one side sweetly.

'Iu raet, smolfela! . . . Reefs Island shells are useless. Fanalei shells the best.'

Now we had all our prejudices present and correct we were most welcome, and no, they wouldn't stoop to accepting anchorage money, but some biros in exchange for freshly speared lobsters later went down well all round, and I had a long, friendly palaver with the chief.

'Send piksa!' cried many voices when we departed next day, and I would. How strange they'd think it if they knew how shocked a lot of nice people in the West would be if they saw the chief's daughter festooned from thighs to brow in a veritable chainmail of dead dolphin's teeth. Whale conservation hereabouts meant dried flesh to chew on, like gum.

Another night of sailing brought us to the Maramasike Passage, between the main islands of Malaita. Here we entered a system of deep salt channels spread like fingers through dense jungle, on whose green canopy the sun brooded heavily, pressing up gaseous odours. It was yet another side of the Solomons – not dream islands these, but a tangle of mysterious worlds whose banks seemed closed against us in the hot, still day, like hooded eyes. Occasionally we spotted habitation, but the stilt houses were often so well hidden, we only glimpsed figures motionless as sleeping bats in the trees when we were all but past, and piccaninnis gazed at us from under subdued bushes of hair (less lime to lighten it here) from deep in the water, their eyes following us like ranks of little crocodiles'.

'I don' like it hia,' said Christine. These were not her sort of islands, but Joe was fascinated.

'You can't write about this place, Mum,' he said. 'People will think you're exaggerating. It's like a dream *film*.'

'I know.'

At the end of the passage, we found a village selling shark fins and Coca-Cola. I had Bacardi with mine and felt even more surreal. But it was open sea again next – a romp across six shades of blue before two islets, straight off the glossiest travel brochure, appeared like glamorous gateposts to still more Pacific surprises, and *Loki II*'s hull was scooped in on a current between them to the last pausing place on our journey before Honiara. This stop was unscheduled but irresistible. On the island of Tavanipupu, just off the edge of Guadalcanal, two white men who'd reassessed their values after twenty years of successful careers in 'civilization' had made a sophisticated haven out of little but palm trees and sun, as well as a new life for themselves. Into this gently designer-tweaked Eden, the grubby contents of *Loki II* poured themselves, and suddenly – after months on tiny wind-whipped Pigeon adhering to a rigorous routine of writing, reef walking, interviewing Hepworths and Islanders – I was sipping wine in the company of a charming couple who stocked their library from *Spectator* reviews, and swirling a silver fork in faultless tomato coulis. How would I know when I woke up from this series of both scary and delicious dreams? Christine, Joe and Benji were ecstatic, too, sauce from a fantasy dessert dripping down now equally tanned chins.

Tavanipupu itself would have its own spell rudely broken the following year, when first one of the partners died then boats filled with gunmen from the Guadalcanal Revolutionary Army swooped into the perfect bay, locked honeymooning guests in the kitchen and visited ancient vendettas on the Malaitan staff. But our evening there was blissful. We were the only guests, and I was allowed to dream my ultimate dream of one-man-forever frolics, in a huge four-poster bed, swathed in sexy mosquito muslin like a wedding dress.

Abruptly, the many-layered private life of the mind was crunched into wide-awake reality when we reached town. Christine became excited as we approached, but I was apprehensive. Sven was surly now, possibly because of a misunderstanding about perks on the voyage. He'd also given up any semblance of hygiene on board, and I wanted the children off before we all went down with belerun (belly run). To give myself a chance to think, I said I needed time ashore to sort out my computer, and visit the hospital on both Christine and Peter's behalf. Christine begged to be allowed to see friends, and I said yes, making only the proviso she be back before dark. It was the beginning of a very unpleasant few days.

First, Joe became ill, and it was clear he needed motherly care as well as medicine. But I had to leave him alone in a seedy hotel room on the second day when, appallingly, Christine had failed to reappear, and Sven had turned nasty. Leaving messages for Christine in half a dozen places, I made my plans. There was a small window of time when Sven and the barman would be away from the boat, and Benji and I could row out and get our gear off. My satellite phone – the only contact from Pigeon with Magnus, not to mention the *Sunday Times* magazine – was on there as well as Joe's wilted but still precious bits of jewellery given him by Christine, which he needed for comfort now. Benji was anxious to rescue his Fanalei shells. He'd gone on liking Sven until he'd upset Christine on arrival in port, by trying to make her stay on board. Now he didn't understand fully what the problem was but knew it was important we moved fast. To reach *Loki II*, I rowed the flat-bottomed coracle affair that was Sven's version of a dinghy, while Benji called out instructions so we didn't get entangled in smarter yachts' moorings. Then he kept lookout while I passed our possessions over the rocking side.

'Don't forget Christine's coconut oil,' whispered Benji as I prepared to descend the frayed rope ladder, and I went back quickly but could find only a bra. Benji rowed on the way back because I was praying I'd be able to tread water holding the satellite phone and computer in the air, if we fell in. With practice in dugouts, he was also a better oarsman. We made it to the hotel beach and had all our gear stowed safely under a table in the midst of a Japanese conference and Sven's dinghy replaced where he'd left it, before our one-time friend, now bogeyman, reappeared. Joe was recovering from vomiting again, and I was cleaning up, when the dreaded banging came on our thin hotel-room door.

'Lusi! Let me in . . . kwiktaem please!'

Not Sven but Christine. When I opened the door she literally tumbled in and lay sobbing on the floor. Finally she managed to squeeze out that she was sorry she hadn't come back, but just couldn't face another night on board, and she hadn't done anything bad, she promised — her boyfriend had flu. She'd returned to confess all, but been met at *Loki II* by a furious Sven, who refused to let her gather any of her remaining possessions aboard until I gave him more money.

''Emi garem all my good kalicos!' she wailed. 'O Lusi, wanem hemi hapen nao? I hate that bastard . . .'

Other reasons for her loathing of Sven emerged. When she'd pushed his hands from her susu (breasts) he'd made her clean the toilet, which made her sick, and he stood over her and touched her at night. He'd even pushed up her kalico and . . . I shushed her gently. Benji, so strong before, was crumpling at her distress; Joe just looked dazed.

'Wasim face,' I told her, 'and lukaftarem piccaninni. I'll be back soon.'

I'd noticed where the police station was earlier. I hadn't wanted to take things so far, but now felt I had no choice. Sven, who'd been well paid, was holding an innocent girl's possessions hostage, had obviously been monkeying with her after promising not to, and I was too afraid to attempt to handle matters alone. But I didn't know what I was starting when I took my complaint to Sergeant Maisa, the biggest and fiercest Reef Island woman I ever saw.

'Siddown,' she said when I entered her office, a bare cube flecked with dead flies, lit both by dazzling sun and the statutory single bulb. 'Tell evryting.'

I did, and when I mentioned that the most offended party was a Reef Island girl, Sergeant Maisa, already dwarfing her desk with a torso that pulled her blouse into juddering lines, grew visibly.

'Hemi hutim disfela gel?' (Did he hurt this girl?) In her outrage she'd broken into Reef Islands Pijin herself.

'Me no savvy,' I said, but indicated what Christine had indicated to me . . . and Sergeant Maisa's hand landed so hard on the desk, it jumped. An order was yelled at the door of the cube and two police constables appeared kwiktaem, one recognizably a Reef Islander, to whom Sergeant Maisa addressed her commands. This pair were to be stationed outside our hotel room, to look after my family and Christine, and Sven was to be brought before her immediately. ('NAO!') My genial guards accompanied me back to the hotel and shook hands with the now smiling Christine and boys, before stationing themselves at either end of the corridor. Joe's medicine had begun to work, and Christine had had a soothing time primping in the relatively primitive but, to her, luxurious bathroom. I dared not think what Sergeant Maisa might do to Sven in that little room, but an eerily cheerful phone call later gave me the gist.

''ello Lusi? Y'oraet? All finis wetem disfela nao. 'Em' no givim trouble no moa. 'Em' leavim Honiara tonaet, an' no kambaek . . .'

Whether Sven's 'deportation' had any official base, I don't know. But I gathered he'd been warned that, should he appear near Reef Islands again, he shouldn't expect to re-emerge with his boat – or possibly his body – intact. Word had gone out on every inter-island radio that a Reef Island girl had been insulted by him, and the police couldn't vouch for his safety should he fall into the hands of her wontoks. Kastom, it appeared, found the greatest of ease working hand in cuff with the law, when it suited. Christine's kalicos were delivered neatly folded by a constable, and she checked everything before our guard departed. Then, all coy smiles now, she asked if I'd managed to get her 'that medicine' we'd talked about, in case her boyfriend no longer had flu. I had, and went over the instructions with her while she giggled helplessly. The condoms I'd purchased as an additional safety measure to the pill had pictures of white women in red stockings on the packet.

'Do girls in Scotland wear clothes like this, Lusi?'

'Not very often.'

When she'd gone out – promising to come back – I fetched food for the boys and a drink for myself, and set up my satellite phone to send an e-mail to Magnus.

'*We've been on a little holiday cruise . . .*'

I left the end of the message vague, as I didn't know yet how we'd get back to Pigeon.

The *Elizabeth Ann* was black and orange – mostly iron and rust – and had an all-Melanesian crew who, when we arrived to enquire about a passage, were heaving petrol drums into the hold. They stopped to watch a white woman and two small boys chatting to the captain. There was no passenger accommodation, but he'd take us to Santa Cruz. The journey could last a week and we must supply our own food. I took enough for Christine but, although she reappeared before we left, it was only to say she was off to Bellona – in another direction – with her boyfriend. She'd wanted me to meet him but he still had flu. I gave her a cuddle and a Lemsip sachet. It was no good trying to persuade her to change her mind. I'd run away when I was her age too . . .

As well as petrol, the *Elizabeth Ann* carried a pick-up truck destined for Temotu Province, roped to the only space on deck. Joe bagged a string hammock open to the elements and barely moved from it, except to fall out occasionally onto the heap of crew beneath, who lifted him back and covered him with a rice bag when it rained. Benji found the shelter of the bridge more agreeable, and discovered he fitted perfectly on the chart table. The captain's wife, on learning I was a wontok of Ross Hepworth, recently President of Temotu (would I still be, after losing Christine?), made an effort to prepare for me the only, coffin-sized cabin aboard: her husband's. This had one small porthole blocked permanently by a ukelele player's head. I rigged a teatowel as a curtain, which bulged under his rasta bayonets. Food for the forty-odd souls aboard was prepared on two gas rings in a six-by-four concrete box a long climb down an iron ladder: rice on one ring, bully beef on the other, three times a day. For tea, a water pump the size of a crane was primed from a kettle dipped into the same black lake under a manhole cover used for buckets to flush the single loo. The shower was a flour drum with a battered tin lid for rinsing. When I used it – clinging to a pipe so as not to be thrown by the heavings of the sea against the studded iron door – fifteen men were gambling outside. Obligingly, they refilled the drum twice. Rain transformed the *Elizabeth Ann* from a cheery tin tub full of smiling crew munching pineapples, to a grim prison complete with caricature figures of black misery propped against nests of oily rope spattered with vomit. Happily the sun was shining when, on the fifth day, Santa Cruz came into view.

How patient my children were – Joe back to daydreaming in his crude hammock; Benji reclining next to the captain on the bridge, checking with binoculars for the far-off ripple that spelled tuna – but how kind strangers were, too. That night on Santa Cruz, when all three of us were sharing half a bucket of water for washing (there was a shortage all over the island), we were protected from the attentions of a drunk by Reef Islanders who'd heard about our troubles on *Loki II*. They arranged our passage back to Pigeon, along with the now recovered chief of Matema, who had, through a bush grapevine more efficient than our radio efforts, reached hospital soon after our stop at his island. It was Ross, in fact, who came next day to fetch us, plus the chief's tiny mother and four enormous logs of taro. The weather was good, and our journey by canoe easy compared to our first crossing, but I felt dreadful about Christine.

'It's all right, Lucy,' Ross said. 'Ben's gone to get her.'

But Ben didn't bring her back. Christine kept on running. The so-called 'simple life' on Pigeon, with its heady mix of values and deep divisions, was too complicated for her. All she wanted right now was the sweet live-for-the-moment oblivion of an apparently caring man's arms around her, and, although I worried about her, I could understand that.

16

1971–1976

BEFORE CHRISTINE CLEMENT WAS SWEPT OUT OF THEIR LIVES, THE Hepworths established a store at Luova on Santa Cruz, run by a local, and Tom opened a post office within the original store on Pigeon – now offering bras and Coca-Cola, as well as white kalico for wrapping the dead, and the same kind of stick tobacco that formed part of the deal for the original 'purchase' of the island. In 1970 the first small aircraft landed on a newly made strip on Santa Cruz, and plans for another on Lom Lom – a dugout ride from Pigeon – promised dramatic changes to lives in the whole area, particularly the Hepworths', who saw the opportunity to open their personal Paradise to visitors from the Outside World. Diana modified the designs for the eight-sided house near the mango tree and began, with great energy, to build. Another useful aspect of civilization came nearer when a small hospital opened on Santa Cruz, serving Islanders from a swathe of scattered islands, plus the Hepworths, although they were still forty-five miles across the risky deep and currently had no boat of their own. Lack of a boat meant that Tom, to oversee the running of the Luova store, had to rely on the erratic movements of mission and copra ships. This again resulted in time away from Diana, which he'd never liked. He was still expanding, seeking more land on Santa Cruz with the idea of building a third store, but it was all more of a strain 'after Christine'. There was an interim period when, with Diana busy on the new accommodation, Tom himself had to take over the schooling. This, he complained privately to his sisters, was '*misery for all*'. His spirits revived, however, when the challenge of advertising the island as a retreat fell to his hand.

'Remoteness *is the unique charm of Ngarando, or "Faraway", as locals call it . . . If you really want to get away from it all, it's perfect! . . . no rats, few flies, no mosquitoes . . . Rare seashells and exciting diving available – or one can simply walk about the villages and study the unspoiled way of life of primitive Melanesians . . . no other tourists within 500 miles, and the Hepworths are always there to tell you all there is to know about the district and its inhabitants.*' Even-handed when it came to exploitation, he wrote the same week to the director of education in Honiara, who'd voiced reservations about development: '*Tourists, in my book, are fine fat sheep to be fleeced with impunity . . . and it's surely too late to save the "Splendid Savages" hereabouts. Too long ago we set their feet on our own damned road.*' Damnation seemed a recurring theme to Tom, for all he recognized the saleable fantasy side of Pigeon, and when hopes for the new airfield at Lom Lom were dashed by lack of funds he confided to his sisters he was writing, not his book, but an essay entitled 'Paradise Receding'. In the same letter, however, he insisted: '*We still love it here, but any picture you have of your brother lying under palms and eating the fruit of the lotus should be erased.*' Tasha suffered from a painful eye condition around this time which forced her to stay in a darkened room all day, and when Tasha suffered, Tom did, too. It was a relief when Christine Clement, true to her word, found a new governess prepared to live on Pigeon for two years. The only problem was, no-one could replace Christine in Tasha's heart, and the new girl, though an excellent teacher, '*took up with a native*', to Tom and Diana's disapproval. It ended civilly – she grew fond of the family, and they of her – but with some sense of disappointment on both sides. A decision was made then to 'drop' two years from Tasha's real age – fifteen in 1973 – so she could fit into a normal high school at the same time it was planned to send the twins to board in New Zealand, when they were twelve.

Ross's passion, at age eleven, was sailing – he was expert at handling a dugout with nothing but a palm leaf correctly angled – and Bressin was 'the quiet one', an avid reader, who liked to go off shooting fish on his own. They had local friends, with whom they spoke Pijin more than they spoke English with their parents, but knew virtually no

Europeans. Picnics at Nbanga, wave-skiing and bonfires built on palm-lattice rafts at the right time of the tide for maximum drama were their entertainments, and Ross swelled in the esteem of Islander companions by daring to sleep alone one night close to the Debbil-Debbil Tree. Tasha had been attached to the Reef Island girl who replaced Sibileh, her previous companion, when Christine was running Pigeon Island School (Sibileh had gone to further her education on Santa Cruz) but to Diana's disgust the new girl had been married off by her father when she was fourteen, meaning another suddenly curtailed relationship for Tasha. The children's correspondence schooling continued under yet another temporary governess but lacked the magic brought to remote island lessons by Christine. Her era with them became something of a dream itself.

The seventies were critical for Tom in his relations with the neighbours. In time he found, and paid for by arrangement with a Kastom landowner, an ideal site for a third store at Luebeva, on Santa Cruz, and Diana – having completed the handsome house named Ngarando on Pigeon, unused because of collapsed airfield plans – took a team to build from dawn to dusk, then herself operated the store at Luova, from which Tom had ousted the local manager, believing he was overgenerous with wontoks – a recurrent problem. When the Hepworths had advertised the job abroad, an Australian claiming to be ideally qualified for the post arrived only to be instantly arrested and deported as a known criminal. He'd had just enough time on Santa Cruz to pass the store key to a delighted Islander, who made off with two dozen bottles of rum, four dozen tin mugs, dark glasses, parasols and a case of spam.

Diana relished the challenge of building the new store, seeing it as the culmination of all her other carpentry efforts. It was large, with integral accommodation and, if the weekly take at Luova were anything to go by, would be a winner financially. She missed Tom – 'When am I going to see you?' was scrawled at the bottom of one letter which took weeks to reach him – but job satisfaction made the separation bearable. As ever, she worked to impress him with progress, and he was impressed. After a quarter of a century of marriage, they still adored each other and were a seemingly invincible unit, even when apart. What they didn't know was that forces that had never stopped rumbling round them, in the form of Islanders frustrated by the use of what they saw as their land, were soon to strengthen, and acquire for the first time something of a leader.

One hot evening at Luebeva, Diana, sweating after a long day's work but proud, nailed up a notice announcing 'Niu PIT Store Open Monday'. Today was Sunday and she'd been working on her own because no Islander would break a church day. Alone, she celebrated completion of the project by writing a triumphant letter to Tom. But when she approached with the keys on Monday morning, her brisk smile – in place for the benefit of a gathering she presumed was composed of eager customers – froze: '*PITs out! PITs out! PITS out!*' was scrawled all over the door. When they'd witnessed her silent reaction, the watchers melted as silently away. The Kastom landowner who'd come to an agreement with Tom earlier was among them, having been convinced that what he'd thought was a bargain at the time, wasn't. The catalyst for this volte-face was a Reef Islander who, in the Civil Service, had seen other ways of life beyond the Islands and decided to bring back the benefit of his experience. He was now head of a land development committee and knew a little about land prices elsewhere, fair wages and Tom's pet hate – unions. Willy Bopali was both a traditional adherent of Kastom and a devout Christian – a perfectly possible balancing act. But he was also a fast learner as a politician, and keen to uphold the rights of fellow Islanders.

Bopali may have opened the landowner's eyes to the idea of exploitation, but the graffiti episode was an act perpetrated mainly by angry young wontoks of families closer to Pigeon itself, who believed the Hepworths to be occupying their land. Their elders might be shy, still bending the knee to the white man, but they weren't going to fall into the same trap – especially now they had a sympathetic Bigman in their midst who was brave and educated enough to confront the enemy. Tom attempted to settle the Pigeon issue once and for all by having the island registered officially, but the requisite notice inviting objections was posted only in Santa Cruz, so no-one in Reefs – it was claimed – ever saw it. But those who objected to the Hepworths' power expanding beyond their entrenched position on Pigeon decided to stop the fresh enterprise on Santa Cruz before it even began, and, backed by many, the landowner demanded his land back.

In what must have been a deeply humiliating act, in front of an impassive audience – because she wasn't going to let the building go with the land – Diana dismantled, nail by nail, rafter by rafter, every scrap of the brand new, never used complex at Luebeva. The *'PITs out'* protest and the ousting of the Hepworths from Kastom land on Santa Cruz were unprecedented displays of hostility, and in the privacy of the back of the now boycotted store at Luova, Diana, after weeks at the heartbreaking job of tearing apart the best building she'd ever made, smudged the sheet of airmail paper on which she spilled out her feelings to Tom with furious tears. She who never cried. But the hostility didn't hurt her so much as the spoilt work. *'Darling Heart, . . . I'm labelling every one of the pieces. Nothing will be wasted but . . . oh darling I'm just so* tired.'

If there had ever been any chinks in the armour that kept the Hepworths distant from their neighbours, these closed now. White, through his tan, with anger so hot it affected his bowels – he'd felt Diana's rare grief in her letter – Tom sat down at the desk she'd made him for his book, and wrote a notice which he nailed to Pigeon's storefront, in case that too was under threat: *'REMEMBER! WHEN IU NO GOT TOBACCO, RUM, TINMEAT, CHOISE WAS YOURS. ASK BOPALI!'* For Tom was in no doubt who was the 'stirrer'. He'd already had dealings with this *'upstart'* about *'nonsense'* concerning *'better wages and working conditions. Hah!'* Tom genuinely believed what he paid his workers was fair, and made the point that if he weren't around, there'd be no regular paid employment in Reefs at all. Bopali's response to the notice was sent by a bearer in a dugout. *'Sir, I regard this as INSULT to put my name in the Public place. I have heard you and Missus complain I am who responsible for recommend you removal from Santa Cruz.* If you can prove this then I will also be the one to remove you from Pigeon Island. *I tell you Tom, I will not be hesitate to see you pull out altogether . . . I warn you rub my name off; when I return and my name not rub off, I will take action.'*

Tom was not accustomed to receiving communications from Islanders on this level. If they wrote at all, it was usually a begging note for a paper screw of sugar on tick, or a polite plea – as from Tangypera, then a youth – to be allowed to work on Pigeon. Wisely, as an 'insult' is serious in Kastom, Tom erased Bopali's name, but kept the bearer beside him to deliver a riposte: *'Sir, I strongly suggest you keep the inconvenience of your own people in mind, rather than your prejudices . . . no-one offers better prices than I can and now your people on Santa Cruz will have to go without.'* It was like a match to a dry coconut husk dipped in kerosene – standard method of lighting an umu for a pig feast – and

Bopali exploded. '*No talking about inconvenience. My people say you rob them. I will look your prices. But if I could be told by anybody of land the size of Pigeon Island which equals same size of land in New Zealand in 1957 which was worth only what you paid for Pigeon, one could well be going to New Zealand and settle there instead of coming to our islands and stealing people of their land.*' Bopali the budding politician would fairly examine Tom's store prices, but Bopali the Christian and Kastom-respecting Reef Islander was accusing Tom of exploitation of the unworldly.

'*By the Living God!*' Tom wrote, changing tack suddenly to air his feelings in another direction – to the sisters who heard from him increasingly often – '*I'll get home to you next year.*' He'd raised their hopes already twice, when things had started to look up – with the airfield, then the new store – and subsequently had to renege when things went wrong. '*It's so sad,*' they'd replied, '*we had the flat re-decorated, so all would be perfect for "when Tom comes" and now "the Bridegroom cometh not" . . . Diana is running a little shop, we understand. Does it make a good living?*' Home? A good living? What did these words mean to Tom at this time? What did he think when he sat mending mugs shattered in yet another earthquake which slopped precious fresh water out of all the tanks, or had to allow his Nenumbo men time off to rebuild their homes after a cyclone which '*just flapped Pigeon with its skirts*'? He noted the prevailing weather conditions, as on the *AR*, but rarely analysed what was going on, either within his family, the community round him or himself. None of this was what he'd planned, except the continuing happiness with Diana. The Queen visited the Solomon Islands in 1974 and Tom, as an expatriate, was invited to be in the capital for her arrival. Drily, he wrote: '*I'm afraid I have neither the time nor inclination for pomp.*' Paradoxically, the Islanders were thrilled, and those with wontoks in Honiara plastered the walls of their leaf huts with photographs from the *Solomon Star* of Her Majesty graciously accepting frangipani necklaces just like the ones they made, from these most far-flung of her subjects. The Bigmen in Honiara presented her with a roll of red feather money, too – which was thoughtfully returned, with ceremony, after Independence, during another royal visit in 1982.

But Tom wasn't going to return anything voluntarily to the Islanders, now or later, because Diana loved Pigeon, so the fight with Bopali and the 'intransigents' went on. So what if £15 and a few sticks of tobacco was cheap for five acres in 1957? The island hadn't been in use then; Nandelli people had *asked* him to become their trader – and he had an official lease. They slugged it out civilly, on the whole, probably aware just how far either could go. Bopali, more hot-headed as a young man than in later years, threatened to take his grievances over the 'insult' to a higher power – the Native Court – but this had no jurisdiction over Tom because he wasn't a native; Tom tried taking his grievances about the dishonoured agreement at Luebeva to an English lawyer but was given short shrift and told it was a 'native' affair. Both knew these were posturings. It *was* a local matter, to be handled using local tit-for-tat methods. Tom provided proofs of the fairness of his prices – with overheads taken into account – and, after much deliberation on Bopali's part, these were accepted. Round one to Tom, and he celebrated by decorating the storefront, not, as in olden times, with heads declaring a victory, but with posies of plastic flowers sent unexpectedly by his Hong Kong suppliers. The question of wages fell more the Islanders' way. They placed a temporary tambu on Pigeon Island's prettified store – no doubt, fulminated Tom, under 'Bopali's baneful influence' – until those most deserving, in the elders' view, got a raise – which Tom then announced he'd been planning anyway. Small points could be gained and lost on both sides, but no-one really wanted PIT's one remaining store shut down, and the issue of Kastom land on Pigeon, although it sank out of sight once more, rumbled on.

With the enforced pull-out from Santa Cruz coming so bitterly, Diana might have slowed down, but she didn't give in for any longer than it took to utter the one strong phrase that jerked from her lips once back on Pigeon with Tom ('*These* bloody *people*'). Something in her made it possible to bounce back, time after time, from major setbacks. Now, airfield or no airfield, she poured all her considerable will and skills into building a forty-foot boathouse for *Kyomie*, a twenty-two-foot motor launch being shipped from New Zealand to bring guests from Santa Cruz. (Tom stuck to his refusal to have anything with a sail.) And on top of *Kyomie*'s house, as well as extending bedroom space for the children – and a new live-in housegirl, Lapoli – she made a dormitory '*ideal for backpackers*' who couldn't afford Ngarando's luxury. Ngarando's only occupants so far had been a group of shellseekers unfortunate enough to arrive at the start of a two-month drought, but Diana believed it was only a matter of time before tourism took off, and asked her friend Amalie to visit *'before we're overwhelmed'*. Not stopping at the boat- and bunkhouse, she went on to raise a seawall, oversee the construction of a firewood shed behind the busy copra shed, and erect an elegant leaf windbreaker for what she and Tom christened their West Patio. There she instructed Tangypera, the houseboy, and Paia, the cook, to serve supper on time for the regular but ever-changing evening cabaret of tropical sunset, and a girl washed up, saving water as Missus had taught her, while Tom and Diana sat side by side in loungers under a system of light bulbs threaded through the palms, reading *Time* and *National Geographic* magazines. Tasha sometimes sat with them, a favourite kitten draped over her shoulders, but more often hung around with Islander friends – increasingly often boys – where they could pull up dugouts below *Kyomie*'s House. Sibileh, now that she, like Tasha's other former schoolmate, had been married off by her father, was too grown up to play at dressing up their twin Amanda Jane dolls, sent from England. In a few months she'd have her own real baby. Bressin and Ross still enjoyed the tree house – from which they rigged a *Boys' Own* dream of a 'flying fox' wire, hurtling them from thirty feet above the ocean straight into it, with a satisfying splash. Up there they took Nandelli male friends, whose ancestors knew about the advantages of defensive battle from on high, and conducted exciting mock battles with 'enemies' below. And onto the growing pile of leaf mats in one corner, where they rested in a heap, Bressin conceived a desire to take Lapoli, who slept naked on hot nights beside the utility room in *Kyomie*'s House.

'Hey! Let's creep in and look at her,' suggested Ross, eyes shining at the mischief of it. Boys only a couple of years older boasted they'd already performed the act of 'durong' with girls – all the way. But Bressin, although longing, was hesitant. It was he, finally, who held the torch, its brightness muffled by mosquito netting, as they tiptoed, skilled as Islanders in silent movement, to the end of her leaf mat. Softly the light, pale as a cloudy moonbeam, brushed her shoulders from where they stood breathless, on either side of the leaf doorway. Her eyes were shadowed, but her upraised chin and outflung arm showed her neat torso to perfection – a living sculpture of quiescent nubility under their hungry eyes.

'Shine the torch lower,' whispered Ross, 'go on.' Under cover of the shadows, he was flushed. Bressin ached to, but said no. They'd agreed not to look below her waist. Like a broad, caressive finger, the beam slid once more over neck, into the erotic declivities of armpits, and over young breasts beaded lightly with perspiration, then the boys were gone. And in the morning Lapoli was gone too, her jobs not begun.

'They're *so* unreliable,' said Diana, annoyed at what she saw as capriciousness. But Tangypera intervened and Lapoli was persuaded to return to work, provided she could share a hut with Aunty Doroti. This was agreed, and the rumours made Diana think. They were only twelve but it obviously wasn't a moment too soon for the twins to be heading off to boarding school where, as she told Amalie, '*they'll meet the class of people we want them to mix with*'.

Housesitters for Pigeon still hadn't been found when Diana left to settle the children in school, so Tom held the fort alone for several months. Since the Luebeva debacle and ensuing angry exchanges, Bopali, rising steadily on the Outer Island political scene, had become keen to find a diplomatic way forward with the Hepworths, even if it took years. He was now a regular store customer, even commiserating with Tom over the absence of his wife and children. 'Sorry nao, cap'n. You'll all be together again soon.' Had they been closer as men, he might, as a father himself and an upholder of moral standards in the community, have mentioned concerns he'd had for some time about the eldest Hepworth piccaninni. Did her dadi know, he wondered aloud to wontoks, how many Nandelli boyfriends Tasha had? 'Cap'n no believim' (he wouldn't believe us) was the general response. Better not to say anything, or Tom might think they were insulting his family. That's how it would work in Kastom, so nothing was said. But a number of boys looked forward to when Tasha, so soft and white and willing, came back. She'd become their communal doll, to undress and play with by moonlight in the bushes, or under an upturned dinghy beside *Kyomie*'s House. She never objected, and sometimes was waiting with blouse removed – Islander girls went topless – to show off a new leaf necklace she'd made. It's not known how far these games went before Tasha went away to school.

Alone on Pigeon, Tom suffered a prolonged bout of malaria, and had his liquor licence revoked on the grounds that crews of cargo boats were abusing the drink he sold to buy, through their fathers, the favours of young girls. The sailors got local Bigmen drunk, in which state they consented to practices contrary to Kastom. Daughters were supposed to be sold as brides only these days, not whores. '*It's all balderdash*,' wrote Tom to his sisters, '*they've no morals.*' Eventually he got the licence back. In the meantime his now seventy-plus sisters corrected his English: '*Balls, dear, no-one says balderdash any more . . . You must come home soon or you'll end up a total anachronism.*' They sensed, too, that their brother was not contented. '*Are you absolutely stuck with being a shopkeeper indefinitely? Not at all the way to live in the romantic Tropics. You might as well be in London.*'

Tom may have echoed this, for in his diary is one word: '*WHOOPEE!*' when temporary managers arrived in May and he was free to go. While Diana worked carpentry miracles on the Auckland flats, he was to spend a full month in London with his dear Elizabeth and Margaret. A full month it was. When Tom, after twenty-eight years away from Britain, flew into Heathrow (via Nauru, Fiji and Japan) he hit the ground running – or maybe still flying – and didn't stop until, bursting to share the joy of all he'd done, he flew back into Diana's arms twenty-eight days later. Elizabeth, her paintings now on show regularly, took him to the opera, the ballet, Sotheby's – where they tried, unsuccessfully, to flog their famous father's family Bible – shopping at Selfridge's and, greatest treat of all, for three days of solid Shakespeare at Stratford. '*I've even seen an International Sex Shop!*' Tom scribbled to Diana like a boy let out of school, and, nostalgically, '*Lunched at Simpson's of Piccadilly again after all these years.*' Handel at the Festival Hall was given ten out of ten in his diary, and Tom received a number of rounds of applause himself when he showed 'Snapshots of a Life in the Tropics' to members of his sisters' artistic circle.

This visit, though brief, wrought a change in Tom. Although he was glad to be back with Diana and enjoyed sharing his new-found street wisdom with his sons, he never again retreated into a remote lifestyle as perhaps he had formerly. Suddenly he'd discovered that the Big Bad Outside World could be enormous fun, and he wanted a share in it while he was still young enough. (He was then sixty-five.) 'Of course we'll travel more in time,' agreed Diana, 'but at the moment there's so much to press on with.' There always would be. But Tom had formidable support for his cultural cravings in his sisters. Back on Pigeon for Christmas 1975, after what was deemed by the adults a successful start at school for all three children, with boarding hosts found for the following year, Tom dug into a bonanza parcel shipped from London five months earlier: books by the score (Evelyn

Waugh, Aldous Huxley, Alvin Toffler, Camus, Angus Wilson) and on tape Saint-Saëns, Telemann, Smetana and Schönberg. Also included were a smart studded collar for the latest dog, illustrated tomes on a diverse array of subjects for the children – and a jar of face cream for Diana. 'Do thank them, won't you?' she said. To friends and family that year she'd sent immaculate cowries, which graced mantelpieces in many fashionable homes. Living where she did, within the fantasy most people wove of her life, she could always have the last word in chic. Tasha showed off new plastic and glass necklaces from New Zealand to old friends down by *Kyomie*'s House.

A fierce kumberra (westerly gale) followed by a cyclone building towards Guadalcanal delayed the start of the children's journey back to school by a week, and Tom tucked letters of apology to head teachers into pockets together with instructions to the twins on how to board a cargo boat from Santa Cruz to Honiara, a trip of several days: take a Solomon Islands plane to Espiritu Santo and another to Vila, capital of the New Hebrides, where they must overnight before hopping on a French airline to New Caledonia. The final leg was a flight to Auckland where they'd be met by one of the ex-Pigeon governesses before going their separate ways to the people with whom they were to board. Ross stayed with a newsagent's family, Bressin with a farming couple, and Tasha unpacked her shrivelled good-luck leaf jewellery – last-minute gifts of wontoks – in the home of a lawyer, whose pregnant wife would be grateful for help with her children and, in return, made Tasha's accommodation fees modest. It says something for the pluck of these youngsters, the twins in early adolescence, Tasha not as advanced in her mind though an adult physically, that they managed this trip without mishap. Fluency in Pijin helped during the Island legs, and Tom revived old contacts in the New Hebrides to see them safely through that part of the marathon. But how they were managing at school was another story.

'*It's remarkable how quickly they've settled,*' Tom wrote to Amalie, the twins' American godmother, but Ross didn't feel this to be the case. In the first term, he beat up fellow pupils at his upmarket school for teasing him because of his Pijin accent. 'Java kid' was the usual taunt, and Ross hated it. The teachers had noticed his unusual English as well, and he was kept in long hours writing the same sentences repeatedly. Not accustomed to this kind of discipline, Ross, during the months his mother was still in New Zealand, one day downed his pen and bicycled away across the fields. Cycling was something 'civilization' had given him that he liked, but surely he wasn't going to have to kowtow to unreasonable demands from '*snooty*' men who weren't a bit like the friendly governesses he was used to on Pigeon? Diana, whose own schooldays had been marred by teasing, told Ross he must learn to be resilient about that – as she had – and would emerge stronger for it, but she was sympathetic about the English 'punishments'; had words with the staff, and accepted that boarding out might be best if he was having trouble in the dormitories. The trouble didn't stop when Ross became a day boy, but meant he escaped his tormentors some of the time. He wasn't afraid – his island upbringing had made him fearless physically – but if he fought, he was jeered at even more: 'Java kid *savage* eh?' Ross's schooldays were not the happiest. It was fine, in Reef Island Kastom, for men to weep openly: absolutely not in the borrowed stiff-upper-lip atmosphere of an old-fashioned New Zealand boys' school, and Ross couldn't, like his mother, choke back his feelings all the time.

Bressin was teased too, but sidestepped problems by disappearing into a book or simply avoiding the company of those who mocked his expertise in primitive fishing techniques. He concentrated on what both absorbed him and, in due course, impressed them: Bressin was exceptional on the athletics field. The arms that had controlled a spear expertly beyond the Edge of the Reef soon adapted to a fine technique with a javelin and, liking the order imposed on daily life by the strict school regime, he began to wonder early on about joining the army.

Tasha, nearly eighteen now – although said to be sixteen – was consistently bottom of her class, and there were gulfs between her and the other girls. Asked to draw her house, she sketched half a dozen childlike boxes looking as though made of straw, and was laughed at; in a home economics class she failed to include a telephone bill or electricity in her 'budget' and, with regard to language, her report read: '*Tasha finds English difficult unless she has individual help.*' Christine Clement had had the time to give Tasha individual help, but it was very different in a class of twenty-five younger, normal girls. Mrs Rose, the woman with whom Tasha boarded, thought her charge struggled painfully at school, and found her less of a help in the house than had been hoped, but without the parents there for discussion –

and with letters taking months each way – all the adults around Tasha felt they'd no option but to let her muddle on. In the last term of 1976, however, her headmistress wrote to Diana advising that, should she return for the forthcoming School Certificate year, '*she would find herself even more out of her depth than she is now . . . She is also, I feel, too old in terms of actual age to be continuing at school, even though in manner and maturity, younger . . . please give this problem your earnest consideration.*' Diana considered. Yes, Tasha no doubt would be better off on Pigeon for the final school year, with a governess to concentrate on her speech and gently bring her to a stage at which she could '*take her place in the world*'. No-one, at this point, suggested to her parents that Tasha's difficulties might be more than a hangover from early hospital traumas. All was settled then. At Christmas 1976 Tasha would come home with the twins for the holidays (they could manage only one visit home annually) but would stay on Pigeon when they went back for their Certificate year.

On the island, Diana was busier than ever, with visits first from Amalie – who found the peculiarly hectic 'simplicity' of Pigeon life a shock – then from Tom's oldest friend, Dennis, and his wife. This couple fitted in admirably, finding it all a lark. His wife didn't mind serving in the store, and Dennis and Tom disappeared for hours to tinker with *Kyomie*'s engine, emerging greasy and grinning to stripwash briskly, as in wartime, then settle on the West Patio to enjoyable evenings of reminiscence over crayfish washed down with gin and bushlime. '*This is more like it!*' wrote Tom to his sisters, who hadn't missed the opportunity to send more literary and musical goodies, and they all dismissed a recent government brochure – handed, offputtingly, to every visitor touching down in Honiara – which said: '*It is not advisable to swim anywhere in the Solomons.*' (This followed a spate of shark attacks.)

'It's Shangri-La, old man,' said Dennis loyally. 'You're far more likely to meet your end under a number nine bus. Only a matter of time till the world's beating a path to your door.' His wife concurred. She'd never seen so many glorious sunsets in her life as on Pigeon. 'Transport, of course, is the only real drawback . . . but the airfield will come. The airfield will come.' Privately, the couple agreed they wouldn't like to *live* on Pigeon – it had been upsetting when a dog left by one of the temporary managers had been punctured by a spear on

Nandelli and left to die, and the red biting ants in the bedding were a pest – but for an unusual break it would be hard to beat. 'Marvellous,' they said as they parted, 'extraordinary spot.' Then Dennis put his foot in it. He'd been concerned to see his old friend ill with a fever twice during his stay: 'But when are you coming home, Tom?'

'Pigeon *is* our home,' said Diana, a little sharply. Why wouldn't people understand? When they'd gone, she aired all the furnishings in Ngarando and repainted the red irons on the roof. Paying guests might arrive any time and they must be prepared.

This might have been the moment for Tom to start writing seriously. His memory had been sharpened by talks with Dennis, and he'd seen the reaction to his slides of sailing days. He'd just wait to unload new stock from an expected cargo boat, then set to. The cargo boat, however, brought disquieting news about Tasha from friends: '*We think she should see a psychologist . . . problems following her most recent ear operation,*' and a strange outburst from Mrs Rose: '*It isn't easy coping with an eighteen-year-old toddler when I've got enough on my hands.*'

'She's being hysterical,' pronounced Diana (meaning Mrs Rose). 'Her hormones will be awry with the new baby. And she probably wants more money.'

Diana was right. Mrs Rose was under strain, with a house move imminent and a demanding family. But Tasha was her biggest worry. To the ex-governess who kept an eye on things from afar, Mrs Rose wrote: '*She's so miserable at school I let her stay at home sometimes. But she won't change her clothes and uses so much lavatory paper I have to hide the spare rolls.*'

I bet she's keeping Tasha off school to look after her children, Diana thought, and wrote to the headmistress with her concerns. The headmistress replied that she'd barely seen Tasha for a month, understanding she was undergoing surgery. Angrily, Diana concluded now that Mrs Rose was keeping Tasha a virtual prisoner, and wrote a strong letter. But in November a frantic telegram arrived: '*TASHA BACK HOSPITAL DUE EAR AND MENTAL DISTRESS . . . MEDICS INSIST TASHA ESCORTED HOME . . . OR YOU COME . . . ADVISE URGENTLY.*' These words were sent by the former governess, who offered to accompany Tasha herself. Tom and Diana, baffled by what was happening, were about to agree to let Tasha fly home, accompanied, when another cable came: '*TASHA PSYCHOTIC PLEASE COME.*'

The page in Tom's diary that might have tentatively celebrated a real start on his book – he'd typed thirty pages about early days on the *AR* – said instead: '*Black Monday. Tasha disaster.*'

Although they were within easy driving distance of each other, no arrangements had been made for the Hepworth children to meet while they were in New Zealand. The twins saw each other in passing at school, but Tasha didn't see any of her family for months. Bressin did once spot her at a bus stop, and approached. She looked agitated but would say nothing. 'I'll come and see you,' he said and, after poring over a cluttered street map – so unlike the simple geography in Reefs – he kept his promise that weekend. A week later, a letter from his school to Tom – though of course not reaching Pigeon for a month – reported that Bressin seemed under the weather, and had asked to have his studies reduced. '*We don't recommend reduction at this stage,*' the letter stated. '*What he needs is more fresh air.*' Perhaps fourteen-year-old Bressin, made pale by suspicions he couldn't pinpoint, said something to Ross, because Ross's guardians telephoned Mrs Rose asking to take Tasha out for a weekend. When Tasha came she clung to Ross and, in a breaking voice, to the best of her limited ability, implored to be allowed to stay, but wouldn't say why. She slept that night in a caravan with Ross and would barely leave go of him to let him sleep. A few days later, despairing at being back where she obviously didn't want to be, she smashed a watch Diana had given her, in the process damaging her most recently operated-on ear. Frantically, Mrs Rose called the hospital and Tasha was readmitted. That was when the first telegram went off and, as what was left of normal behaviour slipped away, the second followed as fast as the slow Island communications system would allow.

When Diana arrived at last to wrap her now full-grown little girl in her arms, Tasha stared at her solemnly through distant eyes. Australia was trying to take over the Solomons, she informed her mother, and she must take off all her rings because they were drug rings. Sometimes what she said made no sense at all. A nursing sister who'd attended Tasha on admission took Diana aside. Tasha, she confided, had refused to remove underwear or take a bath, and when the idea of changing her clothes was more strongly suggested she'd resisted with screams. These, the sister said, could be signs of sexual assault. Did Diana wish this taken further? Tasha could go to a psychiatric hospital for assessment, but if Diana felt other authorities should be informed about this particularly sensitive matter, this could also be arranged.

'No,' said Diana. 'No. I'll take Tasha home.'

For a decade, the Hepworths believed their daughter had been abused by an unknown adult, who had taken cruel advantage of her innocence and naturally affectionate nature. Later they believed the catalyst for her odd behaviour lay in the weekend in the caravan with Ross – with Tasha, the older and more experienced, who had, as Tom put it, '*no inner moral restraints*', as instigator and Ross rejecting her. Diana never set the hellhounds of her anger – or the police – on the stranger she originally accused because 'One did not want that kind of thing to come out into the open . . . it was *different* then . . .' What nobody knew was that Tasha had just gone through an acute phase of an illness that would now go undiagnosed for a further ten months.

Diana believed, one hundred per cent, that in taking her child back to Pigeon without further assessment and without kicking up a fuss that was bound to produce further trauma she was doing the best thing, and certainly there was every sign at first that Tasha was happier back home. A deeply confused girl in white society, who, during hallucinations at Mrs Rose's house thought there was a war on and her dadi killed, Tasha was smiling and dancing with familiar dark faces by New Year 1977. She didn't need to practise the English diction she found so difficult with Reef Island friends. They had another language to share, and whatever inhibitions she'd had about the removal of clothing in New Zealand apparently vanished on Nandelli. That she had some kind of division within herself can be in no doubt, but exactly what occurred, if anything, to trigger behaviour described as psychotic – or indicative of assault – is not known. Tasha was British enough not to talk about 'that sort of thing'. Or maybe she simply couldn't.

17

Lessons in Magic

SOMETIMES WHAT I LEARN ABOUT WHAT'S HAPPENED ON PIGEON, AND to its people, frightens me. I came here thinking I was going to give my boys a safe taste of the 'desert island experience', while gathering notes about an enterprising couple who raised a family in the sun – and now I feel a frisson that's both fear and fascination whenever I open Tom's files – or try to talk to Diana about impossible things . . . I used to think she was hard and cold; now I believe she's one of the bravest women I've ever met – and only ever chilly-sounding because she's suffered so much during her so-called wonderful life.

When we returned to Pigeon from our adventures – complete with Compaq computer part – Diana welcomed me, as on the first day when I'd barged past, with open arms. This time I walked straight into them and held her close.

'I hear you lost Christine,' she said, ticking me off, as I knew she must, even though the warmth of her hug said something else. I apologized but didn't attempt to explain, and she didn't ask. Instead, she ordered Tangypera to take chairs to the West Patio, and I told her of progress I was making with Tom's diaries. Joe and Benji opted for hugs from Pegi and all the wontoks down Ross's end, enthralling their schoolmates with tales of their travels.

'Everyone loved him, you know,' mused Diana, speaking of her husband, and I agreed (Islanders didn't count, and I wasn't going to argue about the Wiens) and told her I thought their marriage, lasting almost half a century, was truly something to celebrate. This pleased her – Tom's arms around her had been key to much of her joy in Pigeon – but it wasn't long before she was spilling out a tale of Ross's latest failings. The problem concerned his method of running PIT, which wasn't, she felt, as efficient as Tom's had been.

'He lies like a Melanesian,' she said – in front of Tangypera, who grinned at me – 'to "avoid trouble". Did Ben tell you how much he's given away to his wretched wontoks in the past? *Thousands* of dollars worth of goods . . .'

I commiserated vaguely – it was hard not to get involved in the family's fights – but assured her the reticent Ben had told me nothing.

'You must start talking to him soon. I'm sure it would do him good.'

I'd been meaning to interview Ben properly for some time, but my embarrassing secret lust – and his shyly evasive ways – made it tricky. It couldn't be delayed much longer though: after Magnus's Christmas visit, Diana was going to New Zealand to have her latest batch of skin cancers zapped, and Ben was going with her.

'Tomorrow then?' I suggested boldly. I could ask about his school-days – no need yet to step into sensitive territory, like asking what form the magic of Reef Island women took. (Did they jump on him in the night?)

'Lovely,' said Diana. 'I'll send down tea. By the way, that shortbread you gave me was delicious.' I left her laughing when I confessed that my final act of vengeance on Sven had been to leave a presentation package of Walker's best, empty, under the greasy pillow I'd refused to share with him.

I went swimming before seeing Ben. For an hour, I let the weight of waves swirling round Poppet Island embrace and buffet me, then lay adrift on a calmer patch, eyes half closed against deliciously dazzling shafts of sunlight. After this, I showered in rainwater, brushed my topknot and tied a kalico firmly over my breasts, adding a pin to the skirt to stop it swinging open. Ben, I noticed, had just taken a shower too. Diana had arranged the chairs in such a way that mine, marked by a cushion for my spine, faced him directly, and he faced the sea. Far away, looking from the West Patio like a ship on the horizon, lay Makalom, an islet inhabited by blue-footed boobies, which Ross in the past had kept as pets. Ben fixed his eyes on this.

'Have you read your father's diaries?' I asked.

'Only a little bit.'

He pronounced 'little bit' 'leedle bit' – close to Pijin's 'lelebet', but with a touch of schoolboy New Zealand, too. I wondered which passages he'd read, but hesitated to press. Did he know how close he had come to being excommunicated from his parents' Will? Did he know what Tom and Diana imagined Ross had done – apart from being inept as a manager of PIT – and was he aware there was a time, after he'd been affected by whatever happened to him in Australia, when his father couldn't stand the sight of him? I groped for topics that might interest but not alarm him. When Ben was alarmed, up popped God like a shield and nothing emerged from his lips but Bible quotes.

'I've been trying to understand what happened to Tasha,' I said, wondering if discussing this might lead to discussion about himself. 'It must have been upsetting, when you were at school, always having her and her – problems – at home during the holidays.' It was a cruder approach than I had intended, but it was out now.

'I suppose so. I don't know. I don't . . . *feel* much.'

Ben's brown eyes were gentle, on Makalom, but vague. He wasn't wearing a shirt, and the glossy hair on his chest went all the way down into the folds of his kalico beneath his navel. I wanted to spread my fingers in it, grip it hard and yank him towards me for a long, rude kiss. I wanted to make him feel. Breathing deep and feeling my nipples tighten, I turned, blushing, to my notes.

'You were interested in joining the army for a time, weren't you?'

'Yes.'

'But it didn't come to anything?'

'No.'

'Was that because you went off the idea?'

'Not really . . .'

Now I pounced. I'd heard he'd begged his godmother, Amalie, to encourage his parents to let him train for a military career. Something in him craved discipline – a set of rules to guide his actions. Somewhere as remote as Reefs, you had to make up your own rules; too much freedom can be frightening. Maybe that's why Tom and Diana had always kept to such a rigid self-imposed routine – why I did, too.

'Was it because you had to come back to Pigeon?'

I wondered how much choice he'd felt he had about how and

where he led any life other than on his parents' dream island. His gaze on the horizon wavered a moment. Less lustful now than sympathetic, I wanted to hold his hand. Slowly, his pale face, the liquid eyes vulnerable as twin Achilles heels, turned towards mine.

'Everything comes back to Pigeon,' he said quietly.

But when our eyes met and I pursued this direction, asking what he meant, his eyes glazed over again and he quickly placed his shield between us:

'The Lord has charge of us all . . . Honour thy parents . . .'

It was no good trying to go on talking to Ben when this happened, but I must somehow get to the root of what had damaged him. Had brainwashing and magic really been involved? Christine Clement's school notes, and the majority of reports from New Zealand, suggested level-headedness, intelligence and potential.

A few evenings later, perched on the southern cliffs from where I'd soon be watching for Magnus's arrival, I observed Ben, Matoko and Joe fishing off the Edge of the Reef. Usually they went far out, in a motorized canoe, but now they were only looking for a local supper haul, using Matoko's dugout. It was the same dugout in which he'd asked if I was married – of blond wood shaped by hundreds of small axe blows, leaving a surface like scales. Joe was boatboy, steadying the craft when speared fish were flung over the side and moving his position to keep the balance right when Matoko climbed in. Once Ben had left the dugout – standing with arms out, Christlike, for a few seconds before throwing himself into a perfect dive – he remained beneath the water, only head, spear and arm appearing from time to time with a catch, so it was Joe and Matoko I watched. Joe, like Mhairi, hadn't tanned deeply, but was sleek on Pegi's generous diet of rice, fish and endless fluffy bananas, and playful as a seal. He cheered whenever a fish appeared, giving a thumbs-up to whoever dropped it in.

Matoko, a head shorter than Ben, was exactly that copper colour described by the *Mohawk* diarist, but with his stack of lime- and salt-bleached hair left wild. For all he had only one eye, he was still one of the most attractive men in Reefs. He was also the only person I could think of who was remotely close to Ben. They'd been fishing companions for years, and he was the only Islander I ever saw paying a social visit to Ben's Box. Once, Tom's diary informed me, Ben had attempted to take Matoko into Ngarando for coffee – a move described briskly by Tom as '*Mistake*', and not repeated. Would Matoko be able to enlighten me about Ben? But how to arrange a meeting without attracting unwanted attention – or assumptions? I'd have to consult Tangypera, who was at this moment working late for Diana, freeing a set of hinges from rust. I watched Matoko's strong arm emerge once more triumphant from the deep, followed by his compactly muscled body launching itself lightly over the edge of the dugout, where he adjusted the rubber on his spear before turning to go. Would I like to be held in those knotty arms? How would it feel to be pressed down onto a pile of banana leaves deep in the bush, legs parting under the doubtless corkscrew efficiency of that hard copper body? Would he smell strange? Would I smell strange to him? In truth, the thought scared me, although I was certain Matoko would be as gentle as he knew how. The problem was, there would be no more of a meeting of minds than with Ben.

Tangypera was quick off the mark. I had only to hiss once, from the bushes, and he was out of Diana's workshed and by my side in a flash, asking what I wanted to learn about now.

'Kastom magic, and the powers of Reef Island women. I'd also like to talk to Matoko about Ben.'

Tangypera rocked on the soles of his bare feet, considering, then told me bluntly it would be better if I didn't talk to Matoko about Ben, because those two were 'kolsap' (close friends) and it would put Matoko in an awkward position. He also confirmed that Matoko still fancied me, and could be confused by a private meeting.

'Beta livim', Lusi.' Better leave it – and him – alone. I wondered who Tangypera was protecting most, Matoko or me, but knew the subject to be closed. What about the magic then? Small, phlegmy giggles shook the leaves by my side.

'Sapos iu mitim Mami b'long mi – an' waef.'

Good. Tangypera was ready to introduce me to his mother and wife. We scheduled it for as soon as Diana and Ben had left for New Zealand. In the meantime I'd try to cram into my mind the contents of another volume of Tom's diary, and make the few preparations needed towards Magnus's arrival for Christmas.

The second best thing, to me, about Christmas in Reef Islands was that the festive period consisted solely of genuine, relaxed happy atmosphere with nil commercial hype; the first, that it meant I saw my fasbon again, after too long. I don't know how many times I ran to the lookout point when Magnus's canoe was due – this being the cyclone season we could rely on long flat calms between violent seas – but do know that by the time 'Sail-ho!' rang out at dusk, I was jelly. How would the rest of his family look, from his point of view, after six months' separation – with him in a vastly different environment, part way through his first year at a moderately conventional senior school, and us by now entrenched in our occasionally wild island ways? The meeting was a shock. I stood in the shallows with a towel in my arms, something I thought he might need, expecting a boy – the boy I'd said goodbye to – and silhouetted against the thin evening light, I saw, climbing out of Ross's canoe, a tall youth.

'O mae wat!' (My word!) cried Kiyo excitedly. 'Magnus kam big laek man!'

He was right. I knew Magnus from the way he moved – lightly and deliberately – as he extricated a backpack from the bows, but these movements came from long arms and long legs and a grown-up-shaped body.

'Magnus?'

'Hello, Mum, is that you? You look minute . . .'

I gasped. His voice had dropped an octave too. Then we were laughing and hugging, my 'little' boy bumping my topknot with his own salt-damp head.

'Is that Benji? Well I suppose you have grown *a bit* . . .'

Benji, whose diminutive size was a family joke, was so awed he couldn't say anything for a moment, then politely invited his very big brother to look at his shell collection any time.

' 'Course I will,' said Magnus breezily. 'Where's Joe?'

I jutted my chin behind me like an Islander, and Magnus did a double-take. Joe was leading the way to Magnus's quarters with a grip bag on his head – followed by four matching-sized piccaninnis supporting his backpack in similar fashion. The procession ended with three smaller children holding the oilskin Magnus had been wearing, rolled like a sausage on their shoulders.

'Amazing,' said Magnus. 'I'm starved. When are we going to eat? We caught a kingfish on the way. What about barbecuing the steaks?' He was still one of us. But his first meal back on the island was taken with Diana, who produced her famous Poisson Cru.

'What does your father do, Jane?' Diana quizzed Magnus's travel-minder, who'd also come on a quest of her own, to introduce beach-friendly sports to the Islanders. Luckily, being a chief scout-master as well as a gentleman farmer, he passed her rigorous test. Magnus, who'd eaten at the children's table before, now sat beside Diana and contributed effortlessly to polite dinner conversation. Afterwards the Irvines and Jane repaired to our eyrie and I had a shot of cognac from the bottle she had clairvoyantly brought.

'You look good, Mum – different,' said Magnus, his own difference showing in his observation. I was relieved he couldn't see all the changes in my mind as well as my body. Then there was a tiny scratching, like a kitten, on the veranda roof – sign of a visitor. It was – oh sweet surprise – Christine Hepworth, returned at last to the fold, in time for Christmas and wanting to be introduced. As though shyly, she presented Magnus with, first, her beautiful face, then the rest of her in tantalizing bits as she sidled round the door. I had a feeling I wasn't going to see much of Magnus after this, but Jane and I exchanged a glance. He might look like a man but he was still only thirteen. Christine was older, doubtless more experienced, and we didn't want any broken hearts.

'You laekem volley ball?' Christine asked in a husky voice, as though she were suggesting a steamy moonlit wander on the beach. Her funny blend of Pijin and English was seductive in itself.

'Yes!' blurted Magnus, although I wasn't sure he'd ever played it before.

'Great,' said Jane. 'We'll get it set up between a couple of palm trees first thing tomorrow . . .'

'You laekem music? I *lavem* music . . .' glimmered Christine.

'Yes!' said Magnus.

'. . . but I only got one tape.'

'Oh? What's it called? I might know it.'

Here Christine curled up, giggling, pulled her long black crinkly tresses over her face, then peeked at Magnus through them:

'*Sex On The Beach* . . .'

Jane and I raised our eyes heavenwards. I had been rather hoping to introduce her – and reintroduce Magnus – to the innocent pleasures of Reef Island singing around campfires. Never let it be said life was slow or dull on Pigeon.

But I needn't have worried. Jane faithfully danced until 3 a.m. to

Sex On The Beach to keep an eye on Magnus and Christine at night, and I did my stint during the risky siesta period after lunch, popping down to the units to chat with the young people – probably maddeningly – for an hour while Jane rested. There was, as well as volley ball, swimming, canoeing, inter-island soccer, and a treasure hunt organized by Peter and Mhairi (tiny but thrilling treasure of Australian lollies sent by the original Christine, née Clement, tied up in palms and concealed in coral cairns) to keep everyone busy at other times. Just once, I caught Christine making graphic shapes out of balloons – also sent by the other Christine – and waving them at Magnus from an inviting pose. On sighting me, she rearranged them into a cute little dog.

'I shouldn't worry,' said Diana when I mentioned this lightly over tea, then nearly caused me to drop my cup by adding casually: 'She's probably just initiating him.'

It was hard sometimes to make out if Diana was ahead of, or behind, her time. If she thought it acceptable for the half-caste granddaughter she'd roared at for behaving tartishly in Honiara to be making passes at my very young son, why had she cut Ross out of her Will when he had 'gone native' and married Christine's mother, under Kastom law, at the age of eighteen? I was to find out soon it hadn't been as simple as that. But for now I concentrated on enjoying the simplest, sweetest Christmas I've ever known, for in the end there was Reef Island singing, umu-baked kokoroko and the traditional daubing of young bodies with pikpik fat, which were then, hilariously, rolled in the sand – as well as *Sex On The Beach*. And when a choir arrived by dugout to sing carols on Boxing Day, Christine, the eldest daughter of the house on Pigeon, performed her traditional task of powdering the perspiring bodies of the singers with fitting modesty. Everyone exchanged flower necklaces, shook hands and danced again when it came to New Year's Eve, and there were sated figures sprawled everywhere when the sun rose. I often took my red kayak way out on the mirror-calm blue during the holiday period, stripping off everything and letting the heat flare through every part of me until I felt so relaxed I never wanted to move again.

But the second week of 1999 came too soon, meaning I had to say goodbye to Magnus again, and again go through the anxious process of checking my satellite phone daily for messages until I was assured he was safely home. '*I'm snow-boarding, having a great time!*' he wrote at last, while we were still sweltering in the – thankfully – long gaps between cyclonic winds. Then, suddenly it seemed, Diana was making preparations to leave too, encouraging me to continue talking to Ben while I could. My interviews with him hadn't progressed much, for, beset on all sides over Christmas by happy young people having a good time – mostly with their bodies – he'd retired even further behind his shield of God. Maybe he was nervous of what talking might reveal, too, for twice he sent messages saying he was 'busy' when Diana suggested a meeting, but was observed lying on his bed humming hymns at the appointed hour. Perhaps that was what being busy meant for him. However, I felt a certain amount of evasion was necessary too. The more I read about Ben in his father's diaries, the uneasier I became, and at least during the quieter cycles of the moon my lustful feelings waned slightly. As Tom had done, I was beginning to see Ben as something of a tragedy – or a victim of circumstance. While he and Diana were away in New Zealand, I would concentrate on Ross and the Islanders. That was the plan anyway, and it looked as though it was off to a good start when, almost as soon as Diana, in a bright yellow oilskin over a red sundress, had disappeared over the horizon in a canoe padded by Stasi's bed, Tangypera turned up to escort me into the bush.

'My women are ready now,' he announced, and I armed myself with a notebook and followed.

As we passed Temotulaki, Tangypera commented that I visited the islet so often, people thought I kept a god on it. I smiled. Certainly, proffered heavenwards as it was, and such a poignant example of island life at its simplest, it meant something special to me.

'Fela laekem faki dea,' he said.

'Pardon?'

'Faki. Iu savvy – jig-a-jig.'

'Ah.'

It was hardly surprising Paradise in miniature attracted lovers.

'Tangypera,' I said quickly, latching onto the subject while it was in the air. 'Do you think Ben has gone in for much faki-ing? In our society, a man that age would usually be married by now.'

'Oh, Ben's married.'

At one point in Tom's diary the question of whether Ben was married or not had raged through the pages for weeks. *'Is he or isn't he? Blast the boy.'*

'Kastom or Christian?'

'Kastom.' Tangypera went on to tell me that silent, celibate, Christian Ben had purchased a Nivali woman from her uncle for approximately £150, and had a daughter by her. Was this the woman Tom thought had magical powers over Ben?

'Yes,' said Tangypera casually, 'every Reef Island girl has magic. Oh look, there's my wife.'

Ahead of us, one of the thin figures I'd often seen in the distance on reef walks, bent sharply as hairpins, straightened, and far-reaching cries like bird calls were exchanged between husband and wife.

'Mae wat, she's pretty!' I said, and Tangypera's leathery features crinkled with delight.

'She *is* nice. We've got plenty of children.'

I thought of a line in Tom's diary that read: '*These people don't suffer, of course, as we do, from "lurve".*' Nine children on, Tangypera and Kaplei ran towards each other and clasped hands. It looked like 'lurve' to me.

'She's shy,' Tangypera explained, as Kaplei covered half her face with a loose end of kalico attached to the bundle that turned out to be a sleeping baby on her back, and he told her in local 'languis' not to be frightened of me because I wasn't like Diana. I wondered if Diana knew how afraid of her people were.

As well as the baby, Kaplei carried a rice bag, its yellow plastic handle round her forehead like an Alice band to keep her hands free. She'd been gathering rif kaikai for a meal. At the rate of one tiny shell, whose rubbery squiggle of an occupant might make half a mouthful, picked up after careful observation of signs in the sand every four to five minutes, this must take a while. 'Solomon Island time,' said Tangypera, smiling. Delicately running a toe along a line, invisible to me on the bleached reef, that led to a pinhead-sized protuberance, he bent forward and scooped up another tasty victim for the bag. There were russet-striped cones tipped by fine hooks concealing 'eyes'; spiny blue urchins hiding in nests of coral, and pearly fanshapes perfect, without their hosts, as earrings. How did one cook them all? 'Bon 'em.' Other figures had, in typical Islander fashion, melted out of sight by now, leaving just the three of us on what must have been over a square mile of reef, edged on three sides by mangroves and raised coral atolls, and on the fourth by a boisterously fluttering frill marking the Edge of the Reef where dipwata began – and from where Tangypera's ancestors were believed to have sprung to claim Nenumbo, in their fancy canoes. Almost in silence we worked, Kaplei never speaking directly to me but teaching all the time by demonstration, her large, expressive toes as busy as her fingers following mazelike patterns on the ground that, read correctly, spelled kaikai. The quiet of the day expanded around us as the sun exhaled its heat from higher and higher, and from where there was no water at all on the surface came the cracks and pops of small creatures awaking or expiring, and the salt scent of exposed reef, like a lightly sweating body from which a sheet has been drawn back. Slowly I began to grasp the meaning of some of the shapes that were as clear to Tangypera and Kaplei as written English to me, and when, finally, I managed to trace a line by myself and swoop on the invisible shell where it should be, and was, Kaplei clapped me on the shoulder and kept her strong, damp, pink-palmed hand there, massaging tenderly. She spoke, and Tangypera laughed.

'She's asking why you're not married.'

'Tell her,' I said, 'that I must lack the magic needed to hold onto a good man.'

Tangypera translated, giggling, but Kaplei looked serious.

'She says that's difficult, because other women's magic may be pulling him away, but there are recipes . . .'

I wanted to know where to obtain the ingredients, in case my awakened state continued back in civilization, but for this I must wait to meet Tangypera's mother. On the way, Kaplei lit a long pipe from a length of bound fibres that had kept a glow at its end all the time she'd been on the reef. She and Tangypera took alternate drags, then she suddenly abandoned the pipe in his hands and squatted down excitedly, beside what looked to me like some kind of shell rubbish tip. It was a rubbish tip, but created by an octopus, which should still be under it awaiting the rising of the tide to move on. First Tangypera tried to dig it out, but came away with only a tantalizing tentacle – white, with spotty orange suckers. He shrugged, accepted the need of his woman's magic and unstrapped the baby from her back. Kaplei, long-bodied and supple – for all her nine piccaninnis – then squirmed down, belly flat to the surface of the reef, and thrust a questing arm down the opening Tangypera had made between broken shells, grimacing with concentration.

'Ahh,' she said quietly, and he echoed her with a grunt.

'Aiyee!' she lamented and he shook his head sympathetically, clicking his tongue and again echoing the sound she made.

'*Ah-ahhhh!*' The two of them uttered this breathy, triumphant cry almost in unison, and there was Kaplei rolling onto her back, clutching the white, gelatinous, slippery prize, over which in a flash Tangypera had slipped a rice bag – mine, with a camera still in the bottom. Kaplei stood up and retrieved the baby, reshrouding its small head against the sun with a leaf used as a hood.

'She says the octopus is for you,' said Tangypera – 'special kaikai.'

'Thank you,' I said, taking the squashy, sticky bag with as much enthusiasm as I could muster, faced with the fact that now I would probably be unable to catch any of the day's events on film. But I was unlikely to forget them anyway.

I'd been to Nenumbo many times since the first, frightening, welcoming ceremony, and it was no longer strange to be greeted in the muddy shallows where the mangroves began by a bevy of naked piccaninnis including two of Joe and Benji's classmates. They swarmed round me as we made our way towards leaf huts built between a shallow beach and thick bush, on land sifted by anthropologists for shards of Lapita pottery 'foreign' to the current inhabitants, who'd been irritated enough by the disturbance to the roots of some of their trees to demand compensation for such disrespectful disinterment of someone else's past – who just might be an ancestor after all. Tangypera's mother, emerging, bent double, through a leaf doorway like a living ghost of the past herself, so old and frail did she appear, tottered forward on legs like birdbones, and grasped both my hands between hers in a grip fierce as a wrestler's. She can't have been more than four and a half feet high – a child's height – but her presence was formidable. Like her son, she had extraordinary, bloodshot, all-seeing eyes and there was immense strength hidden in her diminutive frame. Hoarse words flew from her toothless lips with copious spittle, and she went on yelling – though in fact her voice was barely above a whisper – until a whole collection of woven trugs lay at her feet, brought by lesser females whom she treated as minions. Still clutching one of my hands, she danced away like a sprite, pulling me after her into the bush, the great eyes of girls carrying more conventional, round leaf baskets on their heads slanting to follow our progress into the shadows. Tangypera padded silently behind, smiling and proud. Kaplei stayed back to finish weaving a fresh mat for our return – and, I later discovered, to organize the gathering of a whole range of bush fruits for my inspection and refreshment.

On most of Reef Islands, the bush has remained unchanged, except by cyclones, from the way it's been for thousands of years. Thin soil makes some interiors darkly sparse, but where I was taken on Nenumbo that day there were patches lush as rainforest, the floor matted by deluge-soaked underbrush so that steam rose like conjurors' smoke through layers of leaves to the sky – exactly the sort of place one would expect to find magic a part of everyday life. To me, all the trees tended to look the same at first, which of course they weren't.

'Fo' Mimiopulo,' confided Tangypera, rather suddenly, as a bunch of striped leaves was thrust at me and his mother continued to rummage energetically for more further on. Was it a gift for someone I didn't know, or a cure for some condition of the heart?

'Blood in your pee-pee.'

'Oh.'

Another posy was passed back and laid in a trug.

'Numanio.'

The meaning of this Tangypera demonstrated vividly by pulling his lips away from his gums and showing where they bled. A shouted request brought him shavings from just inside the bark of the same tree from which the leaves came, which he'd later moisten and swallow. This was the medicine for gingivitis.

'Gonorrhea.'

Three different kinds of leaves, combined, were the recommended remedy for this, and instead of giggles from the owners of the big eyes still following us in the shadows, there were serious nods and not a little head craning. Tasha had suffered from VD at least once in Reefs. Had her Islander friends tried this, in their matter-of-fact way, before it had become a scandal among the whites?

The medical tour continued for some time before Tangypera jerked his chin to one side, indicating I should follow, and he whispered, beside a stumpy little tree, that some people believed Sipikoli, Ben's Nivali woman, had, when she feared to lose him, tapped ash from a glowing twig of this into his food. It had seemed to work for a while, but then her magic had been countered by that of a stronger male sorcerer brought in from Malaita. (Here I noticed Tangypera's mother standing still, listening.) Who had brought in this counter magician, I

The hair of a pikpik is singed off before cooking. *Robbie Cooper*

Butchering a turtle, 1998. The Islanders use age-old conservation methods to ensure not too many are killed. *Robbie Cooper*

Pigeon Island School. (*Left to right*) Patteson, Benji, Ngive, Peter with Little Chris, Andrew, Elisha, Joe and Simon Boga. *Lucy Irvine*

Mhairi and Pegi weighing copra, using the method devised by the Hepworths forty years ago. *Lucy Irvine*

Reef Island children fish whenever they're hungry.

Lucy Irvine

Bishop Lazarus, based on Santa Cruz, conducts traditional-style Christian services all over Reef Islands. *Robbie Cooper*

Ben returning, via Temotulaki, from a service at the Church of the Living Word, with Star. *Robbie Cooper*

Diana and Tangypera mending the roof of her workshed, 1998. *Robbie Cooper*

Pegi and Lucy shopping at Otambe. By private arrangement Lucy could get fifty bananas for a Woolworth's exercise book, which would be used to roll tobacco. *Robbie Cooper*

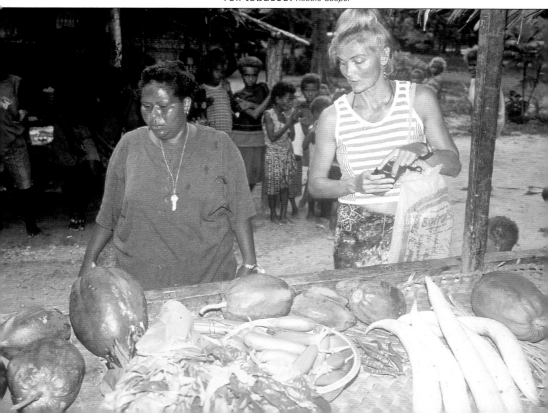

Nupanyi, who Kastom-owns part of Pigeon and has worked for the Hepworths for forty years, ramming copra into a sack. *Robbie Cooper*

This lady at Otambe is cutting up breadfruit to dry into biscuit-like triangles called nambo. Sometimes in the cyclone season it's all there is to eat.

Robbie Cooper

Tangypera, who was Lucy's key to Kastom information. *Lucy Irvine*

Tangypera's mother weaving a basket. She taught Lucy about 'women's magic'. *Lucy Irvine*

One of the elders of Nenumbo who decided Lucy could learn about Kastom matters. *Lucy Irvine*

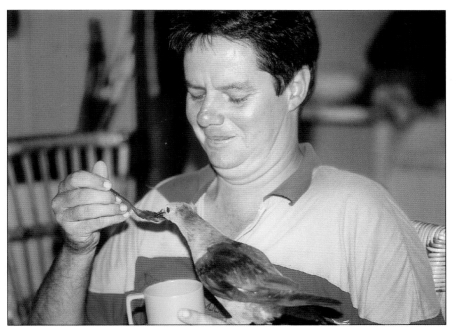

Ross Hepworth, the caring family man, with Nati, a pigeon rescued from the island of Nbanga Temoa. *Robbie Cooper*

Joe, after his terrifying arrival on Pigeon, soon got his confidence back and became an expert at paddling his own canoe. *Robbie Cooper*

Elisha, one of Joe's and Benji's classmates on Pigeon, in another guise at his home village, Nenumbo. *Robbie Cooper*

Pegi squeezing grated coconut for a Kastom pudding. *Lucy Irvine*

Lanebu sheltering Frederic, Ross's and Pegi's son, from the sun. *Lucy Irvine*

wanted to know. Was it a jealous suitor of Sipikoli's who wanted to break up her relationship with Ben?

'No,' said Tangypera. 'It was Ross – with his mother and father's permission. Some say they paid his boat fare from Malaita, too.'

So Tom and Diana had sanctioned the use of primitive forces in the hope of stopping a second son of theirs from going entirely 'native'. Did it work?

'Not for long.'

Unbeknown to anyone, Sipikoli, clearly a determined girl, had secreted a whole sheaf of magic materials into the leaf roof directly above where she slept with Ben, and apparently the only 'magic' strong enough to counter this was an air ticket bought for Ben by his parents. And then, ironically, while he was abroad he'd fallen in with a cult which professed to put its 'volunteers' in touch with special powers ... To get the full sequence of this I'd need to go back to Tom's diary, but now I had to admire the softness of the fresh mat set out for my comfort by Kaplei, in front of her modest leaf hut, into which, somehow, nine children and many wontoks crowded each night, and which had had to be rebuilt from scratch several times since her marriage, after Bigwinds.

'Oki,' said an old lady with such a thin neck, I wondered how she could swallow. She handed me a kidney-shaped object with a smell curiously like roast chestnuts, which, when a papery skin was pinched off, revealed a veined, pinkish interior like a newborn rabbit.

'Kaikai!' (Eat up) I was encouraged, and did, observed by many. The oki proved surprisingly solid and clove to the roof of my mouth, with neither a savoury nor a sweet taste but a disturbing texture of flesh. Six more were slipped into my rice bag with the octopus, which had now ceased to pulsate, but still wobbled, on top of my camera.

'Tevi,' said another woman, and was thrilled to discover I was already familiar with this smooth-fleshed but spiky-centred fruit through my tree-climbing sons. Then I was plied with cutnuts, alite, ngali and ngenumbla – the nuts and berries diet of our primitive ancestors, we are taught at school, but still everyday kaikai to these people.* I used a travel bottle of preboiled water to wash down the

---

* All these fruits and nuts were shown me at Nenumbo under the circumstances described, but over a number of occasions during the year, which I have combined in one scene.

more cloying of the offerings, and Tangypera's mother admired it so much I gave it to her. She immediately filled it with crumbled coral lime, to 'cut' with the betel-nut that, because she was toothless, she ground with a pestle-shaped stone in a mortar-shaped piece of wood. Then, very secretively – but pinching my arm to be sure I noticed – she slipped a twig into my bag for me to take back to my country as magic to enhance the 'holding' of a man. I thanked her profusely, but knew it was unlikely to pass customs. Maybe I'd risk airmailing it to a friend anyway, labelled 'Gift of no value'. Hah. And ask her to save some for me.

Was it surprising that children brought up half in this culture and half in the strict tea-at-four-and-change-for-dinner version of English culture imposed by their parents on Pigeon encountered some confusion at the onset of puberty? Was it, in fact, inevitable, a built-in hazard of the territory? Wading back alone to Pigeon, I met Joe, Patteson, Benji, Ngive and others returning from a spear-fishing expedition in a mix of kayaks and dugouts. Joe was experimenting with the Islander style of extinguishing any life left in a small fish once caught – by biting it in the eye.

'Hi, Mum. We won't need supper tonight – we're just going to cook these.'

'Fine,' I said. I had plans to share my octopus with Star and Stasi, as I knew if I tried to get rid of it any other way it would be found, which could cause offence. It wasn't that I disliked octopus; it had just been blobbing around in the rice bag rather a long time, and it had been a hot day. That night, when I was sure no-one was about, I crept to Diana's house to perform my secret act, and was reminded of a conversation I'd had with her a few days before she'd left for New Zealand, when I'd popped in to request doctors' reports on Tasha.

'You haven't been feeding the dogs, have you?'

'Oh no,' I'd said, lying hopelessly, because I blushed. (On that occasion I'd been given an impossible amount of turtle to get through.) I'm sure she saw through me, because she'd added: 'It disturbs their routine, you see.'

We'd agreed before that routine was important for both children and animals.

'I know.' When, clutching a sheaf of reports, I'd said goodnight that evening, she'd kissed me, and I'd bowed my head.

'Are you all right, darling? You look a little low.'

'I'm fine. It's just . . .' I'd indicated the papers in my hand, diagnosing and possibly condemning in some way her daughter. Or even her upbringing. There was a lot of information about the twins, too, that I knew Diana hadn't looked at for a long time. She hadn't read all her husband's diaries either. 'It's just all such a responsibility.'

'I know, darling,' Diana had said, 'but you have my complete trust. I'm totally in your hands.'

That was part of the trouble. By now I didn't only believe Diana was brave; I was extremely fond of her, and didn't want her to suffer any more hurt than she'd already had in her life, through anything my research uncovered.

18

1976–1981

PEOPLE ON SMALL ISLANDS TEND TO MAKE USE OF WHATEVER SAILS their way, and when a ship came into Mohawk Bay carrying a girl experienced with handicapped children, Tom offered her free board in Paradise in return for care of Tasha. Louise jumped at the unusual job and Tasha, apparently recovering quickly from her crisis in New Zealand, was allowed to go dancing on Nandelli at New Year because Louise was with her. But it is impossible to guard an unchained charge twenty-four hours a day, and when Louise wasn't looking, Tasha slipped away and found a boy named Nokali she liked so much she hoped he'd marry her one day. And so he might have, if it weren't against Kastom practice to form permanent liaisons with imperfect stock. Tom and Diana were to discover more about this, to them, strangely selective rule in due course. But all Tasha knew now was how delicious it was to lie in the warm shallows under the moon, dripping like a princess with phosphorescent jewels, kalico floating above her waist while wavelets tickled her nipples, and Nokali hugged and hugged her, rhythmic as the sea, until a bigger wave seemed to catch them both, leaving him breathless, until he was ready to start hugging her again. They didn't mind if it rained because it drowned the sounds they made, but if it was too windy on the beach they crawled into a cave of leaves they'd discovered one night, holding hands as they crept about seeking a hiding place, and there Tasha turned to flash her pretty smile, still in her crawling position, pulled aside her kalico with one hand, as she'd learned, and he clasped her from behind. Her small, strong hands gripped the roots of box-flower bushes, and her breasts bounced happily up and down on the sandy soil of the island she loved. Afterwards they sometimes made collages of leaves on each other's bodies, glued with their own body juices and Nokali's copious betel spit. She was sad she always had to leave him to go back to Louise, but understood she must or Mummy and Dadi would be cross.

Over the holidays (it was 1977 now) Bressin and Ross reacquainted themselves with old Nandelli friends, and joined in the ritual of smearing pikpik fat over one another then rolling in sand, which adhered like body paint, to celebrate New Year. Ross did a fair amount of rolling about in the bushes, too. Fifteen that year, in Islander terms he was easily ready for intercourse. Bressin read *The Lords of Discipline*, a book about the Citadel, America's answer to Sandhurst, which Amalie had sent. His interest in joining the services was increasing, but his father, always uneasy with the idea of an educated individual having to conform to authority, was not encouraging.

'Join the TA by all means,' he said. 'Learn some skills. But I've never seen the point of signing up as cannon fodder in someone else's war . . .'

Bressin had a different image of army life. On Pigeon and at school in New Zealand he had remained essentially a loner, despite his able participation in sports. As a more permanent member of a recognized 'team', with camaraderie, he imagined, extending beyond physical exercise, he might feel less alone. And it would be good to have a cause you believed in to fight for, wouldn't it? 'Pah!' said Tom. Diana was more ready to listen, in spite of her unhappy experiences in the WAAF, but like Tom she hoped the twins might see a future for themselves on Pigeon – although naturally it would be good for them to see a bit of the world first. The plan was for the whole family to go to England in 1978, when the boys would round off their education in colleges and the Hepworth seniors would do up for sale a house left to Diana by her mother. Tasha should be capable by then of taking on a simple job – factory work perhaps; she was good at making jewellery and for Christmas Christine Clement had sent a craftbox of beads which kept her occupied for hours – although sometimes she disappeared purposefully with them but returned with little to show beyond a grin and dusty knees. Early in 1977 she was sent with Louise to Australia, where her parents thought she might gain useful work experience in caring company. Meanwhile, Tom and Diana prepared a site for two motel-style units along Pigeon's eastern edge, for the guests they still believed would come. They also moved house, deciding, since there were few visitors at present, to occupy Ngarando themselves. This would also take them out of earshot of the tedious drunks who hung around the beach near the store, despite being frequently warned off. Objections to the use of the eastern edge were deflected with promises of jobs.

Diana wasn't madly keen to see Britain again – her last glimpse, in 1947, had left a grim impression of cold grey weather, ration queues and grey, conventional minds – but she knew the only way to hang on to the lifestyle she loved on her South Sea island was to support it largely from outside. The New Zealand flats were letting satisfactorily – mostly to Western Samoans – but income from these still only covered the school fees. The windfall of the house in England was nicely timed to cater for college and travel for the twins, and it seemed the rainbow that occasionally shone like a lucky streak in the Hepworth seniors' otherwise bedevilled lives was in evidence again – until, instead of further stabilizing under Louise's care in Australia, Tasha took a turn for the worse. That tradewind season in Reefs passed with little news from the Outside World, but the Hepworths were accustomed to months between mailbags. Bressin and Ross managed to get sporadic letters through from school, but nothing came from Australia until August, when a note from Louise said the job idea hadn't worked because Tasha was only able to operate under specially supervised conditions. She was currently in a hostel for the handicapped run by a Miss Green, and attending a sheltered workshop.

'I suppose that's all right,' said Tom, and although he was disappointed she wasn't further 'cured' after her upset the previous year, he got on with plumbing for the new units. Diana was concerned that Louise had hived off responsibility for Tasha when a friend invited her to share a flat.

'I hope Tasha isn't feeling abandoned,' she commented, but Tom doubted it. He'd considered Louise a good sort. The next messages, however, seemed to confirm Diana's suspicions. '*MISS GREEN CAN'T COPE*' announced a cable, followed by a letter blurred in parts, having fallen, with the rest of the mail, into the sea on its way from a ship in a dugout. Louise, working day and night shifts in a home for handicapped children, visited Tasha at the hostel as often as she could, but had had to go away to visit her parents. While she was gone, apparently, Tasha had started behaving oddly, and after receiving a letter with a Solomon Islands postmark had, according to Miss Green, whose other charges were only slightly retarded, '*got right out of hand*'. But Diana skimmed over this extraneous information, seeing Louise's 'desertion' of Tasha as the cause of the relapse. No-one knows what was in the letter Tasha received, but it may have told her Nokali was to be married to a Reef Island girl, as this coincided with the time of his betrothal. Whatever, Tasha shredded the letter and flushed it away – followed by sixteen rolls of toilet paper, which wouldn't flush. Then she used the hostel shower as a lavatory. Around this time she started to 'play up' again about changing her underwear, and complained there were teeth underneath the hostel waiting to 'get' her. 'No!' she was heard shouting to herself at all hours, 'No no *NO*!'

Perhaps Tasha had been in love with Nokali, and was suffering, amongst other things, from the twin agonies of disillusion and rejection. She couldn't sleep, and pushed her food away like a grumpy toddler, baring her teeth at anyone who attempted to remonstrate. She tore up other people's letters, and displayed to anyone and everyone the scar from her long-ago heart operation, along with her sanitary towels. 'Lukluk!' (Look!) No wonder Miss Green couldn't cope. Eventually, Tom went to Honiara to make telephone contact with Louise.

'For God's sake, just come!' she almost screamed at him. '*I* can't cope any more either.'

Miss Green had been ready to have Tasha removed by whatever authorities would take her, but Louise had stepped in and brought Tasha to her own flat – which had received similar treatment to the hostel's bathroom. Tom didn't have his passport with him but managed to persuade BSIP officialdom to grant him permission to leave the country without it. He left Honiara for Sydney in the clothes he stood up in and, because no banks were open the day the plane left, no money.

'She's under sedation in hospital,' said Louise, greeting him, pale, at the airport. 'I kept her out as long as I could. I'm so sorry.'

'Oh God, she hates hospitals,' said Tom. He'd never forgotten the big, shocked eyes full of unshed tears staring at him through glass when she was three years old and away from her Island home for the first time; then the lengthy heart operation when she was nine. His Poppet seemed to have such rotten luck. 'Just take me to her and I'll take her home.'

But Tom wasn't taken straight to Tasha. Instead, in a small office three doctors talked to him for over two hours. He was still sweaty from his rushed journey, and hadn't had time to shave. The trousers he wore were from a thrift shop, and still had sand in the seams. '*It was like a grilling,*' he wrote to Diana later, '*but I think I finally persuaded them to approve our "Lifeplan" . . . then they said something about Tasha having schizophrenia, which apparently "undulates regardless of stress" . . . I take it as one of those umbrella terms, but will look into it before we leave.*' The three doctors had concluded, unequivocally, that Tasha was suffering from chronic schizophrenia with acute phases – one of which she was emerging from now, with medication to temper the violence of the symptoms.

'She'll get better at home,' said Tom. 'It was our mistake to send her away with a stranger. She'll be all right when she's back with her family.'

Tom spoke well. He still had much very English polish, despite his dusty appearance. 'But perhaps you'll let me have some of those pills to help on the journey.'

One of the doctors didn't want Tasha to travel at all, and Tom had to enlist the aid of his old sailing friend, Cathy, a qualified nurse, to push permission through, but there was never any question in his mind that home was the place for her, not the hospital she hated. He was given a large supply of contraceptives, instructions on how to look after Tasha during her periods, tablets for epilepsy, others '*to steady her generally*', and sedatives for the flight.

'Hello, Poppet!' he said when he was finally allowed to see her, and she walked into his arms like a lamb.

'Bad men try mek Tas'a prisoner,' she told him.

'I know, but it's going to be all right now. We're going home.'

The acute phase, which he hadn't witnessed, was over, and he frankly thought the whole episode overblown. From Santa Cruz, where they were stuck for days because of bad weather, Tom wrote to his sisters: '*Chemist I spoke to said the doses they've given her are massive. She has awful cramps, poor dear, and I had to hire a couple of girls to carry her down to the boat. We'll cut down on the wretched pills as soon as we can.'*

Back on Pigeon, Diana was up to her eyes in copra, the grass was uncut, and there were queues at the store because an old man on Nandelli had died and there was to be a wake. A kumberra had whacked down palm leaves and coconuts, and it took two days of clearing before Tom was able to get down to mending the Flymo they'd bought on their last trip to New Zealand – writing the manufacturer a long letter of complaint when he discovered it was incapable of keeping going long enough to cut all the parts of the island Diana wanted trim. '*I distinctly recall mentioning five acres in my original letter* . . .' Tasha, in the meantime, got down to looking for Nokali, swishing to and fro in the shallows in front of the area of Nandelli – conveniently out of sight of Pigeon – where he stayed. Betrothed or otherwise, he was soon back in the bushes with her and, without Louise around and with her parents so busy, they discovered, thrillingly, they could extend their activities to Tasha's bed as well.

At certain times of the moon, Nokali found, Tasha seemed almost insatiable. Then he'd invite a few of his wontoks along, which she didn't mind so long as she was always in his arms first and last. He *was* to be married, he told her; his father had, according to Kastom, arranged it, and there was nothing he could do about it. Instead of shouting, Tasha accepted this when it came from his own lips. In many ways she saw herself as a Reef Islander, and Reef Island women were submissive. OK, she couldn't be his wife, but she could be his concubine – and wanted to be for ever. Nokali liked watching his wontoks enjoying themselves, one after another, and sometimes, when there was no-one on top of her, she stroked herself fascinatingly, something Reef Island girls, with the idea of modesty drummed into them by mission churches, never did. As a concubine she was perfect, and he was sorry she'd be going away again soon. Tasha herself wanted reassurance she'd be coming back to Pigeon before long, too.

'Of course,' said Diana briskly.

'But you never know,' said Tom, 'you might find things about England you like.' He knew he would.

There'd been sheaves of replies to an advertisement for partner-managers to look after PIT during the planned period away, starting in late 1978, and Tom had sifted through them carefully. Mike and Sally Pierce sounded excellent: he'd travelled, so would know something about different lifestyles; she'd been in catering, so wouldn't be fazed by crowds at the store. They had two children, who should enjoy themselves on Pigeon, and several weeks to settle in before the Hepworths departed. 'Lukim iu,' (See you) said Ross to the Reef Island girl he last lay with, the night before they left, then they were gone. Bressin was to send home ahead of him a few years later an encyclopedia on sex (confiscated by Solomon Islands customs) but was less informed on the practical side than his more precocious twin. Tasha, the most informed of all, had '*some kind of attack*' at chilly Hong Kong airport, where the family had to wait hours between flights, but was calm enough on eventual arrival in London, several time and culture zones later, to greet the Aunties, whom she'd never seen, civilly. She started breaking down again only when they visited Amalie, the twins' godmother, at a cottage in Devon. Amalie suggested the boys go with her to America before their college courses began.

'No!' Tasha shouted suddenly, very uncivilly, and threw a cup of coffee over Amalie before flouncing out to fill the lavatory with paper.

'She hates the thought of Ross going away again so soon,' explained Diana, which could have been true. Or it could have been just the start of another acute schizophrenic phase. Ross himself was glad to go. At the vulnerable stage between boy- and manhood, he was embarrassed by Tasha's peculiar behaviour, kept away from her as much as possible – and was sometimes unable to restrain his irritation in her presence. She'd already pinched half his pop cassettes, she ranted to herself, disturbing his sleep, and he thought it ridiculous they had to lock up the loo roll. Bressin had a gentler attitude, and was often called upon by Tom and Diana to soothe Tasha if she 'mis-behaved' when they were working on the house they were renovating. But when Ross and Bressin were in America for two months, Tom and Diana had Tasha all to themselves, in a small house close to the English coast, with no warm Pacific Ocean or sunny expanses of reef – or Reef Islanders – around to distract her. It was a shock. Tom's diary, formerly full of jobs to be tackled on a remote tropical island, became, between shopping lists for sandpaper, lino and new recordings of his favourite classical composers, a litany of '*Tasha trouble*': '*T. won't let me drive . . . T. tore telephone out again . . . Worst night yet . . . T. up and down like a yoyo . . . Tasha nightdress walkabout.*'

Was Tasha searching for her lover Nokali, wandering barefoot at night along the cold pavements of Littlehampton, her growing paranoia about being watched fed by twitching curtains? What the neighbours thought of the Hepworths generally, who furnished the house to a high standard entirely from rubbish skips and the dawn pursuit of house clearance advertisements, remains a mystery, but, as ever, their views were of no importance to Diana, who transferred her building skills from raising seawalls on Pigeon to excavating for drain-pipes in the snow with apparent ease – although she did complain of the 'ridiculous' cold. She made her own fitted kitchen when the exact size required was slow to appear second-hand, and they camped in whichever room was not being decorated, heating tins – as on the *AR* and Pigeon – on a primus until a cooker was organized. Tom's job list was full too, but there were days when all their work was wasted: '*Tasha in our bed all night shouting about "Devil" wires . . . wouldn't settle until she'd ripped out every inch of the electrics it took eleven hours fixing.*' There was clearly no hope of the 'simple job' Diana had had in mind to keep Tasha occupied, and finally she was driven to contact a doctor for sleeping pills for Tom, who put her on to Social Services when he heard why sleep was difficult. Did Diana find release in pouring out the story of Tasha's past to a no doubt electrified – and possibly horrified – social worker, describing the beautiful backdrop to her daughter's infancy, the idyllic childhood as an innocent in Eden, until the tragedy of '*rape*' in New Zealand resulting in a terrible change? Possibly because it was Tom who'd been '*grilled*' in the hospital in Australia, and Tom who was told of the schizophrenia diagnosis, this didn't seem to come up. It *was* only an 'umbrella term' anyway, Diana, like Tom, believed. So much had happened to Tasha, it was obvious to her parents that she was just reacting to a whole series of traumas.

'She's fine today,' said Diana, 'just not used to mod cons.' (Tasha's latest voices had emanated from a toaster when two slices of bread popped up. 'Get out! Get out!' she'd ordered them and when they failed to, she'd hurled the toaster across the room, denting a newly plastered wall.)

'But I'm sure you could do with a rest yourselves,' suggested the social worker.

One therapist recommended that the whole family attend sessions with Tasha, but this never happened. Hypnosis was discussed too, and analysis, but neither came to anything. Daycare, however, was found, enabling work to proceed on the house, and another property was bought for renovation, in Wales. Meanwhile Tasha learned to weave baskets – just like in Reefs, but with coloured 'leaves' – had her hair permed, and went to a disco for the handicapped with her dadi, who was now approaching seventy. '*Not as bad as I thought*,' he wrote of this, '*but too many happy morons . . . We must find care for Tasha which brings out her latent potential.*' Just as they'd so often refused to give up hope in other areas in their lives, for years Tom and Diana maintained an unshakeable belief that a cure for their Poppet, damaged from birth, would one day be found. They loved her too much to think otherwise, and hated the thought of her being dismissively consigned to a category.

The twins, in America, made the local newspaper in a Southern state when Ross dived into dangerous waters to rescue a little coloured girl.

'And how do you guys from a tropical paradise island like America?' the reporter asked. 'It's great!' said the cheerful Ross, but Bressin said they'd been ripped off by a cab driver the minute they'd set foot in New York, and wondered why no-one else had dived in to save the girl. Both the twins had slightly out-of-date Beatles haircuts at that time, Ross's glossy black, Bressin's soft blond.

On Pigeon, the Pierce family provided a living soap opera for the inhabitants of Nola and Nenumbo – and active roles in the drama for the people of Nandelli. Sally Pierce, formerly a cook in the south of England, soon adapted to weighing copra and serving Solbrew (Solomon Island beer) by the carton, on a promontory overlooking thousands of miles of scintillating blue. At first it was fun: between stints in the store and copra shed, she sunbathed, and contentedly watched her husband reroofing the Hepworth children's old tree-house for theirs. Discovering they shared the island with flying foxes and exotic birds, and writing to friends about this was exciting, too – at first. But the diet recommended by the Hepworths was dull – endless tins, fish, sticky Solrice and pawpaws, too many of which gave her belerun – and Mike seemed tetchy (he suffered from prickly heat, which often affects the groin) so she wasn't too sorry when the time came to make her first restocking trip to Honiara. In fact, delayed there by the vagaries of suppliers, she took a temporary job at the G Club, which was now undergoing changes as Independence, in 1978, turned from notion to reality, and the capital became a hive of speculation about what would happen when what was left of British influence finally crumbled and 'they' were left on their own. 'They' – Bigmen with clout on Guadalcanal – were already to be found in such bastions of colonialism as the club, the British wishing to make their exit as graceful as possible, and Sally found her ear bent by both black and white barprops beguiled by her bosom. Mike, left with the children, the store and less amenable drunks on Pigeon, sent messages demanding she hurry back, but the delay grew. And into the vacuum left by her absence sailed a white yacht carrying, so Islanders tell, a sympathetic woman with all the right things to help Mike in her medical kit. What fun the Mohawk Bay Debbil was having now! As the wontok grapevine passed on, in languis, via police radios, the information from Honiara that Missus Pierce had been seen leaving the club one night with a man, the bush grapevine in Reefs passed back the news that Mista Pierce was spending a lot of time aboard the ship in Mohawk Bay. As soon as her stores list was complete Sally arranged to return, but by that time Mike was gone, taking the children. He said he'd be away only briefly, to buy turtle shell for PIT, but the Islanders didn't expect him back.

Sally, sleek from meals out during her not unpleasant stay in Honiara, and feeling virtuous for having organized PIT's business there so well, was temporarily fooled by the turtle-shell ploy, but as the weeks passed she was shaken by the dawning truth. She knew Mike had found the sweaty proximity of life on Pigeon less than blissfully romantic, but had never suspected him capable of such a dramatic defection. Despite her own prolonged jaunt away, she was devastated by his 'desertion'. Her old customers, leaning on the counter at Pigeon's store as they sucked from Solbrew cans and spat betel-juice in the sand, watched her change from a big, cheerful lass to a short-tempered and shrivelled middle-aged woman in less than a month. Then she heard Mike was in Honiara, locked up the store and went to fetch the children. No-one knows what these youngsters thought of either of their parents' behaviour, but when they returned to Reefs they found more time was now to be spent on Nandelli, because their mother had a boyfriend there.

Although at first it was strange – the different smells and textures, the crudity of people defecating in the sea yards from where, at other times, people 'faki-ed' or fished – Sally did find comfort in strong brown arms, and the women looked after the children almost like their own. The Islander concerned, Ossi, wontok of one of Nandelli's Bigmen and known as a big ladies' man himself, discovered that the white woman, like Tasha, knew games Reef Island girls didn't. Long into the night, behind an old dugout half hidden under skeins of trumpet-petalled purple convolvulus; in the lap-lapping water, and on sacred-to-lovers Temotulaki, he pleased her, and she pleased him. He began to dream of installing her permanently in a leaf hut that, if they married, his wontoks would help build; and she dreamed of starting a business of her own, on Nandelli. She was fed up with always having to do things 'the Hepworths' way' for PIT. Besides it was in-convenient wading back and forth between the two islands and it meant leaving her new man too long alone. She drank a little, to relieve the stress of what felt like a double life – efficient storekeeper on Pigeon and abandoned 'wild' woman on Nandelli. She never learned to eat blackened reef fish whole, the way 'they' did, with their fingers, but did learn to lick the greasy remnants of it from Ossi's chest, and twist his woolly hair in her fingers while, effortlessly, he gave her more simple pleasure of the flesh than she'd ever known. Especially in the halflight, it began to feel like love to her too, and they split a whole carton of beer between them and his wontoks, on the pink and silver dawn he proposed, toasting the strange fact that he didn't even have to pay a brideprice.

Soon after this, a reminder came from England that it was stock-taking time (could Tom have a note of the figures, please?) and Sally realized she must leave her fiancé to acquire Kastom land for the new store they'd run together while she, sighing, applied herself to PIT's books, the acquisition of a divorce and her children's sporadic education. She'd decided she wanted to make a go of living in Reefs, and did everything to make the foundations for her future there solid, including boosting funds by buying and selling turtle shell on her own account, apparently not realizing that this contra-vened an agreement drawn up by Tom. She continued to run Pigeon Island store, and to develop plans for a store on Nandelli, for over a year.

'Oh dear,' said Tom to Diana at the beginning of 1980, 'looks like trouble back home. Mike has vamoosed, and Sally's saying something about not being able to cope on her own and wanting to "do her own thing". Damn. Why *are* people so fickle?'

'Quite, and *weak-willed*,' said Diana. 'If one sets out to do something, one ought to see it through . . .'

Mike and Sally had intended to stay on Pigeon for three years, and were pulling out prematurely. Diana, by now, had 'seen through' the refurbishing and sale of the Littlehampton house, and had turned her attention to the one in Wales, which required '*total gutting*'. Tasha was successfully installed in a special college close by, and Bressin and Ross were doing fine (according to their father) on their own college courses: business studies and engineering for Ross; hotel management for Bressin. What was the matter with all the people who were so keen on Pigeon at first, then '*flapped at the first hurdle*'?

Sally, three months on from this reaction and still living awkwardly between Pigeon and Nandelli, was currently experiencing a little total gutting herself. One of her sons had '*gone wild*' and was, at an early age, messing about with local girls, and – worse – Ossi, with whom her whole future in Reefs was bound up, had been unfaithful. Men and women on Nandelli recall the 'Bigfela Row' that occurred when, fuelled by a long-awaited replenishment of liquor supplies, Missus Pierce '*go krangge*' (went crazy) and stripped Ossi's new paramour of very nearly all her kalicos on the beach, in public, shrieking '*olsem debbil*' (like a devil). Belying the submissive reputation of Reef Island women, this young woman's wontoks then laid hands on Sally to prevent their friend's thighs being exposed – ruining her marriage prospects for ever – and pulled off a few kalicos themselves before the assembled company melted as one into the bush, leaving Sally staggering up and down, weeping, in a torn bra and skirt, on the strip of silver sand in 'Paradise' that had so often been the scene of her moans of joy. Though embarrassed by her performance, Ossi, softened up by Solbrew, later crept over to Pigeon to offer back a torn T-shirt. Softened by half a bottle of rum herself, Sally opened her arms to him in the bed Diana had made back in 1959 for herself and Tom, and promised she'd take him to the bright lights of Honiara if only he'd give up the other women. 'Yes,' he said, as the effects of the beer receded and this option sounded increasingly attractive. In this house, he could see what he was doing, when he mounted Sally, in a mirror, and after the initial shock this gave him, it made him want to do it more and more. A few yards away, down a coral cliff, the sea licked greedily at the already eroded shoreline, and over on Nandelli, Ossi's 'other woman', leaning languidly against a palm tree under the moon, calmly applied warmed coconut cream to a bruise on her arm, and massaged it slowly over her torso. She knew he'd be back in time; she'd tapped ash from the women's special tree onto the kumera she'd cooked him before he returned to Pigeon – and Island girls were used to waiting.

Bressin did join the Territorial Army. When he wasn't setting his mind to the intricacies of Hilton-sized wage sheets on his hotel management course, he was slithering on eighteen-year-old, South Sea island-grown knees and elbows through English mud, and learning how to handle weapons. He looked at British girls and found them pretty, but wasn't ready to do anything about it. Instead he played hockey, learned to scuba dive, and read. Ross, dashing hot-eyed from disco to disco along the south coast on his moped when he wasn't putting in time on his business course, was another matter.

'How's it going?' his father would ask, when he was briefly spotted grabbing a bundle of clothes for the latest all-night party.

'Fine,' said Ross, although he added every time, 'but I can't wait to get back to Pigeon.'

He missed the constant heat, native fruits unobtainable in Britain, the thrill of body-surfing waves under a silver moon and, most of all, the girls. Although fiercely attracted to young women who gyrated in front of him in English discos, he found himself tongue-tied with them. He knew only how to make moves with Reef Island girls, an art not involving speech, and he desperately missed making moves with them – every night. He could have done another two years at college, but when Tom said there were problems at home, Ross volunteered to go and sort them out.

'If you're sure that's what you want, darling,' said Diana, privately glad he was as enamoured of Pigeon as she, who found life in Britain, with its wretched bread strikes, *cold* rain and unions gaining the upper hand, extremely vexing. 'Daddy will join you as soon as he can.'

When eighteen-year-old Ross arrived on Pigeon after a nine-day journey, he found not a soul on the island, but a letter in red ink from Sally Pierce hung in a bag on the cargo-shed door. Most of it was about how to run PIT – his father had already given him twenty pages on the subject – but the last part told him she was marrying Ossi, currently residing with her in Honiara, and about the venture on

Nandelli. '*I hope you'll be all right,*' she added. '*I found I just couldn't go on on my own.*' Ross raised his eyebrows, Reef Islander style, scratched his head, already full of nits from Santa Cruz, and replaced his travelling clothes with a kalico. He lay down on his parents' old bed but found he couldn't sleep, so he got up and cracked open a beer. It was then, wandering the few steps out of the door onto the beach, that he realized he was no longer alone on the island. There were rows of eyes glinting in the shadows under the coral overhang near where dugouts were pulled up during the day, and – a new addition since his schooldays – a pig tethered to fatten on the island's scraps – something he couldn't imagine his parents sanctioning, but which seemed a good idea. Why open a tin of Chinese spam when you could have your own pikpik? The moon, his old friend, was only part way up, but the soft, warm air on his skin, which had been looking unnaturally white to him for a while, felt wonderful. This was the Pigeon he'd come back for, but he could understand why Sally hadn't wanted to be on her own. He took a lengthy pull of beer, half emptying the can, and thought hard. He longed to break through any barriers his absence had created, but didn't know, now he was actually back sitting on a coral boulder he'd used as a chair from childhood, what was the best first move to make with his old Reef Island male friends – whom he assumed these silent watchers to be. It would be terrible if they didn't accept him – and if the girls who'd been available before were now all married. He'd found plenty to like in Britain, but that didn't mean he felt he could ever properly fit in there. It was hugely important to fit in, and be liked, here. What could he do to show the Islanders he felt more like them than 'his own kind' – and that he didn't want to be categorized with his parents, or even with his brother, as a certain type of white?

'Hey,' he called softly into the shadows, believing he'd had a brainwave, 'iufela wandem mek pati?'

His parents never threw parties for Islanders, and he was of an age now at which, had he been a Nandelli man, he might have started making certain gestures that would be read as a desire eventually to acquire Bigman status. Ross didn't have much money but he'd soon make some, in the store, and in the meantime he could borrow some goods to treat his friends.

'Ross! Brata b'long mitufela!' (our brother) his friends called back. 'Iu kambaek olsem Bigman!'

He'd hit the spot. Soon there was beer for everyone, packets of the lollies they'd shared as children, and young male bodies sprawled companionably all over the beach under a brilliantly star-strewn sky. From time to time small groups got up and danced to their own singing, then lay back down, shared betel, got up again and splashed in and out of the warm shallows, blowing whalespouts of beer and peeing happily into the air. Later, dugouts were paddled away silently under the moon by those still sober enough to balance, returning loaded with girls. Most of the party-goers were back on Nandelli before daybreak so the elders, with their old-fashioned ways, would be kept sweet, but one of the girls stayed three days with Ross in bed, then professed herself too shy to go back to her family. What was she to do?

Ross also felt suddenly at a loss. He'd had a big party, reaffirmed old friendships and made new ones, but it wasn't the sort of event – like a Kastom feast, which took a whole village's co-operation, not just young bloods having fun – to gain him approval where he most needed it, from the elders. He looked at the girl at his side, staring up at him with scared eyes. Her name, he'd discovered some time during the second night, was Teimaliki. When she closed her eyes, hiding her face in her hands and rocking from side to side, he ran his eyes over the rest of her. She was slender-waisted, with the high, pawpaw-shaped breasts typical of Reef Island girls, which would elongate and grow heavier – like the fruit they resembled – as she grew, and a beautifully smooth, delightfully plump bottom.

'O wanem hemi happen nao!' she cried, curling away from him when he tried to hold her and weeping. The gossip would be all over Reefs by now, her marriageability destroyed, her wontoks furious as there'd be no brideprice. Unless . . . ? Ross was still trying to uncurl her. She'd been so willing before but now she wouldn't play. He sat up and looked round. The place was littered with beer cans and there was betel-juice gobbed generously over the floor and walls. His head spun. If he made a mess of things now, he'd be in trouble with his own family *and* the elders. Ross made a decision then that would affect the rest of his life.

'Hey, listen,' he said, in his perfect, unforgotten Pijin, 'let's clean up here, then go and see your parents together.'

Teimaliki stopped crying, got up, wound on her kalico and humbly took a twig broom from out of the leaf roof of the veranda. Ross, after enjoying watching her for a minute, got up himself and put an Abba tape into his new ghetto blaster to help them with their work. While she piled the cans into a leaf basket to chuck from a dugout into the deep at high tide, he checked what was needed in the store and started making a list. Lips folded, Teimaliki shook her rump, experimentally, to unfamiliar beats in the music she'd soon learn to interpret perfectly, and Ross, peeping through the store door, smiled. This could be fun! A day or so later he bought her in marriage for a down payment of the equivalent of ten pounds, the balance to be paid, by unspoken agreement, in favours to her wontoks over time.

They'd been man and wife for four months when Tom came back to Pigeon and had already been offered a baby girl, the child of one of Teimaliki's older sisters, as there were no signs yet of pregnancy. (If a young wife had a baby to look after it was supposed to bring fertility.) Tom mentioned 'wild oats' in a letter to his sisters, but said nothing of the marriage at this stage – perhaps because it was official only in Kastom, and Kastom was after all only an Islander thing. But to Ross it was real, and he wanted it to work, like his parents' marriage had, for ever, even if it had got off to a hasty start.

Tom now applied himself to the task of ridding PIT of the potential rival store across the way. It was the last thing he needed, with bills to pay in Britain and air fares to lash out on as soon as Tasha was ready to come home and Bressin and Diana had finished their business there. Sally and 'her black boy' were away at the moment – probably buying more turtle shell, which should be in his name, Tom reckoned, and he'd start by 'pinning that one on the wench'. He wrote to the Immigration Department, alerting them to 'possibly illegal' transactions between native Solomon Islanders and a temporary expatriate resident. He'd run her out of the country if necessary. But first he'd check PIT's books. Here Tom, irritated to fury at 'very sloppily kept accounts' and suffering from his usual back-to-Pigeon bout of malaria, made a mistake equal to Sally Pierce's bloomer over the turtle shell. He accused her of heisting a sum equating to over ten thousand Australian dollars from PIT's funds, when, it transpired, this figure actually related to a modest profit on beer sales. 'Try not to be too angry with me, darling,' he wrote to Diana when confessing the slip. 'She's still got a lot to answer for . . . Bopali's been paying his store bills by cheque and I'll be interested to see whose name is on those cheques.'

Willy Bopali, who'd continued to be a quiet mover and shaker in Reef Island politics since the days when he'd given fellow Islanders, unintentionally or otherwise, the confidence to oust the Hepworths from Santa Cruz, now found himself in a delicate position. He'd no desire for another European to open a store on Nandelli, but if she did, might it not weaken Tom's position to the point of making him give in gracefully – without blaming the Islanders – and allow Pigeon to return naturally to its rightful owners after all these years? And this white woman was caught up with a Reef Islander with big connections. It wouldn't do to upset the elders on Nandelli, who could profit from the new arrangement by letting their land. But Ross Hepworth had married a Nandelli girl whose family felt aggrandized by their new relationship with Pigeon, and the whole issue of 'rightful owners' would change when they had children . . . '*Come and see me if you would be so good*,' wrote Tom to his old rival, hoping to get him on his side over his new one. Bopali came, listened, promised to produce the desired cheque stubs, complimented young Mr and Mrs Hepworth on their adopted baby girl – named, in the traditional style, Diana after her grandmother – then went to listen to other sides of the story.

The animosity already built up in letters between Sally and Tom escalated on her return to Nandelli, where she and her children shared Ossi's leaf hut. Marching across to parley with Tom, she claimed half the mess in the store's books occurred after Ross came back; Ross said it was like that when he arrived. '*Talk about pots calling kettles black!*' scrawled Tom, exhausted at the end of much shouting, and went to bed with four aspirins. But he came out fighting again in the morning. '*The bloody woman insists she's going ahead with her store,*' he told Diana, '*but I'll have her on the run before you get back, darling. We haven't spent all these years sweating to build up our business to have it taken away by some jumped-up little tart . . . besides, she'll never last with Ossi. My spies tell me he's already "messing about".*'

If Tom hadn't altogether succeeded in pushing Sally out by the time he next wrote on the subject to Diana, he was halfway there, and Ossi was – possibly not entirely unwittingly – abetting him with his infidelities. The magic of Sally's white body was strong but she had a sharp tongue and expected him to work on their joint project almost as hard as the Hepworths expected people to work – a standard of self-punishment incomprehensible to most Reef Islanders. And there was always Teimaliki's sista, waiting for him silently. She might not wriggle and gasp like Sally, but she was restful and always cooked for him after he had lain with her. When Sally went to Honiara to send the children home to her parents for Christmas, Ossi confessed his confusion to wontoks, and several made the interesting point that, even though Teimaliki and her sista didn't come from the highest of Nandelli families, their status *had* now risen, through Ross Hepworth becoming a son-in-law, which also had implications for Pigeon's future. It's not known whether Bopali was present at this meeting, but representatives of claimants to Pigeon were, and Ossi didn't take much persuading to forget the 'krangge' white woman – who anyway drank too much, and liked messing about too much, to make a good wife – and ask the correct uncle for his patient mistress's hand. Sally Pierce left the Solomon Islands a very unhappy woman. And Bopali began to observe, discreetly, how one of Tom Hepworth's sons shaped up now he was married to a Reef Islander. The original ninety-nine-year lease on Pigeon had been reduced after Independence, so that it would run out now in the year 2052 – not long in generational terms, which was how Islanders tended to look at things.

While Tom was battling off competition on Pigeon, Diana faced battles of her own in Britain. '*It's disgraceful,*' she wrote. '*They say at the college they can't have Tasha any more because she's been having sexual relations there . . . I tried to reason, after all, she's a grown woman, but it's no go . . . Another home is recommended, where she'll have more supervision . . . By the way, at the last charity do I picked up a gross of T-shirts at 10 pence each. They're in with the new Seagull engine . . . should do well in the store.*'

Tasha was in the new home in England, with a carer in training to accompany her back to Pigeon in due course, when Diana returned briefly to Reefs and met her daughter-in-law and adopted grandchild for the first time. As with Tom, the relationship didn't seem to impact on her much, although she did comment, in a line to a friend, she thought Ross '*young and foolish to take up with a local. Hopefully it will pass.*' The bargain T-shirts, alas, didn't pass unnoticed through the new Solomon Islands Government customs, who described them sternly to Tom as 'concealed goods'. '*What rubbish we have to put up with!*' he wrote to his sisters. '*The papers got muddled, that's all. Diana's livid. Perfect honesty is the bedrock of her character . . . Incidentally, did I tell you Pigeon's been listed among the Top Ten Most Exotic Properties in the world – according to a Japanese who says he might want to buy it . . . ? I've written back saying it's not all a bed of roses but he's welcome to come and get the feel of it while we fetch Tasha if he likes.'*

The Japanese gentleman didn't come, but Tom felt Ross was capable of looking after Pigeon on his own for a while. Maybe that woman of his would even help. The Islanders watched Tom and Diana depart on the *Southern Cross* to complete their business in Britain and collect Tasha, and as the boat disappeared over the horizon, Ross positioned himself beside the store bell with a spanner and clanged it joyously, a message taken up by the Boo shells on Nandelli and passed on through every village within earshot in Reefs.

'Yee-ha!' he cried, just nineteen, whirling the just eighteen-year-old Teimaliki in his arms, complete with small Diana tied in a kalico on her back. 'Party time again, baby!'

And this time he was going to do it properly: one contingent of male wontoks headed for Matema, using the Hepworths' outboard to reach the best fishing reef; another lassoed the now well-fattened pig – kind contribution of Ossi – and dragged it into the sea for the beginning of the screaming rituals that would end with steaming umu parcels, and women began grating coconuts, plucking kokorokos and massaging coconut oil into one another's hair. When the feast was ready, Ross, for the first but by no means last time in Reef Islands, stood up, cleared his throat and addressed the assembled villagers as his own people.

'Welkam, evrifela. Mifela hapi tumas fo presentim smolfela kaikai fo celebratem samting . . .' (Welcome, everyone. I'm happy to present this small feast to celebrate something . . .) Here Ross hesitated, then, before the gathered crowd of more than fifty Islanders listening to him on his mother's recently retrimmed lawn, put an arm around Teimaliki. 'Waef b'long mi garem baby insaet.' Teimaliki clapped a hand to her mouth with embarrassment, but beamed secretly behind it, as there was a low, then growing animal roar of approval from all the men present. This should help secure Pigeon's future. Teimaliki was pregnant with Christine Hepworth. But they'd keep the adopted girl too as she'd already brought luck, and Ross wanted a big Reef-Island-style family.

19

Cyclones

'LOOK, MUM, I'M GLAD WE'RE NOT CLOSE TO TINAKULA NOW.'

Joe was perched one afternoon on a footstool-sized lump of coral, peeling the bark from a stick to make a fresh arrow for his quiver. Beyond him, the volcano at our back door was sending up a mushroom cloud that in minutes was its own size, then larger, so the cone was dwarfed.

'Have you seen it do that before?'

'No, but Patteson's dadi says it's a sign. It might mean a Bigwind.'

'Oh?'

'Ross is trying to get more information on the radio. Pegi was here during the last one. When she talked about it, she put her hands over her face and – Mum? . . .'

The mushroom cloud was dispersing now, rolling away to form a white streak amid layers of grey veiling the blue. I was peeling a snakebean for a snack, but Joe had stopped peeling his stick.

'. . . while she was talking about the cyclone, saying how she'd run around "olsem kokoroko" (like a headless chicken) I suddenly felt Simon Boga's little hand creeping into mine.'

'Because he was frightened?'

'Yes. But I liked it. It was as though it didn't matter any more whether I was white or black. He just wanted to hold hands – like they do – and I was nearest.'

I hadn't credited Joe with having considered such things – or worrying about his popularity being affected by his colour.

'When I grow up . . .'

I knew what was coming because I'd heard it before but, with the history I'd been reading, the innocent ambition held new slants.

'. . . I want to be a man like Ross.'

'He's a nice person,' I said, and left it at that. But I wondered what sort of price Ross had had to pay to be the kind of man he was. I knew Diana loved him but that he irritated her to distraction, too. As we were talking about him, he appeared, a rare sight up the 'Western' end, almost running in flip-flops, his Bigman's belly wobbling from side to side – not the 'beautiful youth' who looked like Hamlet, as Diana once described him, but a cuddly young paterfamilias.

'Sorry to disturb you, Lucy, but I have to ask you to be ready to evacuate. Cyclone Danny's a few hundred miles away yet, but moving fast.'

'How much warning do you think we'll get?' I wanted to know which to waterproof first – Tom's diaries, Joe's precious project on contrasts between Scotland and Reef Islands, or my satellite phone.

'Impossible to say. Last time we only got fifteen minutes! But that was because Dad insisted on finishing the stocktake first. I've shut the store already and Pegi wants to send the small kids lo' bus' – sorry, into the bush. But Pigeon's the highest island around.'

'Where's Christine?'

Ross looked me square in the eye, and I knew he was going to say something that hurt him.

'My darling daughter is running around with some pot-smoking shit on Malumbo.'* He turned away, busying himself with ensuring a door was properly fastened. 'Seems she's turning out like her mother.'

Teimaliki, whom he'd married as a teenager 'for ever', had quickly acquired a reputation for running around. But he'd been the last to learn of it – or want to believe it.

Joe interjected. He adored Christine. 'Aren't you going to fetch her?'

'Of course. Vili's pulling the canoe out now.'

Ross's big Reef Island family had had, and was still having, plenty

---

* Another island within the Reefs group.

of its own internal storms, but when there was a storm outside they stuck together. In 1993, when Cyclone Nina had struck, he'd even tried to persuade his parents to join him and his new wife, Pegi, in what he considered the safest place on the island, but they'd declined. He checked the shutters on Tasha's House and warned me that if a Bigwind came, the kitchen and bathroom would probably 'get it' first.

'Just pack what you can,' he added as he hurried off, 'and if you get a chance, pop over to Mum's and pick up any stuff on the floor.'

'Sorry to have to ask,' I called, embarrassed by my own feebleness, 'but with this silly spine I can't carry much . . .'

'No worries. If it comes to it, I'll send fifteen guys and have you cleared out in less than ten minutes. I'll send Laloa now to give you a hand. If it gets wild, you'll need to use Ben's place.'

Ben's Box stood only a few feet higher than Tasha's House but if waves were washing right over the island, as they had before, that could make all the difference.

'Go and find Benji,' I told Joe, 'but don't scare him.'

'OK. Can you put my spear and bow somewhere safe?'

'I will.' While he was gone, I shoved a couple of books for the boys into a bag with the last of our cocoa, two torches, a candle claiming to burn long enough for 'prolonged romance', ho ho, and some towels. Then I set to work bagging up the most irreplaceable of Tom's papers, my computer, and changes of clothes for the boys who might for once, if the storm were long, feel cold. Tangypera materialized a metre from my face, as I was bending to fasten a polythene-wrapped box with a belt.

'Sekhan, Lusi. Mifela gogo lo' bus'.' (Shake hands, I'm headed for the bush.) I asked him to pass on my best wishes to his family, and we both said: 'Lukim iu.'* Then he ran away on his bare feet, and I saw him ten minutes later, still running, on the part of the reef still dry between Pigeon and Nenumbo, a slight, bandy-legged figure bent on survival. I knew that, like all his neighbours there, he'd abandon his home and all his few possessions without thought. All that mattered was that the babies were wrapped up and held high above the rising waters, if necessary by the tallest men in the tribe. I noticed that the

---

* 'Lukim iu' can mean anything from a casual 'See you' to a passionate 'I long to be with you again'. 'Take care' is often implicit in the farewell, too.

geckos on Pigeon, many of whom had lost their tails spontaneously as soon as the weather began to change, had now vanished. There wasn't even a crab or a cockroach in sight. Every living creature was battening down in its own way to ride out whatever was coming. Pegi had persuaded Ross to agree about the smallest piccaninnis, Tangypera had let me know before he left. When Vili returned with Christine, the men were going to carry them across the channel, before it became too rough, to Nandelli, and thence to the next island and 'lo' bus''. Pegi wouldn't know exactly where her children were but she could be confident that, with her wontoks, they'd be as safe as physically possible. The wontok system operated on deep trust. Hence anyone who broke that trust fell into deep opprobrium. Like Teimaliki, I thought. Almost everything I'd heard about this woman was negative, yet once she'd been a pregnant teenager in love with an exotic husband, with every hope of a happy future. I kept the diary of Tom's that referred to the collapse of Ross's first marriage for my own reading entertainment if we had to hole up for any length of time. Benji then arrived to inform me that, as Mhairi and Peter had been told they might have to evacuate to the copra shed with people from Ross's house, I'd need to look after Stasi. It wouldn't be a good idea to keep a Rottweiler trained to bark at Islanders shut up in a small space with crowds of them. Mhairi was currently packing the smallest of her fluffy yellow chicks into a crate, while Peter waterproofed his saxophone.

'I'll just carry all my shells in a drawer,' announced Benji calmly. 'I don't need anything else. By the way, where are we going?'

''Lo' ' ouse b'long Missus, fustaem,' said Laloa, who'd come with Benji, ''ouse b'long Ben sapos Bigwind big tumas.'

So it was to be a two-stage process. Current orders were to move immediately to Diana's house, which was less exposed than Tasha's, then if things looked serious, to huddle into Ben's.

'OK.'

Tinakula was now poised puffless between grey sea and grey sky. I didn't want to read menace into the calm, but it was easy to do. Telling myself action was better than speculation, I set Laloa to pack diaries while I pulled out the twenty-one handmade drawers in my bedroom/office and made decisions about what I could live without. Everything, I thought, basically, except my boys. Much as I missed him, I was glad on this occasion that Magnus was far away. In his last message he'd said his team had beaten some old rivals at rugby. '*Great party afterwards, I ate six packets of crisps!*'

'Kwiktaem,' I said to Benji and Joe, who were dawdling over their album, showing scenes of our life in Scotland to Laloa. 'Let's get settled into Diana's while it's still light.'

Taking across the 'emergency' bag first, I assessed the accommodation possibilities at Diana's. Ross had already closed the great barn doors leading from her bedroom veranda by a path straight down to the West Patio – a lovely spot on a fair day. Now Cyclone Danny threatened to barge straight onto and over the patio from the sea – and beyond it, through the barn doors. I would sleep in that room and put the boys behind the next wall, on sofas sandbagged with doubled mattresses in case furniture started moving about. In 1993, I'd heard, the fridge had been swirled into the living room on a wave, and every picture on the walls had crashed down. With this in mind, I removed all glass from high shelves, too. The only loose items on the floor were Japanese fishing floats I knew Diana liked, and these I wedged in a corner. Stasi, chained to a post on the veranda, had her nose between her paws, mournful eyes following my every move. I'd never liked her much but now felt sorry for her; she was gripped, I could see, like the geckos, by instinctive animal fear.

'We'll be all right,' I said, stroking the loose skin on her shoulders, and, black stump of a tail twitching just an inch, she pressed her big, confused head hard against my knee. I could see how she could feel like a friend to Diana. Then she leaped up and growled. Laloa was standing in the doorway with a box on his head, one foot rubbing the other nervously.

'Siddown!' I told Stasi, which she did, and Laloa grinned, left his box and went back for another. Reverently I moved the giant swordfish's 'sword' Tom and Diana had picked up in their trawl net half a century ago, in British Guiana, from where it hung on a wall perilously close to where Benji's head might be in the night, then set water to boil for thermoses on the Calor-gas cooker – in case later it broke loose.

By 5 p.m., when there was usually plenty of light left for a swim before sunset, the sky was so overcast it was hard to see Nandelli, and Tinakula and Matema were blocked out behind walls of grey. Joe and Benji were down at Ross's, now that everything was as prepared as it could be, but it was agreed they'd come back to me before dark.

Mhairi and I ran into each other in the middle of Diana's lawn, each on our way to see if there was anything the other needed.

'You try not to worry, don't you?' she said. Like me, she was not succeeding. 'I mean it doesn't help, does it?'

There was an echo here of Diana's words that had so annoyed me, many moons ago, when I thought Magnus was lost over the Edge of the Reef.

'I know.' Should I ever have put that advertisement in an Edinburgh college and encouraged this nice young couple to risk their lives?

'Well, shout if you need anything,' she said.

'I will.' But we both knew that if the cyclone hit Pigeon, shouting wouldn't help. We'd just be one of those small statistics that don't mean anything in newspapers in 'civilization'.

If there was a sunset that evening, I missed it, even though I was down by the Little Wharf, gazing westwards. The sea was rising fast by then, the channel between Poppet and Pigeon fuller than I'd ever seen it, and there was a tremulousness on the surface of the heavy water, which from time to time broke into thin fast-running waves with white edges; presumably the ripple at the outer edges of the great disturbance heading our way. And Pigeon itself felt like a tiny, inconsequential pebble lightly skimmed on the surface of the Pacific, happening to get stuck on a submerged mountain top, and liable any time to be washed over just like any other stone in an exposed place – with everything on it washed off. I went indoors only when the last light was gone, and Joe and Benji trotted in from under the palm trees (from which the larger nuts had already been cut down as a hazard prevention measure) just as I was lighting candles in Diana's few carefully rinsed-out old cosmetic jars.

'What's for supper? We haven't had any because Pegi's busy. She's hanging all their stuff in baskets from the ceiling.'

I had a few tins hoarded.

'Great! Haven't had beans for ages.'

'When can we have our books?'

'Any time, but remember, we may not be able to get to Tasha's House for more tomorrow.'

If Cyclone Danny in 1999 was anything like Cyclone Nina in 1993, Tasha's House would barely be there tomorrow.

'Don't you think we're making too much of this?' asked Joe, as I pushed towels along the edge of the barn doors after we'd eaten. 'It's barely even windy at the moment.'

'I hope so,' I said.

'I don't. I want to be able to tell my friends at home I've lived through a cyclone.'

I kissed them goodnight around 8.30 p.m. – their normal Pigeon Island bedtime. Each had a torch he could reach easily if we had to get up and make a dash for higher ground in the dark. Stasi was lying like an oversized carving in Westminster Abbey across the end of Diana's bed when I padded through. She smelt, rather, but would keep my feet warm. The weather didn't close in for an hour after I'd settled with Tom's diary, but when it did come, its violence made up for lost time, for rain was hurled through the air by cyclonic winds. Ross struggled down once to check the barometer before turning in.

'Hi,' he called softly, careful not to shine his torch on the sleeping boys. 'I don't think she'll hit us full force till morning – if she doesn't swerve off – but it could be a rough night.'

'Is Pegi OK?'

'She's scared, but not screaming the place down like she did in '93.' I heard a grin in his voice, but he didn't shine the torch on me as I sat primly in his mother's bed in my Marks and Spencer's nightie, spectacles tied on with twine, with his father's diary – containing much of his private past – in my hand. 'I suppose a white woman's stiff upper lip can occasionally be an advantage!'

When he'd gone, I flipped forward in Tom's diary for an account of what had happened in 1993. Both Ross and Ben had been on the island then, with a politician friend of Ross's staying in the guest units. When Nina had struck, the visitor had been attempting to return to Pigeon after checking the safety of wontoks at a village beyond Nandelli, and if he hadn't let his boat and engine be swept from his grasp, he'd have died. Men who spotted him struggling after the boat had shattered on the shore grabbed his arms and hauled him onto a high coral promontory, where they sang until the worst was over, in the knowledge that every dwelling on Nandelli was being destroyed but no-one was in them. Tom acknowledged that his family had been comparatively lucky on Pigeon.

'*Cyclone Nina was travelling at 200 miles a day, which meant the day before it struck, we were outside its influence and had no warning . . . only when we stopped work for tea did we notice the barometer had dropped a mile*

. . . then gale force winds struck, and the sea rose ten feet above normal . . . Ross did valiant work trying to save Kyomie, *lashing her to the boathouse building, but to no avail; huge seas charging along, crashing against Nandelli across the lagoon, and rushing back to meet another wall of water, lifted the 22-foot launch bodily, smashed it against the walls of the forty-foot boat and bunkhouse, demolishing with it kitchen, shower, toilet and laundry, leaving a bare slab . . . I heard a huge tree fall close to us, the seas having sucked away all hold for its roots . . . then a real monster of a wave, which without that fallen tree would have taken out one end of our house, crumpled my hydropod greenhouse like a toy . . . and stove in Tasha's House . . . The store front was smashed and its veranda swept clean away . . . our massive old generator was lifted off its concrete plinth and twirled about in the air, with the Power House completely destroyed. Half the Units were destroyed too, and every stick of furniture . . . The noise was relentless. Water washed through our house but at least our bed was dry.'*

Did Tom recall, when writing that account, his blithe words to his sisters years before, explaining that cyclones are usually narrow and therefore, being small, Pigeon was likely to be missed? *'Famous Last Words!'* Tom was eighty-three, in his penultimate year of life, when he lay in the bed I lay in now, listening to a large part of thirty years' work being destroyed around him in the space of less than three hours. In a separate note to the formal description of Nina he sent to friends, he recorded that he'd tried to read *The Economist* but it was hard to concentrate with the racket outside. When he'd glanced at Diana beside him, who'd done most of the work with her own hands, he'd wondered if, for the first time, he'd see defeat in her, to him, still beautiful eyes. After all, she was in her seventies, 'no chicken' either, and they'd seen many disappointments as well as triumphs together on this island, a sunny dream of which had brought them together years ago.

'Are you all right, darling? Shall I make tea from the thermos?'

'No. Save it. It may get worse yet. I'm drawing up a list of new building materials we'll need.'

'I married a wonderful girl, didn't I?'

She'd said: 'Don't be silly,' when he'd leaned across to kiss her, but smiled – and kissed him back. She'd never give up. To her, a new disaster was just a new challenge.

As I lay there six years later, sensing mounting strength in the storm delivering higher decibels of *'relentless'* noise by the minute, I tried to think of this as some kind of challenge to me, too, but my upper lip would never be as stiff as Diana's. Curling up beside my candle, I looked for distraction in Ross's story, prepared to read through the night rather than lie in the dark and let imagination create scenes in my head, fed by battering thuds and the eerie singing of the wind outside, worse than present reality. I'd wake the boys only if it looked as though a wave were going to burst through the currently merely shaking barn doors. Otherwise I thought it best if Benji didn't have to hear any of that roaring, watery row, except in what I hoped he believed were passing dreams.

'*Bloody girl. I've told Ross he can't allow her to serve in the store any more if she's going to keep giving things away to her wretched tribe.*' This was Tom on Teimaliki, in the early 1980s. He'd looked upon her tolerantly at first, as a 'fling' for Ross, but now saw her as a threat to the success of PIT. Ross seemed to be taking the marriage thing '*absurdly seriously*' too – even sending to Amalie in America for a ring. '*Now she's not even sweeping the house properly, and Diana's furious because they've pushed out her good furniture and replaced it with leaf mats. They lie about in heaps . . . and the child is being brought up entirely as a Melanesian.*' 'The child' (he barely acknowledged the other, adopted girl, Diana) was Christine, of whom his sisters enquired: '*Is she what they call a half-caste, and if so, which half shows most markedly? Do send a picture . . . Bressin, who's been writing us lovely letters, bless him, describes her as quite a poppet.*'

What feelings did these far from condemnatory queries rouse in Tom? Had private disappointment made him, the unconventional pioneer, less liberal in his attitudes than his elderly spinster sisters? Had he become, like his own father in later years, something of a re-actionary? But he felt he had reasons for holding tough views. He knew the practice of '*living among primitives*', while to them it was all just romantic theory. If he had feelings for Christine, his grandchild, they don't appear in his diary, and his suspicions about Teimaliki and her extended family grew, as more and more Islanders were to be seen casually strolling about the 'other end' of Pigeon, '*as though they owned the place*' . . . Where Ross saw a desirable girl whom he grew to love and who, by agreeing to marry him, had handed him acceptance into Reef Island culture on a plate, Tom saw more sinister machinations at work. By '*planting*' Teimaliki in Ross's bed (a woman no doubt imbued with Kastom magic), and '*forcing*' what they called a marriage on him, the locals had inveigled their way further onto Pigeon just when Tom thought his troubles with '*all that land nonsense*' were coming to an end. (Tom had been the first to shake hands with Nandelli landowners when Sally Pierce had finally been driven out, seemingly to everyone's satisfaction.) But Islanders' patience is legendary.

'*It's sickening the way he gives in to her every whim. Now I hear she's demanding her own housegirl!*' Again, responses to this varied: Tom and Diana saw the request as 'putting on airs'; Ross saw it as only fitting, in Kastom, for a wife of Teimaliki's standing to have help in the house. By Reef Island standards, he was wealthy. As I huddled against a pillow right where Tom's head had lain next to his courageous wife's during Cyclone Nina, I puzzled over how he'd apparently not been able to see his own likeness in Christine's face. Could it really be just because it was a different shade? And could no-one see how anxious Ross had been to have his marriage given proper credibility? I'd seen a photograph of Diana taking tea with Teimaliki on a table laid under the palms, with Tom smiling and the two piccaninni grandchildren between them, proof that they *did* attempt to get together at times – if only at the request of Tom's sisters for a picture. But most of the time intense irritation marked Tom's words about his son and his chosen partner. It saddened me because I'd grown fond of Tom – very fond, however irascible he sometimes seemed – through the intimate act of reading his diaries, and of course it was impossible not to like Ross as well.

Wax, flying from my candle as a particularly strong blast rattled the doors, snuffed it suddenly, and Stasi, seeking my hand with her snout, knocked the book to the floor. When I finally managed to right my bizarre research station on a storm-bound desert isle, the diary had fallen open at a page with only two words scrawled from bottom to top: '*THEY'VE VAMOOSED!*' referring to Ross and Teimaliki in mid-1983, and when I flicked forward half a dozen pages: '*WE CAN'T GO ON MUCH LONGER,*' referring suddenly and confusingly to Tasha . . . With six-foot-long palm fronds ripped from their trunks now skittering over the roof irons and adding a sensation of clawing fingers to Cyclone Danny's ever-rising din, I was beginning to wonder how anyone could stand living through the threat of this kind of weather – and worse – annually, on such a vulnerable speck of land, surrounded by family problems even on bright days – and with a running dispute about the 'right' to be there at all on top of everything else. Was it really worth it for the odd truly paradisal days? But PIT was, in effect, Tom's life's work, even if he didn't love the island with the same passion as Diana, and Pigeon was also his only home, so reasons for tenacity were strong, even if the side of him that loved Western culture was – increasingly, as he grew older – tempted away. Tom had a love/hate relationship with his 'dream island', complicated by a love/love relationship with his wife. There were no simple answers to the questions rattling in my head, echoing the crazy activity outside. I realized now, too, that it was going to be hard to tease out the stories of the Hepworth children individually because, raised on and ever returning to this tiny island, this egg in a storm which could be so beautiful and so terrifying, they and their histories were inextricably bound up with it. As Ben once rightly said: '*Everything comes back to Pigeon.*' For better or for worse, a small island's seductive but frightening freedoms, as well as its microcosmically educational but brutal limitations, had created the people they were, their breadth of vision and narrowness; their weaknesses and strengths.

'Mum?'

Joe had crept into the room and stood, with one of our old tartan duvet covers from Scotland over his shoulders, looking at the shuddering doors.

'How long do you think this'll last?' He smiled ruefully. 'It's giving me a headache.'

'No-one knows,' I said, thinking the truth wisest. 'Let's go and see if we can find an aspirin in Diana's cupboard.'

But I'd forgotten, Diana rarely took medicine of any kind – perhaps a hangover from her Christian Science background as a child. I went into the kitchen and poured Joe a glass of water instead. I'd fastened all the louvres but – as Diana had warned – not so tightly that pressure building up might take the roof off. As a result, they shook violently, despite the covered veranda between them and the direct force of the sideways-sweeping wind outside. Even in the dark it was possible to sense furious movement in the air from west to east, flinging every loose object – from footballs to flying foxes, furniture and substantial bushes – off Pigeon altogether, or high into the heads of the stalwart remaining trees and doubtless ragged box-flower hedges along Diana's 'garden' windbreak.

'Yeuch!'

Joe held out the water for me to sniff.

'I see what you mean.'

The hibiscus hedges would be stripped to skeletons, too. With every seed and leaf whirling in the air, the water in the catchment tanks, despite their coverings, must have caught a good deal.

'Hairwashes in "natural floral essences" for a while,' I joked, and gave Joe a few sips from our precious bottled supply.

'Thanks. Mum, are you scared?'

To lie or not to lie, on such a point, to an eleven-year-old? Diana wouldn't have dreamed of admitting to fear. But just then something large hit the barn doors with an impressive crash (it turned out to be a stack of chairs I'd foolishly left outside) and we both jumped visibly.

'Yes, a bit. But I think it'll blow over . . .'

'Ha ha,' Joe said, noticing my inadvertent joke, and returned to his padded couch, where I could see his eyes open in the dark and sense that, like me, he just wanted the cyclone to hurry past us now.

'You can come in with me and Stasi if you like.'

'It's all right. I'll stay here in case Benji wakes.'

'Thanks.'

I wondered, back in my nest, if Diana had ever experienced the sort of intimacy I felt with Joe at times like this, with her sons when they were young. It was hardly likely such moments of mutual support could be shared with Tasha. Back I turned to 1983. What had been happening then to '*that poor child*', an expression Tom used to refer to his firstborn, that brought things to a head that seemingly fateful year when Ross and his Teimaliki suddenly '*vamoosed*' too?

The plan had been to bring Tasha, now twenty-four, back from Britain to Pigeon with a personal carer. Every doctor consulted agreed this was desirable. But en route Tasha suddenly took against the Rudolph-Steiner-trained girl and she was left in Hong Kong.

'Never mind. The main thing is, Tasha's with her family,' said Tom, ever certain that the combination of those who loved her and the place she loved couldn't be bettered by anything 'civilization' offered. Doctors who'd seen Tasha in Britain often came to the same impasse in their studies of her: '*It is impossible to apply the usual methods of assessment to a child brought up on a South Pacific Island . . . The extent to which Miss Hepworth is retarded is hard to ascertain given the unusual circumstances of her background.*' It was an attitude that may have made Tom and Diana defensive. The children's upbringing had been '*idyllic*'. But that they loved Tasha and longed only for her to find happiness back 'where she belonged' can be in no doubt.

If Tasha, somewhere in her muddled mind, equated the return to Pigeon with a return to the arms of Nokali as his concubine, she was to be disappointed. Nokali, with his wife, had moved. But that she found distraction in other arms before long is certain, and this time Tom was all too aware of what was going on, and if in his mind he'd imagined some miraculous 'cure' for her taking place on Pigeon, he was soon disabused of the idea. '*I sometimes think*,' he wrote wryly to his sisters, '*due to her habit of lying down for any randy fellow who'll have her, that the best place for Tasha would be a well-run bordello.*' Sensibly, they urged him to see she 'took precautions' and, because of her un-reliability with pills, an IUD was sent for. But it curled up in the sweltering heat en route, and Tasha acquired a dose of gonorrhoea which had to be treated, before it was uncurled and '*with a struggle*' fitted. In due course it led to another infection. '*Caught her in the bushes again with a crewman,*' Tom recorded, but rather than being shocked or admonitory, he merely added: '*Just hope to God he's clean.*' At the same time, Tom was disgusted with his son for '*indulgence of his proclivities*' when they impinged on Pigeon life as defined by the Hepworth seniors, for of Ross he wrote: '*Had a big blow-up with him. He really has got himself inextricably tied up with a native swarm . . . and the Books are in a shambles. I've had to put Bressin onto it. Thank God for him.*' To Tom, Tasha's actions were always forgivable because she was always essentially innocent. But Ross should have known better than to '*waste his time with these perpetually puerile people*'.

At this point Ross, instead of spending long evenings as his father had, poring over accounts, was out trying to woo back the woman he loved. And if this meant more all-night partying of the type she'd come to enjoy – often away from Pigeon – so be it; he'd find the means to provide the fun she wanted, and to hell with treating PIT as the be-all and end-all of life. He felt his parents never handed him full responsibility for it anyway, failed to accept his wife (one stilted tea party she'd hated didn't count), and let Bressin stick his nose into his business any time. Ross, then, in his turn was becoming angry, and a wedge was beginning to be driven, by virtue of their different cultural identities and relationships with their parents, between twins brought up under the same palm trees.

'*Bressin,*' Tom told his sisters, '*remains a Tower of Strength . . . He shows great patience with Tasha, and is ever the diplomat with his Black Sheep brother.'* Clairvoyantly, at this stage, his sisters sounded a warning note: *'Don't lean too hard on your Tower of Strength, remember he's young and has his own life to lead, too. What of the job opportunity you mentioned?'* Bressin had done well in his hotel management studies in Britain, and the best hotel in Honiara had him under consideration for a responsible and lucrative position. But he was wanted on Pigeon, too. *'I don't know what we'd do without him,'* confessed Tom, as Tasha's – and Teimaliki's – shenanigans escalated, and suddenly, messily, these two young women, each in a different way hampered by the effects of an island upbringing, clashed. One day, it seemed, Tasha was playing happily with toddler Christine and her sista; the next, Tasha was attempting to hit Teimaliki, restrained by a shocked Ross, and spitting at her when she was no longer within arm's reach to bash. Then she threw a spear at a housegirl of Diana's who was hanging up a bunch of bananas, accusing her of stealing her boyfriend; aimed a heavy three-pronged anchor at the legs of another girl, missed, dropped the anchor on her own foot, and screamed through gritted teeth half the night. Teimaliki, in the meantime, sobbing angrily, made as if to vanish 'lo' bus'', accompanied by an entourage of knit-browed wontoks with bundles and babies on their heads and backs, clicking fingers crossly – and Ross had to chase after her, attempting to mollify and reassure in the face of insanity.

Here, for me, reading to distract myself from a cyclone in 1999, the story seemed to spin into a vortex of the hysterical and the bizarre combined, all to the tune of a now steadily screaming wind, and I put the diary down. Time for a cup of tea. Choosing a mug in the kitchen, I noticed, holding a candle shielded from the wind with my hand, that almost all the cups and saucers had been broken and carefully glued. That figured. *'We've hardly any crockery left,'* wrote Tom at one point. But before this another dramatic diary entry read simply: *'BRESSIN'S BOMBSHELL'.* The cargo boat that brought what everyone hoped were stronger pills for Tasha also brought confirmation of the hotel management offer – which Bressin accepted. He was to leave within a month. *'It's a wonderful opportunity for him of course,'* wrote Tom, *'but Oh what vistas unfold if Ross doesn't come to his senses.'*

Trying to ascertain what was going on from diary entries varying in length from one word on a major event to pages on the smallest exchange was surreal detective work, as the wind continued its now jarring, now swooning lamentations. If there was rain as well now, it was so caught up and spun sideways with salt water swept off the sea, I couldn't distinguish it from any other kind of whirled water. Instead, I tried to distinguish threads that told a story – or several stories – in other people's lives. Bressin, it transpired, had accepted the job before the worst of the violence with Tasha, and at a time he thought his twin able to cope adequately with PIT – and get over whatever temporary difficulties he had with his young wife. But Tom was correct in assuming things would deteriorate in the absence of the Tower of Strength. Within weeks of Bressin's departure Ross was complaining that Tasha was throwing chunks of coral at little Christine, and Diana was citing Teimaliki's '*bad*' behaviour as the cause of Tasha's increasingly '*unusual*' behaviour. Sometimes this now twenty-five-year-old child would dance for hours, smiling to herself, or laugh at jokes no-one else heard, but often sobbed unconsolably for hours, too. Or lashed out. A disturbing conversation I'd had with Diana came to mind: '*She saw him as hers, you see, and couldn't stand him being wronged . . .*' Since most of Tasha's aggression was directed against Teimaliki – who'd recently been caught in flagrante delicto on a sofa in Ngarando with a houseboy – the Hepworth seniors wondered if the solution might be for Teimaliki to go back to live on Nandelli, where she tended to flee when things were 'awkward' on Pigeon anyway. But this unequivocal demonstration of how lightly his parents viewed his commitment to his family – an attitude not designed to help his wife feel much sense of commitment either – pushed an already fraught Ross over all boundaries of reserve.

' "*If she goes, I go!*" *he shouted.*' Words recorded by Tom. Ross accused his parents of understanding and caring nothing about how he wanted to live his life. What if Teimaliki just leaves the island when Tasha has her periods? (always a bad time) Tom then suggested, aiming at compromise, and Ross did what he'd never done before: he swore at his parents and told them exactly what he thought of their ' "*impossibly arrogant belief*" ' that they were ' "*always right*" ', and just how much they were feared and hated locally. Tom was deeply affronted by such a show of disrespect in front of Diana, who'd given years of her life to making Pigeon what it was and doing her best for all her children – including Ross. Icily, he asked his son to leave their presence.

' "I'll go all right," ' raged Ross, ' " and you'll be bloody lucky to see me back. Teimaliki is *my wife*. And Tasha's just sick!" '

'But everyone knows Teimaliki is unfaithful to you,' Diana tried to reason. 'Better to face up to it now and let her go and live among her own . . .'

'Shut up! Yes, *shut up* and listen for once in your life, Mum. *I* am her own. It may not seem like it to her, because you treat her like shit, but I'm going to prove I'm not like you, and stand by her whatever!'

'We'll see,' said Diana, also shaking with fury by now. 'You don't know what you're saying or doing . . .'

'That's just it, I *do*! For maybe the first time in my life, I do! I'll come back to get my things when Tasha's asleep. Here are your bloody keys.'

With that, Ross flung the keys he wore, like his mother, round his neck between them on the ground. And just as he would evacuate me, Joe and Benji and all our things from Ngarando and Tasha's House to Ben's Box in ten minutes with the aid of fifteen stalwart wontoks if Cyclone Danny stood square on our path by morning, he swept up his family and all their possessions in 1983 and was across Nandelli channel to start a new life away from his parents in less time than it took them to extract their Will from a polythene-wrapped briefcase kept out of the reach of white ants, and make a pot of tea. Over it, they would discuss the possibility of partially disinheriting him.

That night, in a leaf hut vacated for them, which Teimaliki swept perfectly first, and on a new mat woven by her own hands, Ross's wife came once more into his arms.

'Sore tumas abaotim narakaen samtimg,' she whispered. (Sorry about you-know-what.)

'Y'oraet,' her husband soothed, only infinitely glad to be holding her again, and in the morning they were still locked together as one when Tasha's noises from across the channel came distantly to them amid the lorikeets' dawn squawks. She was lying in their empty bed on Pigeon, rocking from side to side, with the blood from her period seeping over the mattress.

'*Get out! Get out!*' she yelled.

Tasha also, several days into what was to be a prolonged drought, locked herself in Tom's shower with every jar of ointment she could find on the island – from Elizabeth Arden and Gentian Violet to grout – and alternately applied them ubiquitously, then rinsed, until they were empty and the water tank dry. When, eventually, she emerged, half naked and purple splotched, she pushed past her mother and turned on the kitchen-tank tap so hard Tom and Diana between them couldn't turn it off. Tasha's hands were tiny but immensely strong, and her wild acts were driven by immensely strong and uncontrollable impulses. Diana, now wondering, perhaps for the first time, if her daughter really was suffering from some terrible imbalance, started slipping sedatives into Tasha's morning drink, because she was often at her worst 'first thing'. '*Perhaps she dreams of being cured, poor love, and when she wakes finds reality unbearable,*' wrote Tom sadly, his hand-writing dithery with exhaustion. Not long afterwards, following a confession to his sisters that Tasha '*bit my hand through to the bone – then it blew up and is still weeping yellow pus*', the diary entries tail off until the scrawled '*CAN'T GO ON MUCH LONGER.*'

On a dot in the South Pacific, ninety days out of a hundred a blue and gold fantasy isle to the distant eye, the final days of a small family tragedy were being played out. And the long wings of little Pigeon reached out to enfold all its children in the drama. '*Trying to get next cargo boat – or any ship – diverted to stop at Mohawk Bay,*' said a message to Bressin, who was happily and capably catering for a conference hundreds of miles away in Honiara. '*We must get Tasha out. Be ready to meet us any time.*' Bressin responded with a sympathetic telegram. (These were relayed by radio.) He would obtain compassionate leave from the job to see them through Honiara. Good: that was one stage in the journey catered for, and naturally it was assumed that, at this moment of family crisis, Ross would be the one to accompany Tom and Tasha to wherever help could be found for her in New Zealand, and a note was duly sent to Nandelli to ask him to be ready, too. But Ross sent a note back: '*Sorry, Teimaliki does not want me to go. We are busy with family matters.*' This, to Diana, was the last straw, the last word in disloyalty. These wretched Islander girls *must* use sorcery to turn a boy's head so. Distraught over Tasha, and furious with Ross, she sent a piccaninni splashing across the channel with a letter openly threatening to excommunicate him entirely if he failed to do what was his clear duty, at once. '*I'm not coming, Mum,*' he wrote back and, ever one to stick to her word, his mother disinherited him on the spot. Tom's signature was added grimly to her own on the amendment to the Will.

Word then came that the bishop on Santa Cruz had heard the plea for a ship to be diverted, and one was on its way. But Tom, bowels churning constantly from anxiety and with a still swollen hand, was unable to control Tasha on his own. So the first – and only – immediately available and willing strong male Islander was offered a sum to help get Tasha aboard and as far as Santa Cruz: that same Jimson who'd assaulted Tasha when she was five. But whether any memories played upon Tasha's mind is impossible to tell from her behaviour, for she merely did with him as she liked to do with everyone in certain moods: when she felt his touch on her shoulder as he guided her to a seat on the deck of the *Southern Cross*, she insisted he admire the scars over her heart and, when Tom's back was turned for two minutes to search out aspirins for his own aches, opened her legs. The same thing happened throughout the journey, with crew members, strangers met on Santa Cruz and at Honiara airport, until Tom had the brainwave of spiking her frequently swigged bottle of juice not only with day sedatives but with sleeping pills as well. Then she only constantly let go her bladder.

On meeting them at Honiara, Bressin saw his father couldn't travel on alone with Tasha to New Zealand and managed to extend the compassionate leave from his job so that he could help. On the first day, in Auckland, they tried to persuade Tasha voluntarily to enter the psychiatric hospital that was immediately ready to accept her.

'No,' she said. 'Bye mi go lo' Rif.' (I'm going back to Reefs.) So they let her stay one more night with them at a YMCA hostel, eating chips, slurping from her drugged bottle, and looking at necklaces in shop windows. But by the second day the doctors had made their own, fresh diagnosis of chronic schizophrenia and urged Tom to accept the inevitable. She might stabilize, in time, with the right treatment, but at the moment admission – voluntary or otherwise – was really the only option.

'Even if it makes her desperately unhappy?' asked Tom, a slight figure beside his six-foot son, with what was to become, after this, a permanent hunch of the shoulders. He'd always vowed to keep Tasha out of just this sort of institution, full of pastel-coloured corridors and windows that opened only a few inches so inmates couldn't jump out.

'Your daughter requires professional treatment, Mr Hepworth.'

'We wondered about analysis . . .'

'We'll start by trying to reduce the extremity of her mood swings.'

'Yes, she is rather moody . . .'

During this conversation, a nurse, with Bressin, was attempting to lead Tasha towards a chair next to some women with too little hair and too many bags.

'We'll get you a cup of tea, dear,' said the nurse. 'We're all going to have tea, aren't we, girls?'

The 'girls', who smelled, made animals noises and stared at Tasha's dress, which had been ripped en route. But she thought they were staring at her necklaces.

'No wandem tea. Mi go lo' Rif . . .'

Here Tasha turned and headed for the door, clutching her beads. But the door was shut, and her dadi was standing in front of it beside a man in glasses, saying: 'It's for the best, darling, just till you're better . . .'

'Let her go!' Tasha shouted, and lunged at her father, one tiny hand catching him under the chin, so that his head cracked backwards and her way was clear to pummel him in the ribs and boot him in the belly. Bressin and a nurse grabbed her arms from behind but Tom was already crumpled on the lino floor, knees to his chest. '*They pressed a button then,*' he was to write later, '*and Amazons came. She fought, but when four of them laid hands on her, she broke down, and broke my heart.*'

Tom was helped up onto a chair, where he sobbed into one hand while they dragged Tasha away down a corridor to the locked ward. While her noises went on, his other hand was still held out towards her as if he were still trying to offer comfort to – or fend off – his beloved Poppet.

'Let her go! *Let her go!*' Tasha shrieked, over and over, until they finally got an injection into her and she was quiet. After that there was only the sound of Tom's quiet sobs on the edge of the day room of the open ward, until the women further along started clattering their teacups.

'Come on, Dad,' said Bressin, 'we all tried.'

'We did, didn't we?' said Tom, shakily collecting himself. 'You're right. Let's go and write to Mummy.'

'*Darling, darling,*' wrote Tom from the hostel, then stared out of the window onto the blank back wall of another building for a long time. He remembered fearing to lose both Diana and their first child, in the storms that prevented Tasha being born on Pigeon. Why did this feel so much worse? Then he pulled himself together. '*We've done the only thing we could . . . We'll look in on her again tomorrow . . . Now, to be practical, while I'm here, I'll bustle the Hong Kong order and see if I can't find some solar bulbs.'*

When they went to see Tasha next day, she was sucking her thumb and wouldn't look at them.

'Rejection at this stage is only to be expected,' said the doctor.

'Yes, of course,' said Tom. 'My wife and I will come and see how she's progressing next year.'

Sixteen years later, on Pigeon, dawn, a white-out of airspun spray, at which Joe, Benji and I peeped cautiously through only the most sheltered louvres, brought Cyclone Danny close, but not on top of us. Water came through the barn doors from waves washing over the West Patio, but only from the sides and underneath; they were not burst.

'Do you think we can get down to Ross's?' asked Benji, eating rice and banana out of a cup.

'Well, we certainly won't try moving anywhere until we get word,' I said, and at that moment word arrived in the form of an oilskinned Ross, flanked for strength against the wind by Vili, the faithful wontok who'd fetched Christine, and a brother of Pegi's.

'Iufela oraet?'

When Ross was either tired, had had a beer or was stressed, he tended to slip into Pijin. I said we were fine.

'It's close but on its way past, according to Raratonga. The island's going to be a helluva mess, but I doubt there's much structural damage.'

'What about Nandelli?'

They'd seen the first washes go through last evening, right across the postcard palms-and-sand side of the island. The waves would have reached all the leaf huts, giving them a good soak, but since they'd been rebuilt on higher ground after Nina in 1993, most should have remained standing. Vili and Pegi's brother, who never normally went near Diana's house, lolled comfortably next to Joe and Benji on the sofas, gripped by *National Geographic*s.

'Ross, do you mind if I ask you something?'

He shook cyclone water from his dark head and grinned.

'Ask away. I'm not exactly going fishing today, and Pegi's finally gone to sleep now it's confirmed the worst is heading away.'

'When did you last see your sister?'

'Tasha? It must be sixteen years or more.'

'Here on Pigeon?'

'Yes – except I was living mostly on Nandelli then.'

I nodded, wondering how similar his version of events at that time would be to his father's.

'Will you fill me in some time on the years after you and Teimaliki "vamoosed"?'

' "Vamoosed"? Who vamoosed? We were given the Royal Boot!'

'Is that what it felt like?'

'Well – it was the same when Ben had his problems. If you didn't conform to Mum and Dad's wishes, out you went!'

'Did you ever talk much to your dad?'

'No. He and Mum were a complete team. Except for working on the island, they didn't really need us.'

'Is that how it felt?'

But here Ross turned the tables on me, saying lightly: 'Hey! You're really into feelings, aren't you? Which is odd considering you don't let yourself have any.'

I smiled. Giving way to feelings and Pigeon Island seemed a dangerous combination. Did he know how I'd felt, and still felt occasionally, about his brother?

'Watch the clean-up when it calms down,' Ross said as he pulled up his hood to struggle through the fog of whipped water to the eastern end again. 'You'll be impressed. Then come down and party a little. You should let yourself go sometimes.'

Gradually, through the morning, the wind speed dropped, so it was possible to see the movements of the sea all round and, in places, across Pigeon. I was glad the tide had been at its fullest in the early hours, when we couldn't see it, because the power of the suck and surge of massive waves, as they curled around then leaped over the highest coral overhangs close to Tasha's House, was such that I would never have dared attempt to drag the boys up to Ben's Box through the racing rivers that were left in their wake as they receded.

'Look at the Little Wharf,' said Benji later, as the rivers fell away and ceased to form, leaving only gouged channels of mud filled with palm debris. 'It isn't there.'

It was there, only invisible. Where we'd sat so often, legs dangling, munching pawpaw slices in the sun, there was just deep, swaying blue, and all round the rest of the island, where the coral was raised less than fifteen feet, Pigeon had shrunk and its shape was blurred. This was a legacy of pressure in the atmosphere, but the tides should return to normal soon.

'Wow! Look at *that*!' called Joe.

I'd thought he was with Benji and me, viewing the quieter side of the island from Diana's south veranda, but he was standing barefoot in the mud not far from the West Patio, head back and eyes wide as wave after wave struck the already heavily eroded coral under it, was not quite able to make the leap over, and shot up in spouts taller than the tallest palm tree left standing.

'Joe, come here!' I ordered. If one of those waves did make it, as they had all night, his feet would be swept from under him and he'd be a doll bashed on the jaggedly scooped wall under the spouts.

'You worry too much, Mum,' he said. 'It's going down now.'

'I know – but be careful.' There were notes in Tom's diaries about freak waves. But he was right, the worst was over and we'd got off lightly. Now, for us, there remained only the task of shifting our belongings back to Tasha's, which was well drenched by waves hitting it but had lost only some guttering and lumps of leaf thatch out of the roof. The Islanders, however, viewed the aftermath of a cyclone's touch less selfishly.

It was on the third day that a group from Nandelli came to Pigeon, early in the morning, the sound of voices reaching me like a whisper growing slowly into a chorus on the air. Then I saw the heads of the tallest, some topped by leaf baskets, appearing and disappearing close to the middle of the island, on what had been, before Cyclone Danny's attentions, Diana's lawn. Down and up the heads bobbed, from north to south, in a line four deep, with a few stray piccaninnis also stooping and rising at the rear. In front of the Islanders, as they neared Diana's house, was all the litter created and left by the cyclone – squashed bunches of ngenumbla, crab shells, broken-backed palm leaves, whole small trees – behind them, spotless ground that would soon be green again, steaming gently in the sun. As they drew closer, their singing rising and falling as their bodies rose and fell, each time gathering a fragment to add to their baskets, I saw that some carried machetes, to chop larger fallen branches into kindling as they went, while others used long strips of metal curved into scythe shapes to tidy the wind-blasted bushes, whose few remaining leaves were bleached grey with salt. Most, men and women, wore just a kalico tied simply round their waists, but a number had draped cloths around their heads to pad them against the weight of their baskets. At Diana's bungalow, its red roof above the veranda leaf also steaming, they divided, one group bending to the earth with spread and stiffened fingers to rake up stray leaves under the giant satellite dish that, on a good day, could bring Diana Australian soaps, and the rest sweeping over the West Patio like individual twigs in one giant broom. When they neared Tasha's House and saw me, there were grins and waves, and two women, one man and a piccaninni dropped out of formation for a moment to deliver, from folds in their headdresses, tiny pieces of Benji's Lego . . . I heard them all again later, singing different songs, and knew there would be dancing round many fires on Nandelli and Nenumbo. Cleaning up after a cyclone, like rebuilding leaf houses, was a group effort. People didn't just run to their little separate boxes, as I did, and tick off a checklist of possessions undamaged.

Ross was right, I was impressed by the clean-up, but I didn't go down, as Joe and Benji did, to join in the partying, for only on the reef – which I could revisit at last – and in the sea did I feel I dare 'let myself go' a bit, as he suggested. Our little brush with a cyclone had been a sobering experience, leaving me feeling strung out and vulnerable. Maybe some of the things I'd read during that night contributed as well. All I knew was that I couldn't risk 'letting my hair down' and being too much myself with *anyone* on Pigeon – and maybe especially Ross, for I knew he carried within him the seeds of much old pain that might blossom into shapes that could complicate my life here. I could not allow views of my own about this family's story to sharpen into divisions taut as the invisible lines that checkered the island they lived on. I'd just have to go on giving the impression I didn't allow myself feelings.

20

The Mid-1980s

LATE 1983 SAW PIGEON BEREFT OF ALL ITS CHILDREN: TASHA UNDER psychiatric care in New Zealand; Ross away in dudgeon with his Reef Island family, and Bressin in Honiara. '*I'm too old for this*,' wrote Tom, when he and Diana had to unload stock from a cargo boat alone in rough weather, and would have lost several oil drums if Tangypera – who, like Bopali, respected the Hepworth seniors for their remarkable if invasive achievements – hadn't dived in and floated them to land. Everyone was drenched in the process, and Tom felt a fever coming on. He also fell from Diana's seawall when checking nothing had been left to be stolen on the beach, badly winding himself, and it was after this that he wrote to Bressin: '*There just aren't enough hours in the day with the store bell going continuously, and for such trifles – a single fish hook! We must run the business down to just copra and beer. How else will I ever find time to fix the generator, and Mummy clean out the water tanks – never mind the next stocktake, and as for my book, hah! No homeswoppers on the horizon for New Year either, when, as you know, we've a reunion in NZ with the all-girl crew from '54 we don't want to miss . . . and a bang on Mummy's shin from the punt is turning ulcerous.*' Diana's wound was so bad Tom had to help her shower, filling the bucket and rose system rigged to the ceiling with heated rainwater, and applying Epsom salts. While she lurched about trying to keep the store and copra under control, he tried, on arthritic knees, in sweltering conditions, to fix their toilet –

which he needed increasingly in the night – and failed. There was also trouble with the neighbours again, manifesting itself mainly in a spate of thefts and 'accidental' spilling of sacks it had taken hours to fill with sand, but rising on occasion to confrontations with particularly '*reasonless*' individuals – among them one of Ross's old childhood companions, who, Tom reported, '*went berserk one day, God only knows why! whereupon we had no choice but to let Samantha show her face*'.★ Samantha was the new dog, a soft character but of proportions terrifying to the Islanders – a Great Dane. The trouble with Diana's leg lasted eight weeks. Unknown to either, Tom had cancer too, which doubtless contributed to his feeling so weary.

It was some time before Bressin received the letter, as Tom couldn't post it until the next cargo boat came. In the interim, Bressin built steadily on the success of his first months as assistant manager at the Mendana, instigating new regimes for the staff, who liked being addressed in Pijin, and receiving compliments from clients who noticed improvements in the service. He gave lectures, encouraging Honiaran waiters to bring European polish to their work, and planned to introduce silver service the following year. A catering manual was his guide, and he liked the orderliness of 'going by the book' and seeing results. It was very different to his wild upbringing as the best spear fisherman in Reefs, but he relished the contrast and wrote with enthusiasm about his work to Amalie, to Tom's sisters – and to a pretty American girl he'd met as a dinner guest. '*I feel I'm making real personal progress, as well as with the staff training,*' he told his godmother, and to the girl, Angela, he declared boldly that he'd love it if she came to Pigeon Island with him one day, an invitation which, with its exotic overtones, was an ace up the sleeve of an already attractive young man. And she said she'd love to, one day, too. Neither knew how soon they'd be challenged to act on their declarations. Tom's barely disguised SOS reached Bressin when he'd just returned from a weekend picnicking and playing tennis with new-found friends, and he had to make a decision quickly, which he knew, at twenty-one, would impact on his life for years to come. '*We really could do with you back home, you know,*' was the fairly gentle message Tom sent, but the undertone of quiet desperation wasn't missed by this, the quietest of his children.

★ Some of Ross's Islander friends were upset by his parents' 'excommunication' of him.

Bressin, who had a banquet to organize the following day, didn't sleep much that night. Lying under a fan, eyes wide in the dark, he weighed up the pros and cons of leaving the job he was enjoying to return to Pigeon and fulfil what he believed his parents saw as his duty. He saw it that way, too, but he also knew a choice existed, for when they'd cut Ross out of their Will, Bressin had written from his position of new confidence, advising them to forgive his twin and accept his choice of wife and current loyalties, '*for the bread of banishment is bitter to both giver and taker*'. He had no particular religious affiliations in those days, quoting from many sources. He also set down an analysis of his family: '*It's like a play in which we're the characters: 1) Myself, chasing life experience in Honiara. 2) Ross, capable when he puts his mind to it, but liable to have wild ideas and, worse, carry them through . . . 3) Teimaliki, unwilling to take on the benefits of European life but could provide harmony given encouragement; 4) Mummy, linchpin to the success of Pigeon . . . Doesn't get on with Ross because of his wild ideas, his wife, and perhaps deeper emotional reasons . . . 5) Daddy, the most intelligent member of the family, working at something he doesn't really feel is his destiny, but resigned. Life to him is Love and Loyalty. He offers observation, but, like the owl in the tree, 'the more he heard, the less he spoke' . . . 6) Tasha, who fought her handicap for years, dragging us with her until the end that was a bitter pill for all. In turns she's been pitied, ignored, despised, envied, hated and loved, if deep sorrow and patience can be called love . . . And what's the happy ending, you ask? Well, as William Cowper said in 1800, "Happiness depends, as Nature shows, less on exterior things than most suppose."*' Bressin ended this letter with the words: '*I wish I could say more to get my feelings across.*' In another, he told his mother, with reference to Ross, that he believed it unrewarding to try to change people; it was better to adapt to their needs. '*A shallow philosophy, you may think, but will do me until I can find the deep conviction that seems to have borne you through your life.*'

Although Bressin had begun a tentative search for his own convictions, it was not through confusion at this stage. As well as perceptively sympathizing with all points of view over what had happened to his siblings, he was feeling more secure and positive than ever before, so that his father's letter, with all that a decision arising from it implied, disturbed but didn't distress him. He'd been at the Mendana Hotel only six months but had made great strides – especially in the area of relationships. So, switching on a light and finding paper, he prepared to take a still greater one and, instead of feeling restricted by the inevitability of his answer to his parents in their hour of need, allowed the idea of a return to Pigeon to flower into a delicious fantasy that just might prove realizable: 'Dear Angela, How is the Pussy Cat? This is your Owl.'

Ten days later Tom told his diary: '*Bressin's coming, thank God,*' and he and Diana were delighted an American girl might be joining him for a visit in due course. '*How truly like Paradise Reef Islands look from the air,*' Bressin wrote after a flight using the airstrip on Santa Cruz and, while making sensible plans for his takeover of PIT, wove dreams about how paradisal those islands could feel, too, with Angela at his side.

'*Bressin IS a trooper,*' wrote Elizabeth to Tom a few months later when he told his sisters how splendidly things were going now the Tower of Strength was back '*and really taking hold of the reins, so we oldies can even occasionally put our ulcerated legs up!*' And in answer to their interest in 'the young lady', Tom wrote: '*We met her when she came out with her parents – sweet little thing. Not a beauty quite, but has enchanted us with her thoughtful ways, and when they haven't been off on doubtless deep-and-meaningful explorations of the reef, has helped Bressin organize a Pricebook and always helps Diana . . . They're off to Fiji for a fortnight before we head for New Zealand. Fingers crossed he manages to lure her back to Pigeon for keeps once her college course finishes. It looks as though the Gods are smiling on us for once!*'

There was room enough on Pigeon for Bressin and Angela not to feel constantly under their parents' eyes during her visit, and they were allocated – in a way Tom and Diana thought fittingly modern – the privacy of the schoolhouse in which to sleep and take shelter from the warm daily deluges that refreshed the island's greenery. But Bressin, once the day's work was over – or before it began, in the still starlit hours before dawn – elected to take his shy Angela's hand, place her in a canoe, the most precious cargo he'd ever carried, and paddle her silently, Islander fashion, to any of a dozen tranquil spots he knew around Reefs, and there lay her softly on a kalico spread on the sand, and kiss, with the Pacific, her pink nail-varnished toes.

'Hey, that tickles!' she'd whisper in an excited little voice.

'I know. Lie still.'

Then he'd stroke her insteps until she squeaked, a chiffon breeze just hotter than body temperature running over them both all the time.

'Oh Bress!'

When she called his name, he wanted her at once, but he held back, moving to lie at her side, heart skidding at her nearness as she waited – as his Islander friends and his brother told him girls waited.

'Bress?'

If she sat up and bent over him, her long hair a thin curtain over small, bikini-white breasts, he sometimes reached up to touch her reverently, but otherwise flew to complete the intimacy rather suddenly, when all was, briefly, ecstatic. Since it was new for her, too, neither quite understood why, sometimes, she cried a little afterwards.

'I love you,' he'd whisper, kissing her hair.

'I love you too,' she'd answer, smiling between receding sobs, and he paddled her back to Pigeon for the day's work in the store, or to try to sleep in the fanless air of the schoolhouse. They were more relaxed together under the sea, in scuba gear, where she followed, amazed and sometimes afraid, when they descended the cliff walls at the Edge of the Reef, where spinning schools of fluorescent fish could be shadowed unnervingly by the great wings of a ray above or harried into sudden flight by a nosing, lugubrious grouper. Here, Bressin was indisputably Angela's guide, and she basked in his fearlessness and expertise. Everything else would 'come right' in time, she believed, and she looked forward to the holiday in Fiji, where there'd be other young people around and they could dance, have a drink and do 'normal' things. But later (years later, when he'd changed his name to Ben), Bressin was to say he especially loved Angela on Pigeon, because her 'disorientation' there gave her to him more. It was an alien world to her. And Fiji worked less well for Bressin. There, among her type of friends, he was the stranger, and she was too inexperienced to be his guide. Nevertheless, when Tom and Diana left for New Zealand, it was still their hope – and his – that Bressin's proposal to Angela to make a life with him on Pigeon would be accepted. They might even open a restaurant together once the tourists flocked in, for plans for an airfield on Lom Lom were back on the table once more.

'Let us know as soon as you hear, won't you, darling?' said Diana as they set off. 'Then we won't have to bother with any more wretched partners. We'll all be family, and that would be perfect!'

'I will,' said Bressin, the keys of the store and Ngarando, the schoolhouse and the guest units round his young neck. And for three months, managing PIT alone and working every hour the sun was up, and fishing with Matoko at night, Bressin waited.

'Wissway?' Matoko, who at that time had 'stakka' girls to 'messaboat' with, asked his old friend kindly, after a cargo boat which might have brought a letter from Angela had been and gone.

'Nartin',' Bressin would say, with an expressively rueful, Reef Island-style flick of his soft eyebrows.

'Sore tumas.' (Sorry.)

He may have shrugged outwardly, but Bressin was hurting. Deep in the dark, cool, night-time embrace of the sea, his old love, he craved Angela's fluid and elusive young body, which he felt he was only beginning to understand. He wanted a lifetime to learn about it, and missed her small kindnesses, too — the way she'd bring him tea if he overslept instead of ringing the bell loudly (Pigeon's usual wake-up call) and listed books and music she thought he'd like. He loved the idea of sharing these things — sharing everything — with her, and wanted so ardently to believe she'd say yes to Pigeon, and so to him, that at first he allowed himself real hope, not fantasy, and was happy to wait, buoyed by memories of their short but infinitely sweet time together, and writing her into his future plans. But as more mailbags came, bringing no news, his hope faded, the spring vanished from his loping stride over the reefs, and he didn't read poems any more under a hurricane lamp at night but lay quietly staring into the warm dark, her silence and his isolation combining to chip away, like the sea round an island, at his aching heart until he felt hollowed to the core. Finally, she wrote him a 'Dear John' (Tom's description of her farewell letter) and, like his father, Bressin was physically affected by emotional distress, coming out in boils so painful they had to be lanced.

'*The poor boy's rather distracted about his work, as well,*' the disappointed Tom told his sisters. '*I play chess with him in the evening — anything to distract him from what is evidently a blow. Ah, young love!*' Tom had returned to Pigeon later than Diana because his prostate cancer had been discovered during the New Zealand trip. Far from being dismayed by this, at the suggestion of the concerned all-girl crew — described as still '*a gorgeous bunch*' — he had gone to London for his treatment and, apart from '*feeling a bit wuzzly*' on radiotherapy days, he had basically revelled in another non-stop culture fest with his sisters, who were only too delighted to play nursemaid to their beloved brother. One of the all-girl crew, now a distinguished oncologist in London, often joined them too, so that past and present mingled delightfully. But letters to Diana flowed from him too – at the rate of thirteen pages per night – and it didn't matter that they wouldn't reach her for months because she'd know his thoughts were with her anyway. She did, for she wrote to him:

'*My Darling, not a dicky bird from you yet, but I know you'll have written and hang on every mailbag . . . I hope the treatment isn't too vile, and long to hear of 100% success . . . lots of copra here to keep Bressin busy, and your new office is almost complete. Could you find me a loofah and some yeast pills for Samantha? . . . ALL my love, D.*' In the end, as so many were required for the Great Dane, Tom's sisters sent a whole carton of yeast pills, which Bressin took too when his general condition was low. Diana, saddened to see him injured after his first brush with Cupid, tried to console him.

'Look how long it took Daddy and me to find each other. He was thirty-six!'

'I know,' said Bressin. 'Thanks, Mum.'

His parents' relationship had so solid a foundation, and was still so loving, it would be hard to match. He'd wanted to do his best, though, with Angela. When, after Tom had been back some months – with as clean a bill of health as possible before his next check-up – and Bressin still seemed '*in the doldrums*', the idea of sending him on a 'sabbatical' to Australia was discussed. There – who knows? – he might find someone else, as well as broadening his work experience. The three had a quiet Christmas, and Bressin was given an air ticket for the following May, which would give his parents a chance to fit in a check-up trip for Tom, and him time to get PIT into tip-top order for a couple they hoped would join them mid-year. Bressin was grateful, but it seemed a long time to wait – especially as he'd be on his own again while they were away. Would they consider having Ross back?

'Not with Teimaliki. Absolutely not.'

So Bressin continued his full-time occupation with PIT during the day, numbing himself to feeling by exhausting his now much thinner body in the sea at night. '*He'll wear out all our underwater torches!*' wrote Tom, but believed there'd been '*significant improvement*' before he and Diana left the island again. Indeed, Bressin's health had picked up after New Year, and he'd even begun to sketch itineraries for the distant Australian trip. Now he just had to find a way of living through another lonely spell on Pigeon without the focused hopes he'd held onto so eagerly before.

From New Zealand, where they were redecorating the flats that remained the financial bedrock of desert island life, the Hepworth seniors sent Bressin instructions on the handling of PIT's accounts, and lists of the order in which to use tinned food in case he didn't find time for fishing. But Bressin always found time for fishing. He needed the release it gave his pent-up body. In the heavy blue darkness lent by moonlight, not bothering with wetsuit or air tanks, he drifted, massaged by currents, his whole being a suspended arrow, beside crevices and gullies in the coral cliffs until he found his prey, when, with great accuracy, he struck. Again and again he struck, but finally it wasn't enough. Back to the peak of condition on a plain but ample diet of fish, fruit and vegetables, which he preferred to his parents' tins, Bressin ached for a woman. And, as it happened, a young woman from Nivali, a village too far away for commuting by dugout, and who consequently 'lived in' to work on Pigeon, ached for a man. To this woman, Sipikoli, were later attributed sorcery and Sin, but at this stage it looked like a simple case of lonely man meets lonely woman. One day she was walking past the glassless window of the room where he did the accounts, balancing an enormous basket of washing on her head; the next, she was lying with him on the same sun-aired linen, in the first bed Diana had built on Pigeon, also well used by Sally Pierce and Ossi, Teimaliki and Ross. Did she slide her liquid eyes from under her basket deliberately to meet his, or did his liquid eyes seek out hers? Whatever, they entwined, and after they'd finished, she propped herself on one elbow, ran a slender brown finger from his eyebrows all the way down his body, pausing only to swirl it in the soft chest hair unknown to her race, then let it stop at the top of one thigh. Slightly startled, Bressin looked up at the serious, oval face above a perfectly balanced naked body, haloed by a wild bush of lime-streaked hair, and found that, when he stirred involuntarily, she smiled broadly.

'Agen,' she said, for there are exceptions to every rule, and Sipikoli belied the myth that Reef Island women feel no passion. It was 'agen' most nights after that, and when she wasn't slaking him – and herself – happily in bed, she was expertly gutting the fish he caught. All might have been well had they managed to hide the affair, but keeping such a secret on a small island is impossible, and Sipikoli's wontoks were rumbling ferociously as far away as Honiara by the time Tom and Diana returned.

'Good God, what's this about?' frowned Tom when, on checking into the Mendana Hotel, he found a message waiting from the police. Diana had to rush off to see to some split cartons in a shed at the main wharf, but caught up that night, over airline cheese and crackers taken in their room to conserve funds.

'Sounds like the silly boy's got himself involved with some wretched girl whose family are now kicking up. There've been threats of arson on Pigeon, would you believe?'

'A local girl? Oh not again, not Bress . . .'

''Fraid so. But why he couldn't subdue his itch until Australia is beyond me.'

'He won't have to "marry" her, will he?'

'I should think not – and I'll damn well say so.'

'She probably lured him, like Teimaliki. They'll do *anything* to get a white man for their village.'

Back on Pigeon, Bressin didn't attempt to disguise what was going on. After greeting his parents and letting them know all was well with PIT, he announced he'd like to bring Sipikoli to supper on Saturday.

'Don't be ridiculous.'

'Why not?'

'It just wouldn't *work*, that's why.'

'We could try, couldn't we? I'll put two ducks in the umu – one for her wontoks, and one for us.'

'But Saturday's her day for staying late to do the dishes . . .'

'That's fine, I'll do the dishes with her.'

'You'll see, it won't work.'

'Oh God,' said Diana to Tom later, 'the sooner we get him off to Australia the better.'

'Couldn't agree more,' said Tom, and 'I'll speak to her uncle on Sunday – get this nonsense sorted out.'

They went through with the supper party because Bressin politely insisted, but were relieved to see *he* saw it didn't work. And to his surprise – but not theirs – Sipikoli refused to do the washing up, telling him it wasn't 'Kastom' for a guest on such an occasion to do so.

'You just can't treat them like Europeans. It's the Lady Muck syndrome all over again,' Diana, exasperated, tried to explain, but Bressin excused himself. As he'd suspected, Sipikoli had already packed her spare kalico in a basket and was preparing to move out. Persuasively – and boldly for him – he stroked her back as she scrabbled crossly for something under the bed, and, as he felt her relax a little and she emerged, he ran his fingers up to her armpits and tentatively round to her breasts.

'Oraet,' she said, chucking her basket aside and pulling off her kalico. But when they'd finished, she moved back to the labour huts. Sipikoli left because she was upset by the 'insult' shown her at supper. Not yet officially a daughter-in-law, she wasn't prepared to do a daughter-in-law's duties. After this, to Tom and Diana's annoyance, Sipikoli sulked if asked to do any housework, but didn't mind helping unclog drainpipes, hand-cleaning the lawn or any other outside work. It was one of the mysteries of Kastom.

'I told that uncle of hers you're not going to marry her,' Tom told Bressin.

'I know,' answered his son, but volunteered little else. He was feeling confused, understanding far less about Kastom than his brother. He and Sipikoli had slept together because they both wanted to, he'd thought. Had he been thinking about marriage? No. Not then, anyway. What Bressin, following instinctive feelings only, hadn't considered was that Reef Island girls, unlike 1980s European or American girls, weren't 'free' to shack up with boyfriends. Although there'd been talk of it, no-one was actually going to burn down Pigeon because he'd used the body of a Nivali girl to ease his loneliness – but they weren't going to let him off either.

'Yes,' her uncle answered to everything Tom said, 'yes, Cap'n.' That was Kastom manners.

'How much will you pay for her?' he asked Bressin.

'Roll on April,' said the Hepworth seniors, but Tom's sisters, in response to an outburst of irritation, wagged the wise finger of those who see things from a distance. '*What did you expect, dear Tom? It's a long time for a boy his age to be on a "primitive" island without any white girls in his orbit.*' This was the sort of remark that, after vexing him briefly, made Tom think. '*I don't know what the answer is. You're right of course. We've got each other, and can hardly expect our young to do without company of the opposite sex. Having said that, if you knew how complicated this Kastom business is, you'd be more sympathetic! It's the lying that drives me mad, nothing is ever black and white . . . Ha ha I hear your ghastly mirth.'*

Kastom 'complications' were to dominate Tom's life on Pigeon for the next year – and longer. But he and Diana breathed a sigh of relief when, in April, they waved goodbye to Bressin.

'Tell Sipikoli I'll be thinking of her,' he called, as their motorized canoe – the latest form of transport to and from Santa Cruz – drew away, but perhaps they didn't hear over the outboard's roar. Marriage talk had continued, but with no clear result.

Sipikoli, ignoring an unspoken rule that Islanders didn't go up that end, sat with a group of female wontoks on Pigeon's south-western cliffs, staring, knit-browed, out to sea.

'Bye hemi kambaek,' (he'll come back) they tried to comfort her.

'Mi no savvy,' she said. 'Mi no savvy fakin' nartin'.'

She didn't divulge to anyone whether she'd made use of the ash from a certain tree that could help a woman hold onto a man.

Tom, hating a return to long hours in the store and all the other chores that, as he grew older, seemed more of a burden, nevertheless felt they'd done the right thing in *'letting Bressin go'* and cheered himself with the thought that the new partners would come soon. But the next ship into Mohawk Bay brought two blows: the couple due had been forced to postpone their arrival until the end of the year, and Dennis was dead. *'I know he was only here once, and we've been here a long time,'* Tom wrote, *'but he was such a large chunk of my life BEFORE.'* Perhaps because Tom was ten years older than Diana, he had stronger and more positive memories of life before the *AR* and Pigeon than she. It had been thrilling, years ago, to take off into the blue with the woman he loved, and his happiest diary entries were almost all from the sailing years, but things *did* alter over time, and now he began to wonder seriously what they'd do if these obviously not one hundred per cent reliable partners changed their minds and – *'Oh awful thought'* – if Bressin decided to stay in Australia. *'If only Diana would change her spots,'* wrote his sisters, when he confided that he cherished the time with them in London *'like a little gem to take out and gloat over, when all is not wonderful here,'* and would repeat the experience, given the chance, at the drop of a hat – and make it more permanent. *'Talk to her,'* they urged, and, after twenty-five years of desert island life, Tom sat down with his wife and suggested it was time for a change. He was ready to give Britain another try, and teased her gently with the spur that they'd be entitled to pensions now.

'You mean give up Pigeon and go and *live* in Britain?' Diana was aghast, for although she'd proved infinitely adaptable over the years, she saw Pigeon as unquestionably her permanent home. But she also adored her husband.

'Don't ask me to do that,' she said, like someone asked to make an impossible decision between spouse and lover. And, seeing her distress, he let the matter rest. '*You see,*' he explained to his sisters, '*not only has she MADE this place, but there are things about the Outside World she hates . . . top of the list is Housekeeping. Here, she doesn't have to cook, clean, worry about What To Wear, and is never cold . . . and remember, to set up house would be from scratch for us – we haven't a stick of moveable furniture, crockery, you name it.*' His sisters' response was unsympathetic: '*It must be nice for Diana to have the chores we all dislike done by natives, but what does she do with her time? Surely all the building on Pigeon was completed years ago. The place may be perfect for her, but what about you? It's so sad you should be deprived of the intellectual things you enjoy . . . Marriage in this age when we all live so long and change so much should surely be leasehold, not a tie for life.*' Tom had never hinted that Diana was a tie, and said so, but the rest of his reply was measured: '*In the tropics, one can't just put up a building and let it rot. Maintenance is constant, and there's more than enough to occupy us both . . . As to the future, the silly thing is that though Diana and I all too frequently these days do* not *see eye to eye, each of us feels vastly diminished if we're separated. This does not apply to me when I'm with you, and you are not going to be left out of my future, that's* sure. *If we could find a compatible long term couple, there'd be no reason why I shouldn't leave Diana here for such periods.*'

But finding reliable help for PIT had never been easy, and Tom's patience with ecstatic answers to his advertisements – followed by quibbling when realities dawned – was well eroded by now. In his diary he wrote of the future: '*It'll end in compromise, I expect, like most things.*' What he didn't expect was that his level of tolerance for life on Pigeon was to be tested hard in the following months, for in the middle of 1985, '*out of the blue*', the whole of Nandelli village, and others, marched across the channel to Pigeon, with all the Bigmen carrying spears – and they hadn't come to tidy up the island for the Hepworths.

Diana was in the store, and at first thought the advancing Islanders were embarking on one of their fishing drives, when young men blocked off one end of the channel with a twine net, and others drove fish into it. But there were old men, women and piccaninnis in this crowd too. She struck the bell – currently made from the *AR*'s old propellor – four times in succession, a code signal for Tom, typing in his office, to come. They were standing together, at the top of the beach, when the first five Islanders splashed onto it and addressed Tom. One was Matoko's father, also the father of Teimaliki, whom Tom had long ago dubbed '*troublemaker*'.

'Cap'n, evrifela kam fo somaot spialaen.'

He was saying that the elders, over a quarter of a century since the Hepworths' arrival, reckoned the time had come to show the young of nearby islands which sections of Pigeon belonged, in Kastom, to their families. The next generation must learn what to pass on when their time came, and whatever arrangements Tom had made back in 1957, with one headman from one of the clans involved, had no relevance to this process.

Diana moved forward sharply.

'How dare you!'

But Tom, as he had twenty-six years ago when Tasha had been a little thing in his arms, laid a hand on her wrist.

'Let me handle this, darling.'

There was a murmur of approval among the men. It was right for a man to do the talking – and rude of a woman to step in front of him like that.

'But this is nonsense! Pigeon is registered in our name, and the lease doesn't expire until 2052!'

'Darling, getting cross won't help.'

Now the men looked away politely. Cap'n Tom was having trouble with his woman, but sounded firm. When Diana, stiff-backed, strode away furiously, they smiled. It didn't bother them that she was going to radio the police. He was one of their wontoks.

'Sorry, Cap'n. We'll just make our spearlines quickly then go.' And with this, more than fifty Islanders, the elders leading, moved from one end of Pigeon to the other, drawing onto it physically where it was possible to make a track through the soil, the map they believed showed the correct divisions of land among the four main families – all well extended by now – who in Kastom owned it.* Tom walked

* See the spearline map, p. 285.

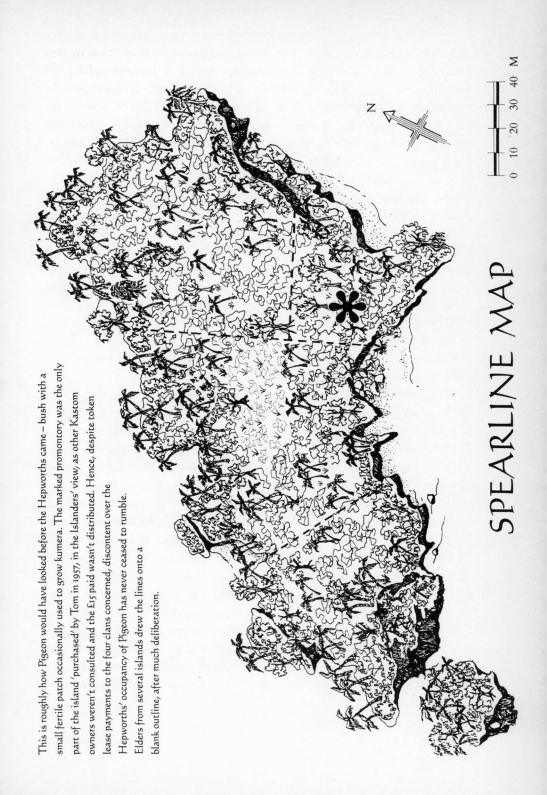

This is roughly how Pigeon would have looked before the Hepworths came – bush with a small fertile patch occasionally used to grow kumera. The marked promontory was the only part of the island 'purchased' by Tom in 1957, in the Islanders' view, as other Kastom owners weren't consulted and the £15 paid wasn't distributed. Hence, despite token lease payments to the four clans concerned, discontent over the Hepworths' occupancy of Pigeon has never ceased to rumble. Elders from several islands drew the lines onto a blank outline, after much deliberation.

SPEARLINE MAP

N

0 10 20 30 40 M

with them at first, his chest tightening with anger when he saw six impassive faces block the light from the window of the radio shack as they peered in at Diana, but forcing himself to remain genial. Samantha, the Great Dane, was so cowed by the sheer quantity of Islanders, she only whimpered. At one point, when they were all standing in the middle of the lawn and entering into detailed negotiations over precisely where a line should be drawn – behind or in front of a certain tree – Tom tried conversing with one of the elders, whose flapping wattles suggested he was old enough to have been around in 1957.

'I say, you remember the *Arthur Rogers*, don't you – numbawan stoa s'ip?'

The owner of the wattles looked at him quickly, but said nothing.

'Well, I'm sure you'll remember how much you chaps wanted a trader in those days. You didn't have anyone to buy your copra, did you? And you liked our tinmeat and tobacco.'

The rest of the elders stood watching and listening now. Tom addressed them all, small, old and grey, but still taller than most.

'You asked for me and Missus to come, didn't you?'

One picked his teeth with a twig; another flexed long black toes in the neatly Flymo'd grass.

'*Didn't you?*'

But not one would own up to having been among those who'd requested that the Hepworths become their traders. Tom left then, his guts aswirl. It seemed ridiculous, with these '*illiterate old fools*', yet it felt like a betrayal. For a fortnight after this Tom was in and out of bed with a recurring fever. And it didn't end there. Within ten days another uninvited party arrived.

'You stay here,' said Diana, who'd rigged up a fan for Tom running off solar power, 'and I'll make sure you're not disturbed.' She was gone before he could remonstrate, but felt he must be with her if there were a confrontation. He understood how some of her ways offended Kastom, and believed diplomacy was wisest where possible.* Despite their differences, he almost wished Bopali, who could at least speak decent English when he tried, were around to translate for him, but Bopali was a Bigwig now, a respected politician, away much of the

---

* Diana's exposed thighs in her swimsuits were a particular offence in Kastom, and the source of much comment among Islanders old and young.

time in Honiara. Tom visited the toilet painfully, then made his way towards the copra shed, from where he heard voices. Diana's was prominent, and he knew immediately from her stance – hands on bikini'd hips and head thrown back – there was trouble.

'Get down at once, you little devils!' she shouted. Two Nandelli boys were up a palm cutting down coconuts with bushknives and throwing them to friends, who tied them into bundles to carry away. Shrieks of laughter followed this command, leaving Diana incredulous, for blatant rudeness was rare.

'Debbil, hemi sae, Debbil!'

The children thought it hilarious she was talking about them as devils.

'They're stealing our coconuts OPENLY now!'

When the next nut fell, Diana, still agile in her mid-sixties, dived on it – but so did a wiry naked piccaninni, and both held on hard. Most of the children were in giggling hysterics by now, but Tom's appearance quietened them, and when Diana looked up and saw him her concentration lapsed, and the quick little boy wrestling with her seized his chance and bore off the coconut in triumph.

'This is disgraceful!' she cried.

At that moment, Matoko's father, the '*troublemaker*', rushed up yelling abuse in a stream.

'Sarrup iu rubas woman! Disfela tri b'long-famli-b'long-mi; Mami-b'long-mi-Dadi-b'long-mi-piccaninni-granipapi . . . iu fakin' bastard!' (Shut up, it's my family's tree . . .)

'This is too stupid,' Tom muttered, a hand to his aching head, and was grateful to see Tali and Nupanyi dissuading two more of this man's extensive kin from swarming up a second tree. What the children were doing – especially the fighting – was against Kastom, and there would be toktoks into the night, and tickings-off. But that wouldn't help the unresolved issues over the land – and every tree on it. And every nut on every tree. The problem wouldn't go away. The Hepworths were there on sufferance. '*Where are our sons now when we need them?*' asked Tom of himself that night, forgetting perhaps how and why each had gone, and was several more days in bed. What happened to Pigeon during Diana's lifetime mattered to him, but Tom didn't write about hopes for its long-term future. If Bressin wanted to take over permanently, however, it was a matter of considerable interest to the Islanders, whose strong family ties spread, weblike, back and forth, over decades, even centuries, with ease.

'*My dear Amalie,*' Diana wrote when things had – mysteriously as ever – 'settled down', but there was a new problem: '*It's four months since we had a supply ship in, and we're low on rice and right out of tea! We're waiting for Tom's new office chair as well, meant to be on the ship, and of course it means we haven't heard from Bressin.*' The rice ran so low that Samantha, without Bressin to catch extra fish for her, lived entirely off coconut for a while, grated by resentful piccaninnis into her plastic bowl, which was like the ones sold in the store their mothers coveted for special occasions. But eventually the long-awaited ship arrived and Tom, thrilled with his '*super-duper typist's chair*', scooted merrily round his office in it, while reading snatches of Bressin's several letters aloud to Diana.

'He's distributed a thousand brochures about Ngarando at a travel show, clever fellow, and he's obviously completely over Angela and that other nonsense . . . Says he's been drinking bubbly, watching top-less sunbathers in Queensland and playing a didgeridoo! And he's enjoying townlife in Sydney, too: "*There's plenty of work available, and the range of specialist bookshops is huge, everything from Anarchy to Zen, and there are open air theatres, universities, beautiful women . . .*"'

'What work is he doing?'

'Doesn't say . . . wait a minute: "*selling Healthfood products . . . and driving a taxi*"! He must have got to know his way around pretty fast to be doing that.'

In fact, Bressin had found his way round the amusements mid-1980s Australia had to offer rather gradually. First, he'd hitch-hiked in Queensland for a month or so, looking for hotel management open-ings with the idea of picking up where he'd left off at the Mendana, but not worrying unduly when he found nothing. He'd watched lovely women, exchanged a few (unused) addresses with fellow youth hostellers, but made no special attachments until he reached Sydney some three months into his sabbatical. There he roamed, tall and dreamy, like other students with rucksacks, and gazed hungrily into bookshops, fascinated that the world contained so many ideas about how to conduct yourself – even your thoughts – each claiming to be the only right one. He flicked through tomes on 'paths' to be found in life from Plato to Tao, pursuing his interest in aphorisms as well, but still gravitated most days, at some point, to the sea, which offered no neat answers but much else. On Bondi Beach, he startled other bathers by swimming further than anyone else, and body surfing off a point thought by most to be too dangerous. '*But it's not a patch on Nbanga*,' he wrote to his parents. One young lady was particularly impressed, and on a sunny Saturday afternoon when he'd gone through his performance in the white waves and was resting afterwards, she made a point of strolling past him slowly on long, smooth legs, C-cup figure well set off by a small bikini, until he looked up. Years later Bressin (when he became Ben) claimed the main reason he went to Australia was to discover the difference between Melanesian and European women. The former he described as 'brideprice women'; the latter, he felt he didn't know much about after his 'failure' with Angela. Now he was about to be launched on a whirlwind discovery tour, for Judith, who went under the stage name of Gloriette – Glori for short – was a professional escort, actress in blue movies and striptease artist. And she offered herself to Bressin free – on a waterbed.

'*I'm sharing a flat with a girl*,' he informed his parents, adding that one of the great things about life in Sydney was there were no Kastom laws to worry about.

'There we go,' said Tom, 'I knew he'd turn the corner once he met a nice girl.'

Diana responded with affectionate encouragement. '*Do ask her to come to Pigeon. Does she enjoy cooking? I thought that restaurant idea you had was marvellous.*'

What Glori enjoyed was teaching Bressin how to smoke hash through a hubble-bubble, while she applied herself expertly to the prolongation of pleasure below the waist. A session with him in the afternoon relaxed her perfectly for work in the strip club, and the sensuousness of her smiles for a dull escort job came more readily when she anticipated what she was going to do with Bressin next.

'Ever thought of being a male model?' she asked once, regarding him appraisingly while she lifted herself gently up and down. 'You've got the body for it.'

He smiled. He had such a lovely, bashful smile, she thought, and tightened her grip subtly.

'Mmmmnnn . . .'

Another time she dressed him, with care, in drag, applying layers of her own make-up, so only his height betrayed him to a few of her underworld friends as a man. In this guise, she sat him in her club while she danced, and back home, shook her tasselled breasts for sheer joy when they played with each other in his ambiguous guise. But this was only one small episode for Bressin in what was to become an increasingly strenuous search for self and direction, and when the next cargo boat reached Pigeon, the tenor of his letters had changed. No longer did he sound like a stranger in the Paradise civilization could offer, but someone who thought he'd found the perfect path through life, and was eager to share it. *'I'll be a new person when I come back, and hope to bring the new skills I am learning to the business on Pigeon.'*

'Wonderful!' exclaimed Diana. 'Will he be home soon?'

Tom's expression was puzzled.

'No – in fact he's asking for more time . . .'

'Oh no!'

'. . . and it doesn't sound like a course he's on.'

Bressin elaborated on what he saw as the positive-for-Pigeon attributes of a group he'd joined that now dominated his time, but Tom and Diana, suffering from a recent spate of thefts so bad they felt they must separate and sleep one at each end of the island, hurried over the detail to find the facts.

'It's some kind of cult, I reckon.'

'What about the girlfriend?'

'They're not living together any more.'

When Bressin joined the cult, advertised as an organization promoting personal development, he found himself caught between two intense forces – the pull of a beautiful woman, and the psychological magnet of a 'highly trained family' of personnel, who promised to nurse him, provided he follow their rules, to the most desirable of mental states in which he'd know great power over consciousness, and no pain . . . He was fond of Glori and revelled in their body games, but knew he didn't feel about her as he had for Angela. The cult persuaded him she had too much power over him, so he moved out of their shared accommodation. But she was worried. She felt *they* had too much power over him, and had grown more attached to Bressin than was her general rule with men.

'I went riding and found I could talk to my horse,' he told her casually, over the phone.

'*What?* Listen, these guys are doing something to you . . .'

Bressin said he'd never met people so dedicated to supporting one another's individual aims with shared spiritual strength. They sat in cubicles and held each other's gaze in silence for hours. Then they sat in a circle and did the same. He said it made him feel good.

'It's crazy,' she said. 'They're either doping your coffee – or it's witchcraft!'

Bressin breathed in sharply.

'What's the matter, honey?'

'Nothing.'

But she'd touched on something that troubled him. When he'd told Sipikoli he was going away, she'd become upset and muttered the Reef Island word for women's magic. Bressin had been brought up with neighbours who dealt in magic and believed implicitly in it all the time, so the idea of its power – even if only over the mind – was not ridiculous to him. This may have made him suggestible – a ripe subject for the machinations of a cult out to fleece the unworldly. And Bressin, for all Glori had taught him in her waterbed, was still very unworldly.

'*We can't allow you any extra time*,' said the next letter from his father, which threw Bressin into a dilemma. He'd dabbled in something he now felt unsure of, in the Outside World, and didn't want to go back to Pigeon until he felt he'd gained something positive from his travels. Gradually – spurred on by Glori – he eased away from the cult but found the intensive sessions he'd undergone had already affected him. Later he was to say, 'It was as though my frame of reference was torn away.' But had he acquired a sure identity before he joined them? Was a child of Paradise not, in a way, the ultimate 'innocent abroad'? His successful but brief confidence-boosting period in the Mendana, drawing security from a catering manual and basking in first love, wasn't enough to keep him steady when filial duty hauled him back to the beautiful but bizarre land of his birth; that first love crumbled, and he had months in which to face what felt like a gaping void over PIT's store counter. In the latter stages he'd had Sipikoli for comfort, but she was seen as just a phase.

The letter Tom next received brought the relieving news that Bressin would come home as planned, but there was an odd note at the end: '*If there's anything you need, let your ideas flow free.*' Tom's ideas – lists of jobs to be done in Honiara – flowed freely over nineteen pages. But before he left Sydney, Bressin returned to the bookshops.

He craved clear guidelines in a world that seemed blurred. His parents had their own black and white set of values, which he admired in many ways, but he still had none of his own. His uncertain hands fell finally, among all the choices available, on the Bible, and he read it for a long time when, on checking in for his flight back to the Solomons from Brisbane, he discovered Honiara airport was closed because of a cyclone. And when at last he did get back, he found all the islands surrounding Pigeon resounding to mourning wails, and a disgruntled New Zealander, meant to be a companion-partner in PIT, scrambling hastily aboard the boat Bressin had just arrived on, eager to get away.★

★ Due to Ben's disassociation from his past, in the 1990s, it was a sensitive matter to glean details of former relationships directly from him, but he confirmed that he connected Angela most closely with Love, hampered, he felt, by sexual inexperience; that Glori was part of an experimental period, and that he felt confused about his relationship with Sipikoli, which was complicated by Kastom issues. A visit to Sydney's red light district, letters written at the time, photographs, Tom's diary, discussion with Islanders, and Diana's and Ross's recollections were further sources for the recreation of the above scenes.

21

Initiations

BEN AND DIANA RETURNED TO PIGEON IN MARCH 1999, ACCOM-
panied by two members of the *Arthur Rogers*'s all-girl crew of 1954. It
was as though images from Tom's diary had stepped off the pages and
were climbing, with girlish giggles, up the ladder of the Little Wharf
– which had reappeared soon after Cyclone Danny blew by. I greeted
the 'girls', now in their sixties, and hugged Diana. She looked paler,
after an eye operation and skin cancer treatment, but her bearing was
as queenly as ever.

'You'll have supper with us, darling?'

I would, but hoped I wasn't placed next to Ben, who, to my horror,
had put on several pounds in all the right places in New Zealand, and
looked completely edible. It was the beginning of a busy social time
for me, taking tea with Diana to catch up on news; fitting in sessions
with the 'girls', and returning to my quarters loaded down with notes,
only to find Tangypera waiting to fulfil requests I'd made for the
Islanders' interpretation of what made the new PIT partner, John, in
the mid-1980s leave in such a hurry, and why all the islands were
in mourning when Bressin/Ben returned over a decade ago from his
Australian adventures.

Tangypera settled himself on one seat-sized root of our Kaikai Tree,
I on another. All I'd gleaned was that there'd been an accident involving the Hepworths' canoe and two lives lost between Pigeon and

Santa Cruz – that stretch of water which had so terrorized my family on the way out. Tom had had a fever at the time, so diary entries were short, but suggested conditions weren't extreme. Later, he added he wished cyclone warnings had been clearer, and wrote to his sisters that he and Diana were '*deeply saddened by faithful old Paia's death . . . but at least the boat was insured*'.

'Was he your friend, Tangypera?' I asked. Paia had been the Hepworths' cookboy. It had been he and his wife, Doroti, who'd shared with Diana the joy of hearing Christine Clement had been found alive after all, when she'd drifted off in her dugout years before. Tangypera said old Paia was everyone's friend, and the wailing at his death had been prolonged.

'What happened?'

Tangypera busied himself rolling chopped stick tobacco in a 'Pigeon Post' article. He didn't look up, or speak, until he'd sealed the cigarette with spit, then stated baldly that Paia and the white man, an Australian tourist, had died because the weather was too rough to make a crossing that day. He himself had refused to go, and no-one else knew how to handle that particular motorized canoe. Jimson, who also nearly drowned, could steer a boat, but not with a wheel. I was curious about the two whites on board, too, one the later dis-gruntled partner, John. Tangypera said he'd been just a learner at sea, but was a good fellow. We exchanged an understanding look. Probably Tangypera had provided similar services for some of the Hepworths' partners as he did for me – information, and a link with the Islander grapevine when required. The white who died was a man named Jardine, who, already delayed too long on Pigeon for his liking, had been anxious to catch a plane on Santa Cruz. Tom's diary implies this man was not only a poor guest (grumbling about Pigeon's lack of facilities) but showed foolish tendencies from the first by fail-ing to treat coral cuts properly. And he'd insisted on leaving, saying the Hepworths had lured him to the island so it was their respons-ibility to get him off.

To visualize the scene Tangypera described – pieced together from tales told by both John and Jimson – wasn't hard. I'd been in an open canoe when waves were wild, sure any moment we were going to drown, and had seen it as a vile but swift end. Here I was wrong. When the canoe capsized that morning in 1986, in sight of Matema but out of sight of Pigeon, John, the shortly-to-be-ex PIT partner, grabbed the anchor rope, and all three others grabbed his trouser belt. There were desperate struggles to right the craft, but it was hopeless. Grimly, aware that letting go meant death, the four clung on, constantly battered by the sea, until, twelve hours on, Paia, the most frail, let go without a murmur and was sucked away. Jardine became a dead weight on the belt until, later the same night, his swollen fingers uncurled of their own accord and his body, face down, waltzed on the waves beside the others a while until a current took it past. Morning found the remaining two off the coast of Santa Cruz. John, a strong swimmer, made a bid for it, but Jimson was exhausted. Alone, he gripped the rope with bloody palms, watching his last companion strike towards shore. Then he became aware the shore was receding, and in a panic tried to follow. The men were separated by the seas, John arriving hours before Jimson, who would have joined Paia and Jardine in death had he not been spotted by fishermen in dugouts, who paddled out to meet him and hauled him ashore, speechless, with chest and arms lacerated by his own attempts to land where there was coral. Difficulties with radios meant it was three days before John's wife was able to speak to him, and the first words he uttered were that he was finished with Pigeon for ever.

'You're not going to leave because of this, are you?' said Tom.

'Yes, and not just because of this.'

Following a by now familiar pattern, there had been 'differences' between the original European occupants of the island and possibly starry-eyed newcomers. Paradise was *never* as people imagined.

'So Bressin will just have to manage alone. Thank goodness he's on his way.'

In his diary Tom wrote: '*What a mess, and there are bound to be calls for compensation from Paia's folk.*' There were.

When Bressin got back in 1986, he sat down to the first meal with his parents for a year, and held up a hand as they lifted their cutlery.

'I'd like to say grace.'

'What? Oh well, I suppose in view of what's happened, if you must . . .'

But Bressin wasn't saying grace because Paia and Jardine had died. He said it because he believed it was the right thing to do, and even when his parents failed to join in the amen, he persisted, at every meal, from then on. I was caught out more than once when dining at Ngarando in 1999 – saying amen when Diana didn't, or not saying it and being glanced at reproachfully by Ben.

'Tasha will be joining us for a month before you leave,' announced Diana, to my surprise. 'It will be interesting for you to talk to her, and good for her.'

Was it possible to hold a conversation with Tasha? I'd have to wait and see. Time was galloping, and I had volumes of Tom's diaries still to study, and also wanted to spend more days at Nenumbo. I hadn't talked to Ross enough yet either and, to add to the several directions of pull, Benji wanted to accept an invitation to spend Easter with Patteson at Otelo, and Joe, paddling his kayak frequently to Nola, I noticed, planned to stay with the family of a little girl called Mata, whose grandfather was the same Nupanyi whose wontoks Kastom-owned a slice of Pigeon, and who had worked all his adult life for the Hepworths.

'Ben would like to take you to Matema over Easter weekend,' said Diana. Is that where he'd taken Angela for picnics? I wondered, and part of me wanted to say yes, by moonlight, with a rug, but I declined. (Whatever my head told me about him, my body yearned again after the new-look Ben.)

'That's kind, but we have other arrangements.'

I planned to make a small contribution to the generous hospitality that would await Joe at Nola, and knew a trip there wouldn't just be a case of dropping a child off, as in Britain, for a weekend with friends. There was an initiation-to-manhood ceremony at Nenumbo I wanted to fit in, too.

'But you'll be back for tea.'

I was about to say no, then hesitated. Now that her friends were gone, there was only me for Diana to talk to about the past, and not for much longer.

'I'll try.'

'Good girl.'

Patteson's dadi overnighted in a hut near Ross's, and disappeared with a happy Benji at dawn the day before Easter Eve. On the same tide, with Joe's white kayak dyed pink by the rising sun and the palms on Nandelli black as Walt Disney cut-outs, I set off to Nola, and knew, as we crossed the calm depths, paddles languidly dipping, that hours like these, as well as tragic moments from the Hepworths' history, mustn't be forgotten, and that they'd experienced them too. On such a dawn, forty years ago, Diana and Tom had made trips to and from the *Arthur Rogers*, unpacking their future; on such a dawn, Ross had woken with Teimaliki, and made a decision that shaped his; and Ben had stared out from his fishing canoe and agreed humbly with his Bible, unsurprisingly, that only God could make such beauty, and should be praised.

'I love this,' said Joe, simply.

'So do I.'

The wind wasn't with us, but the slight effort needed to pull the kayaks across the acres of blue now in full sunlight only added to the immediacy of pleasure – and would speed my lone journey to Nenumbo later.

'Is the wind ever this warm in Scotland?'

'No.'

'Then let's stay for ever!'

I smiled. What greater happiness can a mother have than knowing her children are happy? Diana must have had moments like this too – those that made up her babies' 'idyllic' childhood. But look at her children now: Ben the lonely ascetic; Ross the disinherited;★ Tasha in permanent care. We'd play safe and keep all our options open.

'Let's not think about anything except Now.'

That was easy, with steadily increasing heat kissing our shoulders, and nothing visible of the whole world but twinkling sea and little islands.

'Did you bring your spear?'

'Yes. I want to go fishing with Mata's brother and catch everyone something for lunch.'

Joe was acquiring the same instinctive wish to contribute communally as an Islander.

'Lovely – but don't worry if you don't.'

'I won't. Nobody does, but everyone tries.'

And as the shoreline of Nola became clearer, we were able to distinguish a good cross-section of 'everybody' waiting to greet us. There were the eager male piccaninnis in front of a sprinkling of proud youths rippling their muscles, women rinsing their hands in the sea ready to shake ours, girls peeping from behind them, and olo – the

★ I learned of further changes to the Will later.

important elderly – hanging back, with shy dignity, in the shade.

'There's Mata!' cried Joe, and waved. The entire village waved back and children splashed out to pull our kayaks over the shallows. Joe pointed out Mata's mother, and I waded to meet her, her non-Pijin-speaking husband, bashful but proud at the attention his family were receiving, by her side.

'Kam,' said Mata's mum, and I was whisked under the thatch of a tiny leaf veranda, into the place of honour, and plied with a coconut to drink and a slab of Kastom pudding the size of a laptop to consume under public gaze. Sixteen women with piccaninnis in a packed huddle three feet away jostled one another gently for a view, and Mata's mother, a short, solid woman, sat smiling like a duchess as I pressed as much as I could of the good but heavy pudding into my mouth, moistening it with coconut milk that blew out my belly like beer. Joe was already preparing his spear, with a group of wontoks, to dive. Mata herself, a pretty child of twelve, hair knotted into a shell shape, sat behind me with a leaf, fanning away flies.

'Pua Lusi,' she murmured from time to time. Once she'd visited me when I was working, looking for Joe, and been shocked when I apologized for not being able to entertain her as I must continue working. Such was the general feeling towards Diana, it was assumed I was being kept a prisoner at my desk by her. I couldn't make the Islanders understand I enjoyed my work. Every time I looked at Mata's mother, praying she might share the pudding with me, she beamed and flapped her hands for me to eat up. Had Sipikoli's wontoks treated Bressin/Ben like this, when he'd first visited her village? Diana always maintained that to acquire a white man for a village brought kudos to a family. Did Mata's family have designs on Joe? If both he and Mata had been a year or so older, might she have shaken ash into his kaikai to 'hold' him as a man? Standing up at last, glad of the roominess of my kalico, I shook hands with everyone for the nth time, explaining I wanted to reach Nenumbo before the tide fell. I'd return for Joe after Easter. If the nights were fine, he'd sleep on the beach, among a heap of young; if it rained, he'd be crowded with them on the floor of a dark leaf hut. I believed my trust in Nupanyi's extended family to be well placed, and Nupanyi himself, the most distinguished and land-rich elder in this community, cesspit digger on Pigeon, held my hand in both of his before I left and whispered he'd personally look out for Joe. All he asked for when I said I wanted to make a gesture of thanks was 'lelebet sunga' – a little bit of sugar.

'Sapulo', meaning sailing place, where in the old days all voyages, whether for war or trade, were planned, is the Reef Island name for what other Pacific communities call the Men's Single House. Through this, every youth must pass before becoming a fully fledged member of his clan. At one time, the rites of passage were followed by a period of 'purdah', during which no women must be seen, but on Nenumbo, in 1999, the ceremonies lasted just one day – preceded by pig killing. So shocked the first time, I'd become more or less inured to the shrieking and bloodletting by now, but on this occasion I was relieved to find it was already over. Mouth stained with betel and eyes bloody-rimmed, Tangypera stepped forward to greet me as my feet touched the shore. (Misjudging the speed of the receding tide, I'd had to park my kayak at Temotulaki and walk the rest of the way.) A tall man beside him, red stars daubed on his face, jutted his chin out hard, not looking at all welcoming, and there wasn't another female in sight. But I knew I must brazen it out. Tangypera said there'd been majority agreement to my presence, and that's all that mattered. It was part of Kastom for people still to show disapproval if they wished.

The slaughter of a pikpik marks every major event in Reef Islands, and is itself a stage in the journey to adulthood. Only when he's dispatched a boar may a lad tuck a feathery frond down the back of his loincloth, which waves as he struts, like a cockerel's tail. Pokai, a youth known to Benji and Joe, who longed for this decoration, smiled as I admired the rumpless carcasses of seven enormous pikpiks steaming on frilly beds of wild cabbage. In times gone by these might have been 'long pikpik' – men. The coveted fat was scored inches deep, to be chewed anon. The absence of rumps was because they were considered delicacies, and had already been bagged by the main contributors to the feast. An elder hacked off a head with his machete and wore it, dripping, in a basket, on his own, asking to be photographed. 'Kastom b'long mifela,' I ventured, 'cookboy putim apple insaet maos b'long pikpik.' (Where I come from, apples sometimes accompany roast pork.) Perhaps as a sop to this, I was given a football-sized breadfruit with a portion of semi-raw pig flesh so generous it would have served my family twice.

I was nibbling at this – still full from my second breakfast at Nola –

when Tangypera summoned me to the Sapulo, before which the star-cheeked headman was impressing upon the young the privileges entry entailed. To an outsider, ritual practices in Reef Islands seem disorganized: people sit about sucking on pipes and spitting betel; some sleep. But there are moments of catharsis when everyone, expressive eyebrows knit furiously in concentration, attends. This was one. Sweat streaking his chest and forefinger stabbing the air, the headman addressed each initiate separately, bellowing. A little boy who couldn't have been more than eleven quaked under his tear-stained make-up of powdered lime, one hand clutching a small basket containing betel and a private supply of bananas, symbols of his impending independence; even Pokai, a bold star on the football field, looked nervous. 'He says,' Tangypera explained, 'that now they've left their mother's hut, it's their duty to sharpen their arrows and learn to take part like men in the business of the village.' All important matters would be discussed in the Sapulo; they were permitted to smoke and chew betel, but these days there was a tambu on women sleeping in the house. (Access to a shared concubine was one of the perks of entry in former times, following deprivation.)

When the lecture was over, all the elders' chins were jutted towards the low leaf door, but before the five scared painted boys entered the Sapulo, they were allowed to take the hand of a wontok who'd already been through it. Gravely, a hefty young blood crowned with a black skullcap of hair, from which protruded six aggressive, sea-bleached plaits, approached the small boy, offering a huge, cracked paw; the others found companions, and a short crocodile wove its way into the shadows of the house. There, in the darkness, the symbolic baskets were set down, and old men already in residence acknowledged, with grunts, the presence of the young. The pigs killed to buy the rites of passage lay close together, reeking, in the gloom, and axes and machetes got busy dividing them. No-one inside spoke; there was just the noise of chopping and tearing, but when the boys emerged, hands still linked, everyone smiled and heads were held high. From now on they could use the Sapulo whenever they liked – like a club. And mother couldn't follow.

Leaf platters of pig and parcels of Kastom pudding followed the boys, and gorging and stori-ing commenced. I sat on, uncomfortable among but fascinated by the flower of Nenumbo's youth. One offered me, somewhat ambiguously, a long banana when no-one else was eating them, and there was laughter when I accepted it, but on the whole I was ignored. This was men's business. I moved about as unobtrusively as possible, taking photographs, then saw that, foolishly, I'd let the tide creep back so high I'd have to swim to retrieve my kayak. 'No,' said Tangypera, by now very bleary on betel, and deputed a chauffeur for me named Solomon.

We set off in the flimsiest of dugouts, with only two inches of free-board, but, accustomed to this, I relaxed, asking if he'd passed through the Sapulo yet. But Solomon didn't answer. He just paddled, bailing with one hand occasionally, and stared. Sounds from the feasting grew fainter, and I craned round to see how far we had to go. Why weren't we going by the most direct route? Turning back, I wobbled the dugout, shipping water. Solomon still said nothing, and still stared, and when, with both of us bailing now, my hand inadvertently touched one of his spidery legs, his tongue flicked out and back, like a gecko's. Above the tongue, ecstatic eyes shone. 'Mm-mm,' he said ardently, 'iumi, mm-mm . . .' and in case I wondered what he meant, tried to open my kalico . . . Afternoon sunlight winked on miles of transparent blue. He'd taken me close to the Edge of the Reef, the little devil, to be out of sight of the village, and we wobbled increasingly precariously. 'I'm old enough,' I said severely, 'to be Mami b'long iu.' In and out went the tongue, grope grope went the hand, and finally I had to cuff it away and show I was serious by starting to counter-paddle with the plank I'd been allocated as a seat. We reached Temotulaki, where my red Acadia was tethered, with no injury done other than to my *amour propre*. Why, when I'd been dreaming of love, did I have to be ridiculously propositioned by a randy fourteen-year-old?

'It's all right,' Tangypera soothed me, when word got round next day, 'he only did it because he's krangge.' (Crazy.) Charming.

But I was sorry I hadn't made it back in time for tea with Diana. When, head full of the day's events, I'd crept past her house as evening came on, she was already in her shower. The tea tray, however, was still sitting on the veranda set for two, with only one cup used. This woman had invited me to live on Pigeon for a year, to discover the wonderful story of her and her husband's life there, and trusted me implicitly. What must she think of my gallivanting off to fraternize with what had been to Tom, at times, the enemy? But I couldn't tell any story of Pigeon without including something of the Reef

Islanders' angle on its history – and future. I'd just have to trust, as she trusted me, that Diana's philosophical side would accept this as integral to the tale, even if it upset her. I only wished I didn't have to add to all she'd borne, for, as I'd dreaded, Tom's diary revealed more tragedy than joy in the latter years. Not that it didn't have its comic moments as well.

22

Bressin Becomes Ben

GLORI CAME TO PIGEON IN 1986 – AN EVENTFUL YEAR – ARRIVING just after Sipikoli's magic had restored Bressin to her arms. Did he bring back to the moonlit beaches of Reef Islands lessons learned from his stripper girlfriend, or did he allow his dark mistress's passions to flow over him – and leave him cold soon afterwards – as they had before he went away? Details are shadowy, but that Sipikoli conceived is clear, and that, while Glori stayed and was welcomed by Diana to her table and by Bressin to his bed, Sipikoli retired to the labour huts and went on gutting the fish he caught, and hand-picking leaves from his mother's lawn. *'They're like a pair of lovebirds,'* wrote Tom (of Bressin and Glori), *'coming to breakfast then diving back into bed for more nookie!'* Diana admired the girl for her boldness in undertaking the journey, and was unfazed by her profession. 'She's young,' she told Tom, 'and only needs setting on the right path. I like her.' Pigeon's portals were flung wide to welcome this adventurous refugee from the Outside World, and had she stayed permanently, Diana would have tried to resurrect the restaurant idea. But Glori didn't stay. Did she feel the brooding eyes of the Reef Island girl upon her – even though Sipikoli's head always seemed lowered? Or did the ashes' magic, per-haps more powerful on its home ground than when Bressin was abroad, turn his own eyes back to the little 'sorceress'? Whatever, after a fortnight in Glori's arms, Bressin delivered her to where she could fly back to Sydney's red light district, and within another fortnight was found by Tom back in bed with Sipikoli, reading the Bible aloud.

'Such a pity,' said Diana, and Tom agreed. He'd relished describing the exotic dancer's visit to his sisters. '*Extraordinary!*' they responded. '*What pluck she showed, following him like that.*' 'Pluck' was a quality admired by all the Hepworth seniors, but a Reef Island girl's patience and tenacity failed to qualify, and Tom was seriously irritated when – again – Bressin announced he'd like Sipikoli to come to meals.

'She wasn't conscious of her former Sin,' he argued ambiguously, 'but has repented.'

'I've no idea what you're talking about,' said Tom, 'but your time would be better spent sorting out PIT's accounts than parroting words that can be made to mean anything.'

But Bressin was unswayed, and the more his father mocked his growing religious obsession, the more he retreated into it. In the store, where he'd been so reliable formerly, he showed what Tom considered absurd generosity towards customers, and in his spare time he helped to build a church – donating, to Diana's consternation, two bags of her cement as well as his own labour.

'It's bad for business,' Tom said, but was countered by Bressin reminding him that giving is a Christian act.

'You should read the Bible, Dad.'

'By God, don't you start preaching at me!'

But the Hepworth seniors were grateful when Bressin negotiated positively with some '*malcontents*', who'd been troublesome over Diana's wish to use loose coral from the paths cleared for boats.

'B'long witufela!' (it's *our* coral) said the Islanders, tipping back into the sea all that had been collected for use on Pigeon.

'Rubbish!' said Tom. 'It's just an excuse to stir up that wretched land business again.'

He may have been right, for, although Bressin's non-confrontational methods initially bore fruit – among fellow congregation members – there was never a moment when old scores were forgotten, and although Tom blustered when roused, he now acknowledged privately that some of the Islanders' wrath '*may not be entirely unfounded*'. The chief culprit, he'd concluded, over the years – and possibly through conversations with Bopali, who had a gift for objectivity – was the original headman, Tambi, who'd given both Hepworths and Islanders the impression all was happily agreed back in

1957, when it clearly wasn't. '*The old bastard probably made off with my money and didn't come clean with his friends*,' wrote Tom, his diary style hardening as he aged, '*but that's hardly my fault.*' When Bressin went back to collect more loose coral and Islanders not of his congregation objected, Tom went down with belerun. Then a Lands Officer came out, ostensibly to settle the matter of the coral but in effect addressing the whole issue of land rights. The meeting was held in open court under the palms.

'*Can you believe they found against us?*' Tom wrote to Ross. '*EVERY-THING around Pigeon is theirs below the high tide mark, even the fish, even the sand.*'

Tom was in bed for ten days after this. But Ross, then in Honiara, wasn't unduly worried about his inheritance (excommunication from his parents' Will didn't include Pigeon's disputed land) for he was in closer touch with local feeling – even from hundreds of miles away – than his parents. He'd made himself popular by opening his Honiara house, as an Islander would, when Paia died, and inviting the old man's distant wontoks to mourn with him and share kaikai. It was, as well as being kind, a shrewd move, which may have laid the foundations for his later success as a Reef Islands politician. 'They see me as one of them,' he was to say, 'and even though Mum and Dad have lived in Reefs for forty years, they'll never be seen as anything but outsiders.'

Meanwhile, back in 1987 Bressin told his parents he'd marry the pregnant Sipikoli after all because God had told him to, and this is where entry after entry in Tom's diary reveals his frustration with this once favourite son. From '*Tower of Strength*', who insisted on changing his name to Ben to disassociate himself from a 'sinful' past, the former Bressin deteriorated into '*nothing but a snivelling Jesus Freak awash with half-baked notions*', in his father's view. Tom poured out his troubles to his sisters, who bolstered him with sympathy but were aware also of the tragedy for their nephew. '*It would seem the Gods delight in turning the screw*,' they wrote, '*Tasha born under an unlucky star; Ross, a weak character, and now this disappointment with Bressin, or, sorry, Ben.*' The 'disappointment' took many forms. During the most intense period of his spiritual search, Ben was sometimes not to be found '*in his rightful place*' cutting lengths of kalico in the store, but on his knees before candles in the guest units, a sight which incensed Tom. Unhappy to have upset his father – for the Bible told him to honour his parents – Ben tried to compensate by dropping frangipani blossoms on his bed.

'Get those things out,' demanded Tom. 'They're covered in ants!'

Then Ben tried to kiss him, and took to declaring that ' "*All life is Sex; communion is Sex; villagers are spiritual through Sex . . ." YUKK!*' scribbled Tom, and told his sisters: '*I reckon half his problems are due to poor diet and too much jig-a-jig . . . I caught him yesterday yelling Hallelujahs to the sky . . . But if some of this rubbish has, as is thought locally, to do with Sipikoli's "magic" let's give Ross's exorcism idea a go. I'm prepared to lose my scepticism if that's what it takes! . . . How I long for the sanity of London . . . we* will *come later this year, because the airfield is CERTAIN, now, and we must advertise strenuously for partners or I'll never be able to retire . . .*'

Ross, glad to be asked for help by his parents, who might appreciate him more if he demonstrated clout, as well as popularity, with Islanders, then set in motion plans to send a powerful sorcerer from Malaita to perform ceremonies on Pigeon to reduce Sipikoli's influence. Not currently a claimant to Pigeon, she was seen as something of a nuisance to more local Islanders – possibly including Ross himself. Meanwhile, out of earshot of his hymn-singing son, Tom settled on the West Patio with a notepad and stared out, through its perfect frame of tropical foliage, to the endless bright waters beyond:

'*Imagine living on a South Sea Island, far from civilization's worries, and MAKING MONEY from it!*' he wrote. '*Ngarando-Faraway is For Sale! . . . This small resort on beautiful Pigeon Island only needs capital to become a money spinner. Uniquely, Pigeon is leased until 2052; Tourism will take off when an airfield only 3 miles away is completed in 1988, and NOW is the time to invest . . . Five Hundred Thousand US dollars will purchase everything on the island, including a profitable store, bar one acre to be used in their retirement by Tom and Diana Hepworth.*'

Tom sent this, and advertisements for partner-managers, all over the world, the idea being that they should interview applicants on their travels. Meanwhile, because she'd long expressed wishes to see Pigeon again, Tasha, in pleasant sheltered accommodation now her illness was controlled by drugs, was brought to the island for a fortnight in the care of a friend. Quiet at first, Tasha dodged her medication and disappeared from her bed the second night – to be discovered, after a prolonged search, in the bushes on her back, with four Islanders, who scarpered. '*The police are calling it rape,*' wrote Tom grimly, and Tasha identified the 'culprits' from a photo taken of those who'd caused trouble over coral. But, upset as they were, the Hepworths were aware enough of their daughter's proclivities to see room for doubt. *'Was she called out, or did she go looking for them?'* mused Tom, and there was no clear answer. Diana planned then to build accommodation with a bedroom door that locked, named Tasha's House, and this was done, although Tom felt it would be better if she didn't come to the island again, but took holidays organized by carers in New Zealand. A new dugout for Pigeon was also named after their firstborn. Their original little Poppet might have become almost unrecognizable, but she wasn't forgotten. Ben believed Tasha was suffering from demonic possession.

It was still uncertain how far Ben's wedding plans had proceeded when Tom started packing for a whirlwind tour of Britain and the States to promote the island's sale and visit friends who reminded him of happier times, but when Ben asked that Sipikoli be allowed to stop work because of her pregnancy, he blew up.

'Is she to behave like a Victorian miss just because she's going to have a baby? Ridiculous!'

Ben, hating rows, capitulated, but stuck doggedly to his routine of Bible study, even if it meant neglecting copra-weighing duties. Sipikoli lost the child in the seventh month – *'it died in the womb'*, Ben wrote in a brief, disjointed letter to his parents – but he did marry her, under Kastom law. Tom suspected – as it happened, mistakenly – that he had pinched the brideprice from the PIT till. There's no record of what else happened on Pigeon while Ben was descending into deep dislocation, but that he felt increasingly strange is evident. In 1987, he believed, *'something happened'* to his brain, causing him to cry out in *'deep anguish'* when he was with Sipikoli. Afterwards he felt exhausted and had the impression his *'wealth of feeling'* had left him – meaning all that which through infancy and the growing years is incorporated into 'personality' had died. *'Sipikoli is not of the earth,'* he wrote to Ross, *'but either in heaven or under it.'* The former meant she must be good – he believed she had no knowledge of right and wrong – the latter that she was a victim and perpetrator of lust and deceit, *'both of which I have had my fill of in the last few years'*. Sipikoli retreated to her wontoks when her lover/husband behaved in ways she couldn't understand, but Ben had no-one but God to turn to in the dark and lonely Eden

Pigeon had become for him. Day after day he prayed, fished, and tried to fulfil his biblical duty to his parents by – sometimes at midnight – cleaning the store, which at other times he neglected. He trekked across the sun-sucked reefs and through the torrid soup of the mangrove swamps to church, a mist of sweat – or tears – blurring his vision as he stared heavenwards through the lattice of leaf thatch filtering the midday glare.

But occasionally he addressed a few lines to no-one in particular, which suggest even God wasn't always enough to relieve him of his otherwise unexpressed suffering: '*I can see that, like a blind man who cannot enjoy the things people see, cannot comprehend all the enjoyments of sight, and so sits at the edge of the park, so I sit, waiting patiently for my Lord . . . all for the sake of a cause too deep, or too wide, or too narrow, or too "anything" to give a name . . . Sweet death, no angry consequence, no guilt, no self-desire, no failure.*' Did Ben, who as a youth was not only gifted physically but showed the potential to be able to take his place happily in the Outside World, now, on the beautiful tropical island his parents spent years finding in order to raise a family away from undesirable influences, consider committing suicide there? '*Everything comes back to Pigeon . . . What am I doing here?*'

When his father came back, lugging a bag stuffed with the results of interviews – for partners; prospective buyers were few – *his* first diary entry read: '*THE HORRIBLE HOMECOMING . . .*' for, as Tom had feared, for all his pious intentions, PIT had all but collapsed in Ben's hands, and day after day there were showdowns ending with Tom's voice raised and his confused son either staring silently at his hands or brandishing his shield and sole source of comfort – the Bible – which drove the agnostic Tom to harshnesses he later, if he did not regret them, felt he must justify. One evening, after Ben had '*absconded*' for a week from work to spend time with Sipikoli's family at Nivali, his father delivered an ultimatum, stating that unless Ben pulled himself together and concentrated properly on the business, he'd find himself, like his brother, excised from the financial side of his parents' Will.

'Am I to be a pauper then?' asked their once so articulate son.

'Yes, unless you change your ways . . .'

Ben made an effort, but was soon off to Nivali again, prompting dark comments about native women's magic once more. Evidently the Malaita man's counter remedies worked only on a short-term basis and no-one was prepared to continue paying him indefinitely to keep Sipikoli at bay. While Diana addressed herself yet again to cleaning up the general mess of the island others had left behind – over the years the Wiens, the Pierces, Ross, and now Ben – Tom picked the likeliest of the interviewees he'd seen and arranged for a single man, with his own yacht, to come as soon as possible. Then he once more contacted the banished Ross who, assisting voluntarily with the loading of PIT stores in Honiara, demonstrated the advantages of being liked by Islanders, for his network of wontoks would work twice as hard for him as those raged at by his parents. *'We want you to get your brother on a plane,'* Tom wrote, and offered to pay Ross's own fare to New Zealand should he wish to accompany Ben. *'How wonderful,'* wrote Diana, *'if they'd both get rid of their black wives and make a fresh start.'* But Ross had no intention of leaving Teimaliki and was in fact fighting hard to keep her, as by then her inclination to 'messabaot' amid the temptations of the bright lights had become obvious, even to him. He'd help with his confusingly renamed brother, 'Ben', and, using his distant influence, try to reduce the locals' ongoing demands to Tom for payment for loose coral, too, but then he was going away with Teimaliki and their children to Papua New Guinea to make his own kind of fresh start.

'Ben is departing by mutual agreement,' Tom told Amalie in a letter. *'Diana and I could bear it no longer: his preaching and contempt for our values, sloppy running of the business and his continual LIES, called Avoidance of Conflict by his Melanesian friends: by us, Moral Cowardice . . . Truly even the Melanesians seem relieved at the idea of being without him'* (Ben criticized them for buying drink from PIT) *'and we've had to tell him not to return. If abroad he becomes again the young man we knew and loved, we shall welcome him back, but if he returns in short order in the same con-dition, we don't want him here, we have told him. Sad.'*

But one Melanesian, at least, didn't want him to go. The week before Ben was due to leave, there was a violent kumberra, some say stirred up by the efforts of Sipikoli's magic to combat his parents' dictum. But now, instead of silently tapping ash into his food, she fought more directly for her man, shattering with her fists the red cassette player that had so often played music as a background to their lovemaking, and slapping his face. He turned the other cheek, and, raging helplessly but more quietly now, she waited until he was out of their shared bedroom, then scrabbled among his things until she found his passport – out of which she ripped his picture. But he had another. His parents had safe places for everything of value. At last, Sipikoli simply wept brokenly, like any girl anywhere who didn't want to lose her husband, but no longer felt any power to prevent his leaving.

'Come with me as far as Honiara,' he suggested a few nights later, when perhaps she'd worked a little straightforward feminine magic, and she brightened a little. Tom and Diana furnished her with excellent references in the hope she'd find a permanent job there. Instead, she became pregnant again – as women do who crave to keep something of a man they love – but no-one told Ben, and it wasn't until two years later, when he returned from New Zealand, that he learned he had a little girl. Sipikoli, like Teimaliki with her adopted daughter, had named her according to Kastom practice, after her paternal grandmother. Tom spotted Sipikoli on the cargo boat, returning to Reefs a month after Ben had finally gone. '*But I scarcely recognized her,*' he wrote, '*she was so thin!*' Ten months later, when she boldly paddled the baby in a dugout to Pigeon from Nivali, she was turned away. '*It obviously wasn't his – totally black hair.*' But the hair, when it began to grow, was soft and fair, just like her father's.

Ross struggled fiercely within himself over the rights and wrongs of his parents' failure to let his brother know he had a child, but by then he was having troubles enough of his own. Teimaliki finally left him for another man in Papua New Guinea, and Ross found himself broken-hearted in a strange country with a question mark even over his right to keep his children, for a dispute was raised back in the Solomons as to whether, as a European, he'd ever been legally married to Teimaliki in Kastom. It went to court, and Ross, losing his job as well under a cloud, returned to Honiara to battle with officialdom. As a non-Solomon Islander had no legal entitlement to enter into private deals over Kastom land with indigenous people, did a Kastom marriage between an Islander and a white count as the real thing? It was a controversial case, with the finding – eventually – in Ross's favour: yes, he'd really been married all these years. But that just meant he could be divorced, and Christine, by then a child of eight, elected to stay with her mother and stepfather, as did her sistas. For several months subsequently, Ross, the previously committed family man, went on a bender in the capital, consuming drink and money copiously, and finding distraction among local women who frequented the town's bars, in a bid to forget his hurt. Until he found

Pegi, who just happened to be in Honiara but was originally from Nandelli.

Ben does not recall much of what he did during his two years in New Zealand, but odd lines home suggest he was still *'sitting at the edge of the park'*, looking on rather than able to engage in life. He lived on welfare (his birth in New Zealand qualified him to claim it) and drifted from the cities to the countryside and back again, making no friends. His godmother Amalie, anxious to help both him and his parents, invited him to stay with her for a while in America.

   'Thank you,' he wrote, *'for taking me to Disneyland. I only didn't go on the rides because I wasn't quite myself.'*

23

Complicated Recipes

JOE WAS RECLINING UNDER A PALM AT NOLA WHEN I ARRIVED TO
fetch him after his stay on the island, his hair full of little girls' hands
massaging in coconut oil. On one budding bicep he sported a leaf
armband, and his innocent loins were wrapped loosely in a kalico.

'Not time to go, is it, Mum?'

''Fraid so. I've been invited to watch Kastom pudding preparations
over the way, and we mustn't miss the tide.'

There was a flurry of whispers, springy nests of hair pressed to Joe's
sticky red locks, then beams all round.

'Everyone'll come. They've got wontoks over there to stay with if
they can't get back tonight.'

'Over there' was a village opposite Nola, past an island once set
aside as a leper colony, then left as untouched bush when the 'cure'
came. People suspecting they had leprosy now were meant to report
to Manuopo, but often didn't. We skimmed across the blue with the
wind behind us, in a cheerful flotilla, Mata's mother beside my kayak
in a dugout packed with banana leaves and piccaninnis, Joe's white
Acadia paddled by three boys astride it, and seven smaller dugouts
flying ahead in expert hands, Joe's among them. Preparations had
already started when we drew up, for all dishes needed to be in the
umu before sunset, as they were to be delivered by a recently
purchased bride to her in-laws at sunrise next day – and Kastom

pudding is no instant mix, but a community performance.

Forty coconuts, gathered by the very old and very young, were heaped beside a stake on which they were opened by youths of warrior age, who handed the meat to women to be 'scratched' on two-foot-long graters – where none was available the rasp-like innards of a sago palm were used – until snowy mounds peaked like white Tinakulas in baskets beside each. The strongest hands, male or female, took fistfuls of the grated coconut and squeezed thick cream from it. This cream was used for everything from burn ointment to a balm after birth – or, as in this case, to moisten the cassava which formed the starch base of the pudding. The cassava – thick red cylinders like overgrown carrots – arrived in baskets on the heads of women from an inland village, for the root can only be grown where the soil is deep, and those bringing it would be reimbursed by their solwata (salt-water) sistas with gifts from the sea. Everyone participated – toothless grannies wrapping the grated cassava in thin bark to be twisted in a bamboo tourniquet by the brawniest males; piccaninnis stacking banana leaves beside women softening them over flames to form a pudding 'bowl' in the umu. Only the white woman, the outsider, watched. Young men worked in pairs at the chest-high tourniquet, legs braced and sweat bursting from under tight leaf headbands. Bright yellow liquid spurted from the bark bundles and was caught to be fed to pigs fattening for another feast, and the finally desiccated cassava was flaked through the fingers of young girls, mixed with just the right amount of coconut cream to bind it, flavoured with the green of wild shallots chopped small, then poured and patted into the shaped banana-leaf bowl – an oval declivity four feet long under which even heat was already glowing, to be reinforced by hot black stones from Tinakula and topped by woven parcels of parrotfish tied with twine. Huge heart-shaped leaves sealed the whole, and more stones were placed on top to ensure no steam escaped.

'Finis nao,' said the bride's mother, pipe in mouth, who'd explained the operation to me, her youngest at a breast. 'Bye iufela kambaek fo testim.'

A carved implement with a pronged end was used to 'test' the readiness of a Kastom pudding – essential equipment in the basket every bride took to her new abode – but I was being asked back to taste, not test.

'Thank you.'

Joe had been scouting with the other piccaninnis for drinking coconuts to refresh the workers, but now sprawled close to Mata at the top of the beach, where she trickled sand slowly over his ankles, laughing. Did it matter to him that his mother wasn't married; that no ceremony, heathen or Christian, had marked an alliance with the source of seed from which he was formed? I looked at the bride, barely out of puberty, stalking past on coltish legs, one arm raised to support the basket on her head, to throw the cassava 'milk' to the pigs. Her lips were folded demurely and eyes calm.

'S'ee lucky,' Mata whispered to me, ''usban' naeswan!'

Mata's mother, the duchess, smiled wisely.

'Kambaek wetem Joe nekis yia.' (Bring Joe back next year.)

I wondered how long Magnus would have kept his virginity if he'd stayed with us in Reefs all the time, instead of being a protected schoolboy back in Scotland. Perhaps to lie with a child of nature in the silken tropical air would have made a beautiful beginning to his relationships with girls, but, as I'd seen in Ross's and Ben's histories, it was unlikely ever to be that simple.

Back on Pigeon I recorded the Kastom pudding recipe, and Diana's for Tahitian Poisson Cru, Ben's for fudge and the Nenumbo youths' heatedly debated advice on the killing and cooking of pikpik, then took myself off for a quiet hour at Temotulaki, a tevi tucked into my kalico. It was only weeks now until Tasha came, and I didn't know how this might disrupt Pigeon's normal routine. Ross was dreading the visit; she'd attacked Teimaliki, a fact he hadn't been able to keep from Pegi. Ben, as ever, was reticent about any feelings he had. His new improved body was, I'd discovered, the result of indulgence in ice cream in New Zealand, a decade after his earlier, vagrant trip there, rather than red meat and women. Of all the Hepworth children, his case seemed the saddest, for, unlike Ross, who was essentially a survivor, and Tasha, who after teens and twenties of inner hell had 'settled', according to Tom, better than any of them, albeit under constant supervision, Ben had still not found his place. At one time, he had had the greatest chance of following his father's dream of selecting, eclectically, the best from the Outside World and from a simple, 'natural' existence, and making a happy marriage between the two – but he had failed. Although why should Ben – or Ross – want to follow their parents' dreams? All children have to 'fledge' – like the youngsters passing through the Sapulo, and young men and women the world over who need to strike out from the boundaries of their childhood to discover what they themselves hope to make of their lives. Was Ben's problem to do with the fact that his fledging stage – of which perhaps the Mendana interval had been the most promising episode – had been interrupted? Or (frightening thought) had a combination of the cult experience in Australia, extreme social isolation on Pigeon, and the mysteries of darker Kastom practices caused his personality to fragment, until he became not only disturbed but ill?

A Bible translator with whom I was in satellite e-mail contact, who'd lived in the nearby village of Otambe in the late 1980s, saw a profound difference between true faith and that which Ben displayed in a shield-like capacity. '*I had the greatest respect for Tom, and still do, for Diana,*' he wrote, '*but putting that poor boy on a plane and hoping he'd come back cured was like telling a man with a broken leg to walk off and heal himself.*' I understood what it was like to feel the deepest affection for the Hepworth seniors but still be astounded by them. Couldn't Tom see that Ben was deeply troubled, not just 'being difficult'? Diana had suggested he seek medical advice while he was away, but without supervision this came to nothing. And what did the sympathetic Bible translator make of the long series of failed partnerships in PIT? On two occasions would-be store managers, refugees from Pigeon, had fled to his leaf hut at Otambe, wringing their hands at the seeming impossibility of pleasing their senior partners. We agreed that Tom and Diana, set unshakeably on their own paths, with ferociously high standards – and having had their fingers bitten on several occasions – were wary of handing over the reins of responsibility, or giving trust fully. The newcomers would then become restless, feeling as if an oppressive Big Brother were peeping over their shoulders on a tropical island miles from anywhere, where perhaps they'd hoped – like the Hepworths themselves, originally – to be free of unnecessary rules and regulations . . .

I lay on little Temotulaki and wondered whether there was anything about the Hepworths' lives that did not end in paradox. They'd sailed away from 'civilization' after the war, looking for a life of adventure that would culminate in finding '*a piece of land where we could raise a family in the way we thought right . . . and owe no man*'. That they did experience many years of happy adventuring is fact. In that sense their dream was fulfilled. But in those days, their crews were always birds of passage, and perhaps the Hepworths still saw Pigeon, in some ways, as a ship – on which Tom was Captain, and Diana still the Skipper's Skipper, as the all-girl crew had dubbed her. The power these positions bestowed, bolstered by years of controlling largely submissive local labour – who were also seen as 'incidental', like any Islanders passed on a ship – may, by the time they needed long-term outside help on their dream island, have resulted in ingrained habits which were disagreeable to other independent types. Another part of the paradox was that Diana, who to many appeared overpoweringly autocratic and sure of herself, was still, I was convinced, deep inside, a vulnerable little girl from a background whose basis of faith chopped and changed at her father's whim, and who at age nine had had Sellotape fixed over her mouth when she spoke out of turn at junior school – and later, metaphorically, placed it again over her own lips to prevent them trembling when teased by other children at boarding school. In a sense, through me, I felt, she finally wanted to speak out, and at least tell the world Tasha's story, as well as about the wonderful years. I would try. But there was another important reason not to miss my appointment with her today: she'd asked both me and Mhairi to act as witnesses to a new Will.

The sea was waist high in the channel between Nandelli and Pigeon when I headed back, and calm. I loved striding against the weight of water when it was like this, leaving my own modest wake. Sometimes shoals of translucent fish leaped out of the water in a body as I passed, and there were egrets to watch, as well as the distant shapes of dugouts fishing near the Edge of the Reef. These were the punctuation marks, the stamp of daily life in Reefs – along with the rising and setting of the sun, the moon and tides, the fishers and the fished. There was rhythm and beauty in the cycle; but also occasional shocks – like a crocodile killing a man instead of a man killing a crocodile; a kumberra sweeping a child out of a tree, or a Debbil stirring for reasons that could only be guessed. I had discussed with Tangypera the way magic always worked best with those who believed in it. The Vele man, hired killer of earlier times (but still about, it was hinted), sometimes had only to raise his finger towards a victim and they died of fright. 'But you're not scared of something just in your head, are you, Lusi?' he'd said. In one sense, he was wrong – tricks of the mind unnerved me – but certainly I was sceptical about devilry in general, except the potential powers of man-holding ash, of course . . . I assumed then that the enormous dent in the water – the size of a mini-roundabout – suddenly appearing to my left as I made my way over the channel was merely something to do with fish.

I thought at first it was a cat's-paw effect, as we sometimes see on lochs in Scotland, accompanied by the sudden darkening of a clear sky when there's concentrated pressure from above. But there was further activity, apparently from below, inside the growing circle, which made me think I was lucky enough to have witnessed the gathering of a great shoal I could report to Islander friends. Then the 'fish' all pressed their noses a foot upwards in unison – thousands, quivering as the air above grew darker by the second, and their massed pulses hit my legs. Spray skimmed off the circle's outer rim and gathered rapidly into thick swirls moving round and round, more dense with each revolution . . . Oh God, this wasn't fish . . . Through mist above a heavy, white, undulating band – a hula hoop of cloud – I saw black figures run to stand on Pigeon's highest coral cliff, arms waving. I was the only person in the channel and the path of the whirlwind was becoming clear. A vast outer ripple of quite improbably trembling waves – amid calm in all other parts of the channel – reached me, and I stepped back, and back again, fast. The phenomenon progressed along its path at about the same pace I was trying to run away with splashing strides, but as it passed me – just – on a long zigzag, its force whipped up. Higher and faster, higher and faster it whirled. No wonder these people believed in devils. What else was this white monster, now with only the tip of a cone still attached to the water and the whole, hollow in the centre, spinning and spinning, bulbous as a genie or some nightmare upside-down ice cream . . . It was taller than Pigeon and heading right for the rock where the children played at high tide, hordes of them, laughing, on sunny days exactly as this had been. Thank God they were back in school. When it hit land (Nandelli Point) the whirlwind dispersed. The entire event had taken minutes. In minutes, a child in a dugout could have been battered, then spun, wontoks interpreting nature's obscure whim as part of a deliberate punishment inflicted for reasons discussed for decades, on one particular clan – just as the battering to death of the *Arthur Rogers* in Mohawk Bay, the torture of Christine on her nightmare drift to Utupua, the madness of Tasha and the strangeness of Ben were all seen as part of a curse on the Hepworths.

When I reached land, strong arms guided me, hands patting like paws, to where Pegi sat me on a tree stump; a group gathered, and we told and retold the stori of the whirlwind. There was no time to change my wet kalico before going to Diana's, so I went as I was, running fingers quickly through my topknot to tidy it.

'Lovely, darling. We'll have tea in a minute. I just want you to sign here. You know the coconut trees I mean, don't you?'

Diana was cutting the island in half. I nodded dumbly. How could I refuse to sign her Will, when she must have two witnesses and there was no-one else? Mhairi looked uncomfortable too, but we acquiesced. Tangypera had seen Diana earlier pacing out the land, and knew what was going on.

'It will be decided by the people of Reefs,' he said, appearing at my window that evening, and not bothering to specify what he was talking about.

'I know,' I said. Signing that piece of 'whiteman's' paper would make no difference to the reality of what happened to Pigeon in the future, but I ached for Diana. In 1999, as in 1959, she was still intent on trying to organize her particular Paradise, with the motto 'one way, one heart' – single-minded determination – as her guiding rule. But whether her sons wanted the island or not, and what they'd make of it – or be allowed to make of it by other interested parties – was another matter, and one of the few subjects I judged as potentially too painful to raise with Diana.★

A few days later, Ben, standing up so he could guide the canoe accurately along the narrow coral paths, hummed softly as we headed for Sibileh's village – Sibileh who'd been Tasha's companion at Pigeon Island School more than thirty years ago, even before Christine Clement's time. ''ibileh' pronounced Tasha carefully, smiling up at me from her position on the floor half in and half out of the covered bow, where her carer, Joyce, was trying to protect her charge's soft white shoulders from the mid-morning glare. 'Nobody told me Largactil reacts with the sun,' she sighed. 'She's got no proper reef shoes either. She'll go back with her feet in ribbons.' Then she leaned forward and

★ Naturally Wills are subject to change, and what was set down on that particular day in 1999 may no longer stand.

whispered: 'Well, I suppose it's better than going back with the clap like last time . . .' I nodded, but I'd promised Diana I'd try to talk to Tasha, not just over her, so I slid down opposite her in the bow.

'Oof,' I said as my back complained a bit. 'It's hot, isn't it?' We were between the Deep Blue and the silence of the mangroves, in an open vessel with tropical sun swaying in every dimple of a million wavelets, anywhere in time. Tasha would have made this journey hundreds of times in her childhood, in her own small dugout. The previous evening, there'd been a stilted supper at Diana's, with Ben sitting at the head of the table opposite his mother to say grace, and Tasha, close to my age, perched silently across from me, staring throughout with shining eyes from beneath an Alice band, like a six-year-old on best behaviour. 'Oof,' echoed Tasha experimentally, then pronounced ''ibileh' again carefully. 'Yes, we're going to see Sibileh,' I agreed. After a short reflective pause, Tasha, her small but brilliant eyes ever holding mine, leaned forward to confide something evidently shocking, from her look, but which I was unable to make out. She sat back nodding, like a triumphant gossip, pale knees drawn up to reveal large knickers under an overbright sundress. 'Don't take any notice,' said Joyce, 'she's always imagining terrible goings-on.' ''e 'id!' protested Tasha emphatically, and looked at me confidingly again. Tiny white fingers fluttered on my knee: 'I 'ike icken.' 'I like chicken too – kokoroko.' ''okoroko!' sighed Tasha, as though at a blissful thought, and her eyebrows moved up and down like birds – just like an Islander's. 'Nearly there,' came Ben's flat voice.

Sibileh lived at Otambe, the village which had temporarily housed the Bible translator. It was reached by wading through still water so thick it held tracks like mud. Children lay in those brown shallows staring from under their hair like the silent piccaninnis encountered in the dark Maramasike passage. Were the 'Happy Isles' only the blue and gold ones? On the dark shore stood a heavy middle-aged woman holding the hands of two small girls. Other children, two carrying bundles revealed shortly as younger brothers or sisters on their backs, hung round the folds of her kalico. ''ibileh!' cried Tasha ecstatically, and the woman's grave face broke into a gap-toothed smile. 'Tas'a!'

Along a watery track cut through horseshoes of mangrove roots, which gave way to a slippery jungle path littered with rotting leaves and rooting pigs, we walked in quiet double file until we reached Sibileh's hut. There, her husband, bushknife on knee, rose to greet us briefly before sticking the knife between his teeth and climbing a palm. Sibileh moved wooden bowls, half-peeled breadfruit and the piles of rags that were her washing from a leaf mat on a platform raised above the mud. Her breasts were leaking and she mopped at them roughly. Then she placed Tasha beside her on the mat, all seven of her piccaninnis hanging close, and the rest of us, feeling slightly super-fluous, sat a little way off drinking coconuts. I couldn't hear the conversation, but saw the movements of the two heads: one broad, haloed by a ragged Afro; the other narrow, its mousy rats' tails in their Alice band flopping up and down as Tasha nodded at whatever her friend was saying.

'Isn't it *weird* here,' said Joyce, over her coconut. 'So . . . well, I don't mean it rudely, but *primitive*.' But this was Tasha's background, I thought, doubtless difficult to detail in her casenotes. Ben was pat-ting a dog with horrible sores. The two heads in the corner were both facing out through the web of mangroves now, to the brown channel beyond, and beyond that, to the sparkling ocean that had been their swimming pool as children. They weren't speaking any more but, when Joyce moved her head, I saw that one of Sibileh's large brown hands lay close to Tasha's small white one, and that their little fingers were linked.

'Isn't that nice,' said Joyce – 'almost like sisters.'

Tasha turned round sharply. 'My sista,' she said clearly, and Sibileh's husband nodded. 'Dey sistas,' he said quietly.

'We'd better make a move,' said Ben. 'I promised Mum I'd fix the video for tonight.'

I asked Sibileh if she had any children ready to send to school when Joe and Benji left, because Diana wanted companions for her grand-children, just as Sibileh herself had been a companion to Tasha. A couple of pot-bellied piccaninnis were pushed forward, a nose wiped on a kalico, and I suggested she took them to Pigeon to meet the other children.

'If Missus say,' she said, 'it's oraet.'

Sibileh, who'd been bright at Pigeon Island School, had with Diana's encouragement continued her education on Santa Cruz – until she was married off, like Tasha's next companion, at a young age. Among landed Reef Island girls, it was Tasha who was the odd one out, not being married, not having children. It was well known locally that an arrangement Diana had once tried to make for Tasha to marry the then chief of Matema's son had failed for the same reason Nokali had never seriously considered marrying Tasha. The chief didn't want a daughter-in-law who was – like young Solomon from Nenumbo – krangge, even if she had the advantage of being white and having 'rich' connections. I thought about what it must have taken Diana to reach the point at which she would consider such a marriage, and go through the humble process of asking – only to face rejection. All she'd ever wanted for Tasha was happiness, and if that meant marrying a Solomon Islander – something Diana could not approve in her sons who, she believed, could aim higher – so be it. But although plenty of young men had been happy to enjoy Tasha's body, none of them wanted to be saddled with her mind.

''ideo!' said Tasha, easily distracted by this lure. Diana had asked if I would, for once, join her later to watch a video, power permitting – a film she said might help me understand more about Tasha.

'I've always believed if she'd been able to discuss her problems more,' Diana had said more than once, 'she'd have made better progress. And she can speak clearly when she tries.'

I'd noticed that, but also how much of an effort it was for her. That evening, after watching a cartoon, Tasha strung shells into necklaces with Pegi, who realized she'd nothing to fear from her heavily Largactil'd sister-in-law, and I watched a frightening film about a young girl too sensitive and emotional for her own good,* who'd slept with a cousin for the sheer animal pleasure of it, become violent when he denied her, and was sectioned in a psychiatric institution for years until – when community care came in – it shut. Had Diana watched this film over all the years they'd been able to play videos, and thought: 'That's Tasha'? The girl portrayed was too alive and vivid, too *bright* for a 'normal' life. She reminded me of my friend Addie, who couldn't stand the ploddingness of convention, and who'd lived hard and fast and died young as a result, still dancing, still raging. But Tasha, bless her, was almost the antithesis. Did Diana still deny the diagnosis made by so many doctors of schizophrenia combined with subnormality? I dreaded that she'd ask me to agree that the girl in the film was like Tasha, but when it ended we stood

* *She's Been Away*, screenplay by Stephen Poliakoff, directed by Peter Hall and starring Peggy Ashcroft and Rebecca Pigeon, 1989.

together looking out onto the tropical night and Diana said nothing.

'It was a wonderful film,' I said, as one does, even when the film is upsetting.

'I thought you'd like it.'

'I did try to talk to Tasha,' I said, 'and I'll try again. But I feel the doctors may have been right . . .'★

Diana picked up a book written by a 'self-cured' schizophrenic.

'You should read this.'

I took the book, knowing I'd only skim through it. There are always exceptions to rules, but I couldn't believe Tasha was one of this kind, and when I kissed Diana goodnight I was aware from how she felt in my hug, rather than from what she said, that perhaps she accepted Tasha's condition as permanent now, reluctantly, but a little more than she'd allowed herself to before. She'd written to a friend that she saw me as the daughter she'd lost, a confession that both shocked and touched me.

'Goodnight, darling, sleep well.'

I went back to Tasha's House and, by candlelight, wrote to my mother, no longer living where she'd been when I came back from my *Castaway* island but in a home. I loved her, but I also feared whatever weakness had made her deteriorate gradually after divorce to the point of collapse, and never recover. And I realized I preferred to feel I had more in common with Diana.

★ The last note I saw which gave a confirmed diagnosis related to Tasha's condition in 1983.

The te puke voyaging canoe that sailed from Duff Islands to Nufiloli.
Robbie Cooper

Nbanga Temoa Islanders. *Robbie Cooper*

Ross as President of Temotu Province.
Tom might have been wryly proud
had he lived to see the day. *Lucy Irvine*

A future president? Andrew
Hepworth at Nenumbo. *Lucy Irvine*

Reef Island politicians
in Honiara hope to
blend the best of
traditional Kastom
methods of Outer
Island government
with modern ideas.

Robbie Cooper

Ben maintaining the lawnmower in Paradise.

Robbie Cooper

Diana off to New Zealand to have her skin cancer treated. Vili, one of Ross's wontoks, steadies the boat.

Lucy Irvine

Christine Hepworth making leaf jewellery
with children we met when sailing from
Pigeon to Guadalcanal. *Lucy Irvine*

Benji was determined to blow a blast
through a Boo shell, and finally succeeded.

Robbie Cooper

Joe was our numbawan crab catcher.

Lucy Irvine

One of the many 'private houses' built for fishing. These were also used for romance. *Robbie Cooper*

(*Right*) This elder holds a roll of the red feather money used to buy brides. (*Below*) Drummers at a Nenumbo welcoming ceremony.

Robbie Cooper

Benji was quite awed by Magnus when he came back to visit at Christmas – suddenly a youth, not a boy. *Lucy Irvine*

Patteson and Benji were inseparable. Benji worried he'd never again find a friend like Patteson. *Lucy Irvine*

Joe with Ngive and Elisha, friends in school and out. *Lucy Irvine*

One of Pegi's housegirls peeling breadfruit. Although attractive, she may never marry because her family owns little land. *Lucy Irvine*

On Pigeon, Pokai was a bold football star but he was nervous when he went through the traditional initiation rites into manhood. *Lucy Irvine*

Reef Island girls give each other silent support. Gentle solidarity is very much a part of island life.
Lucy Irvine

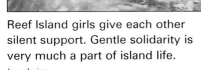

'Bye bye, Lusi, Benji, Joe – bye iu kambaek!' *Robbie Cooper*

24

Tom at Eighty

BACK IN THE LATE '60S, DURING THE CHILDREN'S IDYLLIC DAYS, TOM began to write down his philosophy: '*His own happiness is the goal each individual strives for, whether he seeks it in Power, Wealth, or the Happiness of Others . . . Man is partly Animal . . . and partly Mind, which requires Leisure for development. Our Civilization is on the wrong path because we pursue Knowledge as an end in itself rather than a means to more Leisure in which to think . . . The Greeks, seeing Man's life as an Art, came nearer a solution than most . . . but largely ignored Woman, dividing them into home-makers and the Hetaerae – the "Others" – who were accomplished courtesan types, expected to abandon their babies. But most women want to be mothers and have interests outside the home . . . Men and women should be equal partners but have different spheres. Man's special aptitude is for Reasoning; woman's, Intuition, developed from Instinct. We try to run Civilization on Reason, but happiness comes from creating something, whether poetry or palaces, and that often depends on Intuition.*'

Tom, who spent most days on his tropical island in sweaty toil, dreamed then of leisure and its fruits, and admired an intuitive approach to life. Did he consider his adored spouse as homemaker – faintly insulting to her intelligence – or hetaera – which might question her attributes as a mother? Or, Amazon that she was, perhaps she encapsulated, for him, the best of both. If developed, these thoughts might have resulted in Tom's guidelines for an ideal modus vivendi, based on his experience of life within the microcosm of a tiny island. But twenty years later, when, one by one, his children of Paradise had 'fallen', he added a postscript. Perhaps the excess of 'intuition' afflicting Ben, who tapped into privately imparted guidance from on high, plus a surfeit of the way the Islanders lived by instinct, turned Tom against the idea that unrefined impulses could be healthy. *'People take refuge in Intuition, which attracts those who wish to be "spiritual" without bother, because it promises a Heaven where the Intuitions of others can be ignored . . . Intuition is part of our equipment and Sensitiveness connected with it, but I also know it can get us into a thorough tangle . . . REASON should guide the passions towards Civilization.'* These notes end ruefully: *'Seem to have run out of steam . . .'*

Life wasn't easy for the Hepworth seniors – he to be eighty in 1990, she nearly seventy – when they were alone on Pigeon apart from the neighbours, who continued to take vengeance for perceived old injustices at every opportunity. Growing more sophisticated in their methods, one man made an impression of a liquor store key in mud, carved a facsimile which he poked through wire netting on the end of a spear, and helped himself regularly to nightcaps; others deliberately drilled over-large holes in the cover for a dry dock, so the hatch was lifted easily off its nails and whole cartons of beer removed. *'Saw escaping thieves in canoe and some of "our" boys dashed out – to fight them or to share the loot? No-one can be trusted.'* Tom always had culprits pursued, and many cases reached the homely court on Santa Cruz, resulting occasionally in sentences, but as the deeds committed were not a matter of shame in Kastom, shoulders were shrugged and the pilfering went on. There were times, too, when, for lack of another local with 'initiative', previous offenders were reinstated on the pay-roll. Jimson, fired for molesting Tasha as a child, was at one time rehired as a security guard.

'Blue skies, fair winds, hot sun and beaches by the mile,' Tom was able to write truthfully to the handful of people sounding half-serious about 'buying' Pigeon, but thirty years was a long time for a man with cultural leanings to find these pleasures enough, and the neverending, wordless messages delivered by the Islanders had gradually eroded the notion that life on a small atoll could ever be 'ideal' – for him. *'Stability is only balance,'* he quoted from lines his sisters sent, seeking helpful words to pass on to Ben in 1989, but on Pigeon the balance for Tom had tipped downwards, and yet again he found himself

hanging on the arrival of help from the Outside World – this time in the form of Damian, the American yachtsman who would take charge of PIT, allowing Tom to get away for a prostate cancer check-up, and Diana to arrange for a satellite dish to be shipped from America, bringing the possibility of television for his birthday. Already they could enjoy videos, but fresh supplies often 'disappeared' en route and Diana was aware that, these days, Tom *wanted* to know what was going on in the Outside World; for him the days were over when having an engine to strip down in sunshine was enough. Her plan now was to bring what he wanted to Pigeon. She couldn't contemplate leaving the island permanently – not even for his sake – but would stop at nothing to try to make it as happy a home for him as, for all the 'occasional inconveniences', it still was for her.

But there are lines in Tom's diary that belie his doldrums, and support Diana's view that when people are essentially content they don't bother to record the fact – but miseries need an outlet, so they can give a false impression of dominating the scene. '*Picked seventy mangoes this dawn!*' noted Tom suddenly, in the midst of pages berating Ben – who sent his father a *Good News Bible* from abroad – '*and saw a frigate wheel and wheel on a thermal . . . Diana made fudge which didn't set, so we ate it with spoons looking out on a blue sky with pink pinstripe,*' and a light-hearted 'Pet's Corner' featured in every letter now smartly printed off his solar-powered PC and sent to the ailing Margaret and Elizabeth in London. (Elizabeth, deaf and succumbing to memory loss, now pushed Margaret in a wheelchair to the theatre.) '*Tapushka,*★ *now "upper middle-aged", for a tropical puss, spends his days reclining protected from the rest of the world under the shady spikes of a pandanus – lucky fellow! . . . Samantha's still eating like a pony, but we feel she hasn't long to go and are looking at the idea of a Rottweiler, with all these store breaks. How's Stevie?*' (Stevie was the sisters' elderly cat.) '*Oh my dear,*' responded Elizabeth, in one of her last coherent letters, '*such fun! I picked him up to give him a cuddle and the Alarm thing fitted to my chest went off . . . We had Help the Aged round and could only just get rid of them before Ian McKellen was on the box.*'

Tom had the job of selecting the best spot for each meal, following the sun's arc, for Diana had built dining alcoves into the bush all round

---

★ Originally bought for Tasha in the early 1980s as a kitten, Tapushka survived a rough canoe crossing and clearly enjoyed island life. He died at a venerable age in 1998, not long after we arrived.

the island and it was possible always to enjoy the perfect combination of sun and shade. He seldom wrote '*Bliss!*' in his diary, as Diana did, but would run to '*very nice*' if Diana organized his favourite fried spam and sliced breadfruit for supper, and wrote appreciatively of the '*flash*' of Ginger Rogers's legs caught on film. Perhaps it was the reminder that he'd also once been something of an artist – in photography – that made Tom resurrect, in his eightieth year, the idea of '*the book*'.

'Why don't we find out if anyone's really interested? Nothing to lose.'

Delighted to see him keen again, Diana at once set about packing boxes of old diaries and Kodachromes, and by the time Damian sailed into Mohawk Bay, Tom was all set to gatecrash every publisher in London if necessary to salvage this vital missing link in his old dream.

'Good luck,' said Damian, who seemed as cheerful and adaptable as his letters implied. 'And don't worry about things back home. I'll have the place as shipshape as you've left it when you get back.'

'Wonderful,' said Diana, who related to his seafaring spirit. 'See you in a couple of months.'

On their first night in London, Tom shared Elizabeth's hearing aid at the opera, and borrowed a magnifying glass to read his own diaries, which in parts had faded over the years.

'Here goes,' he said to Diana the following week, and the elderly but still handsome Hepworths began their unconventional tour of publishers. They didn't have to go far.

'Thirty years on a remote and beautiful island, you say, building from bush – and raising a family?'

'Yes.'

'Palm trees, tropical fruit, nature in the raw, away from it all?'

'Yes – and of course there's the story of how we got there. Over a decade of sailing. And before that, the war . . .'

'I'm sure, but I rather think the island's the thing. Anyway, leave me your slides and I'll get back to you.'

'Well, that was easy,' said Diana as they came out of the interview.

'Mmmn,' said Tom. 'Haven't written the book yet!'

Later he confided in his diary: '*I've a nasty feeling that if I miss out the war and minimize the sailing days, it's going to be a dull book. I mean nothing much has really happened on Pigeon, though I suppose that's not really true . . .*'

Back on Pigeon, the Islanders had discovered they could visit the new building, Tasha's House, without detection, by approaching it from the sea. It took only seconds to remove the louvres and crawl in where, on wet nights, it was more comfortable than in some of their leaf huts. Damian had begun his manager duties well but lost sleep over his yacht, which swung about alarmingly, however carefully he anchored it, in Mohawk Bay.

'Yes. Bad luck. There's a Debbil there,' said Nandelli folk, shaking their heads unreassuringly and going over in detail the ends of the *Arthur Rogers* and the *Seaspray*. (The third Hepworth boat to be lost was *Kyomie*, the motor launch, during Cyclone Nina in 1993.)

'Why wasn't I told it was such a dangerous anchorage?' Damian asked himself, and wrote to Tom saying he wasn't sure he could stay the full period agreed, in view of the risk to his property. But by then the Hepworths had moved on to America, where Amalie reminisced with them over crossing the Pacific to Tahiti. She was anxious to help Tom with what she knew was the project closest to his heart – and probably his last.

'You *have* to write your story, Tom.'

'Absolutely,' urged Diana. 'People dream of living on desert islands, and we've done it.'

Amalie mentioned that in the 1980s a book had come out about a young woman who'd lived on an uninhabited island somewhere off Australia, but that was only for a year, and she hadn't raised children there.

'Quite. No-one's done what we have.'

But Tom was quiet, and again confided in his diary: '*I'd know how to begin . . . but how to finish?*' News from Ross after his family break-up in Papua had been minimal, and there was no telling what state Ben would be in if and when he returned. (This was when Amalie offered to take her godson under her wing for a while – and when she did so, she was shocked at how withdrawn he seemed.)

'Anyway I'll give it a go,' said Tom, and plans were finalized when a green light came from the publishers: Damian would be in charge of the store and bring any guests to the units in his yacht; Tom would write his book, and Diana would ensure he wasn't disturbed and take care of the island.

But when they stood once more on Solomon shores, waiting for their store manager to give them a lift back to Pigeon, they faced a surprise. Damian sailed into sight but planned to sail straight on, never returning to Pigeon. His yacht had driven onto the shore one night, and only with great difficulty had he saved her.

'I'm sorry,' he said. 'The life out there just wasn't what I'd been led to expect.'

Tom, sinking down on his suitcase full of history, was too tired to argue or cite the letters that *did*, in his view, explain that Pigeon was not all fun and sun. And, angry though he was, Damian must have seen the old man was exhausted, for he took them aboard after all, cooked breakfast, and they set sail once more for Reefs. When they arrived, however, he stuck to his vow not to stay, and, having dropped them by dinghy, left on the same tide. '*Bastard. Liar,*' Tom wrote two days later, instead of starting his book, and when he discovered the cunning break-ins at Tasha's House added: '*These people are shits.*'

'It'll be all right, darling. We'll *make* it all right,' said Diana, and wrote to Amalie that, despite the nasty shocks on arrival, '*It's Heaven to be Home.*'

Tom sat down to work in his bedroom cum office which was also the radio shack and, later, Ben's Box. Diana fitted a shower in there for him, plus a lavatory flushing thirty feet into the bay below, for he had difficulty reaching more distant facilities in time and was prone to messy accidents. Wearied by efforts to recapture the enthusiasm for adventure he'd had fifty years ago, he slept so soundly that Diana had to rush from Ngarando in the night to close the louvres. So necessary for air, they also let rain flood in onto his gradually shrinking form under its single sheet.

'Is it a crab, darling?' he'd ask as she banged about, protecting him from the elements. Sometimes he forgot they weren't still sharing a room.

'It's nothing. Don't worry,' and she'd bend over to kiss him before making sure any papers left out were safe from the rain. '*One frangipani leaf unfurls, and I write three lines . . . eight fruit on our mandarin tree after thirty years . . . Golly my legs are weak, and prickly heat on my John Thomas, most inconvenient.*' Tom had also begun bleeding anally at this time, but opted not to tell Diana. It would only lead to a ghastly trip on the cargo boat to Honiara, for Santa Cruz no longer had a regular doctor at the hospital. He'd rather save his energies for a more reward-ing journey, to the other side of the world. '*Let the medics regard my bum if they must, but at least with the comforts of Stratford to follow. In*'

Honiara one can't even find an ice cream.' Did he recall searching for an ice for Tasha en route to the locked ward in 1983? It wouldn't be long before Tom had his last sight of his little girl, when, just as they'd done when she was nine and 'miraculously recovered' after her heart operation, they picnicked up a hill in Auckland close to the same hospital where, when she was eighteen, a nurse had detected signs of assault. In her thirties, Tasha, plump from many pills, was panting when she reached the summit, but not as much as Tom. Only Diana was still *'fit as a fiddle'* for all that her cholesterol count had been found to be *'unheard of high'* and she was instructed to cut down on coconuts.

'*I'm an ordinary sort of bloke, I just happen to lead an extraordinary sort of life . . . D'you believe in love at first sight? I didn't, until I met Diana.*' Often Tom broke off new starts to his book to finish instead a letter to his sisters. '*Did you mention water pills – or rather, less water pills? I think I'm in need. By the way, what I'd do about the masturbating ghost if I were you, is take him by surprise – so to speak. Try the old tin can and tripwire trick.*' This suggestion was in response to reports from Margaret of a naked man in her London garden. When confronted by the crippled spinster, the intruder had said: '*I think I'm coming.*' She'd replied calmly: '*Do you? Well don't come near me . . .*' Over the months and miles this became something of a running joke between Margaret and Tom, but Elizabeth was soon unable to complete her half of the sisters' joint letters. '*She's "with us" less and less, but gains something, I think, from staying in her own home.*' Tom, straying from his book again, browsed through a copy of *Country Life* sent by one of Diana's sisters, and ringed an advertisement promising 'Comfort and Dignity in the Autumn Years'. Perhaps he wouldn't have minded moving from his home – especially when Ben reappeared '*ranting less, but by no means in his right mind*' and rumours reached Pigeon that Ross, having finally '*sloughed off*' Teimaliki, planned to marry another Reef Island girl. '*Well at least it looks like the airport might REALLY happen this time,*' wrote Tom, glad to grasp something positive, when an influential Reef Islander who'd done well in Honiara was elected to represent the area, and told Tom transport was high on his agenda. This man, the Honourable Horace Leingalu, was an entrepreneur in politics as well as business. Bopali – with his 'rights for the masses' views and (purported) incitement to passive resistance, such as strikes, in the 1980s – was a wontok and confidant, but Horace saw the advantage of cultivating the Hepworths as friends as well; after all, they owned the most successful private business in Reefs and occupied land that in 2052 would fall back into Islander hands. 'Proper development cannot take off in the Outer Islands until there's a proper means of getting to and fro,' he told Tom on a fleeting visit to his constituency – in a helicopter that was tied to palm trees by only half-joking Islanders who wouldn't let him go until they were satisfied he'd fulfil election pledges.

'You're telling me,' said Tom, enjoying the drop-in – for which Diana had in two days created a helipad outside the schoolhouse. But when his eightieth birthday surprise came – not the satellite dish, which took a year en route, but members of the all-girl crew rallying to their old captain – transport for the ordinary mortal to Pigeon Island was still an open boat across the heaving blue.

'Never again,' whispered one of them, but the joy on Tom's face when Diana sprung them triumphantly on him that evening, like silver-haired bunny girls, complete with cake, made it all seem worthwhile, and – once again – revived memories that begged to be recorded. When they'd gone, he typed out a poem by Longfellow and pinned it up in his office. Goethe, it reminded him, and Sophocles, among others, had produced their best work in latter years:

> . . . for age is opportunity, no less than youth itself, though in another
>   dress.
> And as the evening twilight fades away, the sky is filled with stars,
>   invisible by day.

'That's right, darling,' said Diana and, glancing across from roof repair work a few days later, was thrilled to see him typing energetically. He'd sketched an outline as far as the *Arthur Rogers*'s arrival at Panama, before a series of interruptions set him back.

First, Ben stated that, for all he did not feel in a condition to '*take her to my bosom*' – meaning little Diane – he intended to view his role as a father seriously, once he'd seen Sipikoli's child and knew she was his. This '*set Sipikoli's wontoks off again, and all the old jiggery-pokery*'. Then Ross's now ex-wife, Teimaliki, suddenly reappeared in Reef Islands, to stake her claim on Pigeon. The way she did this caused astonished admiration on Nandelli, for she waded across the channel carrying a traditional digging stick, stuck it into the middle of the ground on Pigeon she considered her own, and stayed there, digging vigorously. Tom was in his office, remembering other times; Diana was completing a platform that was to house his bees – a new interest – soon to arrive from overseas. The suspicion reached her that something untoward was going on when she heard giggles from her labour, and a familiar woman's voice, raised. Tom looked up enquiringly but she waved, mouthing: 'I'll see to it,' and back he went to happy days at sea. Diana downed her tools and headed towards the noise. What she saw – Teimaliki, now a large woman, making deep, deliberate cuts in the best section of her lawn, with a circle of approving wontoks watching – made Diana act before she could stop herself. She grabbed the stick.

'Missus, plis!' cried Nupanyi, who'd been working with her at the hive site. 'Stap fo toktok!' (Let's discuss things calmly.) The patch of ground was close to his.

'Ba iuim!' muttered Teimaliki (up yours) and held on still more determinedly to the stick.

'Get-off-my-lawn,' said Diana through gritted teeth, then wasted no more breath in speech as she pushed the younger woman back, inch by inch, with the stick now gripped horizontally in the air between them. Old, shuddering but still strong white arms combated heavier but less muscular black biceps in a slow dance minimal in movement but riveting, to the gathering audience, in its tension. Nupanyi, deeply distressed, made a sign with his eyebrows and a youth ran for Tom.

'Eh beetch!' shrilled Teimaliki. 'Mifela plandem kumera!' (I'm going to plant kumera, you bitch.)

'Oh-no-you-don't.'

Diana was sweating freely by the time Tom arrived, and Teimaliki all but spitting in her face.

'For goodness' sake!' Tom, meaning only to put an end to the absurd slow-motion battle, made as if to take the stick himself. But Matoko, who'd appeared suddenly, saw this as an aggressive move towards Teimaliki, his sister, and rushed forward, arm raised, betel-stained teeth bared. Diana had always disliked Matoko, with his crude looks and odour, and the way he 'wheedled' favours from Ben. Now she let go the stick and blocked his path, shielding Tom. 'Don't you dare!' she cried. 'Don't you dare!' Then she turned her back on him and stared round all the watchers.

'You are witnesses,' she told them. 'He tried to hit Cap'n Tom.'

'No faet! No faet!' pleaded Nupanyi, wringing his hands.

'It was spur of the moment, darling,' said Tom, stepping forward. 'Everyone hot under the collar. What was going on anyway? You all know Pigeon won't grow anything.' He smiled grimly. 'It's part of the curse, isn't it? Debbil and all that?'

'No true, Cap'n, sir,' said Tangypera quietly, and others nodded. Pigeon, they claimed, had been a thriving garden before the Hepworths came.

'Rubbish,' said Tom, 'it was bush.'

They told him then that when the *Arthur Rogers* had come originally, the soil on the island had been 'resting' (slipslip) between plantings, the implication being that it wasn't so much the island and the bay that were cursed, but Tom and Diana themselves. Remember how Christine Clement, who'd had many Islander friends, grew a garden round the schoolhouse when she was there?

'What about the mangoes?' countered Tom. 1990 was a bumper year. But the Islanders had an answer for that, too. The mango trees were old. They fruited for their old masters.

Teimaliki was now glowering at Diana from a huddle of wontoks, rubbing her arms. Nupanyi moved forward to guide them away, back towards Nandelli, and Tangypera manoeuvred himself into a position that suggested he, Tom and Diana were headed back to Ngarando. The crisis was ending. But before Teimaliki departed – all the way back to Honiara – she raised the stick and jabbed it once more into the ground, like a spear, causing Diana to brace herself to lunge again before Tom's troubled coughing stopped her.

'This island will be the death of me,' he said, unaware of what lay ahead still and what he'd live to see: failure of the latest airfield plans; destruction of most of their buildings by Cyclone Nina, and the death of their last boat, when secondary cancers had invaded his bowel and his mind sometimes felt as incontinent as his body. There were those among the Islanders who wouldn't be surprised that within four years, that body would lie where kumera had grown in time gone by, settling once and for all the future of Pigeon. Others would go to desperate lengths to ensure it never rested on the island at all.

25

Sunshine and Showers

TOM'S LAST LETTERS TO HIS SISTERS TELL HOW SUNSHINE PLAYING peekaboo between downpours on Pigeon made it hard to dry '*nappies*', handwashed by himself and pegged up close to his office, and how he had trouble pottering from his desk to Ngarando and back without stubbing his toes and reopening old sores which suppurated, as they always had, for weeks. Daily he sponged himself '*everywhere*' with Epsom salts to relieve prickly heat, and put a red dot in his diary when there was blood in the doubled trainer pants he stuffed with rags. '*I'm virtually deaf, my bowels are failing, I'm up every two hours all night and can't even remember to take a towel when I wash . . . Gawd!*' Discomforts of the flesh in old age are inevitable, but these erosive indignities were a sad denouement, and I preferred, when I visited Tom's grave, on which our kayaks rested, to think of him still at the helm of his life, a rare man who, after all, had at least in part achieved his dream. And I listened to Diana when she reminded me that the best moments are often fleeting, and that happiness can be the sum of small parts – as was the undeniable achievement of their marriage.

'He always said we were greatly diminished as individuals when we were apart.' I wished I'd seen them together, and she brought out picture after picture – Diana in 1952 tidying Tom's healthy sailor's thatch off Mangareva, love in her eyes, a joke in his; Diana cutting his hair again when he was old and grey on Pigeon in 1992, but the expressions the same; and Tom smiling, slightly self-conscious, slightly self-deprecating, with his arms round the waists of his all-girl crew. *Those* were the days to remember, for him. No ties but to the woman he loved, few money worries, because six months' worth of tins in the ship was all that was needed for a crew to live like sun kings and queens, and no end in sight to roving the bright Pacific. Landfall in 'Paradise' spelt – unknowably, to Tom – the beginning of downfall. Landfall and babies, both of which, so wondrous at first, had finally brought him more pain than joy. In the last days, some of his hope in Ross – once dismissed as '*the Black Sheep*' – revived. He was '*sterling*' during Cyclone Nina and its aftermath, and even hinted that one day, with his new Reef Island family, he might return to Pigeon if he was wanted there. Partially reinstated in the Will, he would be welcome, Tom assured him, but noted sadly that he seemed '*determined to remain Melanesian*', and Ross did not come back to Reefs to stay during his father's lifetime. Of Ben, Tom despaired. When those we've loved most let us down, we can't forgive them, but he wasn't cut out of the Will, for it was recognized that where Ben believed God provided, someone on earth must contribute as well if he were not to end up, in his earthly father's words, as '*truly a despised white pauper*'. Cryptically, and in pain, Tom watched Ben groping in the blue void for '*salvation*' and hoping, year after year, that the lovechild born of '*Sin*' would '*come back to Pigeon*' to be with him. In fact little Diane was afraid of her father's strangeness – or maybe just that he was white – for she was brought up some distance away, as an Islander.

'Look,' said Diana, when, after reading the last of Tom's diaries – broken off abruptly – I was deeply saddened, and she held out a cheeky photograph of Tom clasping a startled but delighted Diana from behind and planting a kiss deep in her grey topknot of hair. He was eighty-two. 'And we lay together during the cyclone, you know,' she said. That's all she said, but it said so much. Lay together. Fade to black. I promised Diana – and Tom, privately – that whatever else I found to write about Pigeon, I would celebrate their love.

Tasha stayed a month on Pigeon in 1999, chemically tamed of her once uncontrolled urges for arms around her, and not visibly in distress. Like her friends the Islanders, she stole a little – a vase from 'her' house, now occupied by me and the boys; store goods which had, daily, to be collected from under her pillow and returned – but there was more mischief than malice in her face when she was caught. I watched her stuff three pairs of nylon knickers, a bar of laundry soap and a handful of sweets down her bra one day when I was chatting to Pegi, and she turned round and twinkled at me before she left, arching her eyebrows playfully. 'Ooh she naughty,' said Pegi, but let her go. Soothed by the evidence she wasn't violent any more, the Islander women treated her kindly, like a child. The men avoided her.

'Tasha's like Solomon, isn't she?' observed Benji. 'Simple.'

Solomon, I now knew, tried it on with everything in a kalico, and seldom stopped grinning and flicking his tongue in and out like a gecko. I rolled the word 'simple' around in my mind, and it seemed not inaccurate. These children of the sun were pared down – or had never grown beyond – their most basic urges: to eat, copulate, sleep, defecate. Left alone – for it was not Kastom practice to taunt the 'different' – Solomon led a not unhappy life. But Tasha, because more hope had been invested in her and because physical misfortune had dogged her from babyhood, too, was tragic as a product of Paradise. She'd been simple as a child, but her later life and its effect on others were anything but. Nevertheless, if you blocked out the unrealized expectations of a European child, it was possible still to glimpse the not unhappy Islander side of Tasha, the little Eve splashing on the reef in the sun. The day before she left I passed her, sitting up to her waist in the sea with Pegi and a circle of sistas.

'Don't forget Mummy's expecting us for tea in ten minutes,' called her carer from the beach, proffering a towel, but Tasha just went on enjoying the warm water, eyes half closed, smiling.

Mangrove mud is repugnant or sensual dependent on mood. It is soft, semi-opaque and visceral to the touch – glorious or obscene. Today I wallowed through it because there's a dead whale where I usually swim at lunchtime, and I didn't feel like asking anyone to help carry my kayak down. No-one's ever refused, but sometimes I just don't feel like talking. Extraordinary how the Islanders seem to sense this: one day a lone fisherman met paddling through the silence will divert his course to chat; the next, he'll just lift his chin a centimetre to acknowledge my presence, and paddle on. I wish I could give out such waves as unconsciously – and inoffensively – back in Britain. I can't believe the bustle and stress that's seen as the norm there. Here, it seems mad. I won't think about it until I have to. Diana's right: joy is temporary by its nature, but maybe, since I get regular doses here, something lasting will have accumulated before I leave.

Before the reeking whale – torn at by seven shark, which the Islanders speared for their fins – blighted, like a grotesque new offering from Mohawk Bay, my favourite floating haunt, I'd taken to swimming to an islet even smaller than Temotulaki, on a rising tide. Only during the roughest kumberra was that rock obliterated, so I nestled amid its casual coating of white box-flowers with eyes closed, confidently, sensing the water rise and feeling the sun weigh down, until consciousness felt pressed to nothing between merging blues. Far away there was the rumble and hiss of spray at the Edge of the Reef where true deep began, but close to, all sound seemed swallowed by the weight of calm liquid welling slowly to meet equally silent and measureless sky. This was vanishing point for me, and I gave myself up to it, gratefully, as often as I could. '*Hold onto that ungraspable blue,*' I instructed myself, smiling at the contradiction, and hoped Benji and Joe, so often seen or heard 'living the moment' to the full, at football with friends under the palms; yelling as they spotted fish; tumbling joyously through waves; edging along branches for bunches of purple ngenumbla, were subconsciously gathering a store of sweet memories too – which would always be there somewhere inside them, waiting to be tapped.

But Pigeon had never been only a *Boys' Own* wonderland, and just a month before we were due to leave we were reminded – this time not through history, but in the present – that remoteness may sometimes feel blissful but has its frightening side too. I was working quietly, towards the end of the afternoon, when a sharp thud followed by a terrified, wobbling scream made me leap up. Benji.

I hadn't even known he was there. So often the children didn't bother to drop in at all after school, but ran, swam or kayaked straight out with friends, and I didn't see them until nightfall. But today Benji had popped to Tasha's to open a coconut because he was thirsty, and, with a machete specially sharpened ready for Tangypera as an advance parting gift, had opened not the coconut but his hand.

'*Ahhhhhhhh!*' He shook all over as he screamed.

His hand was so small and there was such a lot of blood welling, I couldn't see properly what he'd done. Luckily Joe was in sight, preparing, with a group of cronies, to dare-dive off Pigeon's southern end. I sent him for Mhairi, who had first-aid training. Patteson, Benji's best friend, stared huge-eyed as I tried to wash the cut and Benji, collapsed on a stool overlooking coolly puffing Tinakula, howled more. Mhairi was there in moments, but shook her head. The machete had sliced deep between thumb and forefinger, possibly catching a tendon or an artery. It was a needle and thread job – preferably for someone who knew what they were doing. We had stitches but not sufficient expertise.

'I think we should get him to Manuopo, Lucy.' Some four miles away, with the light fading, and at low tide. 'But let's try to stop that bleeding first.'

Mhairi's was a soothing presence, and as she worked, binding up the whole hand with strips of gauze then cleverly making a sling to hold the arm up, and I held him, Benji began to calm.

'Will we really go to Manuopo now?'

I was about to say we'd try, but Ross, whom Patteson, unasked, had fetched as soon as he heard the plan, was suddenly there smiling down straight into Benji's eyes.

'Yes, we will. And you'll have place of honour, travelling with me.'

Patteson, aged nine, walked beside Ross, holding his friend's good hand as he was carried through the island to where dugouts were drawn up at the eastern end. Laloa lugged my kayak.

'You're even going to get starlight,' said Ross, and Benji almost smiled. 'I'll point out the Plough upside-down.'

It was dark by the time we'd passed Nandelli and were heading round Mohawk Bay towards the long, still passage through the mangroves that led, eventually, to Manuopo. Mhairi had come too, paddling Joe's white kayak, but we floundered in comparison to Ross, whose large dugout, with Benji propped in the prow on kalicos supplied by Pegi, sped ahead. As the lapping of open sea receded and the silence of the mangroves closed round us, I could hear Ross's voice, ever steady, telling Benji about the stars, and the time he'd paddled his dadi to Manuopo when he'd nearly cut his finger off with the Flymo. Benji's voice, piping back questions from time to time, reassured me.

'Oh my, I'm all over the shop,' said Mhairi, as she mispaddled into a tangle of mangroves at one point, and stiff grey fingers dangling above quested for root space in her hair.

'Are you all right?'

Our voices were small in the stillness; the faintly gleaming water and irregularly speckled sky huge.

'Och, I'm fine. Don't let me hold you up.'

'Come out of the bushes, you two bad women!' came Ross's voice, not small, and we hurried on. No-one said it, but we hurried because we didn't know what was going on under the bandage; how much blood Benji had lost. It grew so shallow we had to walk, each footfall softly sucked. Only Benji still rode, Ross by his side tugging the dugout by the prow. This was the journey he'd made so many times when Christine, his governess, had been lost. To and fro twice a day, when barely Benji's age. Clawing mangroves in the dark held no fears for him, and the warm mud that kissed his feet then farted them out was as much a component of home, for him, as the sun. Home for Ross, unlike for Ben, maybe, extended beyond Pigeon to encompass all of Reefs – the dark, damp islands, and those like Matema whose skirt of sand was so whitened by exposure to constant sun, it dazzled. He was a man of both the solwata (sea) and the bush. No wonder he'd been elected president in 1997.

At last, the broad stretch like a river that told me Manuopo was near appeared, but there were no lights along it except from cooking fires and the odd coconut-fibre torch. If we did find anyone at the clinic – so mocked by Tom in his diary – would Benji have to be stitched by torchlight?

'Don't worry,' said Ross, reading my thoughts, 'they're just saving power. The cargo boat's so late this time, diesel for the generator's short. I've lent them some of ours before now. Don't tell Mum!'

As we drew into shore, a barefoot girl, eyes luminous, hair like a cloud, held a torch to light the path.

'Ah,' said Ross to Benji, 'you have friends in high places. Patteson's dadi has already sent word.' The girl led us forward to the jumble of cement cubes that was the nearest thing to a hospital in Reefs. 'You should have seen it in Mum's day,' said Ross. 'I've seen pictures. No cement then, just a hut where people came to get their yaws jabs – those that could walk. Believe it or not, there have been some improvements in Outer Island services – though there's still no doctor, of course.'

'No doctor?' queried Benji.

'There's Titus,' Ross said – 'if we're lucky.'

Benji was collected enough to walk, clasping Ross's hand, up the rickety wooden steps leading to the only source of light apart from the girl's torch – a hurricane lamp hanging from the end of a narrow bed off which seven women, perched like birds, visiting a wontok, jumped guiltily as we approached. Ross joshed them, and there was laughter while swift feet ran in four directions to search out Titus. 'Lukluk smolfela whiteman!' came whispers, and Ross filled in details for the curious. Benji's bandage was darkly stained, but not dripping. Then across the dark courtyard, barefoot, came our nurse, rumpled from a nap, in a sweaty T-shirt, but with a face I trusted at once.

'Wissway iufela kutim han' and livim coc'nut?!' he teased Benji gently. (How come you cut your hand and not the coconut?)

'Trae hariap tumas,' Benji responded (I was in too much of a hurry) and allowed his wound to be exposed. Here, my head swam. Part of the inside of Benji's hand had pushed out so there was something like a pouting mouth steadily dribbling blood where the blade had gone in.

'Thass oraet,' said Titus, crossing easily into English, but looked worried after he'd poked in a cupboard for a while and emerged with nothing but a dusty parcel which he explained was his sole emergency pack and *might* contain stitches. Mhairi and I smiled with relief and produced our own – and Boots the Chemists antiseptic wipes which Titus thought very neat. An order was given and somewhere outside a small generator rumbled into life, lighting a white bulb overhead which lent a theatrical effect for the crowd of onlookers, whom Titus gently shooed away. Ross held Benji tightly while the 'mouth' in his hand was pushed shut, and large stitches sewn across it, finished by what looked like fisherman's knots. Mhairi made a perfect bandage, and we headed once more into the warm night, its blackness now thickly dredged with stars Ross said were too crowded for him to disentangle. 'Dad knew them all,' he said, 'but I don't remember him teaching us much.' I thought of Tom, struggling with the illnesses of his later years, as Manuopo closed behind us, when the generator went off, as though curtains had been drawn on a play. I'd promised to bring Titus all our medical gear before we left, for they seemed to have little but kindness and old dressings there – and a paper mobile, twirling limply in the humid air, that read: 'Wash Hand, Wash Mouth, Wash Bum'.*

*

---

* In recent years Outer Island clinics have been equipped with medical basics, but supplies still reach them only irregularly.

Days after this, typically, a cargo boat brought goods ordered four months earlier, only weeks before the end of our stay. It hadn't mattered; we always had fish and fruit, but it reminded me why Tom's days had so often been dominated by irate letter-writing as he chased supplies for the store. While we could happily live on what was available locally, PIT depended on goods from the Outside World.

'This is the boat my father made his last journey on,' said Ross as, outboard switched off, we glided to its side through the usual excited throng of piccaninnis in dugouts, and women, kalicos stacked three feet high on their heads, holding out wiry arms for more that were being lowered down the rusty walls of the hull and passed from hand to hand, dugout to dugout, along with hens, sacks of Sunshine milk, taro and clusters of spear rubbers. The heat and the odour of foodstuffs, livestock and closely clustered bodies on the water were nothing compared to the atmosphere on board, where the sick and healthy spread their limbs side by side at night, and sat propped back to back by day, those unable to find shade shrouded with kalicos against the glare.

'They hauled him up the side using one of Mum's loungers as a stretcher,' Ross said, but he had heard this only by bush grapevine. He'd been in Honiara trying to arrange immediate medical aid that end. 'Ben said everyone stared.'

Tom had been livid when everyone stared at Tasha when he'd travelled with her through the Solomons en route to New Zealand in 1983. '*I wanted to shoot the lot of them.*'

'Was he very sick by then?'

'He was dying. A four-day trip for him in that state must have been torture. I thought he *was* dead when I finally saw him in Honiara. Talk to you later.'

Ross clambered aboard at this point to search for the PIT mailbag. I didn't especially look forward to mail, not wanting to be reminded about the Outside World until I had to face it again – but I knew Peter and Mhairi did. Her mother sent food parcels; his, copies of the *Beano* and the *Scotsman*. I loved their 'normality'. But this time I had a nice surprise: kind responses to 'Pigeon Post' and a copy of the recently reissued *Castaway*. It was difficult to see which seemed the weirder venture at this stage: the fantastically irresponsible year on Tuin, when I'd nearly died, or this year on Pigeon, which I'd thought would be so much safer and more light-hearted. It wasn't safe but, for the boys at least, it had been for the most part light-hearted, and I'd never regret bringing them. Like me, they'd always know now there's nothing like getting down to basics to make one realize just how good life is.

This was Diana's contention too. The war, she said, had made people reappraise their lives – just to *be* alive was something to celebrate. But for her, contrasts were, above all, the key. 'People have forgotten the value of struggle,' she said. Pleasure, for her, meant pinpointing an aim – whether it was making a cupboard or building a home on an island from scratch – then not stopping until she'd achieved it. But during her struggles, often prolonged, she experienced the small comforts she allowed herself as real luxuries. Once I shared a bar of scented soap with her, and her eyes lit up with glee. 'Today's youngsters simply don't know how lucky they are. They think goods and services are theirs by right.' This sounded stereotypical, but coming from her, with her history, I could see the truth of it. We agreed that a number of people might benefit from being dumped on desert islands for a spell. '*Excuse my latent Fascism*,' Tom, who had strong feelings about '*wastrels and scoundrels*', once wrote to his sisters when he'd ridiculed a proposal in the 1980s that Pigeon be turned into a philanthropic drug rehabilitation centre. '*All my life I've been against war, but if these spoilt brats are the result of Peace, for God's sake let's send them off to be shot somewhere.*'

The evening after the boat came in, when the usual partying was over, I sat with Ross on the veranda of the units overlooking Mohawk Bay, and he spoke of his father's death.

'Mum travelled with Dad on the boat. She didn't know the cancer had come back until a medic let it slip on the radio, then she was mad as hell. She'd thought, when he began to shake and sweat, it was one of his malaria bouts.'

I visualized Diana on the radio, Tom in pain on his bed beside her, desperately trying to organize transport. Santa Cruz hospital was no good, the doctor said, it would have to be Honiara, and then onwards for surgery to 'somewhere with better facilities'. Diana knew Tom would most like to go to Britain, so that's what she planned.

'But those four days at sea did for him,' said Ross. 'It was madness. He should have got out months before, by plane from Santa Cruz. I wish I'd been here. Mum thinks everyone's as strong as her, but they're not.'

I thought it a strong decision of Tom's not to tell Diana of his condition, because treatment at an earlier stage would inevitably have meant his absence from Pigeon – possibly for ever – which she'd hate. That was the strength of his love.

Ross was distressed now.

'When I saw him at the wharf . . .'

So often in his diary after a boat trip in later years, Tom had written: '*Felt D.O.A.*' Dead on arrival.

'. . . there was no bloody ambulance, just the nurses' bus, which he was too sick to sit up in . . . and when we finally got him to hospital there was no bloody doctor for ten hours.'

There were tears in Ross's eyes, but he laughed suddenly.

'Mum got so mad she ripped down curtains to put over him because no-one brought a blanket and he was shivering . . . When he came to once, he asked for some apple juice.'

Apples, something English you couldn't get on Pigeon.

'. . . but there was none anywhere. I nicked my boss's truck to try to find some, but there was only this passionfruit shit . . .'

He now wept openly.

'Dad choked on it. Mum was feeding it to him in a cup and he . . . died. Apple juice would have been better . . .'

I put my hand on Ross's back and massaged gently, as he'd done to me when I was upset about Benji, and as Islanders did to comfort one another.

'Lucy? It sounds crazy, but even though I don't think I *liked* my dad very much, I loved him. Can you understand that?'

'Certainly,' I said. 'I feel the same about my own.'

Over the next few days, from Ross, from Ben and from the Islanders, I pieced together the story of the fight over Tom's body that followed his death. For although he might, at last, have felt released from what he'd once described as '*the chains of Pigeon*', the Islanders still had unfinished business with him.

26

Burial

BODIES HAVE TRADITIONALLY BORNE MESSAGES IN THE SOLOMONS. IN
1871, the women of Nukapu, tired of having young men recruited for
plantation work by other whites, then not returned, chose that of John
Coleridge Patteson, first Bishop of Melanesia, to bear notice of their
displeasure to Queen Victoria. On anchoring off Nukapu, the bishop,
with no intention but the gentle onward passage of Christianity in
mind, described it lyrically as '*a palm-covered fleck of sand*'. It's one of
the most isolated islands in Reefs, but Patteson's reputation as a wise
Bigman of his tribe, surprisingly open to discussion of Kastom, had
preceded him, and his death on shore was more calculated than
vicious, coming swiftly from behind with a mallet used for beating
barkcloth.* Other members of the mission party, some wounded, fled
to their mother ship, where arrows tipped with human bone were
removed, and the poison, as far as possible, scraped out. Back on
shore, the women hurried to complete their plan before the *Southern
Cross* disappeared. Patteson was stripped of all but his shoes, and laid
on a fresh leaf mat – a sign of respect. Five young men had been taken
from Nukapu by European marauders, so four further wounds were

---

* A younger relative of the poet Samuel Taylor Coleridge, Patteson, who spoke twenty-three
languages, had made considerable headway in communications with Islanders elsewhere, before his
demise.

added to the body and – in case the white chieftainess still didn't get the message – a palm leaf with five knots in it placed on his chest. A second leaf mat on top completed the parcel, tied with twine at head and feet, which was towed in an outrigger canoe by the mothers and wives of the stolen youths until it was close enough to be pushed out on a current to the ship.

How this message was read back in Britain is another story – later many piccaninnis were named after Patteson – but a belief remained in Reef Islands that a corpse had power to convey meaning, so that what happened to Tom Hepworth's body was crucial to those with a claim on the island he'd 'ruled' so long. In crude terms, if a body was buried on disputed land, it strengthened the claims of the dead man's wontoks; if it was kept away, their claims were weakened. Word flew around the islands when the sick man was seen departing Pigeon. Those who'd studied Tom's face as he was rowed, prostrate, from the shore, then winched up the side of the ship in Mohawk Bay, knew he'd never come back alive. A lot of them didn't want him back dead either. Especially not dead, for that meant for ever.

Ben had been based back on Pigeon since his dreamy two-year exile to New Zealand and his brief stay in America. He sometimes saw Sipikoli, sometimes didn't, and Tom, as his last illness took over, gave up trying to figure out if '*anything was going on*' but dreaded Sipikoli's appearance, as it seemed to increase the '*disturbance*' that manifested itself more peacefully since the trip away, but was still evident in this once prized son. Video sessions, treasured by Tom, were hijacked by '*Ben's people*' who stood in tropical deluges to watch Robert Powell crucified as Jesus of Nazareth. Ben had also taken to evangelizing; Tom once overheard him on the radio asking a stranger in Raratonga if he'd heard the word of God. '*He is improved,*' Tom wrote, '*but – patchy. We can't see him ever getting to grips with the business properly without support.*' Temporary partner-managers for PIT came and went, as ever – one commenting how startling it was for the odd guests there were, to be picked up by '*someone like that*' and given a sermon instead of sustenance and life jackets on their hazardous journey out. But Ben did try. 'God needs good managers for his gifts,' he was heard saying, and he did his best to be one. Knowing that better communications were vital to Pigeon if it were ever to take off as a holiday destination, he wrote to an official in the Solomon Islands postal department, listing numerous delays in the passage of mail to Reefs from Honiara. Incensed by criticism from a European dismissed locally as 'lelebet krangge', the official poured scorn on Ben's already bowed head: '*You think I need be told my job by a ningnong like you? You make too much noise. I suggest is better for you to sit and have nice cold coffee rather than confusing yourself with our work. Let us do that service for you. WE DON'T NEED UNSATISFYING CREATURES IN THIS PROVINCE.*'

Bopali, years before, was one of the few Islanders to have written so brazenly to Tom – but no words of his contained the element of derision in those received by Ben. Tom may not have been liked by all, but he was not despised. What did Ben feel, waiting alone on Pigeon in 1994 after his dying father left the island, when word went out to form a front against his return? But by then Ben had become an expert in not feeling. Only Matoko, his ever faithful diving partner despite the trouble with Diana over Teimaliki's attempt to plant kumera, sensed some deepening of sorrow in him – and Matoko was to be key in the events that followed.

Diana sat alone with Tom for a space after he'd died, then was joined by the Honourable Horace Leingalu, now a close friend of Ross's and a man who, as a Reef Islander but also a businessman and politician, was in a good position to see all the implications ahead. It behoved him, as a Bigman from Reefs, to assist the widow of another Bigman there, and however Tom had set himself apart from Kastom and behaved unlike other Bigmen, that was how he was viewed.

'Where would you like your husband buried?'

Diana, calm, for her grief had not yet welled, said she didn't mind. She planned not to go straight home but to travel on, as she'd hoped to with Tom.

'I advise you to bury Captain Tom on Pigeon Island.'

'On Pigeon? Really, I don't know,' said Diana, suddenly exhausted, 'you must ask Ross,' and she went away to telephone Amalie in the US, someone with whom she could allow herself, just a little, to weep as she gave the news.

Ross, as was fitting both in European and in Reef Island custom, now took the chair by his father's body, his friend beside him.

'I'll book him onto a plane tomorrow,' he said, for he understood some, if not all, of the importance of the place of burial. But when Ross called the airline, he found all places taken for the next fortnight.

This was not unusual; it was a small plane and there were only two flights a week to Santa Cruz, but Horace had clout: some of the passengers would be paying only a part fare, to Kira Kira; a word in the right ear should get them off. But it didn't. Sorry, no places at all, let alone four free seats that would allow a body to lie flat. Tom was in the mortuary now, but burial, in a hot climate, is best done promptly.

'OK, we'll go by boat then,' said Ross.

'Sorry. No seats.'

'We don't need a seat. He can lie in the aisle.'

'Not allowed.'

'Rubas (rubbish), everyone sleeps in the aisle!'

'Sorry.'

'On deck then. I have to get my father home . . .'

'We cannot take your father.' And the phone went down.

Ross had been dealing with cargo vessels visiting Mohawk Bay for years.

'It's crazy! This never happens!'

Horace, who had wontoks everywhere, then visited a few offices himself and found out what was going on. Every carrier between Honiara and Reef Islands had received threats. If Captain Hepworth's body was taken on board either a plane or a ship, 'certain people' would not be responsible for the consequences.

'You mean the landowners are ganging up?' Ross, a Solomon Islander but also Tom's son, felt incredulous at the extent of this power display – then nauseous, because if they refused his father's body, they were, in effect, also denying him and his children any part in Pigeon after the lease ran out. No-one considered involving the police – who doubtless knew already what was going on. This was purely a Kastom issue.

Horace had already seen the makings of a politician in Ross, and the advantages for Reef Islands this could mean. A white man who could communicate with whites but who also understood – and followed – Kastom could be immensely useful.

'If you don't act now, you can forget Pigeon for the future.'

'I'll do it,' stated Ross quietly, 'if it's the last thing I do.'

Diana had gone by then, unable to bear the wrangling, flying to those who'd sailed with Tom, whom he'd loved. He was with her wherever she went anyway. All this Kastom business was irrelevant.

'OK,' said Horace and, recognizing there was a time factor involved, arranged to have Tom embalmed, wearing a suit Diana had packed for him to use in London.

The block on all public transport remained, and while Horace sought to trace the ringleaders, to bend them to his way of thinking, Ross, for the first time in years, donned the useful guise of a European wanting only to do 'the right thing' – in this case get his deceased father to his last resting place – and made the rounds of every high commission in Honiara, until he struck lucky with the New Zealanders. They had an army transport plane available and were pleased to assist in this humanitarian act. But Ross and Horace knew trouble wouldn't stop at Santa Cruz. Everything had to be arranged in secret – and they had to get a representative working for them on the ground. Ross saw this as a stumbling block; people would be afraid. But Horace had already been thinking things through.

'Bopali.'

'But he's Dad's old enemy!'

'Bopali is in favour of what's good for the people – and you're going to be good for the people.'

'I am?'

'Yes.'

Out in Reefs, Bopali, now grey himself and semi-retired from politics, was planted like a mole. He began popping up casually in meetings of elders and slipping in the odd point about the potential loss to Reef Islands if Ross, who'd proved such a friend to Islanders, were shown disrespect. Look at all the feasts he'd given, and his generosity with fish caught from his motorized canoe; look at how he kept open house in Honiara. It's true he'd had trouble with one wife – and not been judged to handle it well – but she was still a Nandelli woman which gave her children the same claims on Pigeon land as her, and although she'd been dissuaded from planting there now, that was only because the *old* Hepworths were in residence. Ross was different, wasn't he – and these were his children, too. In fact, his *two* marriages to Nandelli women (for Ross had married Pegi by now) meant a substantial number of wontoks could benefit eventually from the wealth of PIT – if Ross were not insulted by a refusal to grant his wishes for his father's burial. Insult carries heavy meaning in Reef Islands, and some old men who'd been muttering ominously through their betel about Bopali's attitude to this perfect opportunity to 'pay back' Cap'n Tom looked at him anew. If Ross's *children* in the future took this as an insult, the Islanders could have a 'pay back' war on their hands into perpetuity. It would be a question endlessly discussed in the Sapulo, and who knows, these children might grow into powerful men. Bopali made some headway, but a number of individuals – each with his own circle of wontoks – kept their eyes blank and chins jutted away. *They*, they felt, had been on the receiving end of un-numbered insults from the Hepworth seniors over the years. Why should they show the smallest magnanimity now? It was touch and go what would happen if Tom's body reappeared in Mohawk Bay and an attempt were made to land it on Pigeon. But Ross decided to take the risk.

In silky darkness filled with the sound of crickets, two weeks after his death Tom's body was unloaded from the army plane on Santa Cruz and carried in silence to a waiting canoe. Carefully, Ross covered the coffin – lid not yet sealed – with a tarpaulin, slept a little close by, then set off on a full tide for Reefs, three hours before dawn.

'Harry flatters,' (flat calm) said Ross to his dad – an expression Tom had used. 'No worries.'

Ben was sleeping when, a dot on the horizon in pre-dawn pallor, the canoe was first spotted, but Matoko, on Nandelli, was not. The woman who'd seen it – leaving her hut for a pee – whispered the news to her husband, and he roused a wontok who immediately blew a Boo shell loud enough to be picked up as far away as Nenumbo, with others taken up all over Reefs. As Nandelli people, kalicos round their shoulders, collected sleepily on the point, Matoko, in a loincloth, slid into the channel and across, causing not a ripple, to emerge hidden among the roots of the great liana-strangled tree close to the store on Pigeon. Those who'd chosen still to use them were stirring in the labour huts, and a pair of lovers on Poppet Island, who'd planned to part before sunrise, clutched each other in panic for a moment before taking advantage of the excitement across the way to slip round opposite sides of Pigeon and so appear separately from the water the other end, as if taking an early bath.

Now Ross was close enough for the noise of his outboard to drown the more distant Boo calls, but by then word was already well spread, dugouts were being launched as far away as Otambe, and on their way from Nola. The Nenumbans were abreast of Temotulaki, and in force.

One of their chiefs had a particular grudge against Tom, who'd relegated his restrained diatribes regarding pay for casual labour on Pigeon to a file marked 'Curiosities', and not bothered to reply. Bopali joined the Nola contingent, beside old Nupanyi.

Ross was heading into the dawn, which, flaring to hot pink over Nandelli, cast the gathering flotillas into silhouette. Lorikeets made their morning fuss in a black mesh of treetops. He kept his gaze ahead steady, standing up to steer the boat from the stern, and murmured: 'Nearly there, Dad.' To the Islanders, the coffin was invisible under baskets of cassava draped with betel, but somehow it was known Tom was there. The betel was in fact a clever sign. Nobody had sent word to Santa Cruz for betel in such quantity: Ross, who didn't use it himself, was bringing it to Reefs as a gift.

'Ey!' came a deep voice from the Nola group, positioned in such a way to the west of Nandelli channel that a mere paddle stroke from each dugout would close the formation into a line across the entrance with the now arrived Nenumbans. The people of Nandelli held the centre of the channel, treading water with their paddles.

'Ey!' returned Ross, slowing down momentarily to direct his bow into the coral path that would take him straight into Pigeon's sand beach, but giving no impression of acknowledging any obstacle to his passage.

'Go wea?' called another voice, more blatantly challenging.

'Iu savvy gud,' called Ross. (You know where I'm going.) And when he was abreast of the spread-out line, he shouted three times, for the three main contingents, in Pijin: 'Who will sit up with me tonight?' Meaning who would mourn with him. Nothing moved but the feathering paddles in the centre of the channel; no-one spoke and faces were wiped of expression. On Pigeon, Ben stood on the northern promontory, rubbing his eyes. Matoko ran silently to him and shook his arm. 'Dadi b'long iu kambaek. Hao iu no pray?' (Your father's come back. Why aren't you praying?) Matoko was not a devout convert but he acknowledged the formalities of Christianity, and couldn't understand his friend's failure to call on his god at such a time. Facing square on to the Nandelli phalanx now – the lines behind him closed – Ross slowed the canoe to a chug.

'Dadi b'long mi dae finis!' he yelled, and couldn't keep the grief out of his voice when he had to yell it again against the wall of empty faces, this time striking his chest as well. 'Dadi b'long mi!'

Hands trembling on the engine but carriage still proud, he swerved just before hitting the front dugout, and revved hard so the canoe crunched solidly above the tide line, onto Pigeon land. The Nola and Nenumbo people formed loose ranks with their Nandelli neighbours, and others from Otambe, Otelo and Manuopo glided in to join them. Everybody watched Ross, and Bopali, slightly separating himself from the Nola group, tensed in every muscle as he waited for signs to indicate the way things would go. Ross was wearing his favourite cap, with Porsche in racy letters on it. Stepping out of the canoe into the water but staying close, he flung the cap among the heaped baskets, scratched his head furiously, then opened his hands in a broad gesture.

'Mifela gohed fo berem Dadi b'long mi tumoro. Kaikai afta. Evri nara fela lanona welkam.'

This was unexpected, and some of those still steadying their dugouts against the current in the channel faltered briefly in their feathering as they took it in. Ross was inviting all the 'other' landowners – implying he was one also – to attend the burial of his father, with a feast to follow. Bopali's head was up like a dog's questing for reactions – but all at once there was activity on land. Matoko, leaping down from the promontory where Ben still surveyed the scene, positioned himself with legs wide for balance on Diana's seawall, single eye glinting and hair still wet from his swim spreading shining droplets as he jerked his chin around.

'Ey!' he cried. 'Bokis heviwan. Sapos samfela helpim?' (Hey, the box is heavy. How about some help?) And with that he jumped to Ross's side, tied the bow rope of the canoe to a tree and started lifting baskets off the coffin.

'Ben!' called Ross, looking up at the pale figure of his twin, which began slowly to drift towards them. Bopali then arrowed forward decisively, followed by Nupanyi and a small group of his wontoks who pulled up their dugouts and helped unload the canoe. Significantly, and so everyone had a good view, Bopali lifted the most mountainously piled basket, dripping with green beads of betel, onto his head, turned his back on the crowd and walked up to place it under the veranda of the old cargo-shed house. But some of the Nandelli crowd, unpersuaded, beat their paddles angrily on the water with knit brows. At this, Matoko exploded – for among them were relatives of his. He harangued them from waist deep in the water now, his words coming shrilly in a stream. This was Ross, not his mother, didn't they see? And didn't they want a feast? Couldn't they see all the good things brought in the canoe from Santa Cruz? Becoming in-articulate with frustration – for Matoko knew he might have put his foot in it – he spat to one side, then shrugged, torn, for his own father was glaring at him. One thing at least, in the canoe, was not con-sidered 'good' by some. Now Bopali, sensing a crisis, touched Ross's arm. 'We must get Cap'n Tom indoors, quickly,' he said, and organized four men – among them Nupanyi – to scoop the coffin out of the canoe, still draped with the old tarpaulin. One of the men was of a slight build and when wading out of the water he slipped, so the coffin tipped to one side – but was righted. Paddles thundered on the surface of the sea now – the racket swelled by Nenumbans. 'You must speak,' Bopali advised urgently.

'Plis!' cried Ross, initially at a loss but with words coming suddenly as all his personal longings and grief and dawning beliefs welled into one clear message. 'Hao nao faet?! (Why fight?) Mifela b'long Rif Aelan! (I'm a Reef Islander.) Dis Aelan hia b'long *iumi*!' (This island belongs to *all of us*.) Bopali smiled encouragingly. Already the beating paddles were quieter because people wanted to hear. 'Piccaninni b'long iumi olsem, (our children are all the same) Rif Aelan pipol. *Pigeon Aelan b'long iumi!'*

'Ah-ahh!' Matoko roared, a lone voice, but one that brought immediate echoes from all but a few of the women present, who didn't want a fight, and a number of the men.

'Ah-ahhh!'

'B'long iumi!' shouted Ross again and again, gathering more response every time until he sensed – a natural politician – that the majority of the crowd were with him. It was fully light now, and as the final consensus roar rose from the water, fading up like prayer into the fresh blue day, Ross asked again who was going to sit with him to mourn. Once more, there was silence, then the reedy voice of one of the oldest men present floated from the furthest reaches of the Nandelli ranks, over the water, to land:

'Evrifela!'

Now paddles were raised in the air and shaken for joy and many – the majority – cheered, smiles at last bursting from the restrained faces.

Shunning the 'heathen' night of mourning that followed a busy day of hen plucking and umu building, Ben dug his father's grave quietly, by lamplight, with help from Nupanyi, who knew where the ground was deep enough. Stasi, the young Rottweiler, had to be chained up because she kept trying to join in the digging.

'Sore tumas,' (sorry) said Nupanyi from time to time, brushing away what might have been sweat or a tear as they worked. It was a hot night and Ben sweated too. As a young man, Nupanyi had enjoyed being the most trusted member of the *Arthur Rogers* crew, and Cap'n Tom was always fair with rations. They'd eaten more tinned meat on one fortnight's trip to Vanikoro than in their whole lives before.

'We will build a shelter for your father,' he told Ben in Pijin, 'so he won't be troubled by the wind.'

'That's not Christian,' said Ben reprovingly. 'My family will order a headstone.'

'Yes,' said Nupanyi, but it was confusing. Ross's speech had suggested they were all part of the same Reef Island family, and Nupanyi felt this, in Kastom terms, to be essentially correct, now that Ross had Reef Island piccaninnis. They would build a leaf shelter big enough to fit a headstone inside.

In the morning, the coffin, which had lain open on one of Diana's hand-built dining tables in the cargo-shed house all night, was closed and carried to the waiting grave. Most of the crowd who'd been there to 'welcome' it the previous dawn followed, so that the lawn and West Patio and the area before the schoolhouse were packed solid with Islanders. A brief prayer was volunteered by a local catechist, then Ross, tan yellowed by exhaustion but in command of himself, reiterated his words of the day before, and added: 'The presence of my father's body here lays to rest with it all the troubles that have gone before. No more need for anger or vengeance. This earth I throw down represents land belonging to all of us Reef Islanders to pass down, as is right, in Kastom.' He said it one more time before stepping back to let others shovel in earth: *B'long iumi.**

Diana, returning some months later to Pigeon, while Ross was absent winding things down in Honiara in preparation for a more permanent

---

* I was given more than a dozen versions of these events, some no doubt embellished. But all agreed it was a critical day in Pigeon's history, and that Ross emerged as a fully fledged Bigman.

stay in Reefs, found the proximity of Tom's grave surprisingly comforting. Like Ben, but for different reasons, she couldn't bring herself
to admire the leaf shelter built over it at once, but found that, more
and more, her gaze strayed towards the diminutive structure first thing
in the morning when she rose, and at night before she slept. And as
she had when she was a young woman and he was absent – but not
permanently then – she addressed Tom directly in her diary once
more.

'*Darling, I'm so upset, they've cut back the* one *bush that had grown back
after the cyclone where I do my exercises. It'll take years to come up again . . .
Ross seems to be taking his politics seriously, and Pegi and the children have
settled well, though still far too many wontoks in the store . . . Lanebu comes
from Nenumbo most days and today helped tidy your office. I'd forgotten how
many drawers I'd put in. White ants a problem as usual, but I've put all your
notebooks away safely and plastic wrapped a big file marked Archives.*'

Diana had made over three hundred drawers on Pigeon Island by
1999. And by 1994, when he died, Tom had collected over a dozen
boxes, suitcases and files full of archives, logs, diaries and photographs.
A final letter to the interested London publisher in 1994 read: '*Hello,
remember me, that man on an island? The book we discussed is either still
gestating or has died.*' But Diana was determined Tom's story would not
die, and in 1996 told him in her diary: '*I'm in touch with a woman who
has some experience of remote islands and has already written two books. I
shall see her when I'm travelling with Ben next year . . .*'

27

Final Farewells

'*GECKO SHIT ON MY TOSHIBA AGAIN.*'

There were times when Tom and I wrote the same things in our diaries, only mine was kept on a Compaq laptop and the keyboard clogged with coconut too. Would all the impressions I'd crammed on it survive the halfway-round-the-world journey home – starting with the dreaded canoe trip? And how would I pack efficiently after conveniently forgetting paraphernalia for so long, or organize my happily 'gone native' sons into a frame of mind suitable for readjustment to 'civilization'; how prepare myself? What I shrank from most was making concessions to the Outside World's requirement for image – that version of self reinvented daily in any more social setting than a desert island. Just as on Tuin eighteen years ago, I had revelled in doing without all that on Pigeon. Too easy to say carry on, don't go back to wearing masks and borrowed attitudes, but in the Outside World one has to dress in more than a strip of kalico, and I'd no longer be able to rely on the sun as my sole cosmetic, stress cure, pain reliever, even lover . . . Yes, life on a remote island had drawbacks in the long term, but I also shared Diana's view that much of the time, and certainly in a material sense, it *was* simpler. Determined at least to start as pared down as possible, I began, a fortnight before we left, giving away everything that had value here – ant-proof Tupperware; candles, knives, books – even if they were only used by adults for rolling tobacco – and offered Diana the Missionary Kit solar lantern I'd had shipped out, which I knew she admired.

'I'll just look after it for you until you come back.'

'But I . . .'

'One winter in Britain will be enough, you'll see, and I'll repaint the house while you're away.'

I didn't know what to say. Those words she'd written to a friend: '*She's become like the daughter I lost*,' haunted me as, pretending to be brisk, I took out a notebook and checked technical details about the *Arthur Rogers*. Diana mentioned, before I headed off to see Peter and Mhairi, that Ben was keen to show me where there'd once been plans for a restaurant. This was scheduled for Sunday after he came back from church, but I wondered if it was really Ben who was keen, or Diana, still investing hope in Pigeon and her progeny after all these years; still, despite all, an optimist.

Peter planned to keep the school operational to the last minute. He and Mhairi were leaving a few days after us, and he was preparing reports on each Islander pupil for the teacher to take his place.

'Only problem is, there isn't one yet,' he said wryly, turning to tidy the now impressive little library used enthusiastically by Joe, Benji and local piccaninnis alike. 'Family politics again, I'm afraid. Diana says it's Ross's responsibility to fly out a new teacher; Ross says it's his mum's . . . But you know what it's like, Lucy – you can't get involved.'

I did know. Tiny though it was – because it was tiny – one had to stand back from what went on between the two very different ends of Pigeon. But my heart went out to Peter. He'd brought energy and dedication to his job which had rubbed off on the pupils, and achieved considerable results with Ngive, Elisha, Patteson and Simon Boga, all at first too shy to speak. And he wanted the good work to go on.

'But Diana kept hoping we'd stay a second year, too,' said Mhairi. 'I feel terrible about it but – one's enough.'

I nodded. Apprehensive as I was about facing the Outside World, I was ready to leave too, albeit for different reasons. Much as I liked them, I'd had to maintain a distance from Peter and Mhairi as well as the Hepworths. I was here on a job requiring as much objectivity as I could bring to it, and, just as I couldn't afford to let my hair down with Ross – and must keep my thoughts about Ben private – it would be fatal to relax in the schoolhouse, too. The Hepworths' history was littered with failed relationships with other whites as well as their neighbours; almost without exception partners, carers and temporary managers had come under suspicion, and I knew I must be seen to be alone; must join no enclaves. Only Islanders taking the sea route silently to Tasha's House were the exception to my hermit rules, although it was generally I who sought them out. By the twelfth month, however, when pressure to gather information was heightened by shrinking time, this constant distancing had become something of a burden. I was nervous of the Outside World, but wanted a break from Pigeon's peculiar intensity, too.

'It isn't that we haven't enjoyed it here,' said Mhairi. 'It's been amazing, but we're just' – here she broke off helplessly, then burst out – 'ready for some normality!'

I understood. This well-balanced and not ungregarious couple craved a return to freedoms which 'Paradise' couldn't offer.

'I want to fill a trolley in Safeway!' she cried, making me smile. 'See my folks, go for a meal with friends . . . and have a drink without feeling I'm committing a sin.'

Ben's disapproval of any indulgence extended to everyone, and although Mhairi saw much in him that was kind, she resented – as did the Islanders – his censoriousness. But if I felt isolated on Pigeon through necessity, how much more cut off he must feel, through something no-one fully comprehended. Mhairi attended church with him but, although they shared the weekly trudge through the darkly glimmering swamplands and sang together, he always seemed to her 'miles away'. As Ben himself once said, there was a barrier between him and the rest of the world. But Peter and Mhairi had a life in Reefs of their own: she drew, he composed, they trekked to the tiny 'market' regularly, and on many occasions Peter was garlanded as guest of honour at school functions on other islands; but their clear role as white teacher and wife restricted how close they could feel to Islanders – and how close Islanders could feel to them. Mhairi sat with Pegi and her sistas sewing, and took her turn willingly at handing out stick tobacco in the store, but there was, she felt – as most Europeans would – such a vast difference in educational and cultural backgrounds that any real bond between adults couldn't be expected. With children, however, it was another story, and Peter's innovative educational methods aided what came naturally.

'What did you do in geography today?' I once asked Benji.

'Drew a map of invented islands, Naboomboom and Kracka, then put families on them and a copra-buying place and a monster called the Vanika in the sea, and next week we're writing about preserving food in the tropics – like drying nambo . . .'

He also said they'd discussed conservation in relation to the way Reef Islanders sometimes called a ban on fishing in certain areas – so there'd be plenty for 'later'.

'And sport?'

'It's nearly the finals of the dugout races.'

But nothing gave me such a flood of quiet, maternal joy as when Joe brought me his contribution to Pigeon Island School's composition class halfway through the year. Peter had set everyone the same task: to write a 'Recipe for Happiness'. Most of the pupils – still shy – wrote one word which summed it all up for them: 'Aelan'. Joe went just a little further:

Football, fudge, friends, family and a good book:
Spread on an island, toast in the sun, and SMILE . . .

It confirmed what I longed to be the case, that although most adults on Pigeon seemed to face problems that couldn't always be sanitized by the word 'challenges', the children – local and European – were having the time of their life.

Ben was numbawan fudgemaker on Pigeon. He made a special batch for midnight consumption, and ensured Joe and Benji had a successful last nocturnal spear-fishing session before we left. He *was* kind, which argued that, for all he denied it, some feelings remained. I didn't want to probe too deeply, when we went for the walk round the island suggested by Diana, as by now I believed it could only be painful for him to be quizzed on his past by anyone less than expert, but I was curious to know how he viewed his role on Pigeon in the future.

'This is where the launch broke loose and took the boathouse with it,' said Ben dutifully as we began our tour, adding unnecessarily, 'There's nothing there now.' It was also, I thought, where he, as an adolescent, had disciplined himself not to look below the waist of a naked housegirl, and probably one of the places where, later, he'd lain with Sipikoli. I said 'Hi' as we passed Ross, busy under his veranda on a laptop, piccaninnis everywhere and three women at his feet stitching

a Mothers' Union banner, and he twinkled back, grinning. But Ben
didn't greet his twin, just ducked languidly under the corner of the
leaf roof and reminded me this had been his parents' first house, with
a plank as the storefront. He'd once suggested to his father that
another plank be set outside the finished store when he was managing
it, so customers were on his level, not forced to gaze up from the dirt
outside. But Tom said no, it would only mean they could reach in and
put their fingers directly into the till rather than bothering to break in,
and Ben hadn't argued. 'Mum used to have a three-piece suite
in here,' I was told next, as we passed the cheerful communal area that
was Ross's open house for wontoks.

As we moved on round the leaf, iron and board building, heading
for the units, I heard the tinny bleat of Christine's cassette player from
where she sat moodily twisting her hair into dreadlocks. Repeatedly,
Christine ran away to a boyfriend on another island and was fetched
back. She'd stopped attending Pigeon Island School and, although
they usually kissed and made up, there were frequent disputes
between her and Pegi. 'You shouldn't messabaot. You'll get in
trouble,' said young but matronly-minded Pegi. 'Don' tell me what to
do, you're not my mother!' Christine would retort, then dash up and
hug her and call her Mami next day. Since I'd been cool about the
idea of her coming to Scotland, Christine had avoided me, and I her,
for she was the only Hepworth child I had – nearly – let myself feel
involved with, when we'd gone to Honiara together, and it hadn't
worked out. 'She's out of control,' said Ross, throwing up his hands,
but I knew, if she did get pregnant, he'd look after both her and the
child, which would just be an extension of his big Reef Island family.
Recently Ross had adopted another baby, and he and Pegi said they'd
look after Ben's daughter if she came to Pigeon. Was that what her
father wanted? 'God will decide,' he'd responded when, rashly, I once
asked him straight out.

Now Ben moved ahead to where his mother wanted to install
another water tank, powerful swimmer's back glowing but no bounce
in his stride. 'But Ross thinks it's the wrong place,' he said. Another
'family politics' tussle. 'What do you think?' I asked. At the units, we
stood where not long before I'd sat with his brother hearing about
Tom's death. Ross laughed and cried so easily, letting everything out.
Maybe that's how he survived. 'Me?' queried Ben, and shot a rare
eye-to-eye look from under his lashes before staring out, as he often

did, to sea. 'I know Ross wants something, and Mum wants some-thing.' He was still 'sitting at the edge of the park' – and on the fence. What would happen if, as we stood there, I took his hand and held it in mine? Would he shout 'Jezebel!' and hurl me from him? Or would he understand that my dangerous phases of lust really were over now, and that I wanted only to offer him some sisterly sympathy before we left, and say thank you for being good to my boys? I couldn't risk it, but when our steps took us to the base of the Debbil–Debbil Tree and, listlessly, he said this was where Mum had in mind for a restàurant, I couldn't help saying: 'But what about *you*?' He shrugged. Transport would always be a problem, he said mechanically, unless an airfield came. And if it did, I thought, would customers want their parrotfish served with scripture? I swept my gaze round trying to visualize what Diana saw, and maybe what Ben himself had seen in the past – in the days of his love for Angela. The Debbil–Debbil Tree would indeed make a striking centrepiece, and if the bushes across the lawn were trimmed to make a frame, guests would be able to take breakfast over-looking the shimmering splendour of post-sunrise sea, and, with seats turned round, take cocktails with Tinakula and Matema ablaze, and dinner under a sexy silver moon. To some, it would certainly seem the ultimate retreat – but would Ben benefit?

'Smol brata b'long mi . . .' (oh my little brother) I sighed, the closest I ever came to showing him affection, 'I hope everything works out well for you,' and we walked on to the site of a new labour hut, not yet begun, which looked like a rubbish dump to me.

'God is working everything out all the time.'

'How did you get on with Ben? What do you think?' asked Diana at tea next day.

'I think,' I said carefully, 'it's a lovely site for a restaurant, but I'm not sure if Ben's ready.'

'But he's getting better all the time, isn't he? With the right woman . . .'

I didn't want to say I didn't know, and didn't think it advisable for anyone to seek a solution for themselves in another. Comfort maybe, cure, no. That night she showed me a home video of Ben giving a speech on behalf of a European Union worker who'd been a visitor to Pigeon, at the opening of a wharf at Nialo a few months before Tom's death. Ben stood wreathed in frangipani and spoke of God's gifts, and held the attention of the crowd. Sometimes I wondered if he were just baffled by the particular gift God had chosen for him: his mother's Paradise, but not necessarily his. Both Tom and Diana, on the occasion of the wharf opening, were awarded medals for Service to the Community – and an enquiry was conducted the same day into the death of an adolescent girl whose body was found beneath Pigeon's cliffs at low tide. Had she fallen or was she pushed? Whatever, it was believed she'd been assaulted before being either wholly or half strangled. Was there anything that hadn't happened on this five-acre island? Racial tensions, sexual abuse, sorcery, madness – and now murder as well. No-one ever found out who did it, but what I had to remember was that Pigeon was a microcosm, and a small one at that, in which everything seemed concentrated and extreme. For every moment of horror, there were probably more of joy. *Hold on to that ungraspable blue . . .*

'Ross is going to hold a farewell party for us, a party!' Benji shrilled, sore paw in a grubby Tubi grip waving merrily, and tore off to share the news with Patteson. Those two were inseparable, and it was inevitable they were going to miss each other – but they were also both more expert at the art of 'living now' than anyone I'd ever met. To see those boys diving from the coral boulder off Nandelli Point to swim in unison, like fish in a shoal of two, round it, and help each other up for a repeat performance, or hear them chat in rapid Pijin interspersed with giggles on the Little Wharf, cracking nuts and fanning themselves with leaves, was to witness simple and complete joy in the present. Patteson's mother summed up the situation after she'd delivered Benji back to Pigeon after one of his stays at Otelo. 'Benji olsem Patteson. Sapos em sore, kraekrae – bat em laekem laf moa.' (They're the same. If they're sad they cry – but they like laughing more.) Then she'd paused: 'Bat *mi* gohed fo misim Benji too. Send piksa.' I certainly would.

'Oh Mum, I don't want to go home!' This was from Joe, followed by a smile, but I suspected there was a half-serious element too. At school in Scotland, Joe had struggled with the hearing impairment that was barely noticeable here, and he revelled more than any of us in that other world surrounding Pigeon, under the sea. Day after day he went off, alone or with friends, paddled to a good spot in a dugout, dived for hours, and afterwards, as he rinsed off salt under our gravity-fed shower, sang Reef Island songs. When it rained, instead of sitting in a hut with Islander friends – among whom Benji and Patteson were the stori-yarning stars – he sat under our leaf veranda and added to his project about contrasts between Reefs and the Highlands. Children in Scotland have plenty of toys, he mused, but don't laugh as much as Reef Island piccaninnis; in Reefs it's sunny nearly every day and you can live on fish and fruit; in the Highlands people mostly use central heating to keep warm, and buy food, which is expensive – which means you have to work. Life in Reef Islands could be dangerous – there were stonefish, no doctors for miles, you might get blown away – but essentially it was *easier*, he concluded. And he loved it.

'I've got mixed feelings about leaving, too,' I admitted, 'but now you've had a taste of island life you can always bear it in mind as an option later on.'

He nodded, then pinpointed a few of the things he couldn't imagine finding 'normal' again. 'I just can't see myself putting on trousers – and a top, *and* socks and shoes. And buying bananas in little bunches, instead of picking loads from a whole stem any time.'

'I know.' I didn't want to think about wearing tights again, carrying credit cards and remembering to lock doors. And hundreds of people whizzing around in tin boxes on wheels seemed a mad idea. Just as well I still had an Orange Badge. Dangerous Driver Disabled by Desert Island Life, it should say.

'Are you coming to the farewell party, Mum?'

'I don't know. Diana wants me to go to supper the same night.'

'Oh no – we won't have to go, will we?'

Both boys had learned to like Poisson Cru, but not the formality of Diana's meals. They wanted to sit in a corner clutching a leaf parcel, and shovel in their food with fingers like their friends. Pigeon, to them, had far more to do with immediate fun than with the history – or hospitality – of an elderly English lady. As it happened, Diana herself suggested our last meal together should be adults only. I was going to have to spread myself thin, because Tangypera had issued a kaikai invitation as well. Not wanting to rush either occasion, I moved that to an earlier date.

I usually knew in advance when a squall was approaching, because the lorikeets roosting above Tasha's House shrieked maniacally at the first sign. But the Sunday before our departure, Joe, Benji and I were caught between Pigeon and Nenumbo, dragging kayaks full of goodies for Tangypera's family, so had little warning of the deluge that sent us scampering under Temotulaki's coral overhang. There we rubbed goosepimpled tans and played 'I went out to dinner', imagining all we'd like to eat when back in civilization, until visibility improved enough for us to make a dash. Not a Nenumban was in sight when we arrived, tied up our kayaks and trooped through whiffy shallows towards Tangypera's hut. Maybe they'd given up on us because of the weather – or maybe they'd spring out, painted and carrying spears, as for the deacon's welcome. But no, there was one of Tangypera's older daughters, bulbous with child herself, peeping from behind a screwpine,★ and half a dozen piccaninnis pelting, starkers, to greet us, raindrops sparkling in wild puffs of hair under suddenly brilliant sun. The boldest took my hands, the rest settled our offerings on their heads. Tangypera had said reciprocity is law in Kastom, so I'd kept our gifts modest – linen and my Country Casuals skirt for Kaplei, mother of nine, who through endless bending for shellfish on the reef had stayed svelte; paper tattoos of butterflies for children; pots and pans; buckets for catchment, and fishhooks all the way from Scotland for the dozens of women I knew would hang shyly on the periphery of our modest farewell 'do', and who now parted, as only Reef Islanders can, like a shoal of fish, as we were ushered under dripping palm thatch into an interior reeking of damp leaves and babies. Here I was led behind a leaf screen by Kaplei, and my wet wrap and T-shirt were replaced by a length of yellow kalico falling below the knee. Joe and Benji were loaned both of Tangypera's Sunday best T-shirts, also falling below the knee.

The privilege of kaikai in an Islander's home isn't preceded by small talk. Softly as shadows, women produced food from under heaps of leaves, laid it on woven mats on the floor, then fell back so that only their eyes gleamed from corners where, squatting on haunches, they blew noses into their kalicos, smoked long pipes and chirruped whenever I looked their way. Tangypera, who recently made Kastom magic from tree bark to help heal Benji's damaged hand, averted a moment of awkwardness by stopping me touching my bulging banana leaf of

★ Spiky pandanus palm.

food purely by the power of his stare, while his eldest son completed a soft grace I'd mistaken for a whispered aside. But when the meal began I did the right thing by commenting that, judging from bones the boys were sucking – only they, I, Tangypera and male wontoks ate – there must have been more than one kokoroko included. 'Yes,' said Tangypera proudly, in Pijin, 'I killed a cockerel for each of your sons.' Everyone had already said how sorry they were my fasbon (Magnus) couldn't be here. Flattered, Joe found the wishbones and introduced intrigued Islanders to the British 'Kastom' of pulling them for luck. When I couldn't pack in another mouthful of a foot-long pana root accompanying the chicken, I laid down my leaf with an apologetic smile, but needn't have worried, as the remains were distributed among piccaninnis outside. The women would eat anything left after they'd finished, or not bother with cooked food at all but simply wander off to gnaw wild cutnuts and dig out the lush flesh of paw-paws with their fingers, on a bank of violet convolvulus, with the Pacific washing over their toes and souls . . . When a nervous silence greeted our gifts, I explained that the Islanders' way of living had already given me something precious to carry with me always – perspective – and therefore they owed nothing. Tangypera knew sincerity when he saw it, even if the exchange seemed an odd one.

I sat on with the men after the betel was passed round, toktok began, and the weighty subject arose of more whiteman visitors possibly coming to Reef Islands in the future. Kaplei gently took Joe's and Benji's hands and led them out to play 'lo' bus'' – which they did gleefully, raising many smiles in the hut as their greeting cries in Pijin blended with those of their waiting friends. I asked the Islanders if they *wanted* tourists in their as yet unspoilt 'Paradise'. Tangypera, traditional Kastom chief but father of a churchman, whose main knowledge of whites was still through missionaries and traders – and darkly, though only in his grandfather's time, through blackbirders (on the recruiting ships) – looked at me steadily. 'Wissway iufela tingting?' (What do you think?) Shuddering at the responsibility involved, I said: 'Mi no savvy . . .' Then his tiny, ancient mother hopped on her bandy reef bird's legs to the door and, impulsively, knowing she was one Islander I'd never see again, I jumped up and kissed her. This heralded an uproar of emotional good wishes all round, amid which the impossible question of whether 'development' is desirable in Reefs was, thank-fully, forgotten – for the time being. Joe and Benji and their friends, as ever untroubled by grown-up questions, waved and whooped from the trees in which I'd once seen warriors hide . . .

How can anyone judge if holidaymakers watching Kastom rituals like a floor show – even respectful eco-tourists – would be damaging or useful to such innocents? How could the Islanders work out whether they were being exploited or not? '*Wander the reefs and observe unspoilt primitives,*' Tom wrote in one of his early advertisements for Ngarando. Such words would be censored now, but wouldn't the same message simply be couched in more PC terms? I had a vision of Tangypera selling tickets for the kind of spontaneous topless dancing I'd seen (serious-faced grannies with leaf flounces over their torsos) and guided tours, including paradigms of patience like Nupanyi demonstrating the copra-making process. All this aroused fiercely protective feelings in me, but if, as Diana wished, Pigeon ever *did* become a successful retreat, why should the Islanders miss out on potential benefits to their community? They 'needed' better educational facilities, didn't they, and healthcare? Tom had been of the school that believes 'a little knowledge is a dangerous thing'. What was the good of providing a Western-style education when the faintest possibility of fulfilling Western-style aspirations was off the map for the majority? Did he have a point, or was he being breathtakingly patronizing?

But even Ross believed those who'd pursued jobs and a more 'sophisticated' lifestyle in Honiara (tinned food and nightclubs instead of fresh fish and Kastom dancing) tended to be unintentionally disruptive when they returned to their villages. 'What happens,' he said, 'is that those who've seen the Outside World and then come back and talk about it, bringing with them its almost opposite values – materialism, the idea of the nuclear family – undermine the structure of village life. There's a delicate hierarchy which controls things here – the elders, with representatives from each clan at the top – and these youngsters who go off to the bright lights can easily lose respect for that kind of "old-fashioned" system, and spread discontent without meaning to.' Of course there were always exceptions, such as Bopali, who wanted to strike a balance, bringing back benefits but not threatening Kastom in the process. When Ross was elected President of Temotu Province in 1997, three years after his return to Reefs with his father's body, he'd argued for a reinforcement of traditional Kastom methods of maintaining order in each village – and among the whole scattered population – by investing chiefs and elders with powers also recognized at a higher government level. He didn't want them viewed as old men in loincloths living in a time warp, but treated as valuable assets to the whole process of government. Their methods might seem antiquated – endless toktoks in the Sapulo – but he believed they worked for the average Reef Islander, and should therefore be respected – especially in the absence of any real alternative in the foreseeable future for a far-flung people with extremely limited communications with the capital. Others held similar opinions and Ross was very popular for a while, but when there was an administrative reshuffle higher up, his job disappeared, and by the time a similar position was reinstated his standing seemed less secure. 'Or maybe I just didn't want to run again because being president took me away too much from my family – like those Western politicians who always say that's why they've jacked it in!' But there was also talk that certain elements hadn't been happy with a Hepworth holding power, and had discouraged Ross from setting out again on the campaign trail through the mangroves by poisoning his kaikai – a common method of sending a 'forget it' signal in Reefs. Whichever way one looks at it, Ross's term in office, although brief, was a triumph of a kind. During that time, he'd felt genuinely able to blend within himself his two dramatically different cultural back-grounds, and had endeavoured to use both to the benefit of the people he saw as his own. I liked to think that Tom – albeit seeing it as a wry twist of fate – would have been proud.

Diana's farewell dinner, on our last evening, was served, as had been our first on Pigeon, on her east veranda, with Lanebu clearing the dishes. Ben was there, and Mhairi and Peter, but not Ross. 'Maybe see you later at the fun end of the island!' he'd said earlier, with a wink. Benji and Joe, to my embarrassment, had swum under the coral cliffs past Diana's for fear of being hoicked in and missing a moment of the party.

'She'll grab us to take a message to Ross's, then we'll probably have to take a message back and it'll take ages . . .'

'Her feet are bad and there's no phone,' I said. 'She has to send messages, and you know how rarely Ross visits her.'

'You can't blame him; she always gets cross.'

'She just feels cut off,' I tried to explain, but knew they were too young to understand her sense of helplessness. She who had 'made' this island now felt control slipping away, and her sons didn't run the place the way she'd hoped – as a *civilized* Paradise. 'Tom always opened our library to visiting yachts, you know,' she said. Twelve visitors a year was the average for the 1980s, a few more for the 1990s. Over the years, some of the European classics listed in Tom's diaries – Homer; Flaubert; Graham Greene – had gone the way of all paper in the tropics or been swapped for Harold Robbins tomes, but Diana still read every day, widely: *War and Peace*, Churchill's memoirs and Lawrence Durrell. And not a day went by when I didn't hear classical music coming from her solar-powered CD player – sometimes vying with Reef Island singing borne on the wind. How had she endured the anguish of loss she must have felt, playing arias she and Tom had loved, after he'd died – in this wilderness? Could anything be lonelier than a widow listening to passionate declarations from another hemisphere rising into the ether above the heads of surrounding aliens who'd almost prevented her husband's bones being laid where she could visit him? 'No, it wasn't like that,' she said. 'The music we shared was just another reminder of the wonderful life we shared.'

Her belief that the positives outweighed the negatives of life on Pigeon was total; her fortitude awesome. If Tom had sometimes found the place darkly oppressive, and chosen not to hurt her by saying so, that was his affair. But the welter of emotions crowding the history of that crazy little cupcake of coral made my head spin: from the initial days of joyous pioneering, when both Tom and Diana believed they'd found their perfect home, through shock after shock over Tasha, the rumbling hostility of the Islanders set against idyllic scenes of mixed schooling under Christine Clement – then her horror – to the confusions of the twins' early loves that left them both high with happiness, then plummeted to pain, and drove their Islander partners to desperate measures – everything about Pigeon seemed excessive. It was like a stage set magicked by some mischief-making god into the midst of sunny blue, and used in turn for farce, tragedy, high drama and black comedy. I didn't tell Diana of these views, for fear – like Tom – of doing her pointless injury. But I think she knew nearly all there was to know already, and had chosen to deal with her feelings in the way with which she was most familiar – employing the ultimate stiff upper lip. I looked at her, so elegant at the head of the table, with her hair in a velvet bow that perfectly matched her gown, and ached with the weight of what lay ahead: the revelations I'd have to make to write a rounded history of Pigeon. But had she guessed what was in those of Tom's diaries she hadn't read? The answer was, probably, yes, and she remained undaunted. I smiled, nodding dumbly at the offer of another spoonful of Poisson Cru with coconut cream ('You won't get this in Scotland!') and realized I'd miss her deeply as a unique – and unexpected – friend. If I wasn't careful, I'd fall into the trap of excessive island emotion in a minute.

But to my relief, most of the conversation that evening was practical. I was to take Stasi's bed as padding for my spine in the canoe in the morning, as well as my special seat, and to remind Ross to pick up a basket of kumera for her on Santa Cruz; they were getting so scarce locally. 'When we first came, there was any amount of fruit and vegetables. Now I have to send Ben miles for limes. Ridiculous population explosion.' Statistics bore out her words. More piccaninnis survived to adulthood these days, and fertile land had not increased. 'Solrice is an essential part of their diet now – with added vitamins because they can't grow enough of their own.' I thought of Tom and his hopes for salads from his hydropod smashed in a cyclone – and of comments to his sisters about '*bread and circuses*' being the downfall of empires. The *Arthur Rogers*, then Pigeon, had been his Englishman's castle, and the hordes beyond the moat were almost an irrelevance, except when they impinged.

'You have seen *Came the Dawn*, haven't you?' Diana asked suddenly, referring to a documentary about Cecil Hepworth, Tom's pioneering film-director father, with the same title as his auto-biography. I had, and she went on: 'I hope Ross shows it to the children soon.' I was surprised. Diana so rarely mentioned her grand-children. Then I remembered a throwaway line in Tom's diary: '*Showed the film, at Ross's request, to him and Ben and both their wives.*' So Pegi – or was it Teimaliki? – and Sipikoli had watched footage of Queen Victoria's funeral, shot by their grandfather-in-law. I wondered what it meant to them, and a vision of the silent women who'd towed Bishop Patteson's body out to the *Southern Cross*, their wontoks shooting his with arrows, went through my mind, with its message for the white marauders' female chief. But it hadn't reduced the flow of visitors from the Outside World wanting something – converts, labour, land, customers or tourist attractions – out of Reef Islands. Pigeon was like Britain in miniature, with Diana as queen. She and Tom had been perfectly matched.

'May I pour you more bushlime, Lucy?' asked Ben.

I'd rather have a brandy, I thought, but said yes. I was finding it hard to balance all I felt about Diana: the naturally reserved reaction of one of my generation to her 'imperialist' attitudes jostled with the admiration, and affection, I had for her as a fellow woman – and the toughest instinctive survivor I'd ever met. Maybe I would slip down to Ross's later and have a Solbrew. But no. I wanted to enjoy my last night on Pigeon with a clear head. A dip in the moonlight would be better.

How will I remember this? – the chiffon air, the satin sea, as I roll and surface, roll and surface, all round Poppet Island . . . When I lie on my back, eyes wide, wavelets run over me like gently knowing hands, and beyond, feathery heads of palms glisten, stroked by the softest breeze, kissed by the moon . . .The sky, at its deepest, is blue black; nearer, lightened by drifting silver skeins . . . Afterwards I lay naked under our one remaining sheet (the boys didn't bother) and watched the companions of my solitude. *Night after night the geckos have stalked insects above me like little rubbery-fingered cats. They skitter up the painted tree-trunk post beside my ear, freeze when they reach the open space of ceiling board, inch towards their prey, then pounce, often missing, and sometimes falling on the bed. My favourite is a fat one who lost his tail during a kumberra, and most of his balance with it. It's growing back now – black in contrast to his ochre body – but he's still hopeless, time and again launching boldly across the white wastes at a fly, then plummeting. Evidently the stickiness of his feet hasn't adapted to prevailing indoor conditions on Pigeon yet, but he never gives up . . .* With the battery light on in Ngarando telling me she was still up – probably making tuna sandwiches for our journey – my thoughts returned to the woman who'd brought me to Pigeon. *Diana could be said not to have adapted to prevailing conditions in the Outside World, but she never gives up either, and her determination to see the last wishes of the man she loved carried out has been humbling to witness – as well as a spur.* Una Via Cor Unum. She certainly lives up to all that motto encapsulates. *I'll miss her for many reasons, but not least because the Desert Island Club is a very small one, and there are things about being 'remote' – metaphorically or literally – that I can share only with someone like Diana – and I don't know anyone else like her.*

The boys padded in late, barely needing their torches under the moon. Benji was proud because he'd found a young coconut crab on the lawn of such impressive proportions that Patteson had rushed to fetch his dadi, who'd fetched Ross, and they'd marked it with white paint as 'bagged' for when it grew full size.

'Try to sleep now,' I said. 'Long day tomorrow.'

Benji, stuffed with pikpik and the fizzy 'milk' of young green coconuts, sprawled in abandon across his minimal packing, in their open veranda room, and was instantly asleep, with warm tradewinds ruffling his hair.

'Mum,' whispered Joe, 'I'm still not sure I want to go.'

'Think of seeing Charlie again.' (Our cat.) I was thinking of seeing Magnus, and wondering what his new friends were like. To him, we'd seem so out of touch.

'Yes, I want to see Charlie – and our house. I won't even mind getting the wood in again. But Mum? Will there be Solomon Island sort of children at our new school? I won't know what to say to . . . ordinary ones, after all this time.'

I smiled in the dark. He didn't sound worried – just musing aloud about the next era in his life. But if one of my hopes for the island year had been that my children would integrate well with the local community, I could chalk up a success. Although it was as well for Joe, perhaps, that we weren't staying longer, if he were to make the transition back to his own culture easily.

'You'd be surprised,' I said, 'if you knew how quickly this year away is going to seem like a dream. Don't forget I've done something a bit like this before.'

After a short silence Joe said: 'But you must have missed it, otherwise you wouldn't have wanted to go off again, would you?'

It was a fair point. Maybe I'm hooked on remoteness. And in the event it was my gaze, not Joe's or Benji's, that lingered on Reef Islands until they blurred.

At 4.45 a.m. precisely Diana's light snapped on, the first lorikeet stirred and I checked for crabs, as usual, before putting my feet on the floor. Nothing else was as usual.

'Kwiktaem,' I said to the already stirring boys as I slipped round to our Kaikai Tree and stashed behind it some final gifts for Nenumbo friends – my pillow and sheet for Tangypera's mother, and a washing-up bowl for Kaplei who, it had been arranged, would paddle swiftly across at first light and fetch them before Diana came to Tasha's House, after we'd left, to lock things away. I knew she wanted only to keep things safe for if I came back, but I wanted them used. I'd told Pegi our kayaks were for the Islanders' use now, too.

'Ben!' I heard Diana shouting. 'Go and help Lucy.' But a bark from Stasi told me a bag-carrying contingent were already on their way. In silence, but grinning as they folded the last of our shortbread into their kalicos, four of Ross's strongest wontoks swung plastic suitcases containing Tom's irreplaceable notes – half a century's worth – onto their heads, accepted Joe's and Benji's spears for their piccaninnis, and trotted away.

'Are you ready, darling?' Diana yelled.

'I think so!'

We were to board the canoe down Ross's end, so had now to pass Diana's house for the last time. Joe and Benji ran ahead, stopping just long enough for her to give them a message for Ross and say goodbye to their retreating backs. I'd have to do something about their manners. Ben was hovering on Diana's veranda, sipping tea, watching a blood-orange sunrise flare. 'Go and make sure they're ready,' she said, and when he'd gone she turned to me.

'The tide's perfect,' she said. 'You must go now. Now!'

'I will, I . . .'

'*Now*, darling!'

She was always emphatic, but there was an edge to this repeated command that made me look at her face carefully as she turned to pick up something from a table. She was crying. Diana, who never cried.

'Take this,' she said, ignoring an enormous tear sliding among the lines of her still beautiful face, and pressed a small silk square covered with pink daisies into my hands.

'I'll wear it whenever I need courage like yours,' I said, and we hugged, after which I left quickly. Passing Tom's grave, I closed my eyes a moment. He wouldn't have liked a prayer, so I just murmured I'd do my best.

The beach down at Ross's was busy, Joe already in the canoe to ensure he got the seat beside Ross, but Benji still sitting on the beach with Patteson, who was delicately holding his friend's bandaged hand.

'All aboard,' said Ross, when I'd emerged from an embrace with Pegi, kissed Christine, and shaken hands formally with Nupanyi and all the others who'd got up to see us off. Ngive and Elisha stood close to Patteson when Benji had to leave him, and all three of them, and Ross's small sons, called out a medley of warm wishes for our voyage ending in: 'Bye iu kambaek!' Ben climbed in at the last minute. Then, just as we were setting off, Tangypera made his most spectacular materialization to date – straight out of the water, over the side and into the bottom of the canoe in one movement, where he sat soaked, his eyebrows batting about triumphantly but his head well down in case Missus saw. I'd said, when he told me the story of Paia's drowning, that I'd only make the crossing again if he came, because I knew if he thought it unsafe he'd refuse. It was fine weather, but he said he wanted to come anyway. Even Ben smiled. 'It's all right, Tangypera,' Ross said, 'I'll square it with Mum,' and he shouted for another man to go up and work for her.

Instead of heading directly for Santa Cruz, we passed first along the eastern side of Pigeon, so I could take in the dawn over Nandelli and glimpse Nenumbo a last time, and the boys keep waving and calling to friends who dashed along to the slip by the schoolhouse to chorus their 'bye' and 'kambaek' over and over again – all excited laughter and shouting, no tears. I was still staring out towards Temotulaki when Tangypera said: 'O mae wat! Lusi, lukluk . . .'

And there, on the furthest edge of her east lawn, was Diana on her dicky feet, in her daytime bikini, waving, not her hand, not a hanky, but a great piece of sail – just as she had so many times for Tom, seeing him off and welcoming him home. I ripped the little scarf from round my neck, knelt up in the canoe, and waved and waved back. Twenty minutes later the sun was up, Reefs a blur, and Pigeon had faded into the blinding blue.

Glossary

aelan'	island
afta	after
alite ★	a large green and pink wild nut with a slender kernel
ba iuim	this expression can mean anything from a lightly teasing 'get away with you' to an aggressive 'up yours'
bat	but
befoataem	the time before the coming of Christianity to the Islands
belerun	belly run (stomach upset)
berem	to bury
Bigwind	cyclone
bisi	busy
b'long	belonging to someone or something, e.g. 'nem b'long mi Lusi' – 'my name is Lucy'
bokis	box
brata	brother, but not always a blood relative
canoe	Islanders tend to use this for any kind of dinghy, and it has slipped into general Pigeon usage
cutnut	a wild nut larger than a Brazil, with a hard green skin
dadi	daddy

★ When a word ends in 'e', it is usually pronounced 'eh'.

dae finis	to die, or be dead (interestingly, to 'daedae' for someone is to be in love with them)
Debbil–Debbil Tree	a gigantic tree of the cycad family
dipwata	deep water
durong	from the words 'to do wrong', meaning illicit sexual activity
evri	every
faet	fight
faki	fuck
fasbon	firstborn
fustaem	in the first instance, or firstly
garem	got
gogo	to go, or travel ('longfela gogo' means 'long journey')
gohed	proceed, or go ahead
gummint	government
hao	how or why – often a question
hariap	hurry up, or to be in a hurry
hemi	he, she or it – sometimes shortened to 'emi' or 'em'
hia	here
insaet	inside
iufela	you – often shortened to 'iu'
kaikai	food, or to eat
kam	come
kambaek	return/come back
Kastom	similar in meaning to custom, but used broadly to describe anything to do with traditional ways
kokoroko	chicken, male or female
kolsap	close
kraekrae	to weep, or wail
krangge	crazy
kumberra	fierce westerly gale (phonetic spelling of a Reef Islands language word, not Pijin)
kumera	one of several types of sweet potato grown in the Solomons
kutim	to cut
kwiktaem	fast, or immediately – often a command
laek	like
languis	local language; in the Solomon Islands there are over sixty-five different languages
lanona	landowner
lasbon	last born
lav	love
lelebet	a little bit
livim	leave; some tuna cans in the Solomons have the warning on them: 'Afta openim, no livim fis insaet'

lukaftarem	take care of
lukim iu	basically, 'see you'; for extended meanings see page 251
lukluk	look – this can also mean perception
mae wat!	exclamation, from the English 'My word!'
mami	mummy/mum
maos	mouth
mek	make
mere	woman – from one of the many local languages
mifela	me – often shortened to mi
mitufela	us, we two (or more); with 'b'long', our
naes	nice
nambo	biscuit-like triangles of dried breadfruit, used as snacks and emergency rations
nara	another, or other
nartin'/nuttin	nothing
nekis	next
ngali	a wild nut delicious slivered and toasted
ngenumbla	an attractive wild fruit growing in grapelike bunches, popular with children and flying foxes
niu	new
numbawan	number one – often used as a compliment
oki/ogi	unusually substantial wild nut, served roasted or boiled, like chestnuts
olo	old; this can also mean the important elderly – elders – generally
olsem	the same
openim	to open
oraet	all right, OK
pana	a relative of the sweet potato, or yam, with a slippery skin
pati	party
pikpik	pig
piksa	picture, or photograph
plis	please
prae	pray
propa	proper, or very
pua	poor, to be pitied
putim	to put
raet	right
rif	reef
rubas	rubbish
sapos	what if, suppose, or how about
Sapulo	Men's Single House, where important village matters are discussed

sarrap	shut up
savvy	knowledge, or to know
sekhan	shake hands
seleva	alone/by oneself
sista	sister, but not always a blood relative
slipslip	rest, or sleep
smolfela	small – often shortened to smol
Solbrew	beer popular in the Solomon Islands
solwata	salt water, the sea
somaot	to show or demonstrate
sore	sorry, or sad
spesol	special
spialaen	boundary
stakka	lots, many
stap	stop/stay/remain – 'hemi stap' means 'he or she's alive'
stoa	store
susu	breast, singular or plural
tambu	a ban or something forbidden, similar in meaning to 'taboo'
tanggio	thank you
taro	enormous starchy vegetable
te puke	a traditional voyaging canoe, made entirely out of natural materials available in Duff Islands
tevi	a smooth, peachlike fruit, with a spiky hedgehog for a pit (Benji's description)
tif	thief
tingting	to think
tokabaotim	to talk about
toktok	to talk, as a verb, or discussion in general
trae	try
tri	tree, or three
tumas	too much
umu	underground oven
wan	one
wandem	want
wasim	wash
wetem	with
wissway	often used as a question, this means 'How are things?' 'How come?' or 'Why?'
witufela	we, or us; used similarly to 'mitufela'
wontok	an intimate, relative or friend, with whom one can hold one-to-one talks; more loosely, a clan member
wud	word
yia	year

Acknowledgements

Thank you, dearest Diana, for opening your heart and Tom's diaries to me, and thank you, Ross and Pegi and Ben, for putting up with my peculiar ways and interminable questions. Heartfelt thanks go also to the people of Reef Islands who so generously welcomed me and my children to their shores, and taught us more than I can say. 'Tanggio tumas. Lukim iu.' Particular gratitude is owed to the Hon. Michael Maina, the Hon. Moffat Bonunga, the Rt Revd Lazarus Manamua, Bishop of Temotu – and Tangypera. The kindnesses of Our Man in Honiara (BHC) won't be forgotten either.

People back home to whom I am indebted know who they are, but I should like to mention especially: the guardian angels who cared for Magnus in my absence; Bill Mackenzie of Highland Disability Services' Access to Work Scheme, who ensured a dicky spine didn't limit my aspirations; Highland Canoes; Perception Kayaks (a division of Gaybo Ltd) for expedition rates, and Suresh Paul from DFL Adventure Designs for my Aquabac seat. Among other companies who assisted our enterprise, Walkers take the cake for delivering goodies by cargo boat; Baxters' fare was much appreciated, and our Vango tent, designed for mountains, withstood a tropical kumberra. Cotswold Outdoors Ltd helped, and Scholastic brought smiles to many faces with their surprise gift of forty books for Pigeon Island School. Weetabix and Kelloggs contributed roughage generously.

With regard to gathering information towards the book, I am most deeply indebted, posthumously, to Tom Hepworth, for keeping such copious diaries over the years, and preserving cuttings, letters and photographs which have been immeasurably useful in bringing this story to life. Others to whom I owe thanks include Margaret Fitzpatrick who, unasked, sent pages from the diary her grandfather, William Cock, kept on HMS *Mohawk* in 1898. I am grateful also to William I. B. Crealock, author of *Towards Tahiti*, to Amalie Stone-Walker for sending both letters and articles, and all others who sent material to help trace the Hepworths' history. Very special thanks go to Diana Hepworth's sisters. Among others who contributed to the information gathering were: 'Ferdi' Davies; Mrs V. Williamson; the magnificent members of the 1954 all-girl crew; Christine and Tom Hunter; John Rentz; former District Commissioner Mr W. R. H. Low; Reece Discombe of Vanuatu; Paramount Chief Coloso Cruso Kaveia of Taumako, Duff Islands; Dr Mimi George, cultural anthropologist, and her crew; Mrs J. Maunder; Mrs H. Lear; Mary Clark-Rogers; 'Mop' Openshaw; Mrs Bertram Follett; Margaret Lewis; Mrs A. Meldrum; Mrs J. Nadu and Simon Done. Tom's elder sisters' letters added hugely to my understanding of Tom and his background, and I thank these ladies posthumously. Art critic John Furse added to my understanding of their lives. Studies conducted in Reef Islands by anthropologists R. C. Green, Kaye C. Green and William Davenport assisted my enquiries into local history and customs. The entire Higgins family, Stephen Cook, Clare Morrison, Andy and Justine Hodge, Theo Michell, Haidy Geismar, Alastair Wilkie and Deborah Adams all provided valuable assistance. Other contributors to our venture, and to the book, are too numerous to list, but none will be forgotten. My editors at the *Sunday Times* magazine deserve medals for patience over my unconventional methods of delivery, and I owe much to Joanna Goldsworthy of Doubleday and Hilary Rubinstein of Hilary Rubinstein Books for keeping my spirits up with their endless enthusiasm during the writing of this book – and for sending bikinis when mine wore out.

Lastly, I'd like to thank the total stranger who sent a box of Earl Grey teabags to me on Pigeon Island, without a word, when I was just about to run out. What bliss.

Index